AN UNWELCOME GUEST

Penny Green Mystery Book 7

EMILY ORGAN

First published in 2019 by Emily Organ

emilyorgan.co.uk

Edited by Joy Tibbs

ISBN 978-1-9993433-3-0

AN UNWELCOME GUEST

❦

Emily Organ

❦

Books in the Penny Green Series:

ALSO BY EMILY ORGAN

All I could see of the Hotel Tempesta that foggy evening were the two flickering gas lamps marking the hotel's entrance. In clear light, the building was a cream-and-red-brick structure with decorative tiles surrounding each arched window. Countless chimneys and spires rose from the steeply pitched roof, as if to defy the hotel's tragic past.

A doorman wearing a black and gold uniform greeted me.

"May I take your case, ma'am?"

"Thank you."

I caught my breath as I stepped inside the magnificent foyer, the contrast with the cold November streets felt quite startling. I wiped the grime from my spectacles with a gloved hand and took in the enormous chandelier with its glittering light reflecting in numerous mirrors. A fountain at the centre of the room babbled soothingly, and beyond it lay a grand staircase with red-carpeted stairs. I breathed in the scent of lilies, and my boots echoed on the tiled floor as I approached the reception desk.

"Miss Green, isn't it?" said a slightly built man in an

evening suit. He bowed his sparsely-haired head in a servile manner. "Allow me to take your overcoat for you. Miss Milly here will escort you to your room." He handed my coat to a young maid in a stiff white apron, who gave an unnecessary curtsy. "It's on the second storey, so you may travel there via the newly installed elevator."

The gentle tinkle of a piano accompanied our walk along the corridor, which was lined with portraits of proud-faced men and ladies with hair as glossy as their satin dresses. The light from a row of cut-glass lamps was dimmed by the dark wallpaper, and I felt a slight chill, having been relieved of my overcoat.

⁂

"How do you get on with ghosts, Miss Green?" my colleague Edgar Fish had asked me earlier that day in the cluttered newsroom of the *Morning Express* newspaper. "The Hotel Tempesta is haunted," he had added with a raised eyebrow and a smirk. He was a young man with heavy features and small, glinting eyes.

"And cursed!" added my corpulent colleague Frederick Potter.

"That is nothing but hearsay," I replied. "Anyhow, I don't believe in ghosts, based on the fact that I have never seen one."

"But that doesn't prove that they don't exist," said Edgar. "You just haven't encountered one yet. Have you ever visited a place as reputedly haunted as the Tempesta?"

"Probably."

"You are aware of its history, aren't you?"

"Of course."

"That fire completely destroyed it four years ago, back

when it was the Corinthian. How many guests perished, Potter?"

"About thirty, I think."

"Then that chap who owned the Regency rebuilt it, didn't he?" said Edgar.

"And did a pretty marvellous job," added Frederick.

"Until he went bankrupt and hanged himself in his suite, that is." Edgar shook his head. "Terribly sad."

"That's the curse for you," said Frederick.

"There is no curse," I scoffed. "Mr Gallo wouldn't have bought it if he believed the place was cursed."

"Ah, but he's American," said Edgar. "He doesn't know the full history."

"Of course he does," I retorted. "Besides, he's an extremely experienced hotelier. I'm sure he'll do an excellent job with it, just as he has with the Hotel Maganza in New York."

"In fairness to the American, he has changed the name from the Corinthian to the Tempesta," said Frederick. "Perhaps the name change will lift the curse."

"I doubt it," said Edgar. "Sleep well, Miss Green."

I sighed. "You know that I'm being forced into this because both you and Frederick have refused to go. I can't say that I wish to spend any time there at all, but Mr Gallo seems to believe that inviting a journalist to stay the night will result in something flattering being written about his hotel in our newspaper."

࿇

My bedchamber was a dark, wood-panelled room furnished in blue and gold. Thick curtains hung around the four-poster bed and two easy chairs covered in gold velvet sat either side of an occasional table. A lady in a large hat looked down on me from a painting above the fireplace, and although the fire was lit it seemed to emit little warmth.

"Drinks will be served in the Turkish Salon at six o'clock," said Milly, who proceeded to give me directions on how to find it as she hung my overcoat in the wardrobe. "Before I take my leave, Miss Green, is there anything else you need me to assist you with?"

I glanced at the bed, where my suitcase had been carefully placed. "No, thank you."

"Very good, Miss Green." She gave another curtsy and stepped backwards through the door, so as not to turn her back on me.

I smiled at her obsequious nature once the door was closed, then glanced around the bedchamber once again. I gave a shiver and yearned for the comfort of my humble garret room, ruing the day I had agreed to stay the night in this accursed place. I pushed aside one of the heavy curtains at the window to see thick, dark tendrils of fog pressing up against the pane. Being unable to see anything beyond it left me with a stifling, smothering sensation in my chest. I returned the curtain to its original position and looked up at the lady in the picture, who was steadily watching me. Edgar's talk of ghosts seemed less frivolous now.

I seated myself in one of the easy chairs and took a deep breath.

If only James were here.

I wondered what he would make of this place. Would he share my sense of discomfort?

CHAPTER 2

J ames had shown me a solicitor's letter when we had met outside the Royal Aquarium the previous week.

"I suppose it was to be expected that Charlotte would not accept my offer," he said sourly.

"She plans to take legal action against you?" I skimmed my eyes over the convoluted wording of the document and tried to make sense of it.

"Yes, she and her father wish to have this sorry business discussed in a courtroom. I told you they would, didn't I?"

James shook his head and scowled all around him, as if searching among the passers-by for his former fiancée, Charlotte Jenkins, and her father. There was a bitter chill in the air and his bowler hat sat low on his brow, a woollen scarf was tied tightly beneath his chin.

"I offered them three hundred pounds," he continued. "That's all the money I have saved. Yet they have instructed their solicitor to present a case that suggests it is insufficient!"

"I shouldn't think they would need more than three

hundred pounds," I said. "The real reason behind the legal action is to punish you as much as possible."

"You're right, Penny, and I deserve it. After all, I abandoned a bride on her wedding day."

"You did the right thing," I said softly.

He turned back to face me. "I know that I did."

The sparkle in his blue eyes prompted me to smile. "Once this silly court case is over there'll be no need for you to feel guilty about your actions any longer," I said. "You'll have more than paid your dues. Then Charlotte will seek another husband and leave you well alone."

"I hope so, although I have no idea when my own family will forgive me. I find myself either being scolded or treated with an ill-humoured silence. I don't think my father has said more than five words to me since the day of the wedding."

"He'll forgive you in time."

"I don't think you know my father very well."

It had been almost two months since James had cancelled his wedding, and the joy I had initially felt was now tempered with caution. There had been widespread criticism and disapproval of our conduct, and the news of Charlotte's legal action made me feel that James' obligation to her was not yet over. Our courtship was proceeding tentatively as a result. We were both aware that being seen too often together provoked incessant whispering and gossip. Although I had no desire to wish the time away, I longed for the day when James' engagement was far enough in the past to be quite forgotten about.

"The fellows at the Yard still find it rather amusing," he said. "I don't suppose many bridegrooms have changed their minds just two hours before the big event. It's quite despicable what I did to her when you think about it. And she had long suspected that I held an affection for you. That can't have been easy for her to live with. In fact, I know that it wasn't. I can only imagine how I would feel if you were to treat me that way, Penny, and it's an awful thought."

Although it was natural for James to express remorse for the way he had treated Charlotte, I took no pleasure in hearing it. I wished to forget that they had ever been betrothed.

"You'll need to employ a decent solicitor to defend you," I said.

"Yes, I'll do that." He rubbed at his brow. "The alternative is that I offer them a larger sum and try to keep this case out of the courts."

"It doesn't matter how much you offer them; they'll still sue you for breach of promise. They're punishing you, remember?"

"But it doesn't bode well for my reputation, does it? A police inspector appearing as a defendant in a court of law."

"You have done nothing wrong," I replied. "You simply realised that you and Charlotte weren't well suited. Imagine if you had proceeded with the wedding. You'd have been married to her for almost two months now!"

"Ugh, what a thought."

"So the situation could have been far worse."

He laughed. "Yes, it could, but I wish there happened to be a better way of managing this; a way in which I don't feel as though I have behaved like a complete fool. Although I am certain that I made the right decision, I still feel as though I have done something wrong. I don't like being wrong, Penny. I don't like making mistakes."

"We all make mistakes, James."

"I like to think that I have always tried my best not to, but now there's to be a court case. My father will be horrified! I suppose I should be relieved that my grandfather is no longer alive, or he would also be greatly disappointed in me."

"Surely he wouldn't. He was always very fond of you, wasn't he?"

"Yes, but he wouldn't have understood my current predicament. He was a hard-working police officer who joined the Metropolitan Police only eleven years after its inception. Officers back then had to wear uniform even when off-duty, and they had to seek formal permission to marry. Those were very different times, and I think he would have struggled to understand how his grandson had got himself into this scrape."

"Good afternoon!" trilled my sister, Eliza.

I had just been about to tell James that he needn't be too hard on himself, and that I shared responsibility for what had happened, but instead I turned to greet her.

She narrowed her eyes. "Did the two of you arrange to meet earlier than the time you gave your trusty chaperone?"

"Not at all," I said. "I think you must be a little late, Ellie."

James checked his pocket watch. "Perhaps we were five minutes early in meeting."

"I see," replied Eliza with a wry smile. She was similar in appearance to me, with fair hair and brown eyes, though she stood a little taller. She wore a thick woollen cape over her jacket and a practical divided skirt. "And whose idea was it to visit the Royal Aquarium?" she asked, glancing up at the billboards fixed to the wall. "It's rather tawdry, isn't it?"

"The tawdry idea was all mine," replied James. "I thought it might prove to be a useful distraction on a cold November afternoon. We're just in time for Beckwith's Great Swimming Entertainment."

"What's that?"

"Have you never heard of Agnes Beckwith, who swam twenty miles in the Thames?" I asked.

"Oh, that's right. I remember now," replied Eliza. "She

was only seventeen or so at the time, wasn't she? A remarkable girl. And what about the girl whose job it is to be fired out of the cannon? Is she here today?"

"No but prepare to be amazed by Professor Roche and his pack of fifteen Russian wolves," said James. "And if we're lucky we might catch sight of Madame De Burgh, the Beautiful American Tattooed Lady."

"I shall need a warming cup of tea before we embark on all this adventure," replied Eliza. "Let's step inside before we become too cold to move."

CHAPTER 3

I wandered down to the Hotel Tempesta's Turkish Salon wearing an evening gown which had once belonged to my sister. The bodice was turquoise and gold brocade, and the green satin skirt gathered into a high bustle at my lower back. The corset felt tight and I found the skirts more cumbersome than my usual attire.

The thin-haired servant greeted me, and I was met with the sound of polite chatter as I stepped into a fantastical room of golden arches with swathes of velvet and silk. The ceiling and friezes were gold, red and blue, as was the thick oriental carpet beneath my feet. The paintings on the walls depicted men in turbans and long robes riding horses and playing chess. I felt as though I had stepped onto a theatre stage set.

"Am I in Constantinople?" I asked a waiter with a smile as he presented me with a glass of champagne. He gave a polite nod before announcing my name to the room.

The faces of ten or so people turned toward me, and a jovial man of around forty stepped forward.

"Miss Green! What an honour!" He raised his glass and

smiled widely to reveal parallel rows of neat white teeth, rendered even more impressive by a strong jawline. His handsome blue eyes were close-set, and he had fair, wavy hair, which was parted in the centre. He wore a double-breasted jacket that was buttoned up, and a purple cravat made from silk was tied around his high collar.

"Mr Gallo?" I said expectantly.

"The very same! Thank you for joining us here at the Hotel Tempesta. I'm so delighted that you could make it."

The extended vowels of his American accent gave his words a pleasing flow. My eye was drawn to a small white and brown dog by his side.

"This is Captain, my fox terrier," he added. "He also welcomes you."

"Thank you for inviting me, Mr Gallo. And congratulations on the opening of your new hotel."

He glanced around the room proudly. "Well, we're nearly there with it. We'll be welcoming our first official guests next week. In the meantime," he gestured toward the other guests, "there will just be a select few of you, along with my staff, and I am very much looking forward to entertaining you here tonight. Let me introduce you to some of these people."

I sipped my champagne and made polite conversation with Mrs Mortimer, a lady of around fifty with a double chin, sharp green eyes and grey hair that had been pinned into tight curls. She was a writer for a travel periodical.

"I've lost count of the number of years I've been contributing to *Wonders of the World*," she told me. "I suppose it was all I could do when accompanying my husband on his long voyages. He was an archaeologist and geographer."

"Have you travelled a great deal?"

"I used to. When my husband was alive, he mapped the

area between the Rocky Mountains and the Pacific Ocean. After that we travelled to Cairo, Jerusalem and Constantinople, among other places. I've written several books about my experiences."

"I'm trying to write a book at the moment, but it's not proving to be an easy undertaking," I said.

"What are you writing about?"

"My father. He was working as a plant-hunter when he vanished in Colombia nine years ago. He left a number of letters and diaries, which I have been transcribing into a book about his life."

"How fascinating, and yet terribly sad at the same time. What's his name?"

"Frederick Brinsley Green. An acquaintance of mine has recently left these shores in search of him."

She gave a knowing nod. "I think I recall reading about your father now. Wouldn't it be wonderful if he were to be found? It must be dreadful not knowing what has happened to him."

"We feared the worst when he was first reported missing, and as time passed I began to convince myself that it was unlikely he was still alive."

"How awful."

"Strangely enough, it was easier to think that way because I couldn't imagine any circumstances in which he might be alive and not write to us. It was easier to consider that he had died some years ago than to think of him spending all this time imprisoned somewhere."

"But why should he have been imprisoned?"

"I don't know. Explorers aren't always popular in the countries they explore, are they? Perhaps he upset some of the native people."

A long-faced man with languid eyes and black whiskers joined us. "It's Miss Green, isn't it? From the *Morning Express*?

I believe we recently met while reporting on the murder of Mr Forster."

"Yes, I remember. It's Mr Blackstone, isn't it?" I said. "Am I right in thinking that you write for *The Times*?"

"That's correct." He glanced around the room. "Mr Gallo has done a grand job with this place, hasn't he? I didn't think the hotel would ever reopen."

"I suppose it simply needed the right person to purchase it," I said.

"I stayed here before the fire," said Mrs Mortimer, "back when it was the Corinthian. It was once a marvellous place, but the atmosphere was never quite the same after it was rebuilt. It will be interesting to see what Mr Gallo manages to do with it."

"The chap knows what he's doing," said Mr Blackstone. "The Hotel Maganza in New York speaks for itself."

"Have you stayed there?" I asked.

He nodded and sipped his drink.

"When in New York, there can be no other place to stay!" added Mrs Mortimer with a self-satisfied laugh.

The tinkle of a bell put an end to the conversation.

"Ladies and gentlemen, may I please have your attention?" requested Mr Gallo.

By his side stood a fashionably dressed lady of around forty-five. She had auburn hair, which appeared to be artificially coloured, and wore a black gown made from fine silk. Her lips and face had been reddened with rouge.

"Please allow me to introduce you to Mrs Mirabeau," he continued. "She is the general manager here at the Hotel Tempesta, and this evening was all her idea. Mrs Mirabeau has enjoyed a long career within the hotel industry."

"Less of the *long*, thank you, Nathaniel," she said with a good-humoured pout.

"All right, then. A *distinguished* career in the hotel industry, having worked in Switzerland, France and the United States of America. Anything she doesn't know about hotels isn't worth knowing!"

We all gave a polite laugh and Mrs Mirabeau smiled.

"When Mrs Mirabeau first suggested this idea to me, I told her the fine ladies and gentlemen of Fleet Street would be far too busy to consider spending the night at my hotel. She convinced me otherwise, and here we all are." He surveyed us with a broad smile. "Please join Mrs Mirabeau, Captain and me for the grand tour. I'll try not to bore you too much, and I promise to provide more liquor at the end of it!"

We followed Mr Gallo into the grand foyer, where he paused at the foot of the staircase.

"Now, I know what you're all thinking," he said. "You're wondering why anyone would want to buy this place. I can't pretend that it's had a great history."

"But it's a beautiful hotel," said a slick-haired man with a thin black moustache. "And you've done a splendid job with it."

"Everything I've done is merely superficial. But you're right, it is a beautiful building and I've been on the lookout for a place like this for a long time. I remember hearing about the devastating fire, and we all wondered then whether the hotel would be salvageable. The Corinthian had quite a reputation back then, didn't it?"

"Oh yes, quite the reputation indeed," replied the moustachioed man. "Members of various European royal families stayed here, as well as famous bankers and industrialists. Are you confident that you will be able to entice them back?"

"I'll do my best, Mr Hardy. As a writer for *The Hotelier* I'm sure you'll have some first-rate ideas on how to pull it off. I'll need all the tips I can get!"

His comment was met with gentle laughter.

"Surely not, Mr Gallo," said Mr Blackstone. "You have more experience than anybody else. It's as clear as day that if anyone can make this hotel a success, you can."

"Thank you for your vote of confidence," replied the hotelier with a smile. "Let's go and have a look around, shall we?"

He led us around the hotel with great enthusiasm, pointing out his favourite paintings and elaborating on various items in the display cabinets. I couldn't help warming to Mr Gallo, who had an effortless charm about him. He remembered every person's name and had learned a little about each of our publications.

"We were able to recover some of the items that weren't destroyed in the fire and put them to good use. I've shipped over a few of my favourite items from the Maganza, too. There were a few pieces there that were no longer needed."

"How many bedchambers do you have here?" asked a young man with red hair and freckles.

"Three hundred and eighteen, Mr White."

The young man wrote this down in his notebook.

"Any other questions before we view the Palm Room?" asked Mrs Mirabeau.

"Can Mr Gallo please tell us how he has succeeded so well in the hotel industry?" asked Mr White.

"Succeeded?" Mr Gallo gave a laugh. "I'm not sure I've succeeded quite yet."

"I'd say that you have!" said Mr Hardy.

"I suppose it depends on your definition of success. My story isn't terribly interesting, really. I'm almost as European as you, because my father originally came from Italy. My mother was born in Harrisburg, Pennsylvania, and I grew up in a town called Lewistown in Mifflin County. You won't have heard of it, I'm sure, but it's a place that has undergone a great deal of change. We have the Pennsylvania Canal running through it, and the Pennsylvania Railroad arrived when I was still a boy.

"After the war we had railroads linking us up with all sorts of places, and what with the coal and lumber industries – iron and limestone – all sorts of folk were busy coming and going. My father ran an inn and decided to add a few rooms to it so he could put more of the workers and travellers up. A few rooms turned into ten, then twenty and – well, you get the picture – he was running a few places after a while. We're talking cheap rooms, of course. My father never would have run a place like this. But I helped him run those places, and when I got tired of Lewistown I moved to Philadelphia, and then to New York."

"You have quite a talent for running hotels," said Mr Blackstone. *The Times* reporter seemed keen to compliment the hotelier at every opportunity.

"I merely credit myself with having been in the right place at the right time, Mr Blackstone. It's little more than luck. Come on, let me show you the Palm Room. I'm very excited about this room, as I know it'll be my wife's favourite. She and my daughters are in Paris right now. They've been spending a little time there while I've been overseeing things here. They'll be arriving at Dover this Saturday, and I'm sure looking forward to seeing them."

CHAPTER 4

The Palm Room was a large conservatory with a domed glass ceiling. The foggy evening ensured once again that there was nothing to see beyond the glass, but the arching green fronds of the palm trees were spectacularly lit by small electric lights.

"What do you think of the fish?" asked Mr Gallo, striding over to a large glass tank supported by an elaborate wrought-iron frame. "Captain adores them."

The dog leaned up against the tank, standing on his hind legs and tapping the glass with his paw.

"How marvellous," said Mr Hardy, peering over at the darting, colourful fish. "Quite spellbinding, in fact."

"Try out one of these seats," said Mr Gallo, gesturing toward the wicker chairs.

Mr Hardy sat down. "Very agreeable indeed."

Mr Blackstone joined him, while Mr White scribbled in his notebook.

"Simply remarkable," whispered a large man standing next to me. He had heavy jowls and dark eyes, and was flamboyantly dressed in a red velvet jacket and a gold brocade waistcoat.

"It's all very impressive," I said in return.

"It must have cost a pretty penny," he added, "and this is just one room! He must have spent a fortune on this place altogether."

An older gentleman with a walking stick overheard this last remark and stepped closer to us. "It will have cost him every penny he had, and the rest will have been loaned to him," he said. "Let's hope he makes his money back."

"Oh, I intend to earn every penny back and more, Mr Wentworth!" said Mr Gallo with a grin.

The older man scowled, irritated that his comment had been overheard.

"I'm sure you will, Nathaniel!" interjected the large, flamboyant man. "After all, you have this wonderful Palm Room. It will surely become the talk of the town!"

Two waiters entered, bearing trays laden with glasses of champagne.

"Enjoy a drink in here, everyone," said Mr Gallo, "and then I'll show you the suites upstairs."

I introduced myself to the interestingly attired man.

"It's a pleasure to meet you, Miss Green," he replied. "I'm Mr Philip Somers of *The City Journal*."

"Do you know Mr Gallo well?" I asked, having noticed that he had addressed the hotelier by his forename.

"Yes. I spent some time in New York writing for *The Manhattan Review*, and I met him while I was there. I'm delighted he's finally come to London. I told him to many years ago, of course, and he has finally listened to me! He'll tell you he was waiting for the right hotel to become available, but I can assure you that he was spending far too much time twiddling his thumbs."

"What of the curse, Mr Gallo?" called out a square-faced

man with brown whiskers. He had hard, grey eyes, and he folded his arms defiantly as he waited for the hotelier's reply.

"I've been asked that one countless times, Mr Bolton," replied Mr Gallo with a grin, "and I always reply with: '*Curse? What curse?*'" Light laughter followed. "Yes the place burned down," he continued, "but I think the same has happened to a great many other buildings. And what happens then? They get rebuilt! It happens everywhere. Those fires we had in Chicago, Boston and Michigan... There were scores of buildings gone, and many homes and lives were lost. All that carnage makes a blaze in a hotel seem like nothing at all! I've never been in a fire myself, and neither have any of my hotels. Besides, I have great confidence in the new electric lighting we're installing now. Hopefully there'll be no need for gas or candles in this building at all before long, and that thought fills me with confidence."

"But what of the legacy of the fire?" asked Mr Bolton, his arms still resolutely folded. "People say there are ghosts in the hotel. Thirty-six people died, after all."

Mr Gallo nodded solemnly. "It was indeed a tragic event, but all I can say is that over the past six months I've spent more time in this place than anybody else. When I first set eyes on it, and it was sitting empty, I walked right in and took a look around. I can't deny that it gave me a shiver or two, but empty buildings have that effect, don't they? It was properly rebuilt after the fire, and I can assure you that I have seen nothing of a supernatural nature in this place whatsoever. Now, that's probably to do with the fact that I don't believe in the supernatural. It's interesting, don't you think, that the people who see ghosts are always the ones who believe in them in the first place? I think they're just seeing what they want to see. Captain and I have walked around this building as the only living, breathing man and dog inside it, and we've heard and seen nothing that had us worried. And some say that animals are especially receptive to spirits." He gave his dog an affectionate pat on the head.

"I've never seen anything or anyone unnatural here either," said Mrs Mirabeau.

"Apart from me," added Mr Gallo with a laugh.

"Yes, Mr Gallo, I think it's fairly safe to say that you haunt the place," she replied with a smile.

"I must say, though, that I'm not about to disregard the ghost stories," continued the hotelier. "We should encourage them, in fact! I think a resident ghost or two is good for business. People want to come and see for themselves, don't they? Nine times out of ten they won't see anything, and for those who do, well, it'll just be something in their minds that they wanted to happen. I'll tell you what, why don't we invent something for your readers right now, Mr Bolton?" He laughed. "Let's come up with a headless lady in a grey dress and say that you all witnessed her in the Chinese Dining Room! She'd be like one of those ghosts that supposedly haunt British castles, carrying her head under her arm because she's been beheaded by the king. I think that would be a great tale to tell. I'm relying on you all to come up with something entertaining for your readers; something that'll encourage them to stay here. What do you say, Mr Bolton?"

The square-faced man shrugged. "Can't say that I go in for ghost stories myself."

"But you can't deny the fact that they're good for business, can you?" said the slick-haired Mr Hardy. "I think it makes perfect sense to spread rumours of strange hauntings."

"Rumour and gossip are powerful tools indeed," said Mr Bolton. "What of Mr Thompson's suicide, Mr Gallo?"

"What of it, Mr Bolton?" replied the hotelier. His smile failed to reach as far as his eyes this time, and I suspected that he was growing tired of the square-faced man's challenging questions. There was little doubt that Mr Bolton's manner was deliberately confrontational.

"Some say that his death was related to the curse."

"You claim not to be interested in ghost stories, yet you insist on asking about this nonsensical curse business."

"I'm asking on behalf of the readers of the *South London Reporter*."

"I see. Let me say this, then. There's a well-established claim that Mr Thompson faced financial ruin, and for some people that seems like the end of the world. When everything you've worked so hard for goes wrong it feels like there's nothing left for you. I feel great sympathy for the chap. After all, I know what it's like to put so much into your work, sometimes at the expense of other responsibilities in life, such as spending time with your family. Work of this kind can take over your life, and failure often feels like the end of all your hopes and dreams.

"I actually met the man a few times. He was a rather dour fellow, and he took his work extremely seriously. I'm quite sure that his act of self-destruction was carried out during a moment of madness. Perhaps if someone had been able to talk him out of it he would have found the capacity to pick himself up, dust himself off and get back to it again. The same could surely be said for many suicides, couldn't it? It usually occurs during a despondent moment all alone, when it feels like the world has come to an end. It's terribly sad, and a dreadful waste of a life."

"I agree that it's extremely tragic," said Mr Blackstone. "He died in this very hotel, did he not?"

"Yes, he hanged himself in the room that is now the Venetian Suite."

"Does the room have a strange feel to it now?" I asked.

"No, why should it?" Mr Gallo replied. "It's quite different these days."

"You've never seen him lurking around in there, then?" asked Mr Hardy.

Mr Gallo laughed. "Of course not! We're back to ghost stories again, are we?"

"And the curse!" laughed Mrs Mirabeau.

"Oh, and the curse!" echoed Mr Gallo. "This hotel is supposedly cursed because it once burned down in a fire and then the next fellow who bought it hanged himself here. A good many hotels have experienced similar events in their histories, and countless people have died in hotels. Perhaps none of you realise how common it is. It all has to be dealt with rather tactfully, of course. The undertakers usually bring a coffin shell up the back stairs and take the bodies out that way. It's important that the other guests don't experience any inconvenience or distress during their stay. We simply have to get on with things when the death of a guest occurs. It has to be business as usual."

I noticed the red-haired Mr White scribbling everything down enthusiastically in his notebook.

"I appreciate that similar things have happened in other hotels," ventured old Mr Wentworth, leaning wearily on his stick, "but this one seems to be talked about more than the others. Why do you think that is?"

"Because it's such a beautiful building," replied Mr Gallo. "There's something rather alluring about the combination of beauty and tragedy, isn't there? Something seductive." He gave a suggestive wink and Mrs Mirabeau giggled.

"Isn't there a risk that the stories will make people stay away?" asked Mr Wentworth.

"Some will, of course, but they're probably the kind of dull people who prefer to stay in dull hotels. Those aren't the sort of guests we like here! I've been in the hotel business a long time, and I know that the history of a hotel is part of its appeal. Scandal and gossip can only be good for business.

"I'll show you the Venetian Suite shortly, and you'll see for yourselves that there's absolutely nothing to worry about. There's no hint of any tragedy that occurred in that room. Why, something similar could have happened in a room at your own home and you might not even know about it! That's some thought, isn't it? Have you all finished your drinks? Come on, then. I'll show you around the suites on the first floor."

CHAPTER 5

We followed Mr Gallo up the grand staircase and into a wide, thickly carpeted corridor. Although I refused to believe that the hotel could truly be haunted, I did feel some discomfort knowing that so few of us were gathered in such a large building. I didn't like the thought of so many rooms lying empty behind the countless doors.

A young man walked toward us.

"This is Percy," said Mr Gallo, shaking his hand. "He worked at Claridge's for four years, and then I stole him!" He laughed and patted Percy on the shoulder. "I'll show you all my favourite room first," he said as we continued along the corridor. "I know that I should save the best until last, but I'm too excited about this one to let it wait. This is the Versailles Suite."

He opened the door, and Captain led the way into a bedchamber that glowed with gold and white. Heavy damask curtains hung from a canopy above the enormous bed, mirrors in heavy gilt frames decorated the walls and two elegantly curved chairs had been placed either side of a marble table.

"Are you an admirer of Louis XV, Mr Gallo?" asked Mr Wentworth, pointing his walking stick at a portrait of the king dressed in ermine robes.

"It's the Rococo style that appeals more than anything," replied the hotel owner. "I've always dreamed of creating my own Palace of Versailles."

"I adore it!" announced the flamboyant Mr Somers.

"I find it rather vulgar," retorted Mr Wentworth.

"Yet that's exactly what some guests like," said Mr Gallo. "There's too much ostentation here for your own home – unless you are Louis XV, of course – but you can enjoy it for a night under my roof instead! You can pretend to be a French king and bring your own Marie Antoinette with you."

"I wouldn't be in any hurry to emulate a French king," said Mr Bolton, folding his arms. "We all know what happened to them."

"It's intended to be a work of fantasy," said Mr Somers. "A stay in a hotel like this allows people to escape their everyday lives and experience new pleasures. Perhaps you're happy as you are working for the *South London Reporter* and have no wish to be a French king, Mr Bolton, but plenty of people would."

"Thank you, Philip," said the hotelier. "I've always believed that when people come to stay at my hotels they can enjoy being anything they want to be."

"As long as they pay the bill at the end of it," added Mr Wentworth drily.

Mr Gallo laughed. "Absolutely! That's the most important part."

"I'm guessing there's a view over the Thames from this room," suggested a softly spoken, bespectacled man as he parted the heavy curtains at the window.

"You guess correctly, Mr Goldman," replied the hotelier. "The best rooms have the most delightful views of the river. I believe the foreign traveller likes to rise in the morning, look out of the window and have an immediate sense of where he is. It needs to be a recognisable view; a unique one he can't find anywhere else in the world. A view that says: *'This is London.'*"

"But not so much when the fog sets in," added Mrs Mortimer.

Mr Gallo laughed. "No one in the world does fog like you Londoners. It's not just a bit of mist, is it? It's got a thickness to it that I've never seen anywhere else. And then there's the colour of it. Brown... green... What did *The New York Times* call it? Pea soup, wasn't it? But that's unique in itself. When a foreigner comes to London he needs to experience all of it, including the pea soup. When he opens his curtains in the morning and that's all he sees, well, it's part of the experience, isn't it?"

"Fog is indeed part of the London experience," laughed Mr Hardy. "I like the idea of foreigners paying good money to come and see it!"

"The gentleman and lady staying in this room can expect freshly laundered sheets on the bed every day and service whenever it is required," said Mrs Mirabeau. "Each of the suites has a bell beside the door that will summon the assistance of the staff. Chambermaids light the fire before the guests awake, and the room is dusted every day. On this floor we have a bathroom with running water – hot and cold – for each pair of suites. If guests wish to bathe in their room, the bath can be brought in and filled for them."

"That's a fine painting," I commented, gesturing toward a picture of a lady sitting beneath a tree, reading a letter.

"I'm pleased you like it, Miss Green. It's by Bessette,"

replied Mr Gallo. "I needed a Rococo painting for this Rococo room."

"I've noticed a lot of expensive paintings in the hotel. You must have quite the art collection," said Mr Goldman.

"I have been collecting artworks for a long time, and London is the perfect place to find new treasures."

"Do you buy them at auction?" Mr Goldman pressed.

"I sometimes visit Sotheby's, but I also know the private galleries well, and particularly the Calthorpe Art Gallery. The curator there, Mr Court-Holmes, has been of great help in advising me on the best paintings for my hotel. Each painting requires its own setting, and I have found that a lot of thought goes into choosing its rightful location. You don't want a painting to dominate a room, but neither do you want it to go unnoticed. The furnishing of a room must complement the artwork. I could bore you plenty more about my love of art, but I really must show you the Venetian Suite next door."

The Venetian Suite featured white plaster columns, a bronze statue of a mermaid and a cabinet completely covered in tiny shells.

"My youngest daughter Nancy is sure going to love this room," said Mr Gallo. "Just look at the chairs."

The chair backs had been carved to look like shells, and I smiled as I considered how appealing they would be to a child. The room had an intimate charm to it and was considerably less intimidating than the neighbouring Versailles Suite.

"I usually stay in rooms up in the attic, but I'll be sleeping in this suite for the very first time tonight," said Mr Gallo. "I do this to demonstrate to all of you that the stories associated with the hotel are nothing more than myths and rumours. You couldn't imagine that a tragedy had ever occurred in this room, could you?"

We glanced about the room and collectively muttered that we couldn't.

"On the contrary, this room feels quite pleasant," said Mrs Mortimer.

"I'm pleased you think so," replied the hotelier. "Venice is one of my favourite cities; I dream of opening a hotel there some day. Have you ever been to the Festa del Redentore in Venice? It's a fantastic festival, and an absolute spectacle with its countless decorated barges. I like to bring a little piece of Italy into all my hotels, and each year at the Maganza we hold a masquerade ball. I plan to do the same here at Christmas time."

"It's time for us to sit down to dinner, Mr Gallo," said Mrs Mirabeau.

"Already? Oh, now that's a shame. We've only just begun!"

CHAPTER 6

The Chinese Dining Room was decorated with yellow flock wallpaper and tall porcelain pagodas. A large chinoiserie clock made of gold stood on the gilded mantelpiece.

I took my place between the elderly Mr Wentworth and the flamboyant Mr Somers, with Mrs Mortimer sitting opposite me. Mr Gallo perched at one end of the table, while Mrs Mirabeau sat at the other.

"Now then, tell me what you think so far," said Mr Gallo as we dined on mock turtle soup. "Do you think I can attract the old clientele back to the hotel?"

"I think you have a fair chance of doing so," said Mr Blackstone, wiping his dark whiskers with a starched serviette. "I hear that many in society are already bored with Claridge's."

"That doesn't surprise me," said Mr Hardy, slicking back his hair with his hand. "Claridge's is an exceedingly dull hotel."

"Oh, but I quite like it," said Mrs Mortimer.

"My dear lady, you cannot praise Claridge's within earshot of another hotelier!" scolded Mr Hardy with a gentle smile.

"Of course she can!" said Mr Gallo graciously. "You've been rather quiet, Mr White. What do you think?"

The young, red-haired man earnestly swallowed a mouthful of soup before replying.

"I haven't stayed in as many hotels as your other guests, sir, but I think it's a perfectly splendid place, and I'm quite sure people will enjoy staying here for many years to come." .

Mr Gallo seemed unimpressed with this platitude and addressed Mr Wentworth without further comment. "You find the place vulgar, don't you?" he asked.

"I find some of the rooms are a little ostentatious, but then I'm not the sort of client you're after, Mr Gallo," replied the old man. "Most of your guests will be foreigners, will they not? I think they should be more than happy with this hotel; especially the Americans."

"I didn't buy this place for my fellow countrymen."

"Maybe not, but I think you'll find that a number of them will stay with you here."

"I see. Your thoughts, Miss Green?"

"I like what I have seen so far," I replied. "The history of this hotel fascinates me more than anything."

"You'd stay here for the ghosts, would you?"

"I can't say that I believe in the supernatural, but I do believe that a building holds its history within its walls. I realise this hotel has been extensively refurbished, but I think there is still a sense, a sort of echo, of what has happened here in the past."

"An *echo*. I like that description!" said Mr Gallo. "If you can still sense the hotel's tragic history, Miss Green, would you say that staying here isn't an entirely comfortable experience for you?"

"I'm afraid it isn't, Mr Gallo. Please don't misunderstand me, I—"

"Oh, I don't misunderstand you at all," he interrupted. "I appreciate your opinion. This building isn't just a box of bricks; it holds its past within its walls, as you rightly say. I believe we are supposed to have a complicated relationship with this building. It is beautiful, and yet there's something rather more sinister, too."

Square-faced Mr Bolton sat back in his chair and folded his arms once again. "Mr Gallo, do you wish us to speak frankly?"

"I sure do."

"This nonsense about a building holding its history in its walls and the idea that we somehow have a relationship with it, well, it's piffle as far as I'm concerned."

"Interesting to hear, Mr Bolton."

"In all honesty, Mr Gallo, I think you'll be lucky to attract the clientele the Corinthian once entertained. Hotels are opening up on practically every street corner in London these days, so you'll have a great deal of competition. Your Chinese Dining Room, your Palm Room, your Turkish Room and that – what was it? – oh yes, your Venetian Suite, and so on. They're impressive, but they're also a contrivance. They all claim to be something they're not. I think your desired clientele is looking for something with more integrity. I think the superior classes are looking for modernity rather than novelty."

"Thank you, Mr Bolton." Mr Gallo forced a smile, but the manner in which his eyes coolly remained on the reporter prompted an uncomfortable silence.

"You know what I think, Nathaniel," blustered Mr Somers to my right. "I think this place is simply divine! And I wish you every success with it. I suggest a toast." He raised his wine glass and everyone else followed suit. "To Mr Gallo, and to the Hotel Tempesta! May he have every success with it!"

Turbot, salmon and fried sole were served as glasses were drained, and the mood soon relaxed into idle chatter.

"How did you begin writing for the *Morning Express,* Miss Green?" Mr Wentworth asked.

"I pestered the editor with speculative letters and articles for about a year," I replied. "Writing was all I had ever wanted to do, and journalism struck me as a good way to make a living."

"You surprise me," he replied. "It is not a profession many ladies choose to follow."

"An increasing number of ladies are doing so."

"You must be one of those girls who didn't meet the right chap."

"What exactly do you mean by that?"

"I mean that the right fellow didn't come along. In the absence of a suitor, I suppose an educated lady begins to think about a profession instead."

"My decision to become a news reporter had nothing to do with my marriage prospects, Mr Wentworth."

"Perhaps not. But if you'd fallen in love with a chap and he'd proposed marriage you would likely have acquiesced. And by that token, you wouldn't be here, would you?"

"I don't believe in speculating on what might or might not have been, Mr Wentworth. The fact of the matter is that I wished to become a writer, and that was the profession I followed. Was your career affected by whether you chose to marry or not?"

He gave a snort. "What? Of course not. What an odd question to ask of a man!"

"And yet you ask it of a lady."

"Because it is an entirely different situation."

Mr Somers giggled. "Oh dear, Miss Green. I fear you have offended Mr Wentworth!"

"He offended me first, Mr Somers."

"I suppose he considers it unusual for a lady to be working as a news reporter."

"And I agree," I responded. "However, it has nothing to do with my marriage prospects."

"I can vouch that marriage prospects have never influenced my career, or my life at all, for that matter," replied Mr Somers. "I am not the marrying type," he added in a whisper that only I could hear.

The main roasts were pigeon, poulard, beef, ham, tongue, lamb and mutton. I wondered how I would be able to eat anything more with my corset so tightly laced beneath my evening gown. Every time I took a sip of wine my glass was refilled by the eager waiting staff. I decided to stop drinking it in order to avoid consuming too much. A tight corset and a large quantity of wine would make me unsteady if I wasn't careful.

Mr Hardy and Mrs Mirabeau were conversing animatedly at one end of the table, I observed that the two seemed quite taken with one another. The previously quiet Mr White was talking loudly at Mrs Mortimer, and Mr Bolton had thankfully engaged the insufferable Mr Wentworth in conversation.

The bespectacled Mr Goldman seemed particularly interested in the room's impressive artworks. I could only hear snippets of his conversation with Mr Gallo, but they seemed to be discussing the paintings at great length. Captain sat on Mr Gallo's lap and happily consumed morsels from the hotelier's fingers. Mr Blackstone was addressing Mr Somers, but the latter seemed rather disinterested in what the former had to say.

"That chap from *The Times* is half-seas-over," Mr Somers whispered to me as soon as he was able to take a break from the conversation. "They have a lot of wine to pour down our throats here, haven't they?"

I agreed, then inquired as to when he had first met Mr Gallo.

"Shortly after the Maganza opened about six years ago. I'd been in New York for about a year then, and I interviewed him for *The City Journal*. We're very different, he and I, and have little in common, but for some reason we get along rather well. I introduced him to a few people in Manhattan, and there were a few dinners and parties there. A lot of dinners and parties, in fact; perhaps too many. They are the main reason I'm so large." He giggled and patted his stomach. "I need to put a stop to these parties. Anyway, as soon as Mr Gallo bought this place he wrote to tell me, and I was delighted to hear of it, of course. I have accompanied him to many places in London, though he always wants to visit the art galleries. Paintings are rather boring, don't you think?"

"It depends on the painting, I suppose."

"They're all boring," he replied with a dismissive wave of the hand, "but for Nathaniel they're an obsession. It looks as though poor Mr Goldman has been receiving a lecture on the subject for most of the dinner."

"He appears rather interested," I replied.

"I think he's merely good at feigning interest, as I was with that *Times* man just now. I declare that every *Times* journalist I've ever met swears his publication is superior to everyone else's."

Our plates were promptly cleared as three trollies bearing numerous plates covered with large silver cloches were wheeled into the room.

Mr Gallo lowered Captain to the floor and rose to his feet. "And now we shall enjoy the best part of the meal!" he announced. I gave a small sigh, feeling that it would be quite impossible to eat another morsel.

"Plum pudding!" he announced as one of the plates was placed on the table and its cloche ceremoniously lifted. "Cabinet pudding!" he crowed as the second was unveiled.

Italian creams, Bohemian creams and Genoise pastries followed, along with various tartlets and a lemon cheesecake. Other plates revealed wine jellies and impressive Macédoine jellies, which were ornately moulded and contained whole strawberries and red berries.

"But that's not all," announced Mr Gallo proudly. "There is another pudding that only a handful of chefs in London are able to make. My chef Jean-François has the ability. I stole him from the Langham!" He laughed as a final trolley was wheeled in. "I present to you, my guests, the Nesselrode ice pudding!"

Beneath the cloche was a meringue structure styled to look like the turret of a castle. The waiter handed Mr Gallo a small silver hammer, which he raised in ceremonious fashion above his head. Then he brought it down on the pudding in one swift blow, sending fragments of shattered meringue flying across the table. This action was met with whoops and applause.

"There it is! The Nesselrode!" He pointed at the domed ice pudding. "Made with only the finest Italian chestnuts and maraschino. You must all have a piece of this, I absolutely insist! I shall serve it myself."

CHAPTER 7

I felt nauseous at the thought of eating anything further, but the Nesselrode proved rather intriguing. The clock on the mantelpiece struck eleven. We had been supping for close to four hours.

"Oh dear! What's happened to Mr Blackstone?" asked Mr Gallo as he handed out the plates of iced pudding.

I turned to see that *The Times* reporter was falling asleep on his chair and appeared to be in danger of sliding off it altogether.

"He's three sheets to the wind," replied Mr Somers. "He's utterly inebriated, Nathaniel. You've given him far too much wine."

Mr Gallo clicked his fingers to summon one of his waiting staff. "I think Mr Blackstone requires some assistance," he said. "Take him up to his room and give him some coffee. It doesn't look as though he'll be joining us for our tour of the kitchens."

I groaned inwardly. I longed to retire to bed myself; indeed, the very last thing I wanted to do was tour the kitchens at this late hour.

Mr Gallo noticed our muted response. "But you *must* come and see the kitchens! Jean-François will be extremely offended if no one goes down to pay him their respects."

We watched with bemusement as Mr Blackstone was hauled out of the dining room with his head slumped and his arms draped across the shoulders of two tall waiters.

"The first one to fall!" laughed Mr Gallo. "Who'll be next? You're looking a little unsteady, Mr White."

The red-haired man shrugged, then began to laugh.

The men retired to the smoking room for cigars while Mrs Mortimer, Mrs Mirabeau and I moved into the Lady Jane Lounge. It was furnished in red and gold with polished mahogany tables and a small harpsichord.

"How does Mr Gallo stay so energetic?" asked Mrs Mortimer as we sank into the red velvet chairs.

"He's always like that," replied Mrs Mirabeau. "In fact, he scarcely sleeps. He doesn't seem to need it. He enjoys spending all his time in company. He doesn't particularly enjoy being alone."

"So when he doesn't have guests in the hotel he pesters you for company, does he?"

"He tries," Mrs Mirabeau smiled. "Not in any disreputable sense, of course. He has always treated me very honourably. But if he could keep me talking all night in the smoking room he would. He would happily sit and talk all night with anyone."

"His wife can fulfil that role when she arrives this weekend, I presume," I said.

"Yes, I should think she'll be looking forward to seeing him. Oh, is that the time?" she exclaimed, glancing up at the clock on the mantelpiece, which showed that it was just after half-past eleven. "I must see to something briefly. Please excuse me."

"Interesting lady," said Mrs Mortimer once Mrs Mirabeau had left the room. Her comment had a disparaging tone to it.

"What do you mean by that?" I asked.

"She strikes me as a lady with a past."

"Are you implying that her past is dishonourable?"

"Exactly. You only need look at her rouge and the colour of her hair to see that. And I caught her smoking a cigarette in her office earlier. You know what they say about ladies who smoke cigarettes. It's a pursuit that is usually preserved for a woman of loose morals."

"Mr Gallo seems to think highly of her, and by all accounts she is excellent at her job."

"I suspect she thinks highly of him in return. The pair of them must spend a lot of time together. It makes you wonder, doesn't it?"

Such speculation on the nature of their relationship reminded me of the comments James and I had been forced to endure until recently. Mr Gallo had spoken fondly of his family a number of times, so I felt no reason to doubt his fidelity. Furthermore, I had no wish to be drawn into Mrs Mortimer's gossip-mongering.

"Mrs Mirabeau is a little unconventional," I said, "but I see nothing wrong with that. My own sister is unconventional. She refuses to wear a corset and has adopted rational dress."

Mrs Mortimer gave a groan. "Such ugly clothes those ladies wear. I cannot understand it at all. Since ladies are blessed with such an attractive silhouette, why ruin it?"

"For reasons of practicality. My sister enjoys riding a bicycle, and she can hardly do so in conventional skirts."

"No, she couldn't. However, the best solution would be not to ride a bicycle at all. I don't understand this modern fashion for ladies to behave like men. Men and women complement one another because we have different abilities. That's what makes marriages and communities work; it's all due to a combined effort on the part of both sexes. There is no need for women to have the vote, for example, as the responsibility is shared between husband and wife."

It was rather late in the evening to be drawn into a discussion on women's suffrage, so I felt quite relieved when Mrs Mirabeau returned to the room. A short while later we were joined by the men.

"The consensus seems to be that we must tour the kitchens in the morning," said Mr Gallo. "The hour is apparently too late for some."

Captain sat at my feet, expecting a pat on the head, so I obliged. The clock showed the time to be five minutes before midnight.

"What have you done with Mr White?" asked Mrs Mirabeau.

"Oh, I don't know. I think we lost him somewhere," replied Mr Bolton, his words slurred with drink.

"Maybe he went up to his room?" suggested Mr Goldman.

"I don't even remember seeing him in the smoking room," said Mr Wentworth.

"He was there all right," said Mr Gallo, "but then he took himself off somewhere."

Mr Bolton leaned against the back of a chair to steady himself.

"I believe more drinks are in order!" announced Mr Gallo.

"Not for me, I'm afraid," said Mrs Mortimer, rising to her feet. "I've had quite enough. I shall bid you all goodnight."

"And I shall follow suit," I said, also standing. Captain got to his feet and trotted back to his owner.

"Goodnight, ladies," said Mr Gallo. "Thank you for your company this evening, and we shall see you at breakfast."

. . .

It was a great relief to be free of my corset and gown. I put on my familiar nightclothes and climbed into the large bed, which was comfortable but cold. A small gas lamp provided just enough light for me to read Henry James' *The Portrait of a Lady* by, but my mind kept wandering.

In the dim light I could feel the eyes of the lady in the portrait hovering over me. I considered drawing the curtains around the bed to shield myself from the picture, but I had the irrational worry that doing so would enable someone, or something, to creep into the room without my knowledge.

I got up and checked that I had locked the door. Satisfied that I had, I returned to the cold bed.

I thought of the blaze that had taken hold of this place four years previously. *Could the same thing happen again tonight?* The roar of flames and the screams of trapped people desperate to escape filled my mind. The visions seemed so real that I felt sure I could smell smoke, and my heart began to pound.

I sat up and tried to calm myself. I could still recall the aftermath of the fire. I hadn't reported on it, but I had walked past the ruins and seen the hotel's crumbled walls. Charred masonry and debris had littered the ground. The windows that had remained were like the empty eyes of someone deceased.

I shivered as I thought about the extreme panic that must have consumed everyone in this place that night. I tried to push away the thoughts of people struggling through smoke-choked corridors and stairways. Some of them had chosen to jump from the windows rather than attempt to reach the ground floor.

I got up again and paced around the bed, reassuring myself that the tragic event was safely confined to history.

Then I got back into bed and put out my lamp. Despite the dark, I still felt as though I were being scrutinised by the woman in the portrait.

An image of the doomed hotelier, Mr Thompson, swinging from a rope flashed into my mind. My skin prickled as I thought of the staff who discovered him and how they must have run about the hotel and raised the alarm. I thought of them cutting him down and transporting him down the back stairs in a coffin shell.

I finally managed to calm myself. The bed still felt cold, and I noticed that my body had barely warmed it. I needed my old bed shawl, which I had foolishly left at home. I realised there probably hadn't been a fire in the hearth for some time prior to the unofficial reopening. The cold felt as though it had lingered in the bricks and timber of the building for several years.

Although I wished Mr Gallo well, I couldn't fathom why anyone would ever wish to pay money to stay in this detestable place.

CHAPTER 8

S leep seemed far away as I lay in bed and tried to comfort myself with thoughts of those close to me: James and my sister Eliza. I then pictured Francis Edwards searching for my father in Colombia. I had shown Eliza and James his most recent letter over tea at the Royal Aquarium.

El Charquito, United States of Colombia, 12th October 1884

    Dearest Penny and Eliza

    It is with great delight that I write to inform you that I have reached El Charquito! This is the little village near the Falls of Tequendama, where your good father was last seen. Anselmo and I are enjoying the hospitality of the people of El Charquito at more than eight thousand feet above sea level. The village is little more than a cluster of simple homes clinging to a track that winds down the thickly forested hillside. Although it feels remote here, we are only a short distance from Bogotá.

    The falls themselves are quite a sight, as the River Funza plunges five hundred feet. We are experiencing quite a deluge of rain at the current time, and poor Anselmo is rather disappointed! We have, however, been assured that the rainy season will soon end, and that fine weather will shortly be on its way. I recall you saying that your father always chose his expeditions in Colombia to fall during the dry season between October and March.

I couldn't wish for a better travelling companion than Anselmo. Not only is his knowledge of Spanish invaluable, but he is also agreeable company. I am prone to rumination at times, and his good spirits have lifted my mood on many occasions.

We have visited the hut your father is believed to have inhabited. A delightful family lives there now. The hut sat empty for a few years, so the family knew nothing of your father, but we have spoken to a number of people in the village and some recall a European visitor nine years ago. As you can imagine, other foreigners have passed through this way since then, so we cannot be sure that every supposed sighting of your father is to be believed. However, I feel sure that we have received some accurate reports.

The people who recall your father speak well of him. They tell us he was a pleasant, respectful man who clearly had a love for this country and its flora.

The challenge we face now is to discover which route your father took when he left El Charquito. The people we speak to have differing opinions. I am rather wary of travelling miles along one route only to realise that we have made the wrong decision. So Anselmo and I shall stay in El Charquito for a while and make regular excursions along the various routes that lead out of the village. It is my hope that our enquiries along these routes will reward us with clues about your father's onward journey.

I shall dispatch this letter to Bogotá, and from there it will make its way north to the coast and the transatlantic steamships. Consequently, it will be some time before you are able to read these words. I hear that telegrams can now be sent from Buenaventura, which is a little more than three hundred miles to the west. If my travels take me in that direction, I hope to be able to send these communications with greater promptitude!

I miss London and the company of my favourite sisters a great deal. I hope to receive a letter from you soon.

With fondest regards,
Francis Edwards

"He has spoken to people who remember Father!" Eliza said, her eyes gleaming. "How wonderful! Surely someone must know where he is."

"That depends on when they last saw him," I replied. "I do hope they're telling Francis the truth and not simply saying the things he would wish to hear."

"Why should they do that?"

"I don't know. Perhaps they feel compelled to be helpful."

"I don't see why they should be. I think there is a great deal to be hopeful about here."

I felt wary of becoming too optimistic about our father being found. I had grown so accustomed to him being missing that I was reluctant to raise my hopes only to have them dashed once again.

"This letter is dated the twelfth of October, so it has taken almost a month to arrive here," I said. "Francis appears not to have received my letter by the time he wrote this."

"Your letters presumably passed each other by in the middle of the Atlantic," said James.

"I had hoped my letter would have been waiting for him when he arrived in Bogotá. It must have been held up."

"It had a long way to travel. There is no knowing what sort of hold-ups might be experienced along the way."

"It's rather a miracle that any letters to and from such far-flung destinations successfully make the journey at all," added

Eliza. "What's the matter, Penelope? Your face looks rather serious."

"I'm thinking about the letter I sent to Francis. I mentioned that the wedding had been cancelled."

"And what of it?"

"I felt that Francis should know about it."

"I'm sure he will do by now," said James.

"Not if my letter never arrived."

"Then write him another," said Eliza, "just to be sure."

"If he did receive it, he may not have been overjoyed about the news," I said.

"Because the cancellation of the wedding suggests that a courtship between you and James is now permitted, you mean?" asked my sister.

"Yes," I replied, giving James a gentle smile.

"It is unlikely that Francis would be terribly upset if he were to reach that conclusion," said Eliza. "The reason he left for Colombia was that he knew you would never marry him."

"That makes me sound rather mean, Ellie."

"But it's the truth," she said, taking a sip of tea. "I have no doubt that he swiftly adapted to the idea and is enjoying his exploits in Colombia without giving it any further thought."

"It was sensible to inform him, Penny," said James, "just in case the man were to harbour any hope of a courtship when he returns."

"Oh, I don't think he ever truly did," said Eliza.

"There is no doubt that he's fond of Penny, though," continued James. "I'm sure Francis would be reassured by your concern for his feelings, Penny."

"I'm not concerned," I said.

"Then why are we discussing the matter?" asked James brusquely. I had noticed on previous occasions that he had a tendency to become irritable whenever Francis was discussed. He didn't give the impression that he disliked the man, but the fact that Francis had once wished to marry me sat uncomfortably with James.

"I simply wondered whether he had received the news," I said.

"It doesn't matter either way," said James.

"So what *is* the status of your courtship?" Eliza asked us, her cup of tea poised beneath her chin. "What happens next?"

"My former fiancée pursues me in the courts, that's what happens next," said James with a scowl.

"Oh dear. Really?"

James told Eliza all about Charlotte's legal action for his breach of promise.

"Will you admit to the breach of promise in court?" she asked.

"Of course I will. There can be no use in my pretending otherwise."

"And what was the reason you gave Charlotte and her parents for the cancellation of the wedding?" asked Eliza.

"I told them that I felt I would be making a mistake if I were to go through with the marriage."

"Did you mention Penelope?"

"No, of course not! This has nothing to do with Penny."

"Oh, but it does!" laughed Eliza. "Penelope is the real reason you put a stop to the wedding."

"I knew I was making a mistake," replied James.

"Is that what you intend to say in court?"

"Yes."

"And you have no wish to mention Penelope?"

"Of course not! It wouldn't be fair to bring Penny into this. I have no wish for her to receive any of the Jenkins family's vitriol. I called off the wedding, so I must take full responsibility."

"Although I consider this all rather noble of you, James," I said, "I think perhaps you need to be honest in court about why you have breached your promise of marriage."

"I shall be! I realised the marriage would not be a happy one. I realised I did not love Charlotte."

"But that you loved someone else instead," added Eliza.

"There is no need for the court to hear that point."

"I think you may struggle to keep it a secret," replied my sister.

"It's not a secret; it is simply not relevant. I made the foolish mistake of proposing marriage to a lady I thought I loved, and when the day of the wedding dawned I realised it would be an enormous mistake. There is no need for Penny's name to be mentioned in that courtroom, and I am sincerely hoping that it won't be. Now, that's the end of the matter, and I have no desire for discussions about this whole silly business to take up any more of our Saturday afternoon!"

CHAPTER 9

"Anyway, I'm a fine one to talk," said Eliza cheerily, as if keen to lift the mood of the conversation. "I may be in court myself soon."

"Why so?" asked James.

"To pursue a divorce."

"You plan to divorce George?" I asked.

Eliza and her husband had been separated since he had become involved with a criminal through his work as a lawyer.

"I have been offered a job, Penelope!"

"Have you? How wonderful, Eliza! But why did you just mention divorce and then change the subject?"

"I have wanted to pursue a profession of my own for so long, but George has never allowed it. If I accept the job it will mean turning my back on my marriage."

"Really?" I said. "Are you so certain that George would not tolerate you having a profession?"

"Quite certain, Penelope. His view has always been that it would affect his reputation, you see. If I were to find work it would suggest to others that he is unable to provide for me and our children."

"I don't think George has much of a reputation to salvage these days. I have always found his excuses for your not being able to work rather difficult to understand. After all, the reason you wish to work bears no relation to any shortcoming of his; it is merely something you would like to do for your own fulfilment. It offers you the opportunity to pursue experiences beyond looking after your household and your children."

"You're right, Penelope, and although I think that you work far too hard and take all sorts of unnecessary risks, I must admit that I have been quite envious of the experiences you have had at times. I have been a wife and mother for a number of years, and much as I adore my children it has not been quite enough for me. I suppose that's why I founded the West London Women's Society, because it gave me the opportunity to use my mind a little more and to involve myself in the issues we are faced with today."

"You have done everything you possibly could while married to that curmudgeon."

"Penelope! You mustn't speak of my husband in that manner!"

"I'm sorry, Ellie. I know that you care for him deeply, but the man is a fool, and I have seen how frustrated you have become in having to live according to his antiquated rules. It's wonderful that you have received the offer of a job. What sort of work is it?"

"I would be working for Miss Susan Barrington. Have you heard of her?"

"The philanthropist who manages housing for the poor?"

"That's right. Apparently, my work for the West London Women's Society prompted someone to make a recommendation to Miss Barrington, and I met with her last week to discuss it. The work would involve collecting rent from the tenants and assisting them in any matters they may be having difficulty with. Miss Barrington has been doing this sort of work for around twenty years now, and she strongly believes that people must work to help themselves. She has no patience with people who take no responsibility for their lives and is quite strict if anyone falls behind with their rent due to laziness. The housing estate in Marylebone is called Paradise Place and has been under her management for a number of years."

"It sounds perfect for you, Ellie. I certainly think you should take up the opportunity."

"Even if it means obtaining a divorce?"

"I know the thought is quite dreadful, but it wouldn't be the end of the world. You will likely lose some friends, but the people who matter most will stay by your side."

"Mother won't."

"You might be surprised. She is rather traditional in her views, but she would surely realise that her daughter's happiness is of the utmost importance."

Eliza frowned. "I don't suppose she'll see it that way, Penelope. She's of an age at which duty is more important than personal happiness. I think she will view my actions as selfish and indulgent."

"Even when you tell her about George's criminal connections?"

"I suppose she might view it differently if I were to do so. I haven't told her about that, as it would be so terribly shaming for him."

"Stop trying to protect his reputation, Ellie! His actions give you suitable grounds for divorce. I think you should tell Mother what has happened and then, once she has recovered from the shock, you can tell her that you intend to find employment."

"She would be so ashamed to have a divorced daughter!"

"That's for her to worry about. If you wish to reconcile with George in order to make her happy you are free to do so. But would that make you happy?"

She gave this some thought. "No, I don't believe it would. And I do so wish to work with Miss Barrington."

"I can imagine you being very good at it, Eliza," said James.

"Thank you!" she replied.

I noticed a sparkle in her eyes that I hadn't seen for a long time.

"Well done," I said. "I think it will be just what you need."

"Thank you both for your support," replied my sister tearily. "It means a lot to me at a time like this..." She paused to find a handkerchief.

"Oh, Ellie." I reached out and patted her arm. "Don't be upset."

"I'm fine, thank you," she said, looking flustered and drying her eyes. "Please excuse me. I must pay a quick visit to the ladies' room."

"I think Ellie is making the right decision," I said as we watched my sister's retreating form, "though it is not an easy decision to make. Society takes a dim view of divorcees."

"I think she'll be fine," said James. "The Green sisters are made of strong stuff."

I laughed. "I don't know about that!"

"It's true." James held my gaze and smiled. "I apologise for my ill temper earlier."

"There's no need to apologise. Anyone receiving a solicitors' letter like that would have every reason to be ill-tempered."

"It put me out of sorts, that's for sure. I suppose I had

hoped that once I walked away from the wedding the problem of Charlotte would disappear. It frustrates me that she and her family are lingering on in my life."

"We knew that it would happen, though, didn't we?"

"I suppose we did. It's a shame, as it feels as though our courtship has been rather overshadowed by it. I had hoped we would be able to embark upon a new life together, but it's not that simple, is it?"

"No, it's not. But our time will come once the court case is over. There's no hurry."

"But I can't help feeling impatient about it. Don't you?"

"Yes, I suppose I do. But we will cope with whatever comes our way, James, I feel sure of that. I'm not going anywhere."

He smiled and rested his hand on mine. "You almost did. You nearly bought a ticket to America, remember?"

"Only because you were practically married to someone else!"

"Just think how different our lives would have been," he said with a sigh.

"And look at us now," I said. "Could we ever have imagined sitting together like this without worrying that we were doing something forbidden?"

"And in the tawdry Royal Aquarium with Professor Roche and his pack of fifteen Russian wolves."

We both laughed.

"We shall miss them altogether if Ellie takes much longer in the ladies' room."

CHAPTER 10

I had no recollection of falling asleep that night at the Hotel Tempesta, but when I awoke a short while later my body ached from the stiff position I had maintained. *Had a sound awoken me?*

I had been experiencing a vivid, busy dream, but now that I was awake I could no longer recall it. Voices echoed in my mind, as if I had just been having a conversation with someone only to be catapulted back into a world of darkness and silence.

The quiet seemed to smother everything, like a thick, dark blanket. I moved the bedclothes around just to hear their reassuring rustle.

Could there truly be ghosts in this place?

I had been adamant that there couldn't, but now I feared that if I turned on the gas lamp I would see someone standing at the foot of my bed.

The ghost stories I had enjoyed as a child returned to me; all those old tales of spirits walking through walls and tapping at windows. How silly I had thought those stories, even as a young girl. And yet now, in this dark, silent place, I felt as though they might come true.

I breathed deeply and tried to soothe myself back to sleep. There were only a few hours of darkness left before I could dress and go downstairs to breakfast. I thought of all the food Mr Gallo would provide. I could enjoy a hearty breakfast and then leave. A heavy sensation returned to my body and I hoped that sleep would soon envelop me.

Then I heard a door slam.

The pit of my stomach leapt up into my throat as I sat upright in bed. I stared into the dark, the hairs at the back of my neck prickling.

Then there was a voice – a brief shout – which I began to doubt I had heard as soon as the silence descended again.

Then all I heard was the pounding of my heart in my ears. I noticed that my fists were clenched.

Cold perspiration broke out across my brow as I reached out and illuminated the gas light on the table beside the bed. The room around me flickered into view, and I found some comfort in seeing it just as it had been the evening before. The embers were already cold and the lady in the picture didn't seem to be watching me as intently any more.

Was it possible that I had imagined the door slam?

It seemed to have come from beneath my room. I thought about the circumstances under which a door might be slammed in the dead of night. All I could think of was a disagreement. *But who would be arguing at this hour?* Perhaps the door had been slammed in anger, or perhaps it had merely been high spirits from someone who had consumed too much liquor.

I felt relieved by this thought and released a breath I hadn't previously noticed I had been holding. There was certainly no noise now, and as I glanced around the room again I smiled to myself, wondering why I had worked myself up with so many fearful thoughts. My heartbeat began to return to normal, but as I reached out to turn off the lamp I realised that my hand was shaking.

I tried to laugh at myself as I pictured explaining my irrational fears of this night to James. I knew he would find it quite amusing that I had made myself so fearful over nothing. If he had been there beside me I wouldn't have felt this way at all. I rested my head on the pillow again and felt relieved as sleep began to descend on me once more.

I had no idea of the time when I awoke again, but I felt reassured at seeing daylight between the curtains. With the long November nights upon us I guessed it could be no earlier than eight o'clock.

I sighed as I parted the curtains and saw the fog still clinging to the window pane. The embers of the previous day's fire remained in the grate, and I found this odd given that Mrs Mirabeau had informed us that the chambermaids always lit the fires at dawn.

I dressed hurriedly, keen to breakfast and be on my way. I wondered whether I could somehow escape the proposed tour of the kitchens. Mr Gallo was a talkative man, and would no doubt detain us for as long as possible. I would have to make my excuses about getting back to work.

I put on a thick woollen skirt, thick stockings, a blouse and a woollen jacket. Even with my petticoats on I still felt a chill. I folded up my evening gown as best I could, pushed it hurriedly into my case and left all my belongings on my bed.

I heard voices in the corridor as I stepped out of the elevator on the ground floor. Among the small group of people gathered there I recognised the auburn-haired Mrs Mirabeau. The tone of their voices sounded serious, and I sensed that something wasn't quite right.

Instead of making my way to the dining room, I walked toward the group. I caught my breath as I discerned the blue uniforms of two police constables. The square-faced Mr Bolton was also standing there.

"Is everything all right?" I asked as I reached them.

As Mrs Mirabeau turned to face me I was struck by the way her rouge contrasted with the ashen hue of her face. Captain stood by her side, restrained by the leash she held.

An uncomfortable silence followed. Mr Bolton rubbed at his whiskers and stared at the police officers, as if hoping one of them would reply so that he wouldn't have to.

"Mr Gallo has passed away, ma'am," said a constable with a thick moustache.

I stared at him, then looked down at Captain, trying to make sense of what I had just heard.

"Are you sure?" I asked, instantly realising how foolish my question sounded. "But we dined with him only yesterday evening, didn't we, Mrs Mirabeau?"

"He has been murdered," she replied solemnly.

I took a moment to consider this, unsure as to whether I had heard her correctly.

"But he couldn't have been," I said. "Who would do such a thing? And how? When did it happen?"

"We don't know, ma'am," replied the constable, "but we do know that Mr Gallo was found dead this morning, having been on the receiving end of several stab wounds at the foot of the grand staircase."

"Good grief!" I said quietly. "I cannot quite believe it."

"None of us can," replied Mr Bolton.

"But why would someone do such a thing?" I said, realising once again that my words were risible and couldn't possibly be answered at that moment.

I glanced toward the foyer, wondering whether he still lay at the foot of the staircase.

"Is he—?"

"They have just taken him away to the mortuary," replied Mrs Mirabeau, "and I have sent a telegram to his family in Paris. The staff are cleaning up now."

"Do you know what time he was attacked?" I asked.

Mrs Mirabeau shook her head.

"We've told you everything we know, ma'am," replied the constable. "Chief Inspector Fenton is currently in discussion with the police surgeon, and we'll know more in due course."

"I see." I moved past them as I made my way toward the foyer.

"Excuse me, ma'am!" called out the constable.

"Miss Green!" said Mr Bolton. "You don't want to go down there!"

I ignored them and hurried my step.

CHAPTER 11

A pile of bloodied towels lay at the foot of the staircase, where Mr Gallo had presumably lain. A maid mopped the tiled floor, and I could see that the water had a pink hue. The mirrors had been covered with black crepe as a mark of mourning.

Chief Inspector Fenton was deep in conversation with Mr Blackstone and Mr Somers. I had come across the inspector a number of times during my years of reporting, so I was aware that he was based at Bow Street station. He had narrow eyes and his dark mutton-chop whiskers were tinged with grey.

"Do excuse me, gentlemen," he said. "Miss Green! I have advised the ladies to stay away from here at the present time. It's not suitable for a—"

"I have seen worse, Inspector," I replied. "I was present at the time of the St Giles murders, remember?"

"How could I forget?" Chief Inspector Fenton rolled his eyes. "And it just happens to be my luck that a group of reporters is already gathered here at the crime scene. I won't be able to free myself of you lot now, will I?"

"I'm sure none of us would wish to detain you from your work, Chief Inspector," I said. "Just tell me what you know so far, and then I shall gladly leave you to get on with it." Having left my notebook and pencil in my room, I readied myself to memorise the important facts.

"I had just begun telling these two gentlemen here, but hadn't got too far with it, so I'll begin again for your sake, Miss Green. The deceased was found by a maid this morning at half-past five o'clock. She raised the alarm and reported it to her seniors, one of whom ran up to the Strand, where she eventually found a constable doing his rounds. It wasn't long before we received the summons at Bow Street. A doctor was also called, but it was already evident to the staff here that Mr Gallo was quite dead, and that nothing more could be done for him.

"He was found lying on his back with several injuries to his chest. We suspect that the injuries were inflicted with a knife, though we haven't yet found the weapon. The police surgeon believes that two or three deep injuries to the man's chest caused him to lose his life, but we will know more once the autopsy has been carried out. He also had injuries to his hands, which suggest that he attempted to defend himself."

"Have you any idea how he ended up at the foot of the stairs?" asked Mr Blackstone. "Surely he should have been safely in his room at that hour. He told us all he was to sleep in the Venetian Suite last night."

"He was dressed for bed in a pair of silk pyjamas," replied the inspector. "It is our belief that he was chased from his suite and that the attacker caught up with him at the foot of the stairs. It is possible that he stumbled on the stairs as he tried to flee his attacker. He may have fallen, and then the culprit must have set upon him as he lay at the bottom of the staircase."

"But how do you know that he was chased from his room?" I asked.

"Because that's where the attacker struck first. That's where we found the lady."

"The lady?" I asked. "Which lady?"

"We can't be certain yet, but we assume it's his wife."

"But that's impossible," said Mr Somers. "His wife and daughters are in Paris."

"Are they? Do you know that for certain?"

"Yes," I said. "He spoke to us about them last night."

"Oh dear. You will need to exercise some tact when reporting on this incident, in that case. We don't want the family finding out about this lady."

"This lady," I ventured. "Is she also—?"

"Yes, she is deceased as well. She was attacked with what we suspect to have been the same weapon, and her throat was cut. The attacker clearly wished to be rid of the only witness first."

"I wonder who she was," said Mr Blackstone. "One of the maids?"

"I shouldn't have thought so," said Mr Somers.

"You knew Mr Gallo well," I said to Mr Somers. "Was he the sort of man who entertained lady companions?"

His face coloured. "I wouldn't wish to speak ill of a dear friend who has just lost his life, but for the purposes of the inspector's investigation I can say that he has indeed socialised with certain lady companions, as you describe them, before now. But it is extremely important that his family does not find out."

"Do you know who this poor lady might have been?" I asked.

"I haven't a clue, I'm afraid. I had no idea that anyone would be visiting him last night." He wiped his brow with a handkerchief and turned to face the inspector. "Do you know how the murderer entered the building?" he asked.

"Not yet. My men are searching the hotel from top to bottom, as you can imagine. We are hoping to find the murder weapon, and that will surely yield a few clues. I must ask you all to remain at the hotel for the time being, as we will need to interview everyone about the events of yesterday evening and last night. I understand the staff have laid on breakfast for everyone; not the usual fare you might expect in a place like this, but quite impressive that they have managed to put anything together under the circumstances."

"We need to get out of this place in order to file our stories," said Mr Blackstone.

"I understand that, but you must recognise that it is our duty to speak to you all."

"But the deadline for this evening's edition is midday today."

"It's important that you remain inside the hotel, Mr Blackstone. No one has been allowed to leave since Mr Gallo's body was found. We will do all we can to accommodate your need to contact your offices. Perhaps there will be time for you to attend the telegraph office presently so that you may explain the matter to your editors. For the time being, please go and partake of the breakfast that has been supplied. We shall ensure that the interviews are conducted as quickly as possible."

Bread rolls, bacon and boiled eggs had been laid out on a sideboard in the Chinese Dining Room. The garish yellow decor felt at odds with the subdued mood of the room. I struggled to believe that the man who was now dead had hosted us in this very room just hours earlier. The clock on the mantelpiece had not yet been stopped, which was the usual practice after a death. It read a quarter-past eight.

A waitress rushed over to pour me a cup of coffee as I took a seat close to Mrs Mortimer and Mr Wentworth.

"It's incomprehensible, isn't it?" Mrs Mortimer said. A bread roll sat untouched on her plate. "I cannot understand it at all. It's brutal, absolutely brutal. That's what it is."

"They think he was chased from his room by the attacker," I said. "Did you hear anything in the night?"

"Nothing at all. Did you?"

"I heard a door slam, but I couldn't tell you what time that was."

"Perhaps it had something to do with this horrible business. Did you hear anything else?"

"A shout, I think. The inspector says that Mr Gallo was chased from his room, and they believe he fell as he ran down the stairs."

"And that's where he was set upon, was it not? The whole affair is truly awful."

I didn't like to mention the lady who had been found in his room. For some reason it seemed disrespectful to allude to the secret rendezvous now that Mr Gallo was dead. I wondered how many people knew about her.

"I heard nothing," said Mr Wentworth. "Despite all the talk of ghosts and curses last night, I fell asleep as soon as my head hit the pillow and knew nothing further until half-past seven this morning. I haven't slept that well in a long time. It must be the beds they have here. I awoke in a fine mood and then I discovered that this dreadful tragedy had occurred... And now, well I wish we could somehow turn the clock back to yesterday evening and prevent this awful murder from happening. Gallo must have caused someone a great deal of upset."

"Even if he did, he cannot have deserved to die for it," I said.

"You are quite right," he replied. "There can be no excuse for murder, can there? And whoever did it has got clean away. I don't know how they'll ever find him now."

"Maybe he hasn't got away," I said.

"You think he might still be hiding somewhere in the hotel?" asked Mrs Mortimer with a shudder. "It's possible, I suppose. There are plenty of empty rooms here. The police will be searching all of them, I imagine, though it will be quite a task."

"He might not even be hiding," I said. "It could be one of the guests who stayed here last night."

Mr Wentworth laughed. "Goodness! One of us? That would be quite something, wouldn't it? I cannot think who, though. We were all invited here, and everyone has been such good company. One of the guests a murderer? I think it far more likely that an intruder somehow got into the hotel during the night."

"The police have found no sign of a break-in," I said.

"Not yet. But it's a big hotel, isn't it? As Mrs Mortimer says, there are many rooms to search."

"I suppose that anything is possible at this stage," I said. "I wish we had some understanding as to what the motive might have been."

"He was a powerful businessman," Mr Hardy piped up. "Attaining success in business usually involves upsetting a few people."

"A rival hotelier, you mean?" I asked.

"I cannot imagine another hotelier doing such a thing. Can you?"

"They wouldn't have done it themselves, I'm sure. They would have hired a professional killer."

"And if it were a professional assassin there is probably no hope of finding the murderer at all," said Mrs Mortimer. "They're trained to leave no trace of evidence behind."

"The criminal world has plenty of informants, however," said Mr Wentworth. "Allegiances change and grievances arise. Someone will talk."

"Sometime after the crime has been committed, perhaps, in which case the police will struggle to get this case solved any time soon," replied Mrs Mortimer. "And in the meantime we are all expected to stay here and sit this out!"

CHAPTER 12

I had no appetite for breakfast. I left the dining room as soon as I had finished my coffee, keen to keep up with any progress in the investigation. Scotland Yard had presumably been informed by this time. *Had James heard about it yet?* I wondered.

I followed a corridor in search of the back stairs, which I hoped would offer a clandestine route to the first floor. I wanted to get as close as possible to the Venetian Suite, though I had no doubt that a police officer would stop me in my tracks as soon as I was seen.

The back stairs were hidden beyond a set of plain swing doors. I climbed the steps two at a time and ventured out into the corridor on the first floor. About thirty yards ahead of me I could see two police constables. As I walked toward them, I realised the bedchamber I had occupied on the second storey was likely to have been almost directly above the Venetian Suite.

"I'm sorry, ma'am, but no one is permitted on this floor," said a tall police officer with fair whiskers, who came striding over to me.

The door to the Venetian Suite stood open, but there was no chance of seeing inside the room that lay beyond it.

"I am Miss Penelope Green, a reporter from the *Morning Express*. I've come to find out everything I can about the lady who lost her life here last night."

"We don't know who she is. Some unfortunate wench he found on a street corner somewhere, no doubt. You have no business reporting that, though."

"I won't. I realise it would cause great distress to Mr Gallo's family," I replied. "I cannot imagine that he found her on a street corner. He was entertaining us yesterday evening, and I shouldn't think he left the hotel after that, and especially not in this thick fog. Perhaps he had made a prior arrangement with her."

"We don't know either way, ma'am, and speculation won't get us anywhere. There's no hope of us identifying the lady at the present time, but perhaps she has relatives who are missing her. Someone will turn up before long, making enquiries. Miss Green, may I remind you that you are not supposed to be up here? Please oblige us by returning downstairs to the dining room. I hear that a breakfast has been laid out—"

"I have already breakfasted, thank you."

I turned and walked toward the back staircase, counting my steps as I did so. By the time I reached the door to the stairs I had counted forty-three steps. I climbed the stairs to the floor above, where the room I had occupied the previous night was, and walked forty-three steps along the corridor before stopping. I was only four or five steps away from my bedchamber, which confirmed my suspicion that the Venetian Suite lay almost directly beneath me.

I returned to my room and realised that I had left the door unlocked. I fetched my carpet bag, which had my notebook and pencil in it, then locked the door behind me. My case remained on my bed, ready for one of the hotel staff to transport it to the foyer.

"At what time did you hear the door slam, Miss Green?"

Chief Inspector Fenton and I sat in Mr Gallo's office, which was located just off the foyer. It was a handsome room with mahogany wainscoting and large paintings of pastoral scenes on the walls.

Mr Gallo had evidently not been a tidy man. At one end of his desk sat a pile of papers, which looked as though it had been pushed to one side to make space for the inspector's coffee tray. More papers were scattered across a writing bureau, and a police constable was busy leafing through them.

Sitting beside Chief Inspector Fenton was Inspector Pilkington, whom I recognised from my reporting on the St Giles murders. He had a large grey moustache and a crooked nose.

"I'm afraid I don't know. I had been asleep for a while by that time."

"Was there a clock in your room?"

"No."

"What time did you retire last night?"

"About midnight."

"*About?*"

"It was almost exactly midnight. I remember looking at the clock on the mantelpiece in the Lady Jane Lounge and seeing that it was approaching twelve. It was at that point that I decided to retire for the night."

"By what time would you have been in your room?"

"Definitely by midnight, but I didn't go to sleep immediately."

"How long would you say that you remained awake for?"

"I don't know for sure, but I would say at least an hour."

"So you may have dropped off at about one o'clock?"

"Yes."

"And the door slam woke you?"

"No. I had already awoken and was trying to get back to sleep again."

"What had awoken you?"

"Nothing that I'm aware of. I didn't hear anything immediately."

"But it's possible that a noise you weren't aware of may have awoken you?"

"I suppose that may have been the case, yes."

"Did you hear anything other than the door slam?"

"I think I heard a shout, but I cannot be certain of that."

"Male or female?"

"Male, I think."

"This was after the door slam?"

"Yes."

"But you heard nothing before that?"

"No, nothing at all. And no warning that it was about to happen, such as footsteps or loud voices or anything. That's what startled me so much."

"Which direction do you think the sound came from?"

"I feel quite certain that it came from the floor beneath me, the first floor. And that would tie in with what you believe to have happened, because my room was almost directly above the Venetian Suite."

"Let's not jump to any conclusions just yet. What did you do when you heard the noise?"

"I sat up in bed. I was a little bit frightened, if truth be told."

"Did you leave your room to investigate where it had come from?"

"No, I stayed where I was. It sounds foolish now that I'm saying it aloud, but at the time I felt too nervous to be wandering around the hotel at night."

"That doesn't sound foolish at all, Miss Green."

"I turned on the lamp in my room for a short while and remained awake for a while, listening out for further noises, but I heard nothing else."

Chief Inspector Fenton consulted the notes he had made so far.

"So if you went to sleep at about one o'clock, Miss Green, it is quite feasible that this moment of awakening might have occurred around half an hour later?"

"I feel sure that I had been asleep for longer than that."

"An hour?"

"It might have been, but I can't be sure."

"So this noise occurred nearer two o'clock, and possibly later than that. How long were you awake after that?"

"Once again, it's difficult to say. I felt reassured once I had turned the lamp on and went back to sleep fairly quickly."

"And you awoke when?"

"It was about eight o'clock, I think. After sunrise. Although sunrise is quite difficult to discern in this thick fog. Do you think the door slam had something to do with the murder?"

Chief Inspector Fenton gave a thoughtful sigh. "It's a possibility. Mr Gallo's body was found at half-past five o'clock this morning and the police surgeon believes he died no later than four o'clock. We think you heard the door slam around or after two o'clock, and if the noise is connected to the murder the time of death would likely fall somewhere between two o'clock and four o'clock."

"Was the door to the Venetian Suite left open or closed after the attack?" I asked.

"Open."

"Then why did the door slam?"

"Why indeed? That is something we will need to work

out. Who remained in the Lady Jane Lounge when you retired for the night?"

"Everyone except Mr Blackstone and Mr White, who were in their rooms by then. Actually, Mr Blackstone was, but none of us could be certain where Mr White had got to. Mrs Mortimer left the lounge at the same time I did."

"Interesting."

"The lady wasn't there, though. The lady you found in the suite, I mean."

"I realise that."

"Do you know who she was yet?"

"Not yet. Sadly, the unfortunate found herself in the wrong place at the wrong time."

"Have you any idea who might have wished Mr Gallo harm?" I asked.

"None at all as yet, Miss Green."

"He might have fallen out with someone. A business deal gone wrong, perhaps."

"We are making enquiries."

"And do you have any idea how the intruder broke in? It may not have been an intruder, of course. It may have been one of the guests staying here."

"Still no sign of a break-in as yet. All possibilities are being considered. Thank you for your time. We may need to speak to you again."

"There are countless places in this hotel to hide the murder weapon. So many empty rooms."

"Indeed there are, Miss Green."

"And then there's the staff to consider. You'll be questioning them as well, I presume."

"Yes, everyone will be questioned."

"Did anyone else you have spoken to hear the door slam?"

"My time is precious, Miss Green. Will you please allow me to proceed with my interviews?"

"Yes of course, Chief Inspector. When can I leave the hotel?"

"Not for a good while yet. Return to the dining room for the time being, if you please. In the meantime, we must search your bedchamber. We are searching all the guests' bedchambers."

"I've just locked the door. Shall I go and unlock it?"

"No need. We have spare keys for all the rooms."

CHAPTER 13

News of Mr Gallo's murder spread quickly, and a noisy, inquisitive crowd soon gathered outside the hotel. We were permitted to visit a nearby telegram office in order to send messages to our editors, and as I pushed my way through the onlookers people pestered me for information.

"You can read about it in the *Morning Express* tomorrow," I told them.

"Miss Green!" a man's voice called out.

I looked up to see my rival from *The Holborn Gazette*, Tom Clifford.

"What's 'appened?" he shouted.

I chose to ignore him and continued on my way.

Lunch was served in the dining room when I returned, and although I still had little appetite I managed to eat some ham and cold mutton.

"How much do you know of Mr Gallo's business affairs?" I asked Mr Somers.

He wore a green and red plaid suit, but would no doubt have worn suitable mourning clothes had he brought any with him.

"A little," he replied. "What do you mean specifically?"

"I'm interested in the people he associated with. And anyone he may have fallen out with."

"The New York hoteliers who come to mind are Marshall, Jarvis and Walters. There is a rivalry between them, of course, but I don't think any of them would sink to the depths of having a rival so barbarically attacked in the middle of the night. When Nathaniel opened the Maganza in New York it was reported that he took quite a bit of business away from the Excelsior on Fifth Avenue. It's no secret that the Excelsior's owner, Mr Marshall, bears Nathaniel some animosity as a result. Mr Marshall is a colourful character and is known to have a strong temper."

"Hotels compete with one another all the time," I said. "Surely they are accustomed to it, and there is certainly no call to go around murdering rival owners in cold blood."

"I agree. I met Mr Marshall a few times and believe that his bark is worse than his bite. Besides, I don't think he would go to the lengths of ordering Nathaniel's murder from the other side of the Atlantic. It doesn't make sense."

"Is there anyone he might have fallen out with in London?"

"You're making me feel as though I'm being interviewed by a police officer, Miss Green!" He gave a chuckle. "No one immediately comes to mind. There may be someone out there, and I'm sure the police investigation will uncover whoever that might be."

I lowered my voice to a whisper. "I was surprised to hear about the lady."

Mr Somers gave a dismissive wave with his hand. "Nathaniel has always had a weakness for the fairer sex, but I can tell you that he loved his wife very much, and that he found their temporary separation rather difficult. You mustn't look so disapproving, Miss Green. This kind of thing is more common than you realise."

"I cannot help but think about his poor wife and daughters."

"Absolutely. Mrs Gallo is a delightful lady, she really is. And as for those girls..." He paused to shake his head. "They really will be distraught. I just wish one of us could have stopped it somehow. It can't have happened long after we all retired to bed. One moment he was here with us and then..." His voice broke with emotion, and he pulled a purple silk handkerchief from his pocket and wiped his eyes. "Oh, I do apologise, Miss Green. You don't want to sit there watching an old fool like me lose his composure."

"I understand, Mr Somers. Mr Gallo was a friend of yours."

"Yes, he was. I liked him a lot. He wasn't perfect, but he certainly had no malice about him. None at all. I cannot understand it."

The dark-whiskered Mr Blackstone joined us. "I've heard a rumour that they intend to let us out of this place shortly," he said. "I've interviewed just about everyone I could in the meantime."

"You and Miss Green should form a team," said Mr Somers with a smile. "She was questioning me just now in the manner of a police officer."

"Well, we are reporters, Mr Somers," replied Mr Blackstone. "We're always working."

"I shall have to write up this tragic news for the *Journal*," Mr Somers replied. "But I shan't be interviewing everyone like you, Mr Blackstone. I simply cannot bring myself to do it. I feel too saddened." He wiped his eyes again.

"Have you found out anything useful?" I asked Mr Blackstone.

"I can hardly go around telling rival reporters what I've found out!" he replied with a bemused smile. "In truth, I haven't really found out much more than the established facts. I spoke to the maid who found Mr Gallo at the foot of the stairs. She's in a very sorry state. The police are being careful about what they tell us, as usual. I can't imagine anyone enlightening me any further, and it's as clear as day that Chief Inspector Fenton isn't the sort to let anything slip. That's why I'm so keen to get out of here. We need to discover who Mr Gallo was keeping company with and who might have wished him harm."

"That's what Miss Green was just suggesting," said Mr Somers. "The two of you really should work together."

"Rival newspapers do not work together, Mr Somers," said Mr Blackstone, "as you well know. And if you think I've been busy, you should see what Mr Bolton has been up to. I think he's interviewed every member of staff, and he's been pestering Fenton relentlessly. I think he's the real reason they may be prepared to let us out of here, having annoyed everyone too much!"

"Presumably we are all suspects," I commented.

"But they've spoken to all the guests now and have hopefully ruled a number of us out," said Mr Somers. "All of us, I should think. Why should one of Mr Gallo's guests wish to murder him?"

"Why should *anyone* wish to murder him?" added Mr Blackstone.

"It has to have been an intruder," said Mr Somers. "Someone must have broken into the hotel during the night, even though they haven't yet discovered how he got in. Perhaps they will never discover it. He may have been very clever in covering his tracks."

Mr Bolton strode into the dining room. He helped himself to some bread and meat before joining us.

"I tried warning him about the curse, didn't I?" he said drily.

"Don't even talk about that," said Mr Somers. "It's not the slightest bit amusing."

"I speak quite seriously," replied Mr Bolton. "There was a good deal of talk about the curse before, and now this has happened people will never stop talking about it, will they? They'll have to knock the place down. No one will ever want to run it or stay in it again."

"It's rather hasty to be talking about the future at this stage," said Mr Somers. "And rather disrespectful, too."

"I meant no disrespect, but I can see a certain irony in the situation. '*Curse? What curse?*' Those were his exact words to me last night, and now look what's happened! It was almost foretold."

"What nonsense!" said Mr Somers, jumping up from his chair. "I find your talk rude and careless, sir. Nathaniel was a friend of mine, and I would politely ask you to speak about the man with respect. You don't deserve to have been his guest!"

Mr Somers moved further down the table and took a seat next to Mr White.

Chief Inspector Fenton entered the room moments later with two constables in tow. "We cannot detain you all here any longer today," he said. "You have jobs and families to return to. Keen as you will all be to ask questions, I will simply tell you what we have found out so far and allow you to proceed with the day. I have taken down the names and addresses of everyone here, and the names of your employers, where necessary, so that I or my colleagues can easily make contact with you should the need arise. The first development you will be interested to hear is that we have found the murder weapon: a large knife."

His announcement was met with gasps of surprise.

"Where?" asked Mrs Mortimer.

"I am not at liberty to share that information yet, as there are a few people I need to speak to about it in the first instance."

"But you found it here in the hotel?" asked Mr White.

"Yes, I can confirm that it is here in the hotel. And we have also found some discarded clothing."

There were more gasps and mutters of interest.

"An overcoat was found in Milford Alley, a narrow thoroughfare that runs behind the hotel. This leads us to believe that the culprit either escaped along that route, discarding the overcoat as he went, or threw it out of a window."

"Can you be sure that it is connected to Mr Gallo's murder?" asked Mr Hardy. "It might have been discarded by anyone during the night."

"It might have been, but the fact that the coat is heavily bloodstained suggests to us that it was worn by the murderer. It would otherwise be difficult to account for its appearance. There is a wheelwright's workshop in that street, and the workers we spoke to there confirmed that they did not recall seeing the overcoat in the alley yesterday, so we are certain that it was left there during the night. In addition, I should say that we have been unable to find any windows or doors that show signs of forced entry.

"Thank you all for your help with the investigation so far. We have made a good deal of progress. I would like to request that you continue to make yourselves available to assist me and my colleagues going forward. I am allowing you to leave this hotel on the condition that you continue to cooperate with us. If anyone refuses to do so the matter will be taken very seriously indeed."

Once dismissed, we swiftly left the room and made our way toward the foyer, where our cases were waiting for us. I felt a sense of relief that I would soon be out of this miserable, stifling place. I would be able to get on with my report for the newspaper and I was also looking forward to seeing James. I knew that discussing the tragedy with him would help me feel a great deal better.

"Can you come with me please, Miss Green?" asked Chief Inspector Fenton before I could locate my luggage.

I sighed. "Will it be quick? I really must get back to my office."

I watched enviously as Mr Bolton and Mr Blackstone stepped out of the hotel.

"It may take a little while, I'm afraid," he replied.

"But I don't understand, Inspector. I've already told you everything I know."

"Not *everything*, Miss Green."

I paused and thought about the events of the night, wondering what I could possibly have missed. "Inspector, there really is nothing else I can tell you. I sincerely wish that I could be of more help."

"Oh, you will be, I feel sure of that."

"What is it? What else do you need to know?"

"I want to know, Miss Green, how the murder weapon came to be found in your bedchamber."

CHAPTER 14

I returned Chief Inspector Fenton's stare, struggling to believe what he had just said to me.

"But it couldn't have been in my bedchamber," I responded. "You must be mistaken. Are you sure you're talking about *my* room? It certainly wasn't there earlier. How did it get in there?"

"I have no idea, Miss Green. That's why I should like to speak to you. Come with me, please, and let's get to the bottom of this."

"But I don't know anything about a large knife!"

"I'm sure you don't, but we must still discuss it."

I followed the chief inspector back to Mr Gallo's office, where Inspector Pilkington was waiting, along with the fair-whiskered constable I had seen outside the Venetian Suite.

I didn't like the way the three men looked at me as I took a seat. They watched me intently, as if looking for a sign that I was lying.

"This has to be a misunderstanding," I said.

"It was in your bedchamber, Miss Green."

"Whereabouts did you find it?"

"Perhaps you can tell us?"

I gave an incredulous laugh, unable to believe that he truly believed I might know anything of its location.

"I have no idea, Inspector! Someone has obviously planted it there. My door was locked, although... I had left it unlocked while I went down to breakfast. That must have been when the weapon was deposited there."

Chief Inspector Fenton raised a dubious eyebrow.

"I'm telling you the truth!" I said. The palms of my hands suddenly felt damp. *Surely they had to believe me. They couldn't possibly think that I had carried out this terrible crime, could they?* "Where was the knife found, Inspector?"

He nodded at the constable, who placed a leather bag on the desk before carefully retrieving something from it.

It was a white, bloodstained towel, much like the ones I had seen at the foot of the stairs during the clean-up after Mr Gallo's murder.

I recoiled as the bundled-up towel was placed on the desk in front of me. There were smears of blood all over it.

The constable opened out the towel and I caught my breath as I saw the sharp knife, which appeared to be about eight inches long, laying upon it. It was the sort of knife that might be used in a kitchen. I noticed that its handle and blade were remarkably clean. Judging by the state of the towel, the murderer had attempted to clean the knife with it. My stomach turned as my nostrils filled with the cold, metallic smell of blood.

I covered my mouth with my hands and stared at the knife. I had reported on many murders but rarely came so close to the murder weapon. I shuddered as I reflected on the fact that the implement in front of me had been used to brutally slay two people. I couldn't even begin to fathom how someone might use so much violence against another person. *What could possibly have compelled the murderer to do it?*

Once again, I was aware that I was being watched by the police officers, who seemed keen to assess my reaction when presented with the weapon in this way. I looked away, having peered at the bloodied implement for long enough.

"I have never seen that knife before," I said, staring down at my hands in my lap. "You can take it away now. I don't want to look at it any more."

The constable slowly folded the towel over the weapon and placed it back inside the bag. The movement was carried out slowly and laboriously, as if they wished to continue gauging my reaction.

"I left my door unlocked," I repeated, "while I was at breakfast. That's when the murderer must have planted the knife in my room."

Chief Inspector Fenton regarded me coolly. "What time did you go down to breakfast?"

"The clock said a quarter-past eight when I arrived in the dining room. And you saw me just before that, sir. Do you remember? I joined you in the foyer with Mr Blackstone and Mr Somers. I think that must have been shortly after eight o'clock, but I cannot be completely sure of that. I hope you'll agree that I couldn't possibly have committed this heinous crime, Chief Inspector. I can assure you that I have no idea how the weapon found its way into my room. Someone must have put it there at some time after eight o'clock this morning."

I wished I had locked the door to my room and avoided being implicated in this terrible incident.

"Did you purposefully leave your bedchamber unlocked, Miss Green?"

"No, in fact I didn't give the matter any thought at all."

"Did you return to your bedchamber after breakfast?"

"Yes, I returned to fetch my carpet bag. Everything appeared to be as I had left it, and there was no sign of the knife or the towel at that point. If there had been, I would have summoned you, of course, but there was no indication that anyone had been in there.

"After that I locked my bedchamber, but my case has since been brought down to the foyer. Have you asked who brought it down yet? That person must also have been inside my bedchamber, and would have been in there after me, given that the case was still lying on the bed when I left it."

"What time did you fetch your carpet bag from the bedchamber?"

"I think I left the dining room at about a quarter to nine, so it would have been around five or ten minutes after that, I suppose."

"And I saw you by the Venetian Suite on the first floor at about that time," said the constable.

"Yes, I went there first," I replied, slightly embarrassed that I had been caught snooping about. "I'm a news reporter, Constable. You know what we're like." I gave him a smile, which was not returned. "I wanted to find out more about the lady who died."

"And I told you she was a prostitute, and that there was nothing more I could tell you."

"Yes, and then I fetched my bag from my bedchamber."

"What were you doing on the first floor, Miss Green?" asked Chief Inspector Fenton.

"When I report on a case I like to see the crime scene if possible."

"That is not a necessary part of your work."

"On the contrary, I think it is. If I have a clear idea of what happened when and where I can report it as accurately as possible for the readers of my newspaper."

"Your readers don't require the level of detail you think they do. Now, I believe that my colleagues and I have been more than accommodating with you and your fellow reporters this morning. We have told you the facts of the case as we have discovered them and answered your numerous questions. There was no need for you to go wandering around the hotel trying to conduct an investigation of your own. It is unhelpful and gives us even more work to do. Imagine if everyone did as you have done, Miss Green! My officers would be spending all their time trying to keep control of errant ink-scribblers rather than getting on with the important matter of catching whoever committed this dreadful crime!"

"I apologise if I have caused any inconvenience, Inspector. That wasn't my intention at all."

"Well, you've dropped yourself in it, I'm afraid, because your recent activity can only be regarded as suspicious."

"I was merely gathering information to report on the case!"

He gave a shrug. "I'm sure you will try your hardest to convince me otherwise, Miss Green. However, the facts remain that the murder weapon was found in your bedchamber and that you were seen visiting the scene of the crime. No other guests were seen loitering around there this morning."

"The murderer is hardly going to return to the crime scene, is he?" I retorted. "Especially with so many police officers present."

"On the contrary, Miss Green," replied the chief inspector. "We have found that a number of culprits return to the scene of their misdeeds. Sometimes they do so to derive further warped pleasure from their acts, and sometimes they wish to find out whether the investigating officers are on their trail."

"I went there purely out of interest as a news reporter," I said. "You cannot possibly conjure your theories into a charge against me."

He gave a hollow laugh. "That's what they all say."

"The fact that the knife was found in my bedchamber does not make me a murderer. And besides, I don't have the physical ability to stab two people to death. Neither is there any motive for me to do so!"

"Did you deliberately leave your door unlocked, Miss Green?"

"You have already asked me that, Inspector, and I told you that it was purely accidental."

"Might anyone else have known that you had left your door unlocked?"

"Only if they had tried the handle and found it so, I suppose."

"Did you tell anyone that you had left it unlocked?"

"No! I hadn't given it any thought until I returned to the room."

"Do you understand what I am insinuating here, Miss Green?"

"I'm not sure that I do."

"Collusion. Perhaps you left your door unlocked so that the murderer could deposit the weapon inside your bedchamber. It was something that could have been planned in advance."

"You think I somehow knew who the murderer was and gave him permission to hide the weapon in my room? How ridiculous!"

"It had to be hidden somewhere, didn't it?"

"But why would I ever agree to it?"

"Perhaps you were pressured into it. Bribed, perhaps. Or blackmailed. Or threatened in some other way."

"No, absolutely not. I don't know how the murderer discovered that my door was unlocked, but discover it he did. And now I am having to answer for it."

I thought of everyone who had attended the dinner and wondered who could possibly have carried out this act. *Had the murderer known the bedchamber was mine when the knife was planted, or had it simply been chanced upon? Had someone deliberately wished to frame me? If so, who might have known that I was staying in that room?*

Chief Inspector Fenton nodded once again at the constable, who lifted another bag onto the table. This time he pulled out a heavy brown overcoat. It smelt of damp wool and the same metallic smell that had made my stomach turn on viewing the knife.

The overcoat was laid out across the table. I could see dark staining on its cuffs, and dark spatters on its sleeves and front. I didn't need to be told what the stains were. I quickly looked away again.

"Do you recognise this overcoat, Miss Green?"

"Of course not," I responded emphatically.

"Have another look at it. Can you be completely sure?"

I glanced quickly again at the coat, with its large collar and scuffed, leather-covered buttons.

"Of course I'm sure. It's a gentleman's coat."

"Have you ever seen anyone wearing a similar overcoat?"

"I must have done, I suppose. It is a fairly ordinary-looking coat, though I cannot recall seeing any of the other guests wearing a coat such as this. In fact, I didn't see any of them wearing an overcoat at all. We were inside all the time, so there was no need for anyone to wear anything of the sort. If this is the coat the murderer wore, it would suggest that he came from outside the building."

"He could have put it on specifically to carry out the murder," replied the inspector. "It would have prevented the clothes he was wearing from becoming bloodstained, and would have been quick and easy for him to dispose of. Can you show her the gloves, please, Constable Granger?"

The constable placed a pair of black leather gloves on top of the overcoat.

"These had been placed in the pockets of the overcoat," Chief Inspector Fenton explained. "No doubt they protected the murderer's hands as he inflicted those terrible injuries on his victims. Quite a lot of planning went into this crime. Do you recognise these gloves, Miss Green?"

"No. Perhaps you could show them to the other guests," I suggested. "Or find out which of them is missing an overcoat and a pair of gloves."

"Rest assured that we will be conducting full enquiries," replied the inspector.

"You still haven't told me whereabouts in my room the knife was found," I said.

"That's a piece of information we were hoping you could furnish us with, Miss Green."

"But I have no idea!"

Chief Inspector Fenton gave an odd smile.

"The only person who knows that information, other than you, is the murderer," I continued.

"Exactly. So we must bide our time and wait until someone accidentally lets it slip."

"And what am I to do in the meantime?" I asked.

"You must remain inside this hotel, Miss Green."

CHAPTER 15

I reluctantly returned to the Chinese Dining Room. The staff had cleared away the plates from lunch and I found Mrs Mirabeau sitting at the table smoking a cigarette. She wore a black satin dress with a bodice that was rather low cut for daytime wear. Captain lay curled in the corner of the room, his sad face resting on his paws.

"You must be in a dreadful shock from all this," I said as I joined her.

She gave a shrug and blew out a plume of smoke. "I just don't understand it."

"Have the police told you where they found the murder weapon?"

"No. Do you know?" Her eyes widened with interest.

"It was in my bedchamber."

"*Your* bedchamber?" Her scarlet mouth hung open.

"The murderer must have placed it there, unless the police are mistaken. But they are adamant that it was in my room. I left the door unlocked when I came down for breakfast, and somehow the culprit took advantage of that fact."

"Well, it's quite simple in that case. Whoever you breakfasted with can be ruled out of the investigation and everyone else must be considered a suspect."

"I sat with Mrs Mortimer and Mr Wentworth," I said. "And before that I encountered you and Mr Bolton, and Mr Somers and Mr Blackstone. I'm quite sure that Mr Somers and Mr Blackstone entered the dining room shortly after I did."

"Mr Bolton talked to me for some time," said Mrs Mirabeau. "I don't know how he would have found time to hide the weapon while you were at breakfast."

"So that leaves Mr White, Mr Goldman and Mr Hardy," I said. "Can you remember seeing them at breakfast this morning?"

"They were certainly present, but when it comes to vouching for the time they were here, I cannot be sure."

"It is not only the guests we need to consider, either," I said. "The staff must also be included in the list of possible suspects."

"About twenty of us stayed here last night."

I sighed. "And to think that it could have been any one of them! Perhaps it's not as simple as we think. How easy would it have been for someone to get inside the hotel at night?"

"Not at all easy. The front door is locked at eleven every evening, and I personally have to let anyone in or out after that time. I don't usually retire until midnight or one o'clock. If any of our guests are still out at that time I ask one of the maids to wait up and let them in."

"How did Mr Gallo's companion enter the building?" I asked.

Mrs Mirabeau gave me a sidelong glance and inhaled deeply on her cigarette before replying. "I let her in."

"You knew her?"

"Not well."

"But you were expecting her?"

"Yes."

"You had seen her before?"

"Yes, I had."

"Who was she?"

"A lady he liked." The general manager sucked on her cigarette again.

"Did you know her name?"

"Miss Hamilton is all I know."

"And did he tell you anything about her?"

"Of course not!"

"Why not?"

"What is there to tell? You understand what the woman's profession was, don't you?"

"Yes, I do. And presumably that means he didn't discuss her much with anyone."

"Of course he didn't. Besides, it was none of my business."

"Did you speak to her last night?"

"Just the usual greeting, and I told her how to get to the Venetian Suite. That was it. Off she went, and she used the back staircase."

"When did you first meet her?"

"You ask a lot of questions, don't you, Miss Green?" Her face stiffened. "It was about two months ago. Mr Gallo instructed me to let her in when she called at the door. She visited every Tuesday evening and always came knocking at half-past eleven. Had you been in an observant mood at that hour last night you would have noticed me leaving the room to admit her. I was a minute late in doing so, as I had lost track of time."

"What was she like?"

"I didn't know her at all, really. She was always polite and well-mannered. Tall with dark hair. And of a good back-ground, I would say, from the way she spoke. More of a cour-tesan than a common prostitute, and certainly not the sort of lady who would be plying her trade on the streets. She and Mr Gallo must have met each other through some sort of introduction, but I couldn't tell you who was behind it or when it was arranged."

"What about his wife?"

"She must never find out. And you reporters," she said, pointing her cigarette at me, "must never mention it in your publications. You understand that, don't you?"

I didn't like the admonishing tone of her voice. "I have no wish to upset Mrs Gallo and her daughters any further."

"Good." She extinguished her cigarette in the ashtray beside her. "And will you publish the fact that the murder weapon was found in your bedchamber?"

"No, of course not."

"It's rather interesting," she continued. "The murderer either placed the weapon there opportunistically, or he put it there with malicious intent. Which do you suppose it to have been?"

Her dark eyes fixed on mine, and I returned her stare. "It could have been either," I replied. "But I can't imagine why anyone should wish to frame me for this."

The sound of the door opening startled us, and I stood to my feet, relieved that the conversation with Mrs Mirabeau was at an end. I didn't know what to make of her.

A clean-shaven man with blue eyes and a square jaw stepped into the room, bowler hat in hand.

James.

I dashed over and embraced him, ignoring the fact that Mrs Mirabeau would likely deem my actions inappropriate. I breathed in the scent of his eau-de-cologne and immediately felt better.

"How are you?" he asked.

"Tired," I replied, releasing myself from the embrace. "I

cannot believe what has happened." I took a step back. "This is Mrs Mirabeau."

She gave each of us a bemused smile as James introduced himself.

"I hadn't realised you were on such good terms with Scotland Yard, Miss Green," she said.

"Inspector Blakely and I have worked on a number of cases together," I replied, aware that this did nothing to explain our intimacy. I turned to face James again. "Have you spoken to Chief Inspector Fenton?"

"I've spoken to his men, and they told me all the details, including that of the knife being found in your bedchamber."

"And now he wishes to detain me here indefinitely!"

"I'm sure he won't, Penny. Just make it clear that you will co-operate fully, and he will trust you enough to let you out of here."

"He probably thinks I'm the murderer!"

"I'm sure he doesn't."

"Then why does he speak to me as though I am?"

"He has to ask a lot of routine questions, just to be certain."

"I don't like the way he goes about it. Everyone else has been allowed to walk free, and one of them may be the actual murderer!"

"Hopefully you'll be able to leave as soon as Fenton has all the information he needs."

"Well, there's nothing else I can tell him. I heard a door slam in the night, and I'm quite sure that it was the door to the Venetian Suite, although it was found open, so I don't know how that could be. I wonder how the intruder even got into the room. Presumably Mr Gallo had locked it from the inside."

"He had a key," said Mrs Mirabeau, lighting another cigarette.

"How do you know that?" I asked.

"A key was found on the floor inside the room."

"Meaning what?"

"Meaning that Mr Gallo locked the door when he retired for the night and left the key in the lock. The intruder must have poked something through the keyhole to knock the key out and then inserted a second key to unlock the door. That key was left in the door."

"So he somehow obtained a spare key to the Venetian Suite. But how?"

"He took it from my office," she replied. "Don't ask me when or how, because I really couldn't tell you. I look after all the spare keys, and it wasn't until the police asked me to check for it in my office this morning that I noticed it was gone."

"Was your office locked overnight?" asked James.

"Yes. I lock it every night before retiring."

"At what time did you retire last night?"

"About half-past midnight."

"And until that time the room was left unlocked?"

"Yes, it was rather remiss of me, in hindsight. My office is normally in fairly constant use, but I didn't use it as much as usual last night because we were busy with our guests. I didn't expect anyone to enter my office and steal a key."

"It sounds as though there was quite a bit of planning behind this murder," said James. "A blacked-out lantern was found in the room with three of its sides obscured to help avoid detection. You say you heard the door slam, Penny, but did you hear any raised voices?"

"Only a brief shout after the door was slammed."

"If Mr Gallo and his companion had been awake there would have been a confrontation with the man who had just sneaked into their room. I'm certain you would have heard snippets of that confrontation."

"Mrs Mirabeau says that her name was Miss Hamilton."

"That's a useful piece of information. Have you informed Chief Inspector Fenton of her name, Mrs Mirabeau?"

"Yes."

"The presence of Miss Hamilton may have come as a surprise to the killer," continued James. "The culprit expected to find Mr Gallo alone, and unfortunately for Miss Hamilton he killed her because she had seen his face. Everything had been carefully planned up to that point. He had procured the weapon from somewhere, then dressed himself in an overcoat to protect his clothing and gloves to protect his hands. He had a lantern adapted for secrecy and somehow managed to obtain the spare key from Mrs Mirabeau. He also knew which suite Mr Gallo would be sleeping in that night.

"However, despite all this preparation, I am not convinced that he was a practised murderer. Although the lady had her throat cut, the police surgeon who examined her says that it took several attempts for the assailant to inflict the fatal wound. It was the work of someone who was ill-practised at performing such a gruesome act. If the murderer had planned it better he would have incapacitated one while he killed the other, just so that no one could escape and raise the alarm."

"Incapacitated?"

"With a blow to the head, perhaps."

I shuddered.

"These are not nice thoughts, are they?" he continued. "But at times like this we must try to understand the mind of the murderer. Why a knife? A gun would have made too much noise, I suppose. But what about bludgeoning?"

I shuddered again. "That would have been just as unpleasant as using a knife."

"Smothering? Chloroform? There are other alternatives. Why a knife? There is something rather impassioned about the choice of weapon." James paused to consider this before continuing. "The first thing Mr Gallo did when the killer struck was attempt to escape with his life. He would have run toward the door, which the murderer may well have closed behind him when he entered the room. Gallo would have pulled open the door and then slammed it shut as he escaped to give himself a little extra time to get away. That was presumably the door slam you heard, Penny.

"Then the murderer opened it again and left it open as he chased Mr Gallo along the corridor. It's likely that Gallo headed for the main staircase in the hope of finding someone else there; perhaps another guest or a member of staff. Unfortunately for him there was no one else about at that time, and in his hurry to run down the staircase he tripped and fell. That gave the murderer the opportunity to catch up with him and finish him off."

"And then the murderer returned to his own bedchamber, did he?" I asked.

"We don't know where he eventually went, but we do know that he threw the bloodstained overcoat and gloves from a window on the back staircase. The windows on that side of the building overlook Milford Alley, where the coat and gloves were found. Fenton has men examining the window frames to see whether they can ascertain which was opened most recently. Small splinters of paint may have been disturbed. Fenton tells me the culprit seems to have used the gentlemen's cloakrooms on the ground floor to wash himself and the knife afterwards, as there are splashes of blood-stained water on the floor. The culprit also took a towel from there to wrap the knife in."

"He took a big risk," I said. "He could have bumped into anyone at any time. Then he somehow managed to hide the knife in my bedchamber while I was at breakfast."

"He was unlikely to have known that it was your room. I

imagine he just walked along the corridor trying door handles. He must have been delighted when he came across the unlocked door, and when he saw that the room was empty he quickly hid the knife, still concealed in its towel, beneath your bed."

"So that's where he put it. Chief Inspector Fenton wouldn't tell me."

"Pretend that you haven't been given that piece of information, in that case," replied James.

"So was the culprit a guest or an intruder?" I asked.

"There is quite a lot of work to be done on that front," replied James. "At this stage I would like to learn a little more about Mr Gallo. Mrs Mirabeau, we need to look around his attic apartment. Would you mind taking us up there?"

CHAPTER 16

We took the elevator up to the top storey of the hotel and followed Mrs Mirabeau and Captain along the corridor to a door that was so plain and unremarkable I would have expected it to lead to nothing more than a cupboard. She unlocked the door and led us up a steep flight of wooden stairs and into a narrow corridor with a pitched ceiling.

"We must be in the eaves up here," said James.

"We are," she replied.

Our footsteps echoed on the bare floorboards, which offered a marked contrast to the thickly carpeted floors found elsewhere in the hotel.

"These are the staff quarters," she said as we followed her past a number of doors. "Mr Gallo occupied these rooms at the end." She unlocked the door.

"He allowed you to have a key?" asked James.

"Yes, he didn't mind at all." She smiled.

We stepped into a small, comfortable living room with a sloped ceiling and high wooden rafters.

Captain trotted into the bedroom, which lay just beyond a half-open door, and jumped up onto the bed. Three worn chairs were arranged around a small table in the living area, and the desk was completely covered in piles of papers, just like the one downstairs. Propped up against the desk was a roll of canvas.

"Is that a painting?" James asked, pointing toward it.

Mrs Mirabeau inspected the roll. "Four or five, I'd say. Presumably he was planning to have them framed and hung somewhere. Mr Gallo loved his art collection."

James picked up the roll and began to open it out.

"Be careful with those," said Mrs Mirabeau, stepping forward to assist. "They will be quite valuable, no doubt. Rest them on there." She pointed to the table with the chairs set around it.

"Do you remember Mr Gallo purchasing these?" asked James as he unfurled the first painting. It showed a sunset within a coastal scene.

"No, I don't," she replied, "but then I wasn't privy to everything he purchased."

James unravelled the remaining paintings. The next two were of natural landscapes, while another depicted a shepherdess with her sheep and the last portrayed a group of labourers in a field.

"There are five here altogether," he said.

I surveyed Mr Gallo's living quarters as James and Mrs Mirabeau examined the paintings. I was surprised by the modesty of these rooms compared with the opulence of those in the main body of the hotel.

James rolled the paintings up and placed them back beside the desk. "There are quite a few papers to look through here," he said. "Did Mr Gallo also store papers in his office, Mrs Mirabeau?"

"Yes, and in my office, too. He didn't like to throw

anything out. What would you be looking for among his papers?"

"A mention of anyone Mr Gallo had fallen out with or someone who bore him animosity," said James. "Do any names spring to mind, Mrs Mirabeau?"

"Not really. He was a popular man in general. There were rivalries, of course; most famously with Mr Marshall, who owns the Excelsior in New York. But it was good-natured rivalry, and I have already received a telegram from him expressing great shock with regard to Mr Gallo's passing."

"With whom did Mr Gallo socialise?"

"A great number of people! Where would I start? As soon as he arrived here in London he made every effort to acquaint himself with anyone of influence. He dined at the best restaurants, and he made sure he was invited to parties and opening nights at the theatre... that sort of thing. He did everything he could to get the word out about his hotel."

"What about his acquaintances? Are you aware of anyone he had met only recently?"

"There was Mr Dubois. He's at the Elysian on Essex Street."

"Thank you. And what can you tell us about Mr Gallo's comings and goings in recent days?"

"I've already given his diary to Chief Inspector Fenton."

"Good," said James. "Was there anywhere he went or anything he did that struck you as being out of the ordinary?"

"Not at all. Apart from occasional appointments, he spent most of his time here readying the hotel for opening, which was scheduled to take place next week. And he put a lot of preparation into last night's dinner. He was so keen to create the right impression with his guests that everything had to be perfect. He rose early and worked late into the night, making sure that everything was just as it should be. The bedrooms, the food, the flowers... He had staff to do all that, of course, but he insisted on overseeing everything himself. He was that sort of man." Her red lips parted as she considered this last comment for a moment.

"And what do you know of the lady who visited him?"

"I have already told Chief Inspector Fenton and Miss Green everything I know about her."

"I see." James glanced around the room as if looking for anything that appeared out of place.

"They'll all be saying that the curse has done its work again," said Mrs Mirabeau.

"Only the superstitious people," I replied.

"It might interest you to know that my wedding ring lies within the foundations of this hotel," she said.

"How so?" I asked.

"I happened to be walking past this site when they had just started building the hotel in the summer of 1869. I had argued with my husband. I had left him, in fact. So I pulled off my wedding ring and tossed it into the mud."

"Perhaps someone found it," I suggested.

"Perhaps. I prefer to think that it was soon buried beneath the bricks and mortar. Perhaps it was the ring that cursed the place." She gave an odd smile.

The door opened and Chief Inspector Fenton strode in, followed by Inspector Pilkington. We greeted one another and he gave me a reproachful glance.

"Pardon me for my curtness, Miss Green," he said, "but it really isn't appropriate for you to be here. Firstly because you are a news reporter, and secondly because you are implicated in this unfortunate incident."

"I cannot say that I disagree," I replied. "However, as I'm trapped in this hotel for the time being, I thought I would accompany my friend, Inspector Blakely, as he conducted his inquiries. There is little else for me to do."

"Do you object to me asking Miss Green to leave this area, Inspector Blakely?"

James sighed. "I cannot see any harm in her being here, Fenton."

"This is a matter for the police alone. It won't do to have someone here who could tamper with evidence or benefit from learning certain facts about the case."

"How could I possibly benefit from knowing the facts?" I asked.

"The knife was found in your bedchamber, Miss Green. We haven't yet been able to rule out your involvement in this affair."

"If I may be permitted to leave the hotel and return to my office I shall happily leave you to it, Inspector. May I go?"

He gave a reluctant nod. "Yes, but you'll need to report to Bow Street police station first thing tomorrow morning."

"Is that really necessary, Fenton?" asked James.

"Until we can find a suitable explanation for the murder weapon being found in Miss Green's bedchamber, I'm afraid it is merely standard procedure. I'm sure you're aware of that, Blakely."

"But we all know that Miss Green didn't murder Mr Gallo and Miss Hamilton."

"How do we know that?"

"Well, I can vouch for her good character."

"I'm sure you can." His tone was more than a little derisory.

"As can many other people," retorted James. "The murder weapon was planted in Miss Green's bedchamber because the culprit needed to be rid of it. It's that's simple."

"It's a simple explanation, but there is no guarantee that it is the correct one. I happen to know you have a vested interest in Miss Green's wellbeing, Blakely, and it would be most unfortunate if that interest were to conflict with us carrying out a fair investigation into this case."

James glared at him, so I thought it best to swiftly intervene.

"I shall report to you at Bow Street tomorrow morning as requested," I said. "And in the meantime you will either find me at the addresses I have previously given you or at the reading room in the British Library."

"I'll walk with you to your office, Penny," said James. Then he turned to Chief Inspector Fenton and said, "I'll be back with you shortly."

We pushed through the crowd outside the hotel and James carried my case as we began the short walk toward the *Morning Express* offices. The fog was beginning to lift and much of the street was discernible now, though the chimney tops remained hidden.

"Don't allow Fenton to upset you," said James. "He becomes rather officious whenever he has an important case on his hands."

"I know better than to let him upset me," I replied, "but his manner is rather irritating. I wish you the best of luck working alongside him."

James laughed. "I'm used to his ways. He doesn't always appear to like the Yard getting involved, but privately he'll be grateful for the help. It's difficult to know where to start with an investigation like this."

"Start with Mrs Mirabeau," I said. "I can't get the measure of her at all."

"Neither can I. We'll need to conduct a few more interviews with her in order to do so. I suspect she knows more than she's letting on."

"I feel certain that she does."

We turned onto the Strand, where the tiered spire of St Clement Danes church rose up into the fog.

"I met with a solicitor yesterday," said James. "He has agreed to represent me in this breach of promise case. At the present time we have different ideas with regard to how it should be approached, however."

"What is his idea?"

"He believes I need to be honest about my feelings for you, Penny, and to state that it was those very feelings that put a stop to the wedding. He thinks the jury will take a dim view of me if I appear to be hiding anything."

"That sounds like sensible advice."

"No, it's not! I've already said that this action has nothing to do with you. I have no wish to bring you into it."

"But I must share some of the responsibility."

"It was my choice to propose to Charlotte, and it was my choice to put an end to the engagement. It was also my choice to end it so close to the wedding."

"Immediately beforehand, to be entirely accurate."

"Exactly. What a foolish thing to do. I should have ended it months earlier. I look back now on the litany of mistakes I made, Penny, and it convinces me that you shouldn't have to shoulder the consequences of them."

"But I'm not blameless in this situation," I said. "In fact, I'm fairly sure that I asked you to cancel the wedding while we were walking through the Thames Tunnel."

"You did. And that was a reasonable request given that I had already kissed you several times by then."

I smiled at the memory. "James, I think you should be honest with the court about the nature of our relationship. What happened between us is not completely uncommon, you know. Sometimes betrothed people fall in love with someone else. I think we will be judged fairly if we own up to it."

"There's no *we* in this matter, Penny. This is about me. I have no desire for you to encounter the Jenkins family. Can you imagine how horrible they would be to you? And the jury may also judge you harshly. You will be seen as the lady who ruined an engagement, but I don't want them to view you in that way as it didn't happen like that. My conduct throughout may affect the sum I am ordered to pay, so my solicitor has advised me to speak kindly of Charlotte when we are in court and not to lay any of the blame at her feet. If I attempt to discredit her, the level of damages payable may increase. He told me of a recent case in which the defendant claimed to have put an end to his engagement because his fiancée had taken to drink. The jury didn't believe him, and he was ordered to pay further damages for lying. In that case the sum should have been two hundred pounds, but it was increased to five hundred."

"So what reason do you intend to give for ending the engagement if you don't plan to give the full story?"

"It's going to be rather difficult, isn't it? I think I shall have to say that my feelings for her had changed."

"And not mention us at all?"

"No."

"But you can't lie, James, it wouldn't be right. And besides, you're a police officer."

"I think it's best that you are kept well out of it. I'm planning to visit my parents this weekend to discuss the situation. I hope my father will be talkative enough to hold a sensible discussion with me now. I have endured his disapproval for long enough."

"Hopefully their hostility will have softened a little," I said. "But I still think it would be much better if we were completely honest, as your solicitor suggests."

"My word on this is final."

"It doesn't seem wise to ignore your solicitor's advice."

CHAPTER 17

"**M**iss Green! You survived!"

Edgar Fish greeted me with a wide grin as I arrived back at the newsroom.

"Yes, I did," I replied, "although I don't think I was ever in any real danger."

I sat down at the typewriter beside a grimy window that looked out onto Fleet Street.

"A murderer was prowling the corridors, stabbing people to death, and you weren't in danger, Miss Green?" retorted Edgar. "That's quite preposterous. It's a miracle she got out of there alive, isn't it, Potter?"

Frederick responded with a nod.

"I wonder who had it in for Mr Gallo," continued Edgar. "Are you all right, Miss Green? You look rather pale."

"It has all been quite a shock," I said, "not least because the culprit chose to hide the murder weapon in my bedchamber."

"What?" Edgar said, clearly startled. "While you were in there?"

"No, it must have been done while I was at breakfast. I foolishly left my door unlocked."

"And the devil left the knife in your bedchamber? You must have been horrified when you found it."

"I didn't find it. The police did."

"Oh dear," said Edgar quietly. "That makes it look as though you committed the crime."

"Yes, and it's possible that they still think I had something to do with it."

Edgar laughed. "Just one look at you would tell them you're no murderer, Miss Green!"

"You'd think so, wouldn't you? But experience has taught me that a person's appearance is no indication of their character at all, so I cannot blame the police for being suspicious of me."

"Hang on a minute, Potter. Do you think we might be looking at a murderer here? Miss Green claims the killer left the knife in her bedchamber, but what if she actually did the deed? There's just no knowing, is there?" Edgar laughed again and slapped his desk with mirth.

"What's so funny?" asked our editor, Mr Sherman, as he strode into the room, leaving the door to slam behind him as usual.

"Miss Green is a murderer!" laughed Edgar.

"That's a laughing matter, is it, Fish?" Mr Sherman replied with a scowl. He had a thick black moustache and his hair was oiled and parted to one side.

Edgar assumed a sombre expression. "Not really, sir. I was just having a little joke."

"Does Miss Green look as though she's in the mood for jokes?" asked Mr Sherman.

Edgar gave me an uneasy glance. "No, she looks rather tired, actually. I do apologise, Miss Green."

"It's quite all right, Edgar," I said. "There hasn't been

much to laugh about for the past twenty-four hours, so a little light relief is welcome."

"There you go, sir," said Edgar with a smile. "She doesn't mind."

"But I mind you not getting on with your work, Fish. Where's your article on the dead body that was posted to the Home Secretary?"

"I'm almost done with it, sir."

"Is it typewritten?"

"No, it's just handwritten at the moment. I shall get on with it now."

"Who posted the body?" I asked incredulously.

"A reverend from Lincolnshire," replied Edgar. "Apparently, it was a macabre protest about the fact that his parish has no more room in its burial ground."

"Good grief! What a thing to do."

"Some poor office keeper at the Home Office had the misfortune of opening it," said Edgar. "It had a parcels ticket from the Great Northern Railway attached and was labelled 'perishable'."

"The inquest will be interesting," said Mr Sherman before turning to face me. "I take it you've written all about the recent goings-on at the Hotel Tempesta, Miss Green?"

"I have made a lot of notes, sir."

"Excellent. So you should have something ready by deadline?"

"Of course, sir."

"They found the murder weapon in Miss Green's bedchamber," said Edgar.

"Good Lord! Really?"

"The murderer was hardly going to hide it in his own room, I suppose," I said.

"Good point," said the editor. "Hopefully you won't be considered a murder suspect."

"I'm not in the clear quite yet."

"Ah, but you have the schoolboy inspector looking out for you, don't you, Miss Green?" commented Edgar.

I felt a rush of warmth to my face. "Not really."

"Am I right in thinking that he recently called off his wedding?" asked Frederick.

"He did indeed," replied Edgar.

"Does anyone know why?" Frederick asked.

Edgar wiggled his eyebrows and nodded in my direction.

"What?" asked Frederick, not taking the hint.

"That's enough," said Mr Sherman, a slight smile playing on his lips. "You all have a lot of work to be getting on with. Have you finished your parliamentary report yet, Potter?"

"Almost."

"Not good enough. Get it done!"

CHAPTER 18

T he Horrifying Murder of an Hotel Owner
        The proprietor of the Hotel Tempesta, Mr. Nathaniel
        Gallo, was found tragically murdered yesterday morning.
A knife-wielding attacker broke into Mr. Gallo's bedchamber on the
night of Tuesday 11th November. The proprietor fled and a chase
ensued. The assailant set upon Mr. Gallo after he slipped and fell on
the main staircase. He was discovered by a maid, fatally injured from
a series of knife wounds, at the foot of the stairs at half-past five
yesterday morning.

    Constables from Bow Street police station were soon in atten-
dance, accompanied by Chief Inspector Fenton and Dr. S. Woolston.
The doctor certified the proprietor's death and a search is now
underway for the culprit. The knife used in the murder has been
retrieved, but the police do not yet know the identity of the attacker.
Robbery has so far been ruled out, as many valuables were left undis-
turbed in Mr. Gallo's bedchamber.

    Chief Inspector Fenton said: "This was the brutal murder of a
popular and well-known gentleman in the hotel industry, and the
motive for such a cruel act currently remains unknown. We will of
course do our utmost to find the person, or persons, responsible."

Mr. Gallo hosted a dinner at the hotel, formerly known as the Corinthian, for a select number of guests on the evening of the murder. The special event had been arranged to help publicise the official opening of the Hotel Tempesta, which was to have taken place next week. Mr. Gallo purchased the hotel, which is situated on Victoria Embankment, from the estate of the previous owner, Mr. Boris Thompson, earlier this year. The hotel has undergone an extensive refitting since the purchase, and it was Mr. Gallo's fervent hope that the respected guests the Corinthian had entertained during its heyday would return once again.

Mr. Gallo was 42 years of age and of American origin. He owned a number of hotels in the United States, including the Maganza Hotel in New York. He had stayed in London for the past six months, over-seeing the work being carried out at the Hotel Tempesta.

His wife, Mrs Caroline Gallo, and his daughters, Miss Victoria Gallo, Miss Geraldine Gallo and Miss Harriet Gallo, recently arrived in Paris from New York, and were believed to be making their way to London at the time of writing.

The Corinthian was built in 1869 and suffered a devastating fire in 1880, in which thirty-six people perished. The hotel was rebuilt, but the new owner, Mr. Thompson, committed suicide on the premises after filing for bankruptcy last year. The hotel's chequered history has prompted many to speculate that the building holds a curse for anyone who dares to purchase it. This most recent tragedy at The Hotel Tempesta will do little to dispel such rumours.

I found James waiting for me once I had finished reporting to Chief Inspector Fenton at Bow Street station the following morning.

"Fenton hasn't seen fit to arrest you yet, then?" he said with a grin.

"I think he wants to ensure that I don't jump on a boat to America."

"It is a legitimate concern," he replied. "A good many criminals escape justice that way."

"Except that I'm not a criminal!"

"Well, we don't know about that, do we? The knife was found in your room, remember?"

I gave James a good-humoured nudge with my elbow.

"Fenton and his men intend to focus their investigations on each of the guests who stayed at the hotel," said James. "We've agreed that I will investigate Mr Gallo's acquaintances and any possible enemies. I'm on my way to speak to Mr Dubois at the Elysian now. Would you like to join me?"

"I'd love to."

The fog was gone now, and in its place the low, grey cloud blustered above the rooftops, bringing with it drops of rain.

"Did you sleep well last night after your hellish stay at the Hotel Tempesta?" James asked.

"Of sorts. Actually, not too well at all. The thought that I had been asleep in that hotel while a knife-wielding madman was stalking its corridors felt rather unsettling."

"I can understand that, though you were never his intended target."

"Thank goodness. I wish I could understand why someone should have wished to do such a thing to Mr Gallo. I liked him. He wasn't a particularly good husband, but he didn't strike me as an evil man."

"Hopefully Mr Dubois can shed some light on this whole sorry business."

A strong gust of wind blew up the street and almost took my hat off. James clutched his bowler while I repositioned my hat pin.

"That's what I need," said James. "A hat pin."

"It wouldn't work. You need long locks of hair to loop a pin through."

"Then I shall grow long locks of hair. How do you think that would look?"

"Ridiculous!" I laughed.

"How about glue?"

"That would keep your hat on your head, without a doubt."

"Forever. It would mean that I would have to wear my bowler hat on our wedding day!"

We both laughed and then held each other's gaze. I noticed James' face redden a little, and mine did the same.

He grinned and then looked away again, as if unsure what to say next. He gave a cough, then quickly changed the subject. "My solicitor has informed me of the date when the court hearing will take place. It will be held at Croydon Assizes on the twentieth of November."

"But that's only next week!"

"Conveniently, or perhaps inconveniently, depending on how you view it, there happens to be an assizes session coming up in Croydon. I suppose it means I can get this blasted hearing out of the way."

"Do you feel prepared?" I asked.

"I think so. I can't pretend that I have done nothing wrong, so I think it's best to accept whatever punishment is meted out. I'm hoping the fine won't be more than five hundred pounds."

"If only the Jenkins family had accepted your first offer."

"They were never going to, were they? They wish to punish me as harshly as possible, and who can blame them? If some rascal did such a thing to my daughter I would be thoroughly enraged about it."

CHAPTER 19

We stepped into the marble-floored foyer of the Elysian. James showed his warrant card at the reception desk and asked to speak to Mr Dubois.

"He's usually in his staff meeting at this hour," replied the clerk, "but seeing as you're a police officer I'll try to summon him."

He soon returned and told us that Mr Dubois would be with us shortly. We sat down on a velvet-covered sofa in the foyer while we waited.

"So you're not sure what to make of Mrs Mirabeau?" James asked me.

"No," I replied. "She's quite unlike anyone I have ever met before. She appears to have been loyal to Mr Gallo, and he clearly thought highly of her. He valued her opinion, and they got along well. He told us he met her on a trip to Switzerland, and that she had worked for him in New York for a while before moving to London. She seemed genuinely devastated about his death and yet there's something about her which doesn't seem quite authentic."

"So what isn't she telling us?"

"Good question! I find her manner quite guarded, as though she's protecting herself or someone else. I suppose years of working in the hospitality industry have led to her putting on a persona. It's the sort of job in which you are constantly looking after people and seeing to their every need. It doesn't matter what your own needs are, or even what you think about anything. Perhaps she has become trapped in that way of thinking, but I can't help but think there's something rather suspicious about her."

"I know what you mean, Penny. I wonder what she's really like."

"Perhaps she is the one behind his murder. I can't help thinking she might be, but I don't see what motive she would have unless there had been a dispute between them. They seemed to be getting along very well the evening before he died. There were no signs of animosity."

"That doesn't mean she didn't murder him, however."

"I realise that. But I also saw her talking with the police officers the following morning, quite close to where his body had been found. Her distress seemed genuine to me, and she doesn't strike me as the sort of lady who would be easily upset by anything. If she were the murderer you might expect more of a show of grief, as if she were keen to demonstrate how upset she was by it all. But with that said..." I shook my head, still unsure what to think of her, "she confuses me."

A slightly built, dark-haired man wearing striped trousers glided toward us across the marble floor.

"Inspector?" he asked with a thick French accent. He wore a bejewelled pin in his cravat and several gold rings on his fingers.

We stood to our feet and introduced ourselves.

"I don't quite understand," said Mr Dubois, addressing James. "Why have you brought a news reporter with you?"

"Miss Green is assisting in this case," said James. "With your permission, she would like to print some of the details from our interview in the *Morning Express* newspaper. However, if you object she will refrain from doing so."

"Excuse my impertinence, but can she be trusted? She is a news reporter, after all!"

"I assure you she can, Mr Dubois. I have worked with Miss Green on a number of occasions, and I know her well."

"Ah, I see," replied the proprietor with a grin that suggested he had picked up on the true nature of our relationship. "Welcome to my hotel, Inspector Blakely, Miss Green. Step this way, please."

We followed him into an office decorated in white and gold. Its style was not unlike the Versailles Suite at the Hotel Tempesta.

"Please sit," he said, gesturing toward two elegant chairs. "You'd like to speak about Mr Gallo, would you? I couldn't believe it when I heard the news. He was such a fine gentleman. I don't understand it at all. It must have been a madman or a lunatic of some sort."

"Someone who is in possession of a singular mind, that's for sure," replied James. "But whoever it was had a reason for doing it, and by uncovering that reason we hope to bring ourselves closer to the culprit."

"That makes sense," replied Mr Dubois with a shrug, "but what do you want from me?"

"The most obvious question we have is: do you know of anyone who might have wished him any harm?"

"As I said before, it could only have been a madman or a lunatic. I can think of no one else."

"Did he have any disagreements with anyone?"

"I know nothing about that. Perhaps he did, but I wouldn't have known about it."

A waiter brought in a tray, then made an elegant performance of setting out cups and coffee pot.

"What about the usual rivalry between hotels and their owners?" James continued.

Mr Dubois gave a slight smile, accompanied by another shrug. "Yes, there is always some rivalry, but it is never so bad that someone would kill someone for it. I have spent all my life working in hotels and I never knew of it happening. It's the same as in any business; there will always be rivalry. But is someone often killed over it? No, hardly ever."

"How long have you known Mr Gallo?" I asked.

"I met him in New York, which would be about seven years ago. And then I didn't really know him after that, but he arrived here in London in the summer time, and then I met with him again. And after that we met a few times, actually. He was a fine gentleman, and he knew the hotel trade extremely well. When I heard he had bought the Hotel Tempesta I thought it was excellent news."

"You weren't worried about the effect it would have on your business?" asked James.

"No, why should I? There's enough room for many hotels in London, Inspector."

"Are there any other hotel owners in the vicinity of the Hotel Tempesta that might have been alarmed at the prospect of losing business?"

He gave a dry laugh. "Inspector, you are still holding on to the idea that another hotel owner was angry about Mr Gallo opening the Tempesta and decided to end his life. Does that solve the problem? No, it merely creates more problems than there were to begin with. A rival hotel owner merely responds by making his hotel superior. He offers more comfortable beds, better menus and a level of service that would please even a member of a royal household. That is how all our hotels get better, Inspector, and it is good for everyone.

Nobody decides, 'Oh, I must murder this American because he will steal all my guests.' No, that is not good for business. And afterwards the police arrive and arrest him, and that is the end of it all."

"So you don't believe Mr Gallo's murder could be the result of a rivalry or disagreement within the hotel trade?"

Mr Dubois' next shrug was an impatient one. "How am I supposed to know the answer to this, Inspector? I am not an expert on why someone would want to murder someone else. I have told you all I know, and I feel sure that it won't be another hotel owner who murdered him. But maybe I am wrong, and maybe there is a madman who owns another hotel. Who knows? Anything is possible. So maybe there is a very slight, but extremely small, chance that another hotelier is responsible for it. However, when you ask me if that's what has happened, I must say that I doubt it."

"What sort of man was Mr Gallo?"

"I told you, he was a fine gentleman. I didn't really know him as a personal friend, but I enjoyed his acquaintance and he told entertaining stories. We were always supposed to be talking about business, but he would become distracted by a story he was telling me, and we would never get around to what we were supposed to be talking about. I liked him, and perhaps that's because he was American as well. I have always liked American people. I hope I don't offend when I say that they are easier company than many English people."

"Not at all," said James. "Have you ever met Mrs Gallo?"

"Yes. Twice, I think. She is a fine lady." He sighed and rubbed his brow. "The poor lady. How she must be suffering with this. I don't know how she will ever recover, and those beautiful daughters, too. Ah, it is a tragedy. The actions of a madman and now we have all this. The lives of Mr Gallo's family members are ruined."

"Would you say that Mr Gallo was devoted to his wife?"

"Of course! Why would he not be?"

I thought of the lady who had been found in his room and hoped my expression would give nothing away.

"It can't have been easy for them while he was living in London and they remained in New York," clarified James.

"No, but people manage these things, and it's not a big problem. Mrs Gallo understood the demands of her husband's job, and she enjoyed spending the money he made from it, too." He grinned.

I supposed that if Mr Dubois happened to be aware of any infidelity on Mr Gallo's part he would be too polite to admit it to us.

"When did you last see Mr Gallo?" James asked.

Mr Dubois paused to think about this. "It was last week. A group of us dined at Le Croquembouche. Do you know it?"

"On Westminster Street?"

"Yes, that's it."

"Can you remember the date?"

The proprietor consulted a diary on his desk. "Wednesday the fifth of November."

"And can you recall who else was there?"

"Let me see now. Mr Court-Holmes, Mr Talbot and Mr Ripley."

James wrote these names down. "Was it an evening for discussing business? Or purely a social occasion?"

"A bit of both. There was some business talk, but just a little bit. And then Mr Gallo liked to talk about all sorts of other things as well." He smiled. "It was an enjoyable evening. I can't believe that was the very last time I'll ever see him. It doesn't seem real."

CHAPTER 20

"I recognise the name Court-Holmes," I said as we left the Elysian and walked up to the Strand. The rain was beginning to fall steadily. "I'm sure Mr Gallo mentioned him when he was talking about art. I think he said that Mr Court-Holmes owns an art gallery."

"I'll look him up," said James. "This interest in art intrigues me. Mr Gallo appeared to like paintings so much that he kept a number of them rolled up in his living quarters."

"He gave us the background to many of his artworks during our tour of the hotel. And I noticed that he had quite a detailed conversation with Mr Goldman about the paintings in the dining room while we were eating."

"Fenton is carrying out further investigations into the other guests," said James, "but perhaps you could tell me what you made of them?"

"I'd like to get out of the cold and wet first," I said. "And by good fortune we have found ourselves at the Twinings tea rooms."

The entrance was set beneath a small portico wedged

between the imposing facades of two impressive-looking banks.

"Perfect," said James.

Tea was served to us at a little table in the bustling tea shop, where many others also sought sanctuary from the rain. The spicy aroma of tea mingled with the smell of damp clothing.

"Let's begin with Goldman," said James. "You say that he was interested in the paintings at the hotel. What else did you learn about him?"

"Very little," I replied. "I didn't manage to hold any direct conversation with him. He was young and rather softly spoken, and he went about his business in a quiet, unassuming manner."

"Which publication does he write for?"

"It had Islington in the name, I think. The *Islington Chronicle,* perhaps."

"How sure are you of that?"

"It's the only Islington-based publication I can recall at the moment."

James wrote this down. "Who else made little impression on you?"

"Mr White. He was also young and fairly quiet. He had red hair and asked a number of questions on behalf of his publication, as I recall. Oh, and he went missing shortly before we all retired for the night."

"Where did he go?"

"I couldn't say. After dinner the gentlemen retired to the smoking room and Mrs Mortimer, Mrs Mirabeau and I went into the Lady Jane Lounge. By the time the gentlemen joined us they had lost Mr White somewhere along the way."

"Between the smoking room and the Lady Jane Lounge?"

"Yes."

"And what time was this?"

"About ten minutes before midnight. The general assumption was that he had slipped up to his bedchamber."

"Quite a reasonable assumption, I should think."

"Yes, we had all eaten and drunk quite a bit by that stage. Mr Gallo had been keen for the merriment to continue, but the rest of us wanted to retire for the night."

"Did you see Mr White the following morning?"

"I don't specifically recall seeing him at breakfast, but he was definitely in the dining room at lunchtime. I remember that because Mr Somers went to sit beside him after Mr Bolton had offended him."

"Tell me about Mr Somers, then."

"He was on first-name terms with Mr Gallo, having met him in New York several years ago. He was extremely upset by his death and was moved to tears on one occasion when we discussed it. He knew the Gallo family well, and was also well aware of Mr Gallo's indiscretions."

"Which were?"

"The companion, Miss Hamilton."

"He knew her?"

"No, he didn't know her, but he wasn't surprised to hear about the rendezvous. He said Mr Gallo had always had a weakness for the fairer sex, but that he also loved his wife dearly."

"Very interesting."

"I liked Mr Somers," I said, "and he was probably the person I spoke to the most. I cannot imagine him bearing Mr Gallo any ill-will."

"He may still have murdered him."

"But he's quite a large man. I struggle to imagine him chasing after Mr Gallo with a knife and catching up with him."

"But Mr Gallo fell down the stairs. He may have been

stunned by the fall, which would have allowed time even for a large man to reach him and do the dreadful deed."

"I simply cannot countenance it."

"As things stand, Mr Somers is as likely to have done it as anyone else."

"But I can't think what motive he would have had."

"You barely know him, Penny. He may well have had a motive that we're yet to find out about. Which publication does he write for?"

"*The City Journal.*"

"You needn't look so glum just because I consider your favourite guest to be a suspect!" James smiled.

"I'm not glum, but I suppose I can see that I have formed rather fixed opinions of all the guests, and I really don't know any of them well. It's difficult to view the situation objectively, isn't it?"

"It certainly is. What of Mr Bolton? What did he say to offend Mr Somers?"

"His tone was quite disrespectful yesterday. He has a confrontational manner about him, and I don't think he took kindly to Mr Gallo at all. The feeling was mutual, I suspect. While Mr Gallo was conducting the tour, I felt as though Mr Bolton was constantly attempting to trip him up with unhelpful comments."

"Such as?"

"Asking about the curse and the previous owner's suicide."

"Questions his readers would no doubt have liked to have answered."

"Quite possibly, but he didn't have a polite manner about him. His hands were often stuffed into his pockets or his arms were folded. He gave off an air of self-importance."

"Did he explain his dislike for Mr Gallo?"

"No, it was just the impression I got from him. My feeling was that he resented Mr Gallo's wealth and success. He struck me as the sort of man who would resent anyone who was wealthy and successful."

"I know the type. So his motive for murder could simply have been that he didn't like the hotelier."

"It's probably not a good enough reason to murder him, is it?"

"Not really."

James reviewed the notes he had just written and scratched his chin with the end of his pencil. I felt a warmth in my chest as I watched him, moments together like this were no longer forbidden. Never again would I need to worry that he would choose Charlotte before me.

"What are you smiling at?" James asked when he looked up.

"Nothing."

He gave a bemused grin then consulted his notes again. "There was a lady, a Mrs Mortimer, did you say?"

"Yes, that's right. A writer for *Wonders of the World*. She was an older lady who had once travelled the world with her husband. I think she said he was a geographer. His job was definitely something to do with maps."

"And how was she with Mr Gallo?"

"She seemed to like him. In fact, she was quite a pleasant lady, although she didn't take to Mrs Mirabeau. I had breakfast with her yesterday. I say *breakfast,* but neither of us actually ate anything. She was really quite horrified by the murder."

"As you might expect."

"Yes. And we were joined by Mr Wentworth, an older man who seemed quite grumpy a lot of the time. I don't think he was too impressed by Mr Gallo either. He called one of the rooms '*vulgar*'."

James laughed. "Some of the rooms are a little over the top, aren't they?"

"I liked them. I found myself agreeing with Mr Somers, who pointed out that such places can provide guests with a little fantasy. He said that they offer an escape from people's everyday lives."

"I can see what he meant by that. So Mr Wentworth wasn't too keen on Mr Gallo?"

"I'm not entirely sure. He was quite grumpy with most of us, so perhaps that was just his usual demeanour."

"What else did you learn about him?"

"Not a great deal, except to say that he was one of those old-fashioned types who seemed quite baffled by the concept of lady news reporters. It's possible that he feels quite baffled by ladies altogether. However, I'm quite sure that he couldn't have chased after Mr Gallo with a knife given that he uses a walking stick and is quite unsteady on his feet."

"A ruse, perhaps?"

"That would have been some ruse, but he appeared quite frail to me. I really cannot imagine him having the physical ability to commit such a brutal murder. I know you will still consider him a possible suspect, though."

"Who else was there?"

"The reporter for *The Times*, Mr Blackstone. He was the only guest I had met previously. Quite a dour man; you've probably come across him at some point. He bored Mr Somers senseless at dinner, then prided himself on interviewing as many people as possible yesterday morning. I don't think he managed to interview as many as Mr Bolton, however. I got the impression there was some sort of interviewing rivalry between them. I assume Mr Blackstone's interviews have already been printed in *The Times*, but I haven't had a chance to read them yet."

"If Mr Blackstone spoke to a lot of witnesses it would be quite interesting to talk to him. I suppose Fenton will deal with that, but I'll make a note of it."

"Oh, and he couldn't handle his drink. He had to be helped up to bed by Mr Gallo's staff at about ten o'clock."

"Oh dear, how embarrassing."

"I recall him rather liking Mr Gallo, however, and he seemed quite impressed with the hotel. I'd say that he and Mr Hardy were the most gracious toward our host."

"Mr Hardy, now who's he?"

"Another person I didn't speak to a great deal. He was a slick-looking gentleman who writes for *The Hotelier*. He sang Mr Gallo's praises throughout the tour, in an almost obsequious manner, I would say."

"Do you think he wished to impress his host?"

"It appeared so, though I'm not sure why. I noticed he got on well with Mrs Mirabeau over dinner. They were engaged in deep conversation for a while."

"Did you overhear any of it?"

"Unfortunately, no. Mr Somers was seated next to me and he has rather a loud voice."

James sat back in his chair and sighed. "From what you've told me about the other guests, it's difficult at this stage to determine any motive for murdering Mr Gallo. I can only hope that Fenton has obtained more information from them through his interviews."

"At least we know who we can initially discount."

"I don't think we can discount anyone."

"Some are far less likely to have done it than others. I'm absolutely certain that Mrs Mortimer, Mr Wentworth and Mr Somers lack the physical capacity needed to inflict fatal injuries upon two people."

James nodded. "I suppose that's a reasonable assumption. We can't discount them, but we can consider the others as more likely suspects."

"So that leaves the two young men, Mr White and Mr

Goldman, and the other three, Mr Bolton, Mr Hardy and Mr Blackstone."

"That narrows it down to five. We could certainly concentrate on them in the first instance."

I refilled our cups from the teapot. "Circumstantially, Mr White is the most suspicious because he vanished after the men left the smoking room. He may have used that time to prepare himself for the murder. He needed to obtain the spare key for the room, put on the overcoat and gloves, and arm himself with the blackout lantern and knife."

"I'll speak to Fenton later today and find out what he has discovered about Mr White and the other suspects. With any luck he has reached a similar conclusion. There is also Mrs Mirabeau to consider, of course. There would have been no need for her to steal the spare key to the Venetian Suite given that she was already in possession of it."

"Mrs Mirabeau is a lady of slight build," I said. "Do you really think she could have inflicted such harm on two people?"

"I think this was an impassioned crime," said James. "Whoever inflicted those vicious knife injuries was consumed with anger as they carried out the act. Even a slightly built lady would be capable of doing such a thing if she were filled with sufficient rage. And let's not forget that Mr Gallo was probably incapacitated by his fall on the stairs. Had he managed to get down the stairs and away from his attacker there is a possibility that he might have escaped with his life."

"Are you saying that it would have been easier for the culprit to attack him because he was hurt?"

"Yes, even if the culprit happened to be slightly built."

"And you're suggesting that the murderer was angry, which would imply that the assailant knew his or her victim quite well."

"Yes. Something the victim did must have provoked an

intense anger, so this attack may have been an act of revenge."

"Or jealousy."

"Why do you say that?"

"Let's consider that Mrs Mirabeau is the guilty party," I said, "and that she held a strong affection for Mr Gallo. Perhaps he had rejected her advances and chosen Miss Hamilton instead."

"That would have caused her to be angry with both Mr Gallo and Miss Hamilton, and would provide a suitable explanation for the savage attack on both parties."

"The more I consider this, the more I suspect that Mrs Mirabeau is the culprit," I said. "But why did she wait until all the guests were staying at the hotel to carry out the murders?"

"Because the guests would all be considered as suspects, wouldn't they? Their presence muddies the waters. But let's not get carried away with ourselves, as we have no idea whether Mrs Mirabeau held any affection for Mr Gallo or not. It seems that she respected him professionally, but there is no evidence that she harboured any stronger feelings toward him than that. And I can't help but think about this interest in art, and the paintings sitting beside the writing desk. There have been several thefts from London galleries in recent months."

"You don't think Mr Gallo has been stealing paintings, do you?"

"No, I don't, but there is naturally some convergence between the art world and the criminal world, and I think it may be worth investigating whether Mr Gallo came close to it at all. What was the name of the art gallery owner?" James consulted his notebook. "Ah yes, Court-Holmes."

"The Calthorpe Art Gallery!" I said. "Hearing you say that

name again recalled to my mind the name of the art gallery Mr Gallo mentioned."

"That's a well-known gallery," replied James. "It's on New Bond Street and a painting was stolen from there not long ago. My colleague Inspector Raynes is investigating the case."

"I think I remember Edgar reporting on it for the *Morning Express*."

"I'll put our theory on Mrs Mirabeau to Fenton later, but in the meantime we need to speak to Court-Holmes and find out a bit more about him."

CHAPTER 21

New Bond Street was bustling with gentlemen in top hats and ladies in furs. They stepped in and out of waiting carriages, which conveyed them to luxurious little shops selling fine jewellery and expensive luggage.

The Calthorpe Art Gallery was a pale, ornate, four-storey building with carved decorations around each window. Once we had stepped through a set of polished oak doors, the quiet of the gallery descended upon us. A tangy scent of oil lingered in the air, and I glanced at the paintings of rural scenes, distinguished gentlemen and vases of flowers.

A smart young man greeted us, and by the manner in which he looked us up and down I could see that he had decided we were not his usual clientele.

James introduced us and asked to speak to Mr Court-Holmes. The young man went to fetch the gallery owner, and a short while later a fair-haired man of about forty-five strode through the door at the back of the gallery. He had green eyes, a tidy moustache and a proud, upright posture. His clothes were smart and well-tailored.

"Do you have news for me, Inspector?" he asked James.

"Not of your stolen painting, I'm afraid, Mr Court-Holmes. We've come to see you about a separate matter."

"Mr Gallo?" he asked with a sigh.

"Yes. I understand he was a friend of yours. Please accept my condolences."

"It has come as quite a shock. I really can't understand why anyone should wish to harm him."

"You have already answered one of my questions, in that case," said James.

"He had only been in London a few months, but we spent some considerable time together as we shared a passion for art."

"Do you know of anyone he might have fallen out with? Did he mention an argument or a dispute of any kind?"

Mr Court-Holmes shook his head. "None at all."

"Where did you first meet Mr Gallo?"

"It was during a private viewing at the Royal Academy. Must have been about two years ago now. He purchased a number of artworks for his hotels. In fact, I recall that he was in London at the end of last summer buying paintings from the Royal Academy's summer exhibition. He took a large shipment back to America with him! He was also a good customer of ours, not to mention a gentleman I considered a friend."

"When did you last see him?"

"We had dinner only last week."

"Just the two of you?"

"There was myself, Mr Gallo and Mr Dubois, the proprietor of the Elysian Hotel. And two other friends, Mr Talbot and Mr Ripley. We enjoyed a very pleasant evening at Le Croquembouche."

James wrote this down as if it were a new piece of information, not letting slip that he had already heard a similar account from Mr Dubois.

"Mr Gallo was keen to acquire artworks for the hotel, and I saw him a number of times at Sotheby's auction house," Mr Court-Holmes continued. "He always enjoyed visiting us here, and as you can see we have quite a variety of works. I'm rather fond of Realism," he pointed at a painting of peasants toiling in a field, "and I find Neo-Classicism rather pleasing." This time he gestured toward three paintings depicting bored-looking women in diaphanous clothing reclining on Grecian terraces. "However, my first and most persistent love is Rococo. It's what some call Late Baroque. I'll never forget seeing Boucher's *Triumph of Venus* in Stockholm. It is such a vibrant artwork. Our stolen piece, the *Madame Belmonte*, is another Rococo painting. It was painted in 1775."

James and I gave an appreciative nod.

"You'll notice an absence of French Impressionism here," he added, adjusting his silk cravat. "It doesn't do much for me. Just a blotch here and another there. It's said that the artwork reflects one's first impression of a scene, and that is why no further detail is required, but I prefer a painting with greater depth. Some would consider the works in my gallery to be old-fashioned, but I have always admired the old masters and will continue to celebrate the paintings inspired by their style. What is your view of impressionism, Miss Green?"

"I find it quite pleasing to the eye. In fact, I see the world as an impressionist painting whenever I remove my spectacles!"

He laughed at this. "And you say that you're a news reporter."

"Yes, for the *Morning Express*."

"Then I have met your colleague, Mr Fish."

"I recall that he reported on the theft of the *Madame Belmonte* painting."

"They knew what they were looking for when they came here. The robbers propped a ladder up against the rear of the building and broke a window on the first floor to get inside. The *Madame Belmonte* was cut from her frame quite skilfully. Oddly enough, the theft has actually increased business. People have been interested to see the empty frame, and for a while we kept it hanging on the wall! Just for a day or two, while our visitors' curiosity was piqued."

"I believe my colleague, Inspector Raynes, has been assisting you with the investigation," said James.

"That's right. And a detective from Pinkerton's is over from America at the moment working on the case with him, having followed a criminal fellow over the Atlantic. Stealing and forging paintings is the sort of thing this chap goes in for, apparently. They're trying their hardest to find evidence that he has something to do with our missing *Madame Belmonte*, but these people are very good at covering their tracks, aren't they?"

"Are all your paintings for sale?" asked James.

"We're not a shop, so we don't put prices on our paintings. However, if someone is interested in purchasing one we will happily discuss it over a glass of champagne. I like to choose which clients I sell my paintings to, and even if someone offers a decent price I won't necessarily sell to them. I have a strong attachment to every artwork here, and I like to feel reassured that if we sell one it will be looked after in a responsible way. If a person is not a good match with a piece of artwork I simply don't sell it to them."

"You like to learn about your buyers before selling to them?" James clarified.

"Exactly."

"We found a roll of paintings within Mr Gallo's living quarters in the hotel's attic. Might he have bought them from you?"

"The works he bought from us were always framed. He might have removed them from the frames, of course, but I'm not sure why he would do such a thing. We pride ourselves on ensuring that each frame complements the picture in question. Do you know which paintings they were?"

"There were two landscape scenes, a painting of a sunset and two paintings with rural workers in the foreground. Was one of them a shepherdess, Penny?"

"Yes, I think so," I replied.

"I didn't look at the artists' names, I'm afraid," added James.

"Interesting."

"Admittedly, my descriptions of the artworks are rather poor, but do any of them sound familiar?"

"No, I can't say that they do. I'm quite confident they are not the artworks Mr Gallo purchased from us."

"The stolen one is definitely not among them?"

"No, indeed. The *Madame Belmonte* is a portrait."

"Of course. I should have realised that it would be." James gave an embarrassed laugh.

"Mr Gallo would never have had anything to do with a stolen painting," said Mr Court-Holmes. "It would be completely out of character."

"Even if he hadn't realised it was stolen?"

"I suppose any one of us could buy a painting without realising it had been stolen. You're not suggesting he was murdered over a stolen painting, are you?"

"We don't yet know what the motive was; that's what we're trying to find out. I find it odd that the paintings in Mr

Gallo's rooms are all rolled up together in the way they are. It suggests some sort of secrecy, or perhaps I'm dwelling on them too much. Do you think they might be of any significance, Mr Court-Holmes?"

"It's impossible to say, Inspector."

CHAPTER 22

I resolved to spend some time working on the book I was writing about my father's travels over the weekend. I had transcribed many of his letters and diaries, but there were still a good few to work through.

The week's events had left me feeling quite tired, and I soon found myself gazing out through the window beyond my desk at the rain drumming down on the rooftops. I wondered how James was faring on his visit to his parents' house given that they hadn't yet forgiven him for ending his engagement. He had previously told me that his and Charlotte's mothers were friends, and that this was how they had originally come to meet.

As my cat, Tiger, decided to stretch herself across my page, I took the opportunity to pause from work and make myself a cup of cocoa. There was a knock at the door as I placed the kettle on my little stove.

"Only me!" called my landlady, Mrs Garnett. "There's another letter for you here from the lovesick librarian!"

"There's no need to call him that any more, Mrs Garnett," I replied as I opened the door. "He has left the library now and is far too busy enjoying the travelling lifestyle to be lovesick."

She gave me a knowing smile as she handed me the letter. Her steel-grey curls were contained beneath a white cotton bonnet, which contrasted beautifully with her dark skin.

"Let's hear what he has to say, then," she said as she walked into the room and sat herself down on my bed.

"Why are you so interested, Mrs Garnett?"

"I'm always interested to read something written by a person who's off travelling the world! I won't be travelling anywhere myself any time soon... possibly never again. So I like to hear about other people's adventures instead."

"Very well."

I sat on the chair at my writing desk and opened the letter, which had been written almost a month earlier.

El Charquito, United States of Colombia, 17th October 1884

  Dearest Penny and Eliza

  Your letter has reached me at last! It found its way from Bogotá via a messenger from the British Embassy.

  I must say that I was very sorry to read of the cancellation of Inspector Blakely's wedding. It must have caused great upset to both parties, and I can only hope that the decision was made for the right reasons. Please extend my regards to Inspector Blakely.

  Hopefully you have received my previous letter by now, which explained that Anselmo and I plan to stay in El Charquito for a while in order to take excursions out into the countryside and make enquiries among the people we find there in the hope of discovering news of your father's whereabouts. We have employed the services of a local guide who knows this area well.

  We have made two excursions so far, and I can already see why your father was so drawn to this country. The vegetation is lush and verdant, and in the densely forested areas around us I have espied some of the orchids your father loved so dearly. I couldn't possibly know the species as well as he, so I cannot name them, but I can certainly vouch for their beauty.

The incessant rain has finally stopped, and I am hoping the low cloud will lift before long. We have been assured that this is the beginning of the dry season!

Our first excursion took us through the forest twenty miles south of here to a small village called Las Fronteras, but our enquiries turned up no word of your father. The following day we travelled south-west for just over twenty miles to a pleasant little town called Subia. My spirits were lifted by the many colourful flowers thriving there despite the damp weather.

I have eaten my fill of potatoes, sweet potatoes and cassava root. The Colombians enjoy their meat, but it is rather over-salted for my taste. I am also savouring figs and mangos, and of course the wonderful Colombian coffee.

The air here is to be recommended. It is rather different from the smoke of London, although I must say that we haven't quite escaped the fog!

Tomorrow our guide will take us north across the River Funza, and we shall continue our enquiries there. I feel sure that it won't be long before we encounter someone who recalls your father and can give us some valuable information.

With fondest regards,

Francis Edwards

"What a lovely letter," said Mrs Garnett. "Doesn't he have a wonderful way with words? If the poor fellow is truly disappointed that the inspector's wedding was cancelled, he doesn't obviously show it."

"He has other more pressing matters to consider now, Mrs Garnett. Important matters such as finding my father."

"Won't it be fantastic when he finds him?"

"*If* he finds him. He may never pick up Father's trail."

"But it sounds as though he knows what he's doing with all this talk of the various places he's visited and the suchlike. He's a very clever man, and brave, too. Why didn't you ever agree to marry him?"

"Much as I like and respect Mr Edwards, I don't love him. I'm quite sure we've had this same conversation before!"

"We have indeed," she said with a sigh. "Will you marry the inspector now?"

I felt my face redden. "We haven't really discussed it as yet. It's too soon after the cancellation of his last wedding to consider another."

"Two months, isn't it? Surely that's long enough. Get on with it, I say, as you never know what might befall you. You've met my friend Mrs Wilkinson, haven't you?"

"I have indeed."

"Her husband's cousin died in a fire last week. He was fast asleep in bed, and then, whoosh! Everything caught fire and he was dead. You never know when the good Lord will decide your time is up, and that's why you shouldn't waste it."

"I wouldn't say that I'm wasting time at the moment, Mrs Garnett."

I heard footsteps beyond the open door.

"Hello?"

It was my sister's voice, and I felt relieved that the topic of conversation was about to change.

"Penelope! Mrs Garnett!"

I noticed my landlady frowning at the sight of Eliza's practical tweed jacket and divided skirt as she strode into the room.

"Did you arrive here on your bicycle, Mrs Billington-Grieg?"

"I did, Mrs Garnett, but don't you worry. I know you

don't allow bicycles in the house, so I left it next to the privy."

"We've just been reading the latest letter from Francis," I said, standing to my feet and passing the letter to Eliza. "He has been busy making daily excursions."

Mrs Garnett excused herself while my sister read the letter.

"How wonderful," Eliza said once she had finished reading. "He's working hard, by the sound of things, though I think he was hoping for a little more sunshine! Now then, Penelope, tell me what happened at that accursed hotel. I've been in Derbyshire this week visiting Mother, and I recalled you telling me you were going to be staying at a new hotel some American chap had opened. Then I read in the newspaper that he had been murdered! Please don't tell me you were there."

"I was, actually. Would you like a cup of cocoa? The kettle is almost boiled."

I made our drinks and my sister listened intently as I recounted the events that had taken place at the Hotel Tempesta.

"I thought my own life had been quite eventful of late, but once again you have beaten me to it."

"Unfortunately, I am still having to report to Chief Inspector Fenton at Bow Street station every morning because the murder weapon was found in my bedchamber."

"Surely he knows that you couldn't have possibly done such a thing."

"I'm quite certain that I am not considered a suspect in the murder itself, but I suppose he sees a possibility that I might have colluded with the killer and allowed him to hide his weapon there."

"Well that's utterly ridiculous, too."

"I suppose they cannot rule anything out at this point. He wants to conduct a longer interview with me on Monday."

"He needs to leave you alone!"

"All the guests are being interviewed in this manner, Ellie. James and I think that a number of them could be ruled out as suspects, including me. We just need to persuade Chief Inspector Fenton to concentrate on the more suspicious guests."

"You mustn't undertake any police work yourself, Penelope."

"I realise that, but James and I have worked on a good few cases together now."

"As long as you remember that you're a news reporter and not a policelady." Eliza blew on her cocoa to cool it. "I wonder whether ladies will ever work for the police force."

"I don't see why not. There are already several female private detectives. I know the Pinkerton Detective Agency employs some."

"That's the American detective agency, isn't it? I've heard the name before."

"Apparently they have a man in London at the moment looking for a criminal who may have stolen a painting from an art gallery that belonged to a friend of Mr Gallo's."

"Well that sounds rather convoluted. I was going to say that I wouldn't mind becoming a lady detective, but I think I'd become too easily confused by situations like that. Anyway, I'll be starting a job of my own on Monday."

"Congratulations, Ellie! You must so be looking forward to it!"

"I am. I thought I should tell Mother the news of my situation before she heard it from anyone else. It wasn't easy, but I feel better for it now."

"What did she say?"

"Not a great deal, really. I think she's still coming to terms with the idea. I did place considerable emphasis on George's behaviour, perhaps unfairly at times."

"Why would it be unfair? He consorted with criminals."

"But not knowingly."

"How can you be so sure? He's an intelligent man, and I don't believe he was unaware of what his client was embroiled in. I think you persist in flattering him too much."

"I didn't flatter him to Mother!"

"Good! Was she surprised?"

"Yes, extremely. Quite horrified, in fact. She couldn't believe that a lawyer would get himself into such trouble."

"No, I don't suppose she could. Many people struggle to believe that a professional gentleman might be capable of any wrongdoing."

"She was rather uneasy when I introduced the idea of divorce. I had to stress the point that I couldn't possibly remain married to a man who had behaved so despicably. Although she was opposed to the idea, she eventually agreed with me. She is so extremely disappointed in him."

"As you were when you discovered what he had done."

"Yes, although I am quite recovered from that now. I mentioned my offer of employment to Mother."

"And what did she make of it?"

"She sighed and made a comment about having two daughters who are determined to be as modern as possible. She enquired about you and asked whether you were courting. I didn't dare tell her you had caused a man to cancel his marriage just hours before his wedding. I don't think she would have coped well with that news on top of mine."

"No indeed. I suppose she would have been even more despairing of us if you had."

"You'll have to visit her and explain the situation to her soon. It's only fair."

My stomach turned at the thought.

"It's been some time since you last visited her," continued Eliza. "I suppose you're always rather busy, aren't you? And you'll be even busier now that you've decided to become an unofficial police constable."

"I have done no such thing!"

"There's no need to take offence, Penelope. Your closeness to James makes it inevitable."

"Not at all, Ellie. I haven't forgotten that I'm a news reporter. The reason I'm so involved in this current case is that I was staying at the hotel when the murders were committed."

"That may be so, but it is important to remember where *your* job ends and *his* begins. I realise there is always some justification for these situations, but how does your editor view your romantic involvement? And how about James' superiors? I shouldn't have thought it would be too long before something is said."

CHAPTER 23

"When did you first hear of Mr Gallo, Miss Green?"

Chief Inspector Fenton sat across the table from me in a small room at Bow Street station that was lit by a gas lamp and a narrow window. Inspector Pilkington was also present and had been tasked with writing down everything I said.

"I was aware that the Corinthian Hotel was being refurbished," I said, "as I saw the work being carried out when I walked past it. My office is only a five-minute walk from the hotel."

"But when did you first hear of Mr Gallo himself?"

"I didn't know the name until an invitation arrived at our office for a reporter to spend the night at his new hotel. Before that I had heard that an American hotelier intended to reopen the Corinthian, but I didn't know his name at that time."

"What had you heard about him?"

"Just that."

"When did the invitation arrive at the *Morning Express* offices?"

"It was some time in September."

"Was it addressed to you directly?"

"It was addressed to the editor, Mr Sherman. He had no wish to stay at the hotel, so he passed the invitation on to my colleague, Mr Fish. He wasn't keen to take up the invitation, and neither was another colleague, Mr Potter, so it fell to me to accept it."

"Why was it refused by your three colleagues?"

"It didn't interest them enough, I suppose, and Mr Fish was rather preoccupied with the rumours about the hotel being haunted. I wouldn't say that he was frightened about staying there, but I believe the thought unnerved him."

"Was Mr Sherman well acquainted with Mr Gallo?"

"Not to my knowledge, no. I think it was a speculative invitation. Mr Gallo most likely invited writers from all the publications he enjoyed reading. Or perhaps he chose the publications he felt would provide favourable reviews. I'm sure Mrs Mirabeau would know more about his reasons. In fact, it was Mrs Mirabeau who recommended the idea to Mr Gallo. You should ask her about it."

"There's no need to make suggestions as to how we carry about our investigation, Miss Green. I'm more interested in what *you* know at the present time. So the first time you met Mr Gallo was on the evening of the dinner?"

"Yes."

"And you got to know him during the course of the evening."

"Not particularly. He gave us a tour of the hotel and fed us well – a little too well, actually – and then we all retired for the night. The Mr Gallo I saw was the man he wished us to see. It came as a great surprise to me to learn that he had entertained a female companion that evening. He had given us the impression that he was devoted to his wife and daughters. From what I did know, though, I liked him. He was pleasant, amusing and a good host. Inspector, I realise you're trying to establish any possible motive I might have for murdering Mr Gallo, but I really didn't know the man! There were other guests there who were much better acquainted with him."

"Which of the guests did you know before you arrived at the hotel?"

"Mr Blackstone was the only person I had met before, and I must add that I am not particularly familiar with him. I just know him to be one of the reporters for *The Times,* and as a result our paths cross now and again."

"Was Mr Blackstone acquainted with Mr Gallo before that evening?"

"I'm not sure. He didn't mention that he was."

"There is a strong possibility that two or more guests colluded to carry out this heinous act."

"If you're suggesting that Mr Blackstone and I colluded you are sorely mistaken, Inspector. We are practically strangers!"

"You must have had an opportunity to collude with someone, though. Did anyone ask if they could store something in your bedchamber?"

"The murder weapon, you mean?"

"Perhaps you didn't know they were referring to the murder weapon. Perhaps they came up with an excuse to visit your room. This wouldn't mean that you were complicit in the crime at all, as you were assisting the murderer unwittingly."

"No one asked if they could put anything in my bedchamber, or asked to visit it at all, Inspector. Have you asked the staff? I think it would have been perfectly easy for a chambermaid to hide the knife in my room without arousing suspicion."

"The staff have all been interviewed."

"Did you happen to learn anything about the relationship between Mrs Mirabeau and Mr Gallo? She was particularly well-placed to carry out the attack because she is so familiar with the hotel and had access to a spare key for every room. If it could be established that there was an intense acquaintance between her and Mr Gallo—"

"Are you concocting a motive to fit the crime, Miss Green?"

"No, I'm only wondering if you or your officers have discovered any sort of untoward relationship between Mrs Mirabeau and—"

"Not a bit of it!" he interrupted. "And if I hear any rumours of this sort again I shall assume you have been the source of them. Please don't share any of your far-fetched theories with anyone outside these four walls, Miss Green. We don't need your wild guesswork confusing matters even more. I'm aware of the cordial relations between yourself and Inspector Blakely, but I must warn you against working with him on this investigation."

"But it's my job to report on it."

"By all means report on it, but you should not be involving yourself in the investigation. Firstly because you're a news reporter, and secondly because you are still listed as a person of interest in this investigation."

"Why on earth would I be of interest, Chief Inspector?"

"I'm afraid you will be until we can explain how the knife came to be found in your bedchamber."

"It was discovered there because I foolishly left my door unlocked when I went down to breakfast!"

"I can't just take you at your word, Miss Green. There might well be another explanation for it."

"Has Inspector Blakely told you about the guests we – I mean to say *he* – thinks are most likely to have committed these crimes?"

"We have discussed them, thank you. That's all for now, Miss Green. Please report back here tomorrow morning."

"Must I continue to report here every day, Chief Inspector? Can we not try every second day, or even every third? I have no plans to go anywhere."

"We will see you tomorrow morning, Miss Green."

I encountered Mr Blackstone as I stepped out of Bow Street police station.

"Miss Green." He gave a polite nod. "Have you just visited Fenton for a report on the progress of the case?"

"There was a little more to it than that, unfortunately. Seeing as the weapon was found in my bedchamber, I have to report here every day. He asks me questions and then I ask him some in return, but he's never very keen to answer them. Are you here to get an update from him?"

Mr Blackstone nodded.

"Well, good luck," I said. "He's rather grumpy today. I think he resents the press taking such an interest in the case."

"Oh, I always find that he's all right with me."

"Good," I replied with a bitter taste in my mouth.

I should have liked to discuss the case further with Mr Blackstone, but I was mindful of Chief Inspector Fenton's warning that I wasn't to go around sharing my theories too widely.

CHAPTER 24

"Watch out, Potter, here comes the chief suspect," said Edgar as I arrived back at the newsroom.

"I would find your remark amusing had I not just spent the last hour at Bow Street station with Chief Inspector Fenton," I replied, pulling my papers out of my bag and tossing them onto my desk.

"The man clearly has no idea what he's doing," replied Edgar. "Surely he must know that a mild-mannered lady reporter couldn't possibly be capable of such a crime."

"I'm not sure I like the description *'mild-mannered'*," I replied. "It suggests that I'm rather feeble."

"Women *are* feeble. That's why they're generally incapable of murder."

I gave a dry laugh. "I've encountered a few murderesses in my time."

Edgar pondered this for a moment. "That's true. There have been a few, haven't there? You've got me feeling worried now. Perhaps you're the guilty party after all."

"I wouldn't rile her, Fish," Potter chipped in. "You never know what she might be capable of."

"Who is capable of what?" asked Mr Sherman, the newsroom door slamming behind him.

"Murder, Mr Sherman," replied Edgar. "We've decided that Miss Green would be quite capable of committing a murder."

"Is your article about Lord Northbrook's report on Egypt written yet, Fish?" asked the editor.

"Almost, sir."

"Then may I suggest that you finish it instead of sitting there spouting nonsense? And what are you grinning at, Potter?"

"Nothing, sir."

"Your parliamentary report last Friday was rather thin on detail. Are you sure you didn't nod off?"

"The discussion in the House of Commons can be pretty dull at times."

"It's dull most of the time, Potter, but it's your job to report on parliamentary proceedings all the same."

"The Under Secretary for Home Affairs fell asleep on Friday afternoon, sir."

"And that means you're entitled to follow suit, does it?"

"No, but his job is surely more important than mine."

"Are you arguing with me, Potter?"

"No, sir."

"You just argued with him, Potter," whispered Edgar.

"Quiet, Fish!" scolded Mr Sherman. "Mr Potter, if I have a parliamentary reporter who keeps falling asleep I shall find a simple solution. Do you know what that might be?"

"A replacement parliamentary reporter, sir."

"Very good. Perhaps fewer beverages in the House of Commons' bars will encourage a more alert mind."

"Might do, sir," he replied meekly.

Mr Sherman turned to face me. "How's the Hotel Tempesta investigation going, Miss Green?"

"There are numerous potential suspects, sir."

"Including yourself?"

"Chief Inspector Fenton informs me that I am still a person of interest."

"Foolish man. What is Inspector Blakely's view?"

"He has various possible suspects in mind, but the real challenge is finding the evidence."

"Isn't that always the challenge? By the way, a telegram arrived for you." He passed it to me. "The messenger boys are all out on errands, so I thought I'd better bring it to you myself."

"Thank you, sir."

The telegram was from James, asking me to accompany him to dinner that evening. My initial joy was tempered when I read that Inspector Raynes and a man named Mr Russell would also be joining us.

◈

James arrived at my home in Milton Street in a hansom cab at six o'clock.

"You're getting in the cab with just him, are you?" asked Mrs Garnett in a reproachful tone as we stood in the hallway.

"There's a cabman, too," I replied, looking in the mirror as I pinned my hat in place.

"But he sits up top, right at the back. That's no good for a chaperone."

"Inspector Blakely and I have travelled in many hansom cabs together before now."

"That makes it even worse!" She sucked her lip disapprovingly. "What would your mother say?"

"I don't know," I replied. "I'm thirty-five years old, Mrs Garnett."

"That makes no difference! You're a spinster, and he's a bachelor."

James was quietly listening to the exchange from the doorstep.

"Miss Green is quite safe with me, Mrs Garnett." He gave her a reassuring smile.

She sucked her lip again. "It still makes no difference. It's not the way two grown people should behave!"

James kissed me as soon as we were seated in the darkness of the hansom cab. "Don't tell Mrs Garnett I did that," he said.

"Well, I just might. She would never allow you inside the house again!"

We both laughed.

"How was the visit to your parents?" I asked.

"They were initially better-natured than when I last saw them."

"That's good to hear."

"But then I told them about the impending court case and Father became rather quiet again."

"Oh."

"I think he feels ashamed that his son is to appear as a defendant in court. It's not fitting for a police officer, as far as he's concerned.

"Did he say that to you?"

"He didn't need to; I knew that's what he was thinking. And I know myself that it isn't proper."

"I don't know how you could have avoided the situation."

"By not proposing marriage to Charlotte Jenkins in the first place!"

"Your mother introduced you to her, didn't she?"

"Yes, but I certainly can't blame Mother. I foolishly thought that I was in love when I evidently wasn't. It was only when I met you, Penny, that I realised what love really felt like."

I reached out in the darkness and laid my hand on his.

"The same applies for me, James. I don't think any of this could have been helped, and it is difficult enough without your father making you feel worse."

"He's disappointed in me, and I suppose I would feel the same way if my son had done such a thing. But nothing can be done to change the situation now. I can only hope that my father will come round before too long. Are you looking forward to our dinner tonight?"

"I would be if it were only the two of us dining," I said. "Why Inspector Raynes? And who is Mr Russell?"

"Raynes is to tell us more about the American art thief, and Mr Russell is the Pinkerton chap who is chasing after him. The thief calls himself Mr Rigby Pleydell-Bouverie."

"An impressive name."

"Not his real one, however. He was christened Jack Shelby, and Inspector Raynes describes him as a gentleman criminal. I'm not sure he is truly a gentleman, as such, but apparently he has made a convincing pretence of being one."

The Royal Adelaide Grand Cafe Restaurant was a large, busy establishment located opposite Charing Cross Hospital. Inspector Raynes waved us over to his table when we arrived and stood to his feet to greet us. I remembered meeting him at Scotland Yard before. He was a tall, long-limbed man with a large nose and a fair moustache.

"You look rather sorrowful sitting here on your own, Raynes," said James. "Where's the Pinkerton fellow?"

"He should be here shortly," he replied. His voice had a nasal tone to it. "Have you dined here before?"

"No," replied James. "Have you?"

"Oh yes, a number of times. I can strongly recommend the Dover sole." He knocked over an empty wine glass as he sat down again.

"Dover sole sounds good indeed," said James as we took our seats. "I thought you might like to know that Miss Green and I met with your friend Mr Court-Holmes last week."

"He's not a personal friend, you know," replied Raynes with a puzzled look.

"I realise that; I said it in jest. But he was a friend of Mr Gallo's, so I was interested to find out whether he would be able to tell us anything more about him."

"Was he helpful?"

"I'm not entirely sure. There is no doubt that Mr Gallo had an interest in art. The question is whether he had any involvement in the criminal side of the art-dealing industry. Mr Court-Holmes seems certain that he wasn't mixed up in it, but it could provide a motive for his murder if he was. What do you know about Mr Court-Holmes?"

"He has owned the Calthorpe Art Gallery for eight years now. Pleasant chap, isn't he?"

"He seemed to be. What did he do before he opened the gallery?"

"He was a private collector. Apparently, he was born into a wealthy family, so he had access to plenty of capital to buy all the paintings he wanted."

"Have you discovered whether he has any connections with the criminal fraternity?"

"My investigation has been focused solely on the stolen painting, the *Madame Belmonte*. I can't find any evidence that he has been involved in any criminal activity. Do you think he could be?"

"I have no idea. That's why I asked you, Raynes. So you suspect that the painting was stolen by this American chap who calls himself Mr Pleydell-Bouverie?"

"It's rather a coincidence, don't you think? I heard that he arrived in the summer with a couple of associates, and that the *Madame Belmonte* was stolen a short while after his arrival. However, it's not the only painting to have been stolen recently. Oh, here comes the Pinkerton detective now. He'll be able to tell us more."

A dark-haired man approached our table, and I noticed there was something strikingly familiar about him, though I couldn't quite put my finger on it.

"This is Mr Russell," said Inspector Raynes.

We introduced ourselves, and as his eyes met mine he gave a faint smile, as if he were also aware that we had met before.

"Mr Russell?" I asked as we sat down. "I feel sure that I know you by another name."

CHAPTER 25

Mr Russell smiled again. "You know me by the name of Hardy."

"I knew it!" I said. "I felt rather confused for a moment there. You attended the dinner at the Hotel Tempesta, did you not? Were you working undercover? But I don't understand... You had a British accent that night..."

"I was born in Britain but I've been living in New York for the past twenty years."

His hair was styled quite differently compared with the oil-slicked hairstyle he had sported at the dinner. He was clean-shaven, but I felt sure he had worn a moustache previously.

"You are quite the actor, Mr Russell," I said.

"Sometimes one has to be."

"At least there is one less suspect for us to consider now," said James with a smile. "It's a pleasure to meet you, Mr Russell."

A waiter arrived and we quickly placed our order.

"Have you informed Chief Inspector Fenton of your true identity?" James asked the detective.

"Only on Friday. I could have told him earlier, I suppose, but I wanted to keep my cover going for as long as possible."

"What exactly were you doing at the Hotel Tempesta?" I asked. "Were you investigating Mr Gallo?"

"We suspect that he had something to do with Pleydell-Bouverie's schemes. Let's call him by his real name, Jack Shelby, as it's easier to say without getting our tongues twisted. We know that Shelby and Gallo met two weeks ago, and I was hoping to find out whether Shelby had offered him any stolen artworks at that time. We haven't found out yet whether he had."

"So Mr Gallo may have been involved in some sort of criminal activity?" James asked.

"Perhaps unwittingly. Shelby's Pleydell-Bouverie character can be quite convincing."

"Do you know where he is now?"

"He's staying at Claridge's presently. We have our men watching him around the clock."

"Why don't you simply arrest him?" I asked.

"If only we could, Miss Green. Shelby is wanted for a series of bank robberies in the United States, and that's why he has fled to Europe. Bank robbery isn't an extraditable offence, so we are powerless to do anything at the moment. Had he committed murder it would be a different story, but Shelby doesn't seem to be the violent type."

"Then you don't think he could have been behind Mr Gallo's murder?" I asked.

"It wouldn't be his usual style of crime. We know that he is a thief, but we also know that he abhors violence.

"Isn't bank robbery violent?" asked James.

"Not his sort of bank robbery. He prefers a degree of sophistication. The modus operandi of his gang is to break into the bank and crack open the safe in the dead of night. But with regards to Gallo's murder, I wouldn't rule Shelby out completely. Something may have changed that prompted him to commit such a terrible act."

"So you're just following him around at the moment?" asked James.

"We'll have him extradited to America if we can prove that he has committed forgery. We are convinced that he has, but we need the evidence. My colleagues back home are working on that. We're certain that Shelby and his men are behind the thefts of paintings in New York and Boston, and we know that forgeries of those paintings have been made."

"Why forge stolen paintings?" I asked.

"The forgeries are sold to people who believe they are buying the real thing."

"Even though they know that the original painting has been stolen?"

"Yes. Astonishing, isn't it? Some people are willing to buy a painting they know has been stolen at a much lower price than it would fetch at auction. We believe that Shelby has made several copies of each forgery, which must have brought in quite a bit of money."

"And he just keeps the original?" I asked.

"Now this is where he makes even more money. The owners of the stolen artworks are so keen to have the original painting returned to them that they are usually happy to agree a compromise with the thieves in order to buy the painting back. We know that Shelby employs a lawyer specifically to negotiate with the people he has stolen from."

"Then he gets away with it and makes a lot of money in the process!" I exclaimed. "Why can he not be arrested?"

"He can only be arrested if the victim of the crime wishes to prosecute. Whether they are art galleries or banks, many of his victims are more interested in having their property returned than in having men like Shelby arrested. If they prosecute, they may never see their stolen goods returned to them. They are not particularly interested in seeing the thieves behind bars, even though locking them away would ultimately make society safer. Fortunately, there's a bank in America that wishes to prosecute Shelby, and that's why I'm here in London. My aim is to arrest Shelby, and when my colleagues are able to prove that he has been involved in the forgery of paintings I shall pounce on him."

"But in the meantime you can do little more than watch."

"We cannot afford to lose sight of him. With a bit of luck we might catch him committing a crime here in London. That way, Inspector Raynes here could arrest him. If we can prove that he stole the *Madame Belmonte* from Calthorpe Art Gallery Raynes has a reason to put him behind bars, where he can safely stay until we're able to extradite him."

"Does he know that you're after him?" asked James.

"Oh yes. The Pinkerton agency has been interested in Shelby for about six years now, and he has spied me here in London. In fact, one evening a few weeks' ago I followed him into the Cafe Royal and he had a drink sent over to my table."

James laughed. "How brazen!"

"And that's not all. We have exchanged pleasantries a few times. He'll occasionally ask me how my day is going, then I will reply with the information that it's going well and ask the same of him."

"It sounds like a veritable game of cat and mouse," I said.

"Oh it is, though I sometimes wonder which of us is the cat and which is the mouse."

"Have you heard about the roll of paintings we found in Mr Gallo's rooms?" James asked him.

"No, I haven't. That sounds interesting."

"You and Inspector Raynes might wish to visit the hotel and examine them. I've had a look through them myself, but I know so little about art that I couldn't tell you much."

The conversation paused as the waiter served our soup course.

"You'd probably be interested to see a photograph of Shelby," said Mr Russell.

He reached into his jacket pocket and pulled out a photograph of a sullen-looking man with thick, wavy hair and dark whiskers. He looked about thirty years of age.

"This photograph was taken when he was arrested on a charge of robbery in 1878. Quite a minor offence, and unfortunately he was released without charge. Bear in mind that it was taken six years ago, and that Shelby is quite adept at changing his appearance. Sometimes he has whiskers, sometimes he doesn't. On occasion he grows his hair longer, and at other times he has his head shaved. Sometimes he wears spectacles and sometimes he doesn't."

"So he may look quite different now?" I asked.

"I'm sure that he does, but you have a picture of him now at least. That's better than nothing, isn't it? If you turn it over you'll see that I have described his height and build there. It's commonplace for the criminals we're pursuing to change their appearance, and that's why we Pinkerton fellows are also adept at doing so. I always say that you can recognise a man by his eyes. There's something about his eyes and brow," he circled a finger around the upper part of his face, "that is always recognisable, even when he chooses to put on spectacles or to pull his hat down to shield his face. The other unmistakable trait is a man's gait. If you watch for long enough you will get to know the way he walks. If he's paying attention he'll try to modify it, but the moment he's distracted he'll revert back to his usual way of walking. I've seen a few supposed limps disappear when men have realised we're in hot pursuit!" He laughed.

"Are you not concerned that Jack Shelby might escape to the continent?" I asked.

"We've alerted the customs officials at your ports on the south coast, so if he tries to travel to France, Belgium or Holland someone will hopefully catch sight of him. If he's well disguised, however, he will probably slip through the net. I think he'll stay in London for a little while yet. I should think he has his eye on another gallery or two, and most likely a few jewellery stores as well. He'll want to make the most of his stay here as much as I'd like to ruin it for him!"

"Both Mr Gallo and Mr Shelby lived in New York. Do you think they might have become acquainted there?" I asked.

"We're not aware that they were. I have never known Shelby to visit the Maganza or to dine at any of the establishments Mr Gallo liked to frequent in New York."

"What is your opinion of Mr Gallo?" asked James.

"I didn't know the man well, but from what I saw that evening at the hotel I'd say he was a decent sort of gentleman. If you're asking whether he ever got caught up in anything of a criminal nature, I never heard that he had. I can't say, hand on heart, that he wasn't, but no papers ever crossed my desk with his name on them."

"Someone clearly wanted Mr Gallo dead," said James.

"They did indeed. I don't envy you, given the scale of this investigation."

"I can't help but think that there must be a connection," I said. "A friend of Mr Gallo's ran the art gallery Mr Shelby possibly stole the painting from. Can it be a coincidence that a painting was stolen from Mr Court-Holmes' gallery shortly before his friend was murdered?"

Mr Russell shrugged. "It's difficult to know at this stage, but these connections and coincidences do not provide sufficient proof that Shelby had a hand in Gallo's murder."

"But they're both from New York," I said.

Mr Russell smiled. "There are a lot of people in New York, Miss Green. Being from the same city doesn't prove anything. The two gentlemen may never have laid eyes on one another."

He must have noticed my disconsolate face, as he acquiesced a little. "All right, we can't rule anything out. Having a well-known hotel proprietor murdered isn't the sort of thing Shelby would usually do, but I am ready to admit that anything is possible. We'd be foolish to ignore any possible involvement. I can imagine you're struggling to identify possible suspects, you probably have hundreds of people to consider and still can't uncover a motive. I certainly sympathise, as I know that feeling well. Meeting here, as we are tonight, and sharing what we know, goes some way to helping each other. I have a deep respect for the work of Scotland Yard, and thankfully the Atlantic Ocean is no obstacle to us working together. Unfortunately, it's no longer much of an obstacle for the criminals either!"

"What was your opinion of the other guests who stayed at the hotel on the fateful night when you became Mr Hardy?" I asked.

"I can't say that I took to Bolton or Wentworth. White was a bit suspicious, too. I'd like to know where he disappeared to after we'd had our cigars in the smoking room."

"Perhaps he was just tired and retired for the evening."

"Like Blackstone, you mean? He over-indulged himself, didn't he?"

"It was difficult not to," I said. "Our wine glasses were never empty! What about Mr Goldman? He took quite an interest in the hotel's artworks."

"The quiet ones are usually hiding something, aren't they?" he said with a smile.

"What did you make of Mrs Mirabeau?" I asked. "I noticed you were in conversation for a while. Did you learn anything interesting from her?"

"I was trying to ascertain what she knew about Mr Gallo's

art purchasing, but she didn't let on too much. Either the lady is ignorant of it all or she was holding back."

"Did you notice whether she seemed to hold any particular affection for Mr Gallo?" James asked.

"She was fond of him, there's no doubt about that. But it's likely that it was nothing more than a healthy respect for his success. She gave the impression that she was very loyal to him."

"Might she have murdered him and his companion in a fit of jealous rage?" I asked.

Mr Russell sat back in his chair as he considered this. "Goodness, do you think that could be a possibility?"

"It's not impossible," I said.

"No, I suppose not. Who were the other guests there? Mr Somers and Mrs Mortimer, I recall."

"I think it unlikely that either could have murdered Mr Gallo," I said.

"Mr Somers is a large fellow, isn't he? I think Gallo would easily have got away from him. And from Mrs Mortimer, too. She is a lovely lady, but rather mature in years. I agree that you could probably rule both out."

"So that leaves us with Bolton, Wentworth, White, Goldman and Blackstone," said James.

"Blackstone was far too inebriated," said Mr Russell.

"That leaves us with four, then," said James.

"And Gallo would likely have escaped from Wentworth, too," said Russell. "The old man uses a walking stick."

"White may also have been too drunk," I said. "I suspect that's why he disappeared, I believe it was nothing more than intoxicated tiredness. I also think the killer was unlikely to have noticeably disappeared so shortly before the crime was committed. The man who killed Mr Gallo would have acted as normally as possible until the time of the murder."

"When he skulked about in an overcoat and gloves with a

blacked-out lantern and large knife," added James. "So we have Bolton and Goldman to consider, and possibly Mrs Mirabeau."

"It's best not to rule the others out too hastily," said Inspector Raynes.

"We won't forget about them," said James, "but with so many suspects we need to concentrate on those who are most likely to have done it."

"Bolton didn't like Mr Gallo," I said. "He made that quite clear."

"I noticed that as well," agreed Mr Russell. "But perhaps the murderer wouldn't have made his distaste so obvious."

"That leaves Goldman, then," said Inspector Raynes.

"The quiet one," added Mr Russell with a smile. "It was either him or the delightful Mrs Mirabeau, I would say. I am reluctant to consider the notion that such a charming lady would have wished Gallo any harm, but who can be sure in a situation like this?"

CHAPTER 26

"The Pinkerton detective, Mr Russell, would like to look at the paintings in Mr Gallo's rooms," I informed Chief Inspector Fenton the following morning. "Inspector Blakely and I had dinner with him last night."

The inspector groaned and struck the table with the palm of his hand. "It's bad enough having the Yard involved, but the Pinkertons as well? What were you doing dining with that man?"

"I am perfectly entitled to do so. He was a fellow guest at the hotel."

"Yes, I'm aware of that, and it would have been helpful if he'd informed me of the fact that he was a Pinkerton detective sooner than he did. But this sort of conversation shouldn't be held without me present."

"There has to be a connection between Mr Russell's case and Mr Gallo's murder," I said.

"I'll decide on whether there's a connection or not, Miss Green. I don't need Scotland Yard or Fleet Street instructing me on these things. Or the Pinkertons, for that matter!"

"I can't see any use in denying it, though."

"You can leave now, Miss Green. I'm quite satisfied that you have reported to me as usual this morning. Though I shall make no secret of the fact that I spoke with the deputy commissioner at Scotland Yard yesterday about the nature of your relationship with Blakely."

"What of it?" I asked.

"This... *intimacy* you appear to share does not give you licence to involve yourself in police work."

"I have done no such thing; I'm simply reporting on the investigation. If you don't want me to be involved in any police work, requesting that I report to Bow Street police station every morning is hardly helping matters, is it?"

"I would just like to say that the deputy commissioner is aware."

"Thank you, Chief Inspector Fenton," I said, getting up from my chair. "Who is your chief suspect in this case, by the way?"

"If I tell you, Miss Green, you'll print it in your newspaper and jeopardise my entire investigation."

"Do you need me to report to you again tomorrow morning?"

"Perhaps once a week will suffice from now on."

"Thank you, sir."

I walked straight to Scotland Yard, passing Covent Garden market and then Charing Cross station, where the elegant facade of the Charing Cross Hotel was almost lost in the tea-coloured fog. The November morning had taken on a strange twilight appearance.

I found James in the smoky office he shared with several other inspectors and nodded at Inspector Raynes, who occupied a desk nearby.

"Penny!" James greeted me with a grin. "What brings you here?"

"I've come to tell you that Chief Inspector Fenton only requires me to report to him once a week from now on."

"That's good news."

"I think my daily visits annoy him too much. He won't even tell me who his chief suspect is."

"He either has no idea or he's deliberately choosing to be secretive. The deputy commissioner had a word with me this morning. Fenton's been complaining that I'm treading on his toes in the case."

"And he has also complained to the deputy commissioner that I'm too closely involved in the investigation."

"How do you know that?"

"Chief Inspector Fenton told me so himself."

"Well, let's just ignore him for now. I was all set to begin investigating Mr Goldman today, but I'll let Fenton get on with that. I've decided to find out more about the poor lady who lost her life alongside Gallo instead."

"Good. She doesn't seem to have been given much consideration so far. It's almost a week since she lost her life, yet no one seems to have noticed she's even missing. The ban on reporting about her death has hardly helped the case."

"Meanwhile, she lies in the mortuary, now the property of the Strand Poor Law Union. The Board of Guardians is keen to have her buried in a pauper's grave, but its members have been urged to wait until her family can be informed. They won't be willing to wait forever, so it's quite urgent that we discover who she was. I've been given possession of her bag, which was found in the Venetian Suite."

He led me over to a table upon which a green canvas bag had been laid out. It was edged with red fringing and had a red braided strap. Around it lay various belongings that had presumably been stored inside it. Hard-wearing canvas was not the standard fabric for a lady's bag, and the fringe and braid appeared to have been sewn on to make it look more attractive.

"The only other lady I know who carries a bag as practical as this is you, Penny," said James. "This bag is designed for durability, and would suit a lady who needed to carry a number of important items around with her. Miss Hamilton was clearly not the sort to be content with a decorative purse looped around her wrist."

I felt a lump in my throat as I examined the other items on the table. I thought of the mysterious, unfortunate lady who had chosen each of these things and tucked them inside her bag that fateful evening. There was a small mirror, a pot of rouge, a purse embroidered with beads, an ivory comb, a toothpick, a sizeable key and a folded-up copy of the *Morning Express*. I picked up the newspaper and saw that it was the edition from Saturday the eighth of November. A pencil and small notebook also lay on the table.

"She was wearing a silk nightgown when she was found," said James. "It was delicate enough to fold down to a size that would fit inside the bag. She had evidently planned to spend the night with Mr Gallo."

"Mrs Mirabeau told me that she visited him every Tuesday. Perhaps she stayed overnight on each occasion. I wonder why she had a three-day-old newspaper with her."

"There must have been something in there that interested her."

"But what?"

James shrugged. "The decoration on the purse seems to depict two initials."

I picked up the purse and examined the beadwork. Among the floral motifs I was just about able to discern two letters marked out in pale blue beads.

"A and D," I said. "No H for Hamilton, though."

"And this is even more mysterious," said James as he picked up a scrap of paper I hadn't yet noticed. It was crumpled and appeared to have been torn from the notebook. I could see that something had been written on it in pencil. He handed it to me, and I tried to read the words before realising that the letters were jumbled.

"Is it a code?" I asked.

"It must be."

"Why has she written something in code?"

"Did she write it or did someone else do so?"

"Mr Gallo, perhaps?"

"We'll have to compare it with other samples of his handwriting."

"What else have you learned about her?" I asked.

"She arrived wearing a red and green satin evening dress, so I'd say that she had dressed to impress him. A red and green hat decorated with an ostrich feather was also found in the room. She wore an overcoat for warmth and a good-quality woollen scarf and gloves. The dress bears a label from Webb and Courtney, a ladies' outfitters on Albemarle Street in Mayfair. Fenton tells me his men made enquiries at the outfitters, but the assistants couldn't recall a customer matching Miss Hamilton's description."

"What did she look like?"

"She was a tall lady of slim build with long brown hair. She appears to have been about twenty-five years of age. Examination of her hands and nails suggests she wasn't accustomed to rigorous labour. However, they were not the hands of a lady, either. Her fingers bore the customary stains of an ink pen."

I glanced down at the ink stains on my own hands.

"Her hair was well kept, and she looked after her skin, so she obviously cared about her appearance," continued James.

"There were no scars or wounds, and she appeared well-nourished. There was no indication that she drank a great deal, and she seems to have been in good health, with no sign of any troubling illness or disease. She appeared to have given birth to at least one child, however."

"Goodness. Where is that child now, I wonder?"

James gave a sad shrug. "She was clearly literate," he continued, "because she read the newspaper and was in possession of a notebook and pencil."

I placed the coded message back on the table and picked up the notebook. I flicked through its pages but saw nothing written within them. There were a number of rough edges where pages had been ripped out.

"Is there any money in her purse?"

"Six shillings."

"That would pay my rent for almost three weeks," I said. "Do you think that was the amount Mr Gallo paid her?"

"It's possible."

"And the staff at the shop where she bought the dress had no recollection of her?"

"No, so I'm wondering whether the hat and dress were borrowed."

"Miss Hamilton was a mother," I said, "which means someone must be missing her. A common-law husband perhaps? A child? Not to mention parents, brothers, sisters, and friends... I cannot understand it."

"It's likely that she was leading rather a secretive life, so those closest to her may have been completely unaware of her profession. She may not have seen them for a good while."

"But she had a child. Or maybe more than one."

"Perhaps someone else is bringing up the children. Miss Hamilton was unmarried, so perhaps the child or children went to a foundling hospital. We have a lot of questions and

CHAPTER 27

James and I walked down Whitehall toward Westminster. Ahead of us, the clock tower of Big Ben was only just discernible in the fog.

"How are you feeling about the court case?" I asked.

"I've been trying to forget about it."

"But it's only two days away."

"I prefer not to be reminded of it!"

"May I accompany you?"

"I would rather you didn't, Penny."

"But you won't have anyone else there with you," I remonstrated. "Your family won't be attending, I presume."

"No, they won't. But I'll have my solicitor with me."

I gave a hollow laugh. "A solicitor is hardly good company."

"A solicitor is pragmatic and does this sort of thing on a regular basis. His company will be all I need."

"But it will be terribly difficult for you! I suspect the entire Jenkins family will be there."

"They will be, but that doesn't mean that I need an army with me."

"It would just be me, James, and I wouldn't exactly consider myself an army. We needn't even be seen together; I could hide myself among the public benches."

"I won't have you involved."

"I wouldn't be involved! I can simply hide there, and perhaps just the thought that I am there with you might help a little. I can't bear the thought of you having to cope with it on your own."

"I will manage perfectly well."

"Will you?"

James stopped and turned to face me. "You never give up, do you?"

"Please, James. I promise I'll stay out of the way. I just want to be there for you."

He sighed and shook his head. "If the Jenkins family see you..."

"They won't!"

Little Smith Street was a short lane tucked between Westminster Abbey and the gas works.

The housekeeper who answered the door led us up a narrow staircase and into a room that was hazy with tobacco smoke. Bookshelves lined the walls, and a man with thin wisps of white hair was bent over a desk beside the window.

"Mr Hobhouse?" enquired James.

The old man turned to face us. He wore a pair of spectacles and a second pair rested on his large forehead.

"Blakely, isn't it?" he said, after squinting at James for a short while. "You're Roger's boy, aren't you?"

"I am indeed, Mr Hobhouse."

The old man rose up out of his seat and walked over to us with a lopsided gait.

"And how is your father?"

"He is enjoying his retirement."

The old man tutted. "I don't believe in retirement."

"It's probably just as well, Mr Hobhouse, as there's something I need your help with. I must introduce you to Miss Green here. She's a reporter for the *Morning Express* newspaper and is helping me with a case I'm working on."

Mr Hobhouse surveyed me. "I like to see a lady doing something useful. A reporter, you say? I'm delighted to meet you, Miss Green. Now, what have you got for me, young Blakely?"

James gave him the scrap of paper he had found in Miss Hamilton's bag. Mr Hobhouse removed his spectacles and lowered the pair he had worn on his head.

"Hmm. I can't immediately see an indication of commonly used letters," he muttered. "Did you find any other pieces of paper with notes written on them?"

"No."

"It would have been a little too convenient to have done so, I suppose, but I need more than this to crack the code. Are you sure you haven't come across a key?"

"A door key?"

"No, no." Mr Hobhouse gave a dry cackle. "A cypher is solved with a key, you see. The recipient of this message needs another piece of information in order to decypher it. That's what we call a key. It's no good sending someone a jumble of letters and hoping they can make sense of it. The key must be agreed between the sender and the recipient. Are you certain there was nothing else to accompany it?"

"No. We found this piece of paper among the belongings of a lady who was tragically murdered. There was nothing else written down anywhere."

Mr Hobhouse hobbled back to his desk, picked up a magnifying glass and examined the piece of paper again. "She must have had the key somewhere," he muttered. "It was either written on a piece of paper or committed to memory. She's deceased, you say?"

"Yes."

"Oh dear. If she memorised the key, this message will be rather difficult to decypher."

"Can you do anything with it at all?"

Mr Hobhouse sighed and switched his spectacles over again.

"Well, I can try, I suppose. But it may take me some time and I can't promise anything. I'm not getting any younger, Blakely!"

"I realise that, Mr Hobhouse."

"In fact, my brother died of old age two months ago, and he was three years younger than me."

"I'm sorry to hear it."

"I'm not asking for sympathy, Blakely. I'm merely emphasising how ancient I am."

"Do you think you'll be able to help us?"

"I might and I might not. Leave it with me and I'll see what I can do."

"Can we be sure that it's even a cypher?"

"What else could it be?"

"Well, I don't really know."

"Of course it's a cypher, young man. Why else would someone write down a series of otherwise meaningless letters?"

"Let's take a cab to Albemarle Street and speak to the ladies' outfitters that supplied Miss Hamilton's dress," said James once we had stepped back onto Little Smith Street.

"Haven't Fenton's men already made enquiries there?"

"They have, but there can be no harm in visiting a second time."

James hailed a cab and we climbed inside.

"I hope Mr Hobhouse will be able to decypher the secret message," I said. "He didn't seem particularly enthusiastic about doing so, did he?"

"Oh, I think he was just being cantankerous, it's his manner. He's been like that for as long as I've known him; all my life, that is."

Brightly coloured fabric gleamed through the leaded glass windows of Webb and Courtney on Albemarle Street. We stepped inside.

"This is the dress," said James, pointing toward a gown with a red and green bodice trimmed with red ribbon. The voluminous skirt was a startling green satin decorated with red fringing. I pictured the dress being worn by a tall, dark-haired lady wearing a matching hat with an ostrich feather in it. She must have been a sight to behold when Mrs Mirabeau answered the door to her that fateful evening.

"Can I help you?" asked a lady in a violet bustle dress, who had been regarding us coolly. Her brusque question suggested that she immediately suspected we had no intention of buying anything from her.

I introduced myself and James, and she seemed more bothered by the fact I was a news reporter than him being a police officer.

"Inspector Blakely and I regularly work together," I said. "My discretion in this matter is assured."

My words did not appear to convince her.

"If this is regarding Mr Gallo's murder, I've already spoken to the police," she said.

"So I understand," said James, "and I am very sorry to trouble you further, but we are extremely keen to establish the identity of the poor young lady who lost her life at the same time as Mr Gallo."

"I can't tell you any more than I've already said."

"I didn't catch your name, madam," said James.

"Miss Webb."

"Miss Webb, I was wondering whether the lady might have borrowed the dress from someone, and if that person was perhaps one of your customers. I have written down the measurements of the dress." He took out his notebook and showed her the notes he had made in it. "This should give you a good idea of the sizing. Could you tell us who has bought that particular style and size of dress from you?"

"The customers I was able to tell the police officer about didn't match the description of the lady who was murdered at all."

"I realise that. But I should like to speak to those customers, as it is more than likely that one of them will know who she is."

"Much as I'd like to help, Inspector, I don't know how you'd go about finding the customers who bought this gown. I don't keep a record of their addresses, I'm afraid."

"If any of them returns to this shop, could you please ask them to contact me at Scotland Yard?" James handed her his card. "We are extremely keen to establish the identity of the lady who was wearing one of your dresses the night she was killed. No one has come forward to report her missing yet, so her body lies unclaimed."

Miss Webb looked at the card in her hand and gave a long sigh. "There is one address you might like to try, Inspector. I know that a few of my customers live there. I don't recall any of them buying the red and green dress, but it might be worth making enquiries with them."

CHAPTER 28

The address Miss Webb had given us turned out to be a smart, four-storey, terraced house on Old Cavendish Street, just north of Oxford Street. A young maid opened the door.

"Hello. Do you know a Miss Hamilton?" James asked her.

"Can't say as I do." The girl shook her head.

"I apologise, I had hoped you might. I am Inspector Blakely of Scotland Yard, and my companion here is Miss Green, a reporter for the *Morning Express* newspaper. Can you tell me who lives here, please?"

"There's a few people what lives 'ere."

"Could you tell me their names?"

The girl bit her lip.

James drew his warrant card out of his pocket and showed it to her. "No one's in trouble, but I should like to have as much information as possible about the tenants in this building, if you please."

"There's Miss Larcombe, Miss Biden, Miss Kay, Mrs Marsden and Miss Evans," blurted the girl.

"I should like to speak to all of them, if I may."

"Only Miss Kay's at 'ome."

"Might I speak with her?'

The girl bit her lip again and left us on the doorstep while she went to fetch the lady in question.

"Five women sharing a single house makes me wonder whether they are all employed in the same profession as Miss Hamilton," whispered James. "Perhaps it's a vain hope, but I pray that one of them may have encountered her."

A short while later, a pale-faced lady came to the door. She wore a simple grey dress and assumed a sullen expression when James explained who we were.

"You have heard of the unfortunate death of Mr Gallo, I presume?" James asked.

"Yeah."

"Did you ever meet the man?"

"No."

"Did you ever see him anywhere? At a restaurant, perhaps? Or at the theatre?"

"No, an' I wouldn't know what 'e looked like, anyway."

"Do you have a profession, Miss Kay?"

"Of sorts." She folded her arms and leaned against the door frame. "I'm a companion."

"A gentleman's companion?"

"Yeah, but I don't solicit if that's what you're askin'. It's all done by way of introduction."

"Are you aware that Mr Gallo's companion lost her life on the night of his murder?"

Miss Kay's eyes widened. "No, I can't say as I did."

"We're trying to find out who she was. All we know is that the name she went by was Miss Hamilton. Do you know that name?"

"No."

"Do you know of anyone with the initials A D?"

"No."

"Do you have any friends you haven't heard from for a while?"

She considered this for a moment. "Can't think o' none."

"Do you share this house with friends of yours?"

"Yep."

"Are they in the same line of work as you?"

"Can't speak for 'em."

"I will make the assumption that they are, in that case. The maid informed me they are all out at the present time. Is that right?"

Miss Kay nodded.

"When they return, would you please ask whether they knew of a lady called Miss Hamilton, or whether they have a friend they haven't seen for a few days? We're desperate to uncover this lady's true identity."

"And what if you 'appen ter find out who she is? What then?"

"If we can learn more about her, we will hopefully discover more about the person who has done this to her. Miss Hamilton's body currently lies unclaimed at the mortuary in Macklin Street. If her identity remains unknown she will receive a pauper's funeral. She deserves to have her family with her, and she deserves a respectful burial."

Miss Kay gave a laugh. "I'm sure the coppers treated 'er with nuffink but respect while she were alive!"

James sighed. "I cannot speak for the lady's past experiences, Miss Kay, but it is my duty to find out who she was and who has done this to her."

"You wouldn't care a bit about 'er if Gallo hadn't croaked it as well."

"That's not true."

"Women like 'er are murdered ev'ry week, an' the coppers ain't never interested in finding out who did it to 'em."

"That's rather an exaggeration, Miss Kay—"

"No it ain't!"

"Arguing isn't going to help anyone!" I interjected. "Please, Miss Kay, will you just ask your friends? Someone somewhere will be missing this Miss Hamilton. We know that she had at least one child."

The young woman's sullen face softened slightly.

"And we think someone lent her a dress," I said. "It was a beautiful red and green satin gown from Webb and Courtney on Albemarle Street. In fact, the shop still stocks the dress. Perhaps you could go in and take a look, as the sight of it may spark a memory of Miss Hamilton. Perhaps you saw a lady wearing that dress, or maybe your friends would recognise it."

She gave a sigh. "I'll take a look if I'm passin' that way."

"Here's my card," said James, handing it to her. "If you or your friends can help at all, please come and find me at Scotland Yard."

"Anythin' in it for me?" she asked with a hostile stare.

"Yes. The knowledge that you will be helping to bring about justice for poor Miss Hamilton."

She continued to stare at James.

"Very well." He extracted a half-crown from his pocket and gave it to her. "Now I really do expect you to help us, Miss Kay."

"I intend to put out an appeal for help in the *Morning Express*," I said as we walked along Oxford Street.

"We mustn't upset Mr Gallo's family," replied James.

"We needn't say that Miss Hamilton had anything to do with Mr Gallo; it will be a simple request for help. She cannot go on lying in the mortuary unclaimed, and as you rightly say she will end up being given a pauper's funeral with no one in attendance before very long. She won't even have a headstone. What could be written upon it when we know so little about her?"

"Very well. But you won't mention murder or Mr Gallo, will you?"

"No, I shall be discreet. You can trust me, James."

❧

An appeal for information was printed in the *Morning Express* the following day.

Information requested in relation to a lady believed to be called Miss Hamilton, but who may be known by another name, with the initials A.D. Aged between twenty-five and thirty years of age, she is five feet and seven inches in height with a slim build and long brown hair.

"It is not a long description, but I suppose someone who knew the girl would recognise her from it," said Mr Sherman, surveying the lines I had written in the morning edition.

"I feel sure that if we had been allowed to make her death public knowledge we would know who she was by now," I replied. "It angers me that her murder is receiving less attention because everybody feels the need to protect Mr Gallo's reputation."

"And the feelings of his family," added Mr Sherman.

"Yes, I understand why that's important, but it hardly seems fair to Miss Hamilton's family."

"This is what happens when one pursues a certain profession in life," Edgar chipped in. "One devalues oneself."

"Something unpleasant must have happened for her to have pursued such a profession," I said. "Women don't willingly seek out that kind of work."

"There is good money to be made from it," said Edgar.

"It's the only way for women in desperate circumstances to earn money, and perhaps it was something she turned to as a last resort. If only we knew more about her we might be able to understand why she made that choice."

"It's easy, though, isn't it?" Frederick piped up.

"What is?"

"This profession you speak of. There is no need for education or an apprenticeship of any sort. A lady can merely put herself out there, so to speak."

"And it's not just ladies who put themselves out there," said Edgar.

"So I've heard, but I have no wish to dwell on such matters."

"It is certainly *not* easy," I retorted. "For some women it is the very last profession they turn to in order to feed themselves."

"Or to buy drink," said Edgar. "They're drinkers, a lot of these women, and that's what they want the money for."

"Miss Hamilton wasn't a drinker," I said. "In fact, she appeared to be in good health."

"There's always the possibility that she happily chose that type of work," said Mr Sherman. "Do you think she was untypical for a lady of her profession?"

"Possibly," I replied. "She seemed well educated enough to have done something else instead. She had a copy of the *Morning Express* from the eighth of November in her possession. Can you think of anything significant about that particular issue, sir?"

"No."

"Neither can I."

"Well, why not have a look through it for yourself?" asked Mr Sherman. "Perhaps something you read will strike you as being pertinent. In the meantime, please obtain a copy of the paper the Farmers' Alliance has just published. It's called *The Present Crisis in Agriculture,* and a meeting will be held to discuss it."

Edgar tutted. "There is always a crisis in agriculture, according to the farmers."

"Were you asked for your opinion, Fish?"

"No, sir."

"I think they're convening down at the Holborn Restaurant today, so see if you can get down there, Miss Green. I realise the Gallo case is taking up a lot of your time, but we will need some other work from you, too."

"I shall follow up on it, sir." I folded up the latest edition of *The Times,* which I had been reading to see how Mr Blackstone was reporting on the Gallo case. Despite his supposed rapport with Chief Inspector Fenton he didn't appear to have gleaned any more information than I had. "May I request permission to spend a short time in Croydon tomorrow, Mr Sherman?" I ventured. "I ask because it's not strictly to do with work, but I should very much like to be there."

"What's happening in Croydon?"

"The breach of promise case against Inspector Blakely is to be heard there."

"Goodness, is that so?"

"You're a brave lady if you plan to attend the hearing, Miss Green!" said Edgar with a laugh.

"Why is she brave?" asked the editor.

"Because it's her fault!"

"That'll do, Fish," scolded Mr Sherman.

"Edgar's right," I said. "Inspector Blakely has urged me not to attend, but I must take responsibility for what has happened. The punishment shouldn't be his to bear alone."

"If he doesn't want you to go, why on earth are you setting yourself up for it?" asked Edgar. "I should be glad of the opportunity to keep my head down if I were in your shoes."

"That's because you are considerably less honourable than Miss Green," said Frederick. "You've always been one to shirk responsibility."

"That's a tad harsh, Potter!" exclaimed Edgar. "If I've done wrong I'll always own up to it. But if someone tells me they're going to shoulder the blame instead I'll happily step aside and allow them to do so!"

"Good luck, Miss Green," said Mr Sherman, solemnly. "Unusually for me, I must say that I agree with Fish on this occasion. If Inspector Blakely is happy to accept the punishment single-handedly, why not allow him to do just that? There's a risk that you may attract the ire of the spurned woman."

"Then it will be no more than I deserve," I said.

"I know why you're doing this, Miss Green," said Edgar. "It's because you feel terribly guilty about what has happened. If you can give the offended party an opportunity to scold you, perhaps you'll feel as though you've received your just rewards."

"My intention is to go there in support of James," I said. "But I think there may be some truth to what you say, Edgar."

CHAPTER 29

Croydon Town Hall was an imposing, classical-style building situated just off the high street. I paused when I saw the gathering of people standing outside it and pulled my silk scarf up over my chin. I wore an old-fashioned bonnet with a wide, soft brim, which would help to shield my face.

The fog had lifted, and the sun was doing its best to make an appearance between the heavy grey clouds. A man in a dark coat and bowler hat caught my eye, and I smiled as I recognised James' familiar mannerisms. He was talking with another man, whom I guessed was his solicitor. The two men walked up the steps of the town hall and disappeared inside.

A few moments later a brougham pulled up and a fair-haired young lady in a burgundy skirt and jacket stepped out, followed by an older couple. It could only be Charlotte Jenkins and her parents. I felt my heart pound as I watched them ascend the steps to the town hall. Once they were safely inside, I cautiously approached.

A noticeboard in the town hall foyer stated that *Jenkins vs Blakely* was to be the first case of the day. I stepped inside the noisy, wood-panelled courtroom and seated myself as quickly as possible on the public benches. I dared not look up for a while, and when I finally did I saw James sitting with his solicitor. He kept swallowing nervously, and there were spots of colour high up on his cheeks. I prayed that the hearing would be over quickly.

I surveyed the press benches and felt a snap of anger when I spotted Tom Clifford from *The Holborn Gazette*. Although it was quite usual for the press to report on cases such as these, I felt sure that his presence was fuelled by personal interest. *Why else would he make the journey from London town to Croydon?* Fortunately, I felt sure that he hadn't noticed me. Perhaps I shouldn't have been surprised to see Mr Bolton, who worked for the *South London Reporter*, seated near Tom on the press benches. However, it felt odd to see him in the courtroom, and I fervently hoped that he wouldn't spot me here.

Heads turned as Charlotte entered the room. Her hair was pinned up beneath a small burgundy hat, and there was something more refined about her than I remembered. Her face was a little thinner and her jaw jutted forward in a defiant manner. She didn't look over in James' direction at all as she sat with her solicitor on one side and her father, who was a large, red-faced man with thick grey hair and whiskers, on the other. He kept turning toward James and glowering, and I noticed that James studiously avoided his gaze.

Mr Justice Meeks eventually began the proceedings and the jury was sworn in. I breathed deeply in an attempt to calm the pounding of my heart. Perhaps I was imagining it, but I could feel people's eyes resting on me as if they had worked out who I was.

Charlotte's counsel, Mr Duncombe, rose to his feet and

began: "The plaintiff is compelled to bring this action in order to recover compensation for the suffering she has endured in consequence of Mr Blakely's breach of contract. The promise of marriage and the breach of promise has been admitted by the defendant, so the only matter for the jury to contemplate this morning is the sum Miss Jenkins is entitled to in damages.

"Miss Jenkins is twenty-six years old, and is the daughter of Mr Napier Jenkins, an accountant. She resides with her parents in Garland street, Croydon. She is respectably connected as the niece of a vicar and the cousin of a magistrate. At no point can any criticism be made with regard to her reputation or conduct. She has remained entirely blameless throughout."

I felt a bitter taste in my mouth.

"The defendant, Mr Blakely, is thirty years old, and is the youngest son of Chief Inspector Roger Blakely of the Metropolitan Police, now retired. Mr Blakely is an inspector at Scotland Yard and resides at Henstridge Place in St John's Wood.

"The facts of the case are as follows. Miss Jenkins and Mr Blakely first met in April 1882. They were introduced through their families, with Miss Jenkins' mother, Mrs Mary Jenkins, already being quite well acquainted with Mr Blakely's mother, Mrs Eleanor Blakely. The introduction, made at the suggestion of Mrs Jenkins and Mrs Blakely, culminated in a marriage proposal from Mr Blakely to Miss Jenkins on the third of September 1882. Miss Jenkins agreed to marry Mr Blakely with the full consent of her parents, and the parties became engaged from that hour.

"Mr and Mrs Blakely expressed their approval of the engagement. At the time of the proposal, their son was employed as a sergeant at Scotland Yard and received an annual wage of one hundred and ten pounds. In 1883 he was promoted to the rank of inspector and his salary increased to one hundred and sixty pounds.

"The engagement progressed well, and the wedding date was arranged for the twelfth of January this year. However, this coincided with a period of time Mr Blakely had to spend in Manchester for his police work, so the date was rearranged to the thirteenth of September.

"The wedding was due to take place at St John the Baptist Church in Croydon at eleven o'clock. Shortly after nine o'clock that morning the defendant called at the home of Mr and Mrs Jenkins and requested to speak with them and their daughter, Miss Jenkins. In no uncertain terms, Mr Blakely stated that his feelings for the plaintiff had changed, and that he could no longer consider marrying her. An angry exchange of words between the defendant and the plaintiff's father, Mr Jenkins, ensued.

"Mr Blakely promptly left the family home, and two days later wrote a letter to Miss Jenkins offering a payment of three hundred pounds as recompense. Miss Jenkins and her father felt that Mr Blakely had not offered suitable compensation and decided to place the matter in the hands of their family solicitor. This is why we are here today presenting this breach of promise action."

Charlotte was then called upon. She stood to her feet and avoided James' gaze.

"Can you confirm that the statement I have made is complete and correct?" asked Mr Duncombe.

"Yes, I can."

"Did you notice any sign of Mr Blakely's feelings toward you changing before the day of the wedding?"

"No obvious signs, no. But a matter had caused me some concern prior to the wedding day."

"Can you explain to the jury what that matter was?"

"I had become concerned about a lady with whom Mr Blakely had made an acquaintance."

My heart thudded heavily, and I stared down at my hands in my lap. James' hope that I wouldn't be mentioned in the case had been futile. Charlotte clearly intended to ensure that everybody knew about me.

"How did Mr Blakely make this lady's acquaintance?" asked Charlotte's counsel.

"Through his work. She is a news reporter."

I heard mutterings around me and felt my face heat up. I wished now that I hadn't attended the hearing. I wasn't aware that anyone around me had realised who I was as yet, but I felt sure that it would only be a matter of time before they did.

"And what concerned you most about this acquaintance?"

"Mr Blakely spoke of her often. A little too often."

"Your words suggest that he possessed a certain level of affection for her."

"I believe that he did."

"Enough affection for him to change his mind about your engagement?"

"Yes, I believe so."

"So it is your belief that the reason behind Mr Blakely's change of heart was that he held another lady in his affections."

"That's right, yes."

I still daren't look up. I had no idea what James made of this revelation, but I imagined that he felt every bit as uncomfortable as I did.

I felt relieved when James' solicitor was finally permitted to cross-examine Charlotte.

"Miss Jenkins, you mention that Mr Blakely spoke of another lady a little too often for your liking."

"Yes."

"Did he talk about her within the context of his work?"

"Yes."

"Did he talk about her as if he knew her personally?"

There was a pause. "I was aware that he was quite well acquainted with her."

"As a result of his work?"

"Yes."

"But he wasn't acquainted with her on a personal level?"

"I don't know." I sensed a growing impatience in Charlotte's voice. "He carried out a substantial amount of work alongside her."

"And was it necessary for him to do so?"

"I couldn't really say. She's a news reporter, so presumably she pushed her way in as these people often do."

"Miss Jenkins, I wish to ascertain whether your former fiancé was intimately acquainted with this lady or not, in your opinion."

"I don't have any evidence of it, if that's what you mean," she snapped. "But I could tell there was something between them. They used to meet at the Museum Tavern in Bloomsbury."

"In the course of their work?"

"That was his excuse, but I believe they also met there for personal reasons. My fiancé was attracted to another woman. Her name is Miss Penelope Green."

As I sank down into my seat I felt the person sitting beside me glance sideways; not because he recognised me, but in an attempt to ascertain why I was trying to hide from view. I realised that my attempts to avoid being seen were having the opposite effect.

I felt relieved when Charlotte sat down, but then her father was called upon. He had a scowl etched across his large face, and he glared at James as though he were little more than a naughty schoolboy.

"You approved of your daughter's engagement to Mr Blakely, Mr Jenkins?" Charlotte's solicitor asked.

"At the time I did, yes." He spoke loudly and brusquely. "He was a sergeant at Scotland Yard, and I thought he was a thoroughly decent, respectable chap. I couldn't have been more wrong."

"So you had no concerns about his conduct or standing during their courtship?"

"None at all. I had no knowledge of this other woman Charlotte has mentioned. It's a disgrace! The fellow has behaved despicably!"

"When did you first become aware of this other woman?"

"I wasn't aware of her at all. It was only after the ignoramus called the marriage off at the last minute that my poor daughter told me about her. '*This is because of Penny*,' she kept saying, over and over. The poor girl was distraught. No man should have to see his own daughter in that condition. I wouldn't wish such a thing on my worst enemy. It is a dreadful state of affairs, and he should be thoroughly ashamed of himself. And he calls himself a police officer! If this is the manner in which the officers at Scotland Yard conduct themselves I fear for the future of this country, I surely do! This man isn't fit for any profession. If those in charge at the Yard have any sense they'll dismiss him at once.

"And as for this woman who calls herself a reporter, it is said that she writes for the *Morning Express* newspaper. She should also be dismissed from her position. The pair of them should be thoroughly ashamed, and I should like to see them both publicly disgraced!"

CHAPTER 30

I felt a bead of perspiration trickle down between my shoulders and into my corset. I closed my eyes and willed the hearing to be over.

"Mr Blakely has offered your daughter some form of recompense for the breach of promise, I believe?" Mr Duncombe asked Mr Jenkins.

"Oh yes, he was quick to do that. The very last thing he wanted was an action to be brought against him. He offered me a paltry three hundred pounds, and I told him, 'To hell with it!'"

"I must remind you to respect the order of the court, Mr Jenkins," said the judge.

Mr Jenkins sniffed in response.

"So Mr Blakely offered you damages of three hundred pounds."

"Three hundred pounds, and I told him—"

"So you have already said. In summary, you and your daughter decided that the sum offered was insufficient, and that was why you decided to pursue this action."

"It is nowhere near enough!"

"Thank you, Mr Jenkins." The solicitor turned to face the judge. "I have no further questions, Your Honour."

Fortunately, James' solicitor declined to cross-examine Mr Jenkins. I felt sure that the jury had already heard enough.

Then James was called upon. He stood to his feet, cleared his throat and gave a nervous smile. This was the first time Charlotte had looked directly at her former fiancé, and she stared at him with her upper lip curled. Mr Jenkins' face was red, his frown even more pronounced.

James' solicitor asked him, "Mr Blakely, may I ask when you realised that your feelings for Miss Jenkins had changed?"

He cleared his throat. "It was the night before the wedding. I couldn't sleep that night, and when the day of the wedding dawned I realised I didn't have the strength of feeling toward Miss Jenkins that would have been necessary for a long and happy marriage."

"And you informed Miss Jenkins of this at your earliest convenience?"

"I did, yes. I travelled by cab to London Bridge station and took the train down to Croydon as swiftly as possible. I arrived at Miss Jenkins' home at approximately nine o'clock."

"Which the jury will recall Mr Duncombe stating in his opening statement. And you offered Miss Jenkins three hundred pounds in damages, did you not?"

"Yes, that is the full amount of money I have in my savings account."

"And if you were to pay Miss Jenkins the three hundred pounds that would encompass all of your savings?"

"That is correct, yes."

The time came for Charlotte's solicitor, Mr Duncombe, to rise to his feet.

"Who is Miss Penelope Green, Mr Blakely?" he asked.

I held my breath.

"She is a reporter for the *Morning Express* newspaper," replied James.

Charlotte kept her steely eyes fixed on him.

"Do you hold her in your affections?"

There was a long pause. James glanced around the silent courtroom, then swallowed nervously.

"Yes, I do."

There were gasps and mutterings around me.

"How long have you been harbouring these feelings?"

"It's not easy to be precise. I suppose I have been fond of Miss Green since I met her."

"Which was when?"

"In the October of last year."

"So you have held her in your affections all that time?"

Perhaps I should have shielded my face more effectively with my bonnet, for it was at this precise moment that James spotted me. He stared, his lips moving slightly, as if they were about to form words. I smiled, but my presence had obviously distracted him from the proceedings.

"Mr Blakely?" continued Mr Duncombe. "Could you answer the question, please? Have you possessed an affection for Miss Green since the October of last year?"

James tore his gaze away from me. "It has been a very gradual realisation. I would like to stress that it was always my intention to carry out the promise I had made to Miss Jenkins, which is why the decision was made at the very last moment. I sincerely apologise for the upset and inconvenience it has caused. I am only too aware of how difficult this time has been for Miss Jenkins and her family. I have already apologised profusely; however, I would like to assure Miss Jenkins and her family that the breach of promise was preferable to continuing with the marriage proceedings."

"Your reason for the breach of promise is not merely your changed feelings toward Miss Jenkins, but also the fact that you have romantic feelings for Miss Green."

James dwelt on this before giving a slight nod. "Yes."

"It would have helped the Jenkins family and the court here today had you been honest from the start about the real reason behind your cancelling the wedding. In reality it is because you wish to marry Miss Green instead, is it not?"

"Miss Green and I have never discussed marriage. In fact, we have chosen not to pursue an official courtship in light of recent events. I wished to resolve my differences with Miss Jenkins and her family before embarking upon another courtship. I acknowledge that I have done wrong and wish to make recompense to Miss Jenkins."

"It is all well and good demonstrating your contriteness to the court now, Mr Blakely, but the fact of the matter is that you have been deceitful for many months. You stated to Miss Jenkins, and subsequently to this court, that your reason for cancelling the wedding was that your feelings had changed. At no point did you acknowledge that your affection for Miss Green was the true cause of this change in feelings. There was further deceit in the months leading up to the wedding, when you at no time discussed your affection for Miss Green with Miss Jenkins or her family. Had you done so, they would have had a much better understanding of your state of mind. You continued with the pretence that you were to marry Miss Jenkins right up until the day you were due to marry her. If that is not deceitful, may I ask you what is?"

"I had no intention to deceive anyone."

"No, I'm quite sure that you didn't. However, the facts speak for themselves, and this is why the jury must now consider a higher sum in damages than the one you previously offered to the Jenkins family."

James opened his mouth as if to argue with Charlotte's solicitor but seemed to think better of it. This was his punishment, and the best thing he could do at that moment was to keep his demeanour calm and respectful.

I breathed a sigh of relief when Charlotte's solicitor sat back down. James also took a seat as the judge addressed the court.

"Mr Blakely, you are a respectable man with a responsible profession. I am certain that there is no stain on your character other than what we have heard this morning. It is more honourable to break off an engagement than to marry with a lie in one's heart. However, it would have been wiser for you to acknowledge the true reason for the breach of promise and your changed feelings for the plaintiff: namely, your affection for another lady."

The judge asked the jury to retire in order to consider the level of damages payable. James glanced over at me again, and this time managed a slight smile.

There was light chatter in the courtroom while we waited. James spoke with his solicitor to pass the time and Charlotte conferred with her father. I wasn't sure how James would be able to afford much more than the three hundred pounds he had already offered.

Ten minutes later the jury returned to the courtroom.

"Have you reached an agreement with regard to the sum owed in damages?" the judge asked the foreman.

"Yes, Your Honour."

"Please tell the court the total sum payable to the plaintiff."

"Six hundred pounds, Your honour."

I sighed. It was a lot of money, but hopefully it would mean that James would finally be free of all obligation to Charlotte and her family. He gave me another subtle smile, and it was then that I felt someone else's eyes upon me.

I glanced at Charlotte and saw that she had noticed me. Her expression was frozen into a haughty stare, and her blue eyes were cold and unblinking. I felt a shiver run through me.

Never before had I seen anyone look at me with such a deep intensity of hatred.

CHAPTER 31

I left the town hall as quickly as possible. It didn't feel appropriate to be seen with James at that moment.

"Miss Green?"

I felt a sickening turn in my stomach knowing that someone had noticed me there.

A man with a square face and brown whiskers caught up with me.

"Mr Bolton," I said, forcing a smile.

"It's not often that a news reporter becomes the news," he said with a wry smile.

"I'm not news," I retorted as I continued my brisk walk. "This has all just been an unfortunate sequence of events. It really isn't of any consequence to anyone else."

"No, I suppose not. Although I wouldn't be doing my job properly if I didn't report on the case. There is always a great deal to write about when the assizes are being held. I never imagined you would be caught up in one of them!"

"Neither did I."

"The Scotland Yard inspector you've been, er, associated with... He's working on the Gallo case, isn't he?"

"Yes, he is."

"And what does he make of it?"

"He feels there are quite a few possible suspects."

"There are, aren't there? And to think that it was likely to have been one of us who stayed at the hotel that evening. That's quite a thought, isn't it?"

"Whom do you think it might have been?" I asked, stopping so that I could better gauge his reaction.

"Gosh." He blinked a few times and shook his head. "I simply don't know. That Mr White seemed an odd character to me. And Mr Goldman, too. But it could just as easily have been a member of the hotel staff, couldn't it? They were best placed to plan the attack, find the spare key and hide the murder weapon... I hear the weapon was found in your bedchamber. Is that right?"

"Yes."

"So you could be a suspect yourself, Miss Green!"

"Something else to put me in the news, don't you think?"

"I can't imagine you bearing Gallo any sort of grudge."

"You didn't like him much, did you?"

Mr Bolton avoided my gaze. "I don't like men of his type, as a rule."

"Which type is that?"

"The type that has made a lot of money rather quickly. It makes me wonder what they've been up to."

"He ran a successful hotel business."

"He did, but I have a feeling he was involved in more than just that."

"Such as?"

"I don't know, but I should have liked to find out."

"Your manner was quite confrontational toward him that night."

"Do you think so? I don't like to mince my words, as a

general rule. There are so many more questions I wish I had asked him."

"Such as what else he was involved in?"

"Yes, but I wouldn't have received a straight answer, would I? Anyway, I'm supposed to be heading toward West Croydon station, so I shall leave you here. Nice to see you again, Miss Green." He doffed his hat and went on his way.

I watched him for a moment, feeling that he had cut our conversation short rather suddenly.

I strode on toward East Croydon train station, looking forward to the anonymity I would soon enjoy back in London town. As I walked, a carriage drew up alongside me. I glanced up at the occupants and immediately wished I hadn't. Charlotte Jenkins' face glared out at me from the window.

To continue walking would have seemed cowardly. I decided my only choice was to stop and listen to what she had to say. The carriage door flew open and Charlotte stepped out, closely followed by her parents.

"So this is her, is it?" demanded Mr Jenkins, surveying me with great distaste. "This is the harlot?" His top hat made him seem even taller and more intimidating.

"I would like to apologise," I began. "I never intended for it to come to this."

"You made eyes at a man who was engaged to be married!" boomed Mr Jenkins as he took a step closer to me.

"The matter has been settled in court," I said, desperately desiring to step back but resolving to stand my ground.

"The matter is far from settled!" shouted Charlotte. "You put a stop to my wedding. You are little more than a manipulative Jezebel!"

I tried to remain as calm as possible, but I could feel my legs trembling. "I have apologised," I said, "and the court has found in your favour. I don't think there is anything more to say on the matter."

I turned to continue on my way, but as I did so a hand grabbed at my arm. I stopped and looked back to see Charlotte's twisted face just inches away from mine.

"You have no idea of the harm you've caused," she spat. "You think you can just walk off with my husband and I'll leave you be! Well, you're wrong. I know where you live, and I know where you work."

"That's because I helped you once, Charlotte. I helped you find James when he was missing, if you recall."

"You didn't want to help me; you only wanted to find James. I was a fool to ever ask you for assistance. You betrayed my trust and ruined every chance I had of finding happiness!"

I tried to pull my arm free, but she strengthened her grip. I was surprised by her strength.

"You won't get away with this," she continued. "I intend to make your life every bit as miserable as you have made mine."

"Let go of me, please," I said, staring into her cold eyes.

She ignored my request. "You'll regret this," she continued. "I'll make sure of that."

"And it will be nothing more than you deserve," her father added with a grim smile.

I gripped the handle of my bag and resisted the urge to hit Charlotte with it. I had no wish to get into a physical fight.

"I have listened to all you have to say," I said. "Now let go of me."

The grip on my arm loosened, but it was only after Charlotte had struck my face that I realised what she had done. For a brief moment everything turned black, then my ears rang and a searing pain ran down my cheek. I clenched my teeth and glared at her crumpled, bitter face.

"Oi!" came a shout.

It was James.

"Leave her alone!" he demanded as he ran toward us.

James had almost reached me when Mr Jenkins raised his arm and shoved him away with his elbow.

"This harlot's not even worth it!" he growled. "She'll lose interest in you soon enough and start looking for another marriage to destroy."

"Don't you dare speak about Miss Green in that manner!" retorted James.

"Why are you defending this whore?" growled Mr Jenkins.

James lunged at Mr Jenkins and a scuffle ensued.

"Stop it!" I cried. "Ignore him, James! Just leave him be!"

Mr Jenkins struck a blow that sent James tumbling to the ground. I ran to his side and helped him up.

"Let's go," I pleaded. "We need to get away from here."

There was a horrible red mark below James' left eye.

Charlotte's face was wretched and awash with tears.

"It's too late," said James as a constable ran toward us, blowing his whistle. "We're in trouble now."

CHAPTER 32

"I never should have come to court," I said.

James and I sat in an austere waiting room at the police station next to Croydon Town Hall. He pulled a grimace and said nothing. The large red bruise on his cheek was already turning a nasty shade of purple. Charlotte Jenkins and her father were being interviewed in a nearby room.

"You agree that I shouldn't have come, don't you?" I said.

"What's done is done," he said bitterly. "Ruing our decisions won't make any difference now."

"But you tried to talk me out of it and I didn't listen. You were right."

"I know the Jenkins family well," he replied curtly. "I know what they're like. But I suppose some good might come out of this, as Mr Jenkins will likely be charged with assaulting a police officer. Other than that, it's a rather sorrowful state of affairs. I'm so sorry that Charlotte struck you."

"It wasn't as damaging as the punch you received," I said. "And there's no need to apologise for her behaviour. I suppose we all bear some responsibility for what has happened."

❦

The Holborn Gazette, Friday 21st November 1884

    The Argument for Keeping Women Out of the Workplace

    By Thomas Clifford

    There is little doubt that members of the fairer sex are increasingly occupying positions in the workforce that were previously the sole domain of men. Ladies have been admitted to the medical profession, and it will surely only be a matter of time before other professions make the same concessions. Female clerks are not unheard of in London's offices, although readers will be reassured to know that the sexes are properly segregated in these instances.

    Fleet Street – as is seemingly customary – follows its own rules in this matter. We have become accustomed to seeing a number of lady writers working in our midst, and I count among them the esteemed Mrs Linton, who celebrates achievements in both journalism and novel writing. However, the capricious nature of journalism does not allow for the rightful segregation of men and women. Instead, female news reporters must do what their male counterparts do, and therein lies the problem.

    At a breach of promise case yesterday involving Jenkins vs. Blakely, it was determined that a female news reporter for the Morning Express, *Miss Penelope Green, had been responsible for the cancellation of the nuptials on the wedding day itself. In the course of his work for Scotland Yard, the defendant and prospective groom, Inspector James Blakely, had been forced to work alongside Miss Green on a series of investigations. It was perhaps inevitable that while the inspector was busy catching criminals, Miss Green was set on catching his heart.*

    The sad result is a broken-hearted former fiancée and a family thrown into dismay, their only consolation being court-ordered damages to the sum of six hundred pounds.

    Let this be a lesson to any gentleman who is tempted by the fair gaze of a lady worker! The admission of women to the workplace presents a pathway fraught with difficulties. If the trickle becomes a river it can only be expected that this type of legal action will be keeping the courts busy morning, noon and night.

"Oh dear," said Eliza, folding away the newspaper and placing it on my writing desk. "That's not very charitable, is it?"

"Tom Clifford is clearly enjoying this golden opportunity he has been given to ridicule me," I said, slumping down on my bed. "And for some reason his editor allows him to do it!"

"His editor is a disgrace. What did James make of this article?"

"He hasn't seen it yet, and I don't want to show it to him for the time being. He wasn't at all pleased that I attended the court hearing yesterday."

I told Eliza about the confrontation with Charlotte and her family.

"How dreadful, Penelope. While I have some sympathy for Charlotte, the woman needs to learn how to conduct herself with decorum! The court has awarded her six hundred pounds and her former fiancé has been made an example of. You'd think she would have been satisfied with that. I have to agree with James, though. It was rather foolish of you to attend."

"I feel partly responsible for the breach of promise case."

"But how was your being there in person likely to help or change anything? It sounds as though you only made matters worse."

"I realise that now, thank you, Ellie."

"So what now for you and James?"

"I shall have to wait for him to calm down."

"It never takes very long, does it?"

"What doesn't?"

"For these things to turn sour."

'No, it doesn't take long at all."

"And to think that you seemed so happy together when we visited the Royal Aquarium."

"We were, and I feel sure that we will be again! All we need is for Charlotte and her awful family to leave us alone."

'This is what happens when you fall in love with a betrothed man. Did you think his fiancée would simply disappear without saying a word?"

"No, I didn't think that. I suspected she would bring about a breach of promise action, but I didn't think it would be as awful as this. And now James is angry with me because I didn't listen to him!"

"You never listen to anybody, Penelope."

"That isn't helpful, Ellie!" Hot tears began to prick my eyes. "What if he is never able to forgive me?"

"Now, now," said my sister, walking over and sitting beside me on the bed. "Of course he will. James loves you *because of* all your insubordinate habits, such as not listening to people and doing whatever you please, not *in spite of* them. There are plenty of ladies who would listen intently to him and obey his every word, but I'm sure he would find them extremely dull. He'll forgive you quickly; if he hasn't already, that is."

She gave me her handkerchief and I wiped my eyes with it.

"Thank you, Ellie. Let's change the subject. How are you finding your work with Miss Barrington?"

"I'm enjoying every minute of it. I've been collecting the rent from the tenants and ensuring that repairs to the housing have been carried out. I have to check that the tenants are keeping their living spaces clean and tidy, and that everything is in order. I have also been assisting them in various ways. Some of them are unable to read or write, so I have been reading their letters aloud. I also helped a lady write a letter and played with her young son while she carried out some chores. I had forgotten how difficult it can be to get anything done with young children running around!"

"But you have a nursemaid."

"Indeed, and it can still be difficult, even with a nursemaid! I don't know how these poor women get by. This particular lady takes on sewing work in order to pay her rent. She is almost continually sewing something and is just about able to watch over her children as she does so. It's far preferable to working in a factory, I suppose. This new work of mine has made me realise just how little other people have. Some of the tenants own nothing more than the clothes they are wearing, and they must toil all the time, every single day of their lives. Even when they have worked hard all week they will only have earned just about enough to cover their rent and food.

"Anyway, I console myself with the fact that Miss Barrington's housing project provides these people with homes, and that people like myself do whatever we can to assist them. It's not about offering charity, because otherwise they will never learn to look after themselves. Instead, people like me can help them care for themselves. I am enjoying the feeling that I can be of some use."

"It has given you a measure of independence, Ellie."

"It has indeed. And it has encouraged me to proceed with the divorce. I have instructed a law firm to assist me."

"That's extremely brave of you. Congratulations!"

"I can't say that I feel happy about it. In fact, it's all rather sad, but the matter must be resolved. I have already received a number of disapproving comments from the housekeeper."

"It's likely that many people will disapprove, Ellie, and there is nothing much you can do about that. But there are reasons why you have chosen to take this course of action, and very good ones, too. Many people will be unable to understand them, and I cannot see that there would be a lot of use in explaining it all. I think you are displaying a great deal of bravery in this matter, but then I always knew you were a brave person from the way you go careering around London on your bicycle."

"Thank you, Penelope. Now, shall we burn this *Holborn Gazette* in the fire?"

I finally received some good news later that day. A letter had been received at the *Morning Express* offices from a lady called Miss Margaret Davies. She had seen the appeal for information about Miss Hamilton and her letter said that she might be able to help. She had offered to call in at the *Morning Express* offices on Monday the twenty-fourth of November at four o'clock.

CHAPTER 33

"Your bruise is looking a little better," I said to James as we met in a rainy Westminster the following Monday morning.

"It feels a little better," he replied, holding out his umbrella so I could join him beneath it.

"Are you still angry with me?" I asked.

He sighed. "No, not with you, Penny. I'm just angry about the whole silly court case in general. I don't know where I am expected to find six hundred pounds. Anyway, that's by the by. The good news is that Mr Jenkins has been charged with causing an affray."

"Good!"

"You could have agreed to have Charlotte charged as well."

"I didn't see the need. I effectively stole her husband, so perhaps the score is settled now."

James shook his head. "You're too forgiving, Penny. Her behaviour was despicable."

"Let's hope that we will neither hear nor see anything more from the Jenkins family from now on."

"I hope not. I'm also hoping that Mr Hobhouse has managed to decypher the message we gave him. Shall we go and find out?"

We walked down Whitehall, avoiding the puddles as best we could.

"The lady we spoke to at the house on Old Cavendish Street, Miss Kay, left a message for me at the Yard," continued James. "Apparently, she or one of her friends encountered Miss Hamilton a few times at various restaurants. Her name was Clara Hamilton and she was usually in the company of some gentleman or other."

"Was that all she said?"

"Apparently so. At least we know Miss Hamilton's first name now."

"Did Miss Kay know where Clara lived?"

"She didn't say. We'll have to continue with our enquiries."

"Young Blakely! I presume you're here to find out whether I've had any success with your cypher."

"That's right, Mr Hobhouse."

"What have you done to your face?"

"Just a minor altercation."

The old man tutted, swapped his spectacles around and handed James the piece of paper that had been found in Miss Hamilton's bag.

"What you're holding there, Blakely, is an example of the Vigenère cypher."

"What does that mean, exactly?"

"Blaise de Vigenère was a Frenchman who came up with a clever method of encryption during the sixteenth century. Actually, there was an Italian chap who proposed it before him, but Vigenère always gets the credit. Here's his table."

Mr Hobhouse handed James a piece of paper with the alphabet written on it in multiple rows.

"What's this?"

"A to Z written out twenty-six times. You will see that each row is shifted along by one letter. So on the second row, Z is below A and A is below B. On the third row Z is below B and A is below C and so on. There is a shift of one each time."

"I see that."

"You've probably come across the Caesar cypher before, Blakely."

"I can't say that I have."

"You will have done, though perhaps without realising it. It's the simple substitution of one letter for another. So for example if you wanted to send the delightful Miss Green a message in Caesar cypher you could substitute 'B' for 'A' and 'C' for 'B' and so on. The system is named after Julius Caesar, who apparently used a shift of three letters. So he substituted 'D' for 'A' and 'E' for 'B', and the rest followed in the same sequence thereafter. Its weakness is that it is rather easy to decypher because some letters are used far from frequently than others. For example, 'E' is used a great deal, but 'Z' is not. So identifying the frequency of the substituted letters means you can eventually decypher it. You look for patterns as well. Not many letters appear side by side as a general rule, but 'O' does in words such as '*book*' and '*look*'. The Caesar cypher is quite simple to work out in a short space of time; usually a matter of hours."

"I'm sure it would take me longer than that," said James.

"What Vigenère did was invent a cypher in which each letter had twenty-six possible substitutions. That's what you see written in the grid I have just given you. You can see there that 'A' can be represented by any of the twenty-six letters beneath it."

"I do see that," said James. "But how on earth do you use it?"

"That's where the keyword comes in. The writer of the message comes up with a keyword, which is applied to the first column of the table."

"I'm afraid I don't follow," said James.

I couldn't help smiling at the intense concentration on his face.

"Let's say you come up with the keyword 'sun', and you want your message to the charming Miss Green to say 'Good morning'. First of all, you let Miss Green know that you will be using the keyword 'sun'. That's something that must be agreed between you. Then when you send the message you spell out the keyword in the first column here. So you find the alphabet line that begins with 'S' and read along it until you find 'G' which is the first letter of 'Good morning'. Then you go to the line at the top and that will be the letter you substitute it for. Then you find 'U' and correspond it with 'O' to find the letter substitute. The keyword has fewer letters than the message, so you simply repeat the keyword until you reach the end of the message. Good morning would read *'yibv gbjhvfa'* in this case."

"I think I understand it now," said James.

"I don't think I do," I said. "How do you know that Miss Hamilton's message was written in the Vigenère cypher, Mr Hobhouse?"

"I didn't immediately. I tried a few different approaches before I realised it was likely to be Vigenère."

"Have you managed to decypher it?" I asked.

"I believe so, yes."

"But you didn't have the keyword."

"No, but with careful analysis there are ways and means of working it out. I think the keyword used to code this message is 'nemesis'."

"How on earth did you work that out?" asked James.

"Well, for three hundred years no one could solve the Vigenère cypher. It was so difficult, in fact, that the French named it *le chiffre indéchiffrable*. That was until twenty years ago, when a Prussian officer published a deciphering method."

"But how did *you* do it?" asked James.

"I have probably bored you enough for one day, young Blakely, but in summary I firstly looked for sequences of letters that appeared more than once. I looked at the spacing between those sequences and that information helped me narrow down the length of the keyword. I then proceeded to use this assumption of keyword length to analyse the frequency of letters that corresponded with the first letter of the keyword, the second letter and so on. From this analysis I began to come up with some ideas of what the keyword might be. It took a few attempts, but I decided that the keyword had to be 'nemesis'. And when I deciphered the message using that keyword, this is what I found."

He gave James a piece of paper with the following message written on it:

Sunset at Arromanches, The Bountiful Harvest, Shepherdess at Thirlmere, Rural Scene North of Trieste, Summer Scene at St Moritz.

"Quite poetic," I commented.

"Perhaps they're the names of poems," suggested Mr Hobhouse.

"They could be," said James. "Or songs."

"I can imagine a song about a bountiful harvest," said Mr Hobhouse, "but it's not a song I'm familiar with. I'm quite sure there's one about a shepherdess, though."

"Thirlmere," said James. "Where's that?"

"The Lake District," replied Mr Hobhouse. "Wordsworth liked it up there, so perhaps these are poems after all."

"A shepherdess," I said as an image came to mind. "Wasn't there a painting of a shepherdess in Mr Gallo's rooms?"

"Yes!" said James. "And there was a sunset, too. Perhaps that was at Arromanches? And another of the paintings had mountains in it, so perhaps that was St Moritz. There were some farmworkers in fields... Could that be the bountiful harvest?" He grinned. "It's beginning to make sense!"

"Well, I'm relieved that it makes sense to you because it was completely meaningless to me," said Mr Hobhouse, swapping his spectacles over again.

"But why were the names of these paintings written down using a cypher?" pondered James. "And was the message sent to Miss Hamilton or did she write it herself?"

"Perhaps Mr Gallo wrote it," I suggested.

"Either way, it seems the lady was engaged in a kind of secret communication with someone," said Mr Hobhouse. "It's all very intriguing indeed."

"Might the keyword give us some sort of clue?" asked James, carefully folding and placing the message in his notebook. "Nemesis sounds rather threatening."

"She is the Greek goddess of retribution," replied Mr Hobhouse. "I don't know anything about art, but I know my goddesses."

"Nemesis was a goddess?" I said. "I didn't realise that. In fact, I had never given any thought to where the word might have come from."

"Interesting indeed," said James. "Miss Clara Hamilton seems to have been rather more mysterious than we first imagined."

CHAPTER 34

"These are the names of the paintings discovered in Mr Gallo's room all right," said Mr Russell, examining the decyphered code in James' office at Scotland Yard.

"Are you absolutely certain of that?" James asked.

"Absolutely sure. We visited the Hotel Tempesta last week and took a good look at them. Inspector Raynes and I managed to identify them all, didn't we, Raynes?"

"Our work was made slightly easier by the fact that all the paintings had already been listed as stolen," said Inspector Raynes. "I'll go and fetch the ledger to show you."

"The names of the paintings were written in code, you say?" Mr Russell asked James.

"Yes, using the Vigenère cypher."

"Intriguing."

"Is that one of the cyphers Jack Shelby uses?"

"He prefers the Playfair cypher, which would be quite complicated to decypher if he didn't use the same keyword each time."

"The keyword isn't 'nemesis', is it?"

"No, it's not."

"Have you encountered the word *nemesis* anywhere else during your investigation?"

"Nowhere, I'm afraid."

James sighed. "I feel there must be a connection between Shelby and Gallo, but it's proving rather difficult to establish one."

"It is extremely difficult," replied Mr Russell. "That's why I was at the dinner in the first place pretending to be Mr Hardy from *The Hotelier*. All we have to go on is a sighting of Shelby at Gallo's hotel a few weeks ago."

Inspector Raynes returned with a heavy, leather-bound volume, which he placed on his desk. "We've found the paintings listed in here; all of them stolen within the past twelve months." He opened the ledger and proceeded to show us the relevant entries.

"But it says here that *The Shepherdess at Thirlmere* has been recovered," said James. "Does that mean it was stolen, recovered and then sold on to Mr Gallo?"

"No. It means that Mr Gallo was in possession of a clever forgery," said Mr Russell. "Two of the other paintings have also been recovered. I think Mr Gallo was in possession of five forgeries in total."

"Did he know that they were forgeries?" asked James.

"I should think it unlikely. He probably thought he was buying stolen paintings, which isn't a particularly admirable undertaking. But he did love his art, and it seems he was willing to take a few risks in the way he acquired it. As I explained to you when we met last, the paintings are stolen and then forgeries are made. The forgeries are sold to people who think they are getting their hands on the real thing, and then the genuine painting is sold back to the owner. Inspector Raynes and I have visited the owners of all three recovered paintings, but they remained tight-lipped about those they had done a deal with to recover their artworks. They're worried about possible recriminations if they talk."

"All they really care about is getting their paintings back," added Inspector Raynes.

"Two of the owners haven't had their paintings returned," said James. "Are you encouraging them to negotiate with the criminals in a bid to find out their identities?"

"We're doing exactly that, Inspector," replied Mr Russell. "Hopefully we'll soon discover that Shelby is behind all this."

"But what about Miss Hamilton?" I asked. "The coded message found in her bag suggests that she also had a vested interest in these paintings. Where does she fit in with all this?"

"I haven't come across any connection between Shelby and a Miss Hamilton as yet," replied Mr Russell. "That doesn't mean there isn't one, though."

"She was up to something," I said. "She was more than a paid companion, I believe. Her supposed profession was just a cover, but for what? Why was she so interested in those paintings?"

My question was met with blank expressions all round.

⚜

"Clara Hamilton was a spy," said James as we left Scotland Yard and made our way toward Bow Street. "That explains why no one has reported her missing, and why barely anyone seems to know her. I'm assuming that Clara Hamilton is a false name because she was working undercover for someone, that would also explain why we can find no official record of her. Let's hope Miss Davies will be able to tell us more about her when she visits you this afternoon."

"It also provides a possible motive," I said. "Someone may

have realised she was spying on Mr Gallo and wanted her to stop."

"But why would he have been murdered as well?"

"Because he was a witness to her murder, perhaps."

"Possibly. But this Shelby chap might have wanted him dead as well, mightn't he? Perhaps he sold the forged paintings to Mr Gallo, who told Miss Hamilton whom he had purchased them from."

"Perhaps Gallo showed her the paintings," I said, "and told her the names of them. How else could she have written them down?"

"He was probably quite proud of his acquisitions and couldn't resist sharing the news with her."

"There is certainly a motive here for Shelby having them both murdered. Mr Russell says that he abhors violence, though."

"Perhaps he has simply managed to avoid the need for it so far. But if he is the one behind these thefts and forgeries, he's making good money from his victims. Mr Gallo's carelessness was a risk, and Shelby couldn't afford to let Miss Hamilton discover his identity."

"I have a copy of the *Morning Express* with me from the same date as the one Clara Hamilton had," I said. "I looked through it a number of times but cannot work out what might have interested her in it. Maybe you could have a look through to see whether you are able to find something. I wonder who she was working for."

"Someone who was looking for confirmation that Gallo was caught up in this stolen art and forgery business, I should think. It may have been a police detective, I suppose, although you'd think he would have stepped forward by now to explain the situation. It could also have been someone from within the art world."

"If Shelby is behind these murders, someone who stayed

at the Hotel Tempesta that night must have a connection with him."

"It could be Mr Bolton or Mr Goldman."

"Mr Goldman was discussing art with Mr Gallo over dinner."

"And then there's Mrs Mirabeau."

"Do you think she might know Jack Shelby?"

"It's possible, isn't it?" he said. "Much as Chief Inspector Fenton resents my involvement in this case, I think we need to ask him what he has discovered so far."

"Mr Goldman interests me the most," said Chief Inspector Fenton as we sat with him in his Bow Street office. "But I don't want you publishing that sentiment, Miss Green. I see you're still determined to accompany Inspector Blakely wherever he goes."

"Has my presence affected your investigation in any way, Chief Inspector?" I asked.

"No." He gave a scowl. "But that doesn't mean I consider it appropriate, and I have made my feelings on the matter very clear to the deputy commissioner at Scotland Yard."

"So I heard,' said James. "But let's return to Mr Goldman. What have you learned about him?"

"He's a Jewish gentleman, twenty-seven years of age and lives in St John's Wood."

"As do I," said James.

"Have you seen him around those parts, Blakely?"

James shook his head. "Quite a few people live in the area, Fenton."

"Goldman's an ink-slinger," continued Chief Inspector Fenton. "He writes for a range of periodicals on an ad hoc basis. He likes to write about hotels and restaurants, then give them a mark out of ten or something like that. I'm not sure what qualifies him to be more of an expert on these matters than anyone else, but there you have it. He's one of these self-proclaimed experts, I suppose. They're two a penny these days."

"He has an interest in art, does he?" asked James.

"Yes. He's one of these high-minded chaps who considers himself well-versed in the arts. It's not just paintings, but the theatre, opera, music recitals and that sort of thing. The sort of leisurely pursuits a chap enjoys when he has time on his hands and isn't working every hour the Lord sends investigating crimes."

"What motive might he have for murdering Mr Gallo and Miss Hamilton?" I asked.

"I'll be frank with you, Miss Green," he replied. "I just don't like the man. There's something about him that doesn't seem right. His profession sounds rather vague to me."

"He's a writer," I said.

"You're entitled to stick up for your own, Miss Green, but his vagueness suggests to me that he is hiding something from us."

"Have you spoken to his associates?" James asked. "Friends and family?"

"Yes, the chaps have been doing that, but nothing particularly untoward has emerged so far."

"Is it possible that he might have known a chap named Jack Shelby?" James asked. "He calls himself Rigby Pleydell-Bouverie."

"That's the fellow the Pinkerton chap's after, isn't it? No, I haven't found any evidence that Goldman knew him."

"We think Shelby may be behind the murders of Mr Gallo and Miss Hamilton," said James. "He most likely wouldn't have committed the deed himself, but he might have somehow persuaded one of the guests to do his bidding that fateful night."

"That's rather a hasty assumption, isn't it?" replied Chief Inspector Fenton.

"Are you aware that Miss Hamilton was a spy?" I said.

The inspector gave a laugh. "That's one word for her, I suppose!"

"You're not taking this seriously, Fenton," snapped James. "She was in possession of quite a complicated cypher that detailed the forged paintings Mr Gallo had bought. He may have bought them from Shelby."

"*May have*. But there's no evidence that he did, is there?"

"Not yet. But if you could find a connection between Goldman and Shelby that would strengthen your case. Similarly, if you could prove a connection between Shelby and one of the other guests the puzzle might be solved."

"And this loose woman, Miss Hamilton, may have been some sort of spy?"

"Someone certainly wished to silence her. Maybe she knew Shelby."

"But there is no evidence," said Chief Inspector Fenton. "And I don't see where this conversation is getting us, Blakely."

"You need to find out whether any of the people who stayed in the hotel that night were acquainted with Shelby."

"But we don't know for sure whether he orchestrated the murders, do we? All this is merely conjecture, Blakely, and I must get on with the job rather than entertaining any more of your wild theories."

"Have you considered Mrs Mirabeau as a suspect?"

"Mrs Mirabeau has been exceptionally helpful."

"Some culprits prefer to stay close to the investigation."

"Are you suggesting that she is the murderer now? I thought you said it was Shelby."

"She may have been working for Shelby."

Inspector Fenton gave a loud snort. "What nonsense."

"You will ask her about him, won't you?"

"I shall add that task to my ever-growing list, but I cannot promise to make it a priority."

"How deeply dissatisfying," said James as we stepped out of the police station. "I think we should go and speak to Mrs Mirabeau ourselves. Have you the time to accompany me?" He consulted his pocket watch. "It's almost one o'clock now."

"Yes, I have three hours before I need to meet Miss Davies," I replied. "The Hotel Tempesta is only a short walk from the office, so I have plenty of time yet."

We walked along the Strand and had almost reached the Hotel Tempesta when I saw the familiar large frame of a man walking toward us. He wore a deep blue cape over a burgundy velvet jacket along with a tall top hat.

"Mr Somers!" I called out. He was initially startled but smiled when he saw me.

"Miss Green! What a pleasure it is to see you again."

I introduced James, then said, "We're on our way to visit Mrs Mirabeau. Have you just come from the hotel yourself?"

"As a matter of fact, I have." His expression grew sombre. "It sounds foolish, I know, but I cannot keep away from the place. My thoughts are consumed by that dreadful night, and I have been unable to escape them. Have you been feeling the same way, Miss Green?"

"Yes, my feelings have been quite similar."

"Poor Mrs Mirabeau has remained there to help the police with their investigation," continued Mr Somers, "and all she has now are two maids for company and that poor little dog. She misses Nathaniel terribly. We all do. She wants to get away to France, but she's stuck here while the investigation is ongoing. It doesn't seem fair."

"I suppose each one of us is considered a suspect," I said.

"But that's ridiculous! How can we all be suspects? It's been almost two weeks since the dreadful event and the police are no closer to catching the culprit!"

"We're doing what we can, Mr Somers," said James. "We've been trying to establish whether Mr Gallo had any criminal connections—"

"Of course he didn't!"

"My statement was not intended as a slur on Mr Gallo's character, but the fact remains that he bought several artworks which he believed to have been stolen."

"And that was why someone killed him?"

"We don't know yet. His companion that night, Miss Hamilton, has become increasingly interesting to us as well."

"I just don't understand why it's taking so long."

"Our job would be far easier if everyone we spoke to was completely honest about what they know."

"I've told Chief Inspector Fenton everything I know countless times! I have nothing to hide, Inspector."

"I'm sure you don't, Mr Somers, and thank you for being so obliging to date."

"What do you intend to ask Mrs Mirabeau about?"

"There are a few things we need her to elaborate on."

"Such as?"

"Let's leave that between us and Mrs Mirabeau for now, shall we?"

"Well, you must be gentle with her. She has suffered terribly."

"I'm aware that this has been a very difficult time for her."

"Have you seen any of the other guests since that night?" I asked Mr Somers.

"Only Mr Bolton and Mr Blackstone. Oh, and I saw Mrs Mortimer in one of the tea rooms just off Oxford Street. We are all desperately impatient for this case to be resolved."

"In which case we need to be getting on," said James. "It has been a pleasure to make your acquaintance, Mr Somers."

CHAPTER 35

Mrs Mirabeau appeared weary as she admitted us to the Hotel Tempesta.

"I have never liked British winters," she said as we followed her into her office. "I prefer to be in the south of France at this time of year."

I felt my skin prickle as I glanced around me. The hotel felt even more sinister now that the fountain in the foyer no longer trickled and the blooms of lilies had vanished. The mirrors remained covered with black crepe, and the windows admitted pallid rays of daylight that were too weak to chase away the shadows.

Despite the emptiness of the place, Mrs Mirabeau had clearly taken considerable care over her appearance. Her bright auburn hair was neatly pinned and embellished with black bows. Her black silk dress rustled as she walked.

"You're not staying here at night, are you?" I asked.

"Oh yes," she replied. "I have a room here on the fourth floor."

"All by yourself?"

I shuddered, and her scarlet lips formed a bemused smile.

"Why ever not?" she replied. "It's the same room I've been using these past few months."

"But when you consider what has happened here of late..." My voice trailed off and I glanced over at the grand staircase, which ascended up into the heavy gloom.

"Two maids have remained with me here," she said. "We keep each other company."

The only light and warmth in the building appeared to be coming from Mrs Mirabeau's office. We sat in comfortable chairs beside a cheerful fire, and Captain nuzzled his nose into my hand.

"I should add that Chief Inspector Fenton and his men are regular visitors to the hotel these days," she added. "Do you mind if I smoke?"

We shook our heads and she lit a small cigarette.

"So how can I help you, Inspector?" she asked James. "I've answered so many of Inspector Fenton's questions that I don't think there can be anything left to tell."

"Have you heard of a man called Jack Shelby?" asked James. "He also uses the name Rigby Pleydell-Bouverie."

"No. Who is he?"

"An American gentleman criminal," said James. "Although I use the word '*gentleman*' in its loosest sense. Did Mr Gallo ever mention his name?"

"Not that I remember."

"Do you recall the paintings we discovered rolled up in his chambers?"

"Yes. They're forgeries, aren't they? The man who I had assumed to be Mr Hardy turned up to take a look at them. Then I discovered he's a Pinkerton man! It was completely brazen of him. To think that he spent the night here pretending to be someone else! I would say that he is the most suspicious of the lot."

"What do you mean by that, Mrs Mirabeau?" asked James.

"Well, no one's going to consider him a suspect if he claims to be an American detective. Do we know for sure that he is?"

"My colleague, Inspector Raynes, has been working with him for some time now. I don't think there can be any doubt that he is who he says he is."

She parted her lips and puffed out a plume of smoke. "But you don't know for certain, Inspector."

"The problem with this case is that we don't know anything for certain," replied James with a sigh. "Can you tell us anything more about Miss Hamilton?"

"I have already told you everything I know."

"We suspect that she may have been a spy."

Mrs Mirabeau raised an eyebrow. "Are you sure? For whom?"

"That's what we are trying to ascertain."

"Why would she spy on Mr Gallo?"

"We believe the forged paintings were of interest to her."

"I don't know how she could have known about them."

"Someone told her, and I would like to know who. Mr Gallo may well have shared information with her himself, and that may be why they were both murdered."

Mrs Mirabeau sucked on her cigarette. "Your theory is beginning to sound rather far-fetched to me."

"Can I ask what *your* theory is, Mrs Mirabeau?"

"I can't say that I have one, Inspector. I'm as baffled by this situation as the next person."

"But you think the Pinkerton man is suspicious."

"I do, as a matter of fact. Why pretend to be someone other than who you are?"

"He was working undercover. The Pinkertons are very good at it."

"Well, he certainly fooled me. Did he fool you, too, Miss Green?" she asked.

I nodded.

"Can you describe your relationship with Mr Gallo?" James asked.

The only sign that this question had riled Mrs Mirabeau was an extra blink in her otherwise calm gaze.

"Nathaniel and I got along exceptionally well. We understood each other."

"On a personal, as well as a professional, basis?"

"Yes, but not in the manner you're probably thinking, Inspector. He was a married man, after all."

"It didn't prevent him from having a secret liaison with Miss Hamilton."

"She meant nothing to him!" she snapped. "I'm talking about a relationship founded on mutual trust and respect. That's what Nathaniel and I had."

"Did you have a particular affection for him?"

"Of course I did, but only as I would for a brother. It was nothing more than that; quite unlike the fondness you and Miss Green obviously have for one another."

"That has no relevance to, or bearing on, our discussion, Mrs Mirabeau."

"Have I spoken the truth, then?" she asked with a smile. "I must say that it was quite obvious to me when you greeted each other in the dining room that morning."

James scratched his chin and glanced around the room. "It is exceptionally tidy in here, Mrs Mirabeau," he commented.

"I've had a lot of time to spare. I've been going through all the papers and sorting out any unresolved matters. I do hope that I'll be able to leave here soon."

"Where will you go?"

"To the south of France, of course."

"Will you work over there?"

"Yes. I know a number of hoteliers in St Tropez."

"That sounds very appealing. It begs the question as to

why you ever bothered coming to London, with its grey skies."

"Because Nathaniel asked me to, Inspector."

"I should like to look inside Mr Gallo's office again if I may, Mrs Mirabeau."

"Of course."

James rose to his feet. "I don't mind if you prefer to accompany me," he said to her.

"I trust you to look in his office without my being present," she replied with what struck me as an insincere smile.

"It's just as I said to Mr Somers," muttered James as we walked toward Mr Gallo's office. "My job would be far easier if everyone was willing to be honest with me. There's something Mrs Mirabeau doesn't want to tell us, and it is frustrating me enormously. I also found Mr Somers' manner rather prickly when we spoke to him."

"He's just annoyed that no one has been arrested yet."

"That's one possible explanation, but there could be another reason entirely. Why does he keep returning to the hotel? It makes me wonder what his motives are."

We reached Mr Gallo's office and stepped inside.

"Just as I thought," said James, glancing around. "Everything in here is remarkably tidy, too. Do you remember the mess he left it in?"

"Mrs Mirabeau said she has had a lot of time to spare."

"The papers that were on the desk have disappeared," said James. "Perhaps Fenton has taken them." He walked over to the other side of the desk and opened the drawers. "Can he really have taken everything? Let's find one of the maids," he whispered.

I followed closely behind him as he strode out of the

office. We turned right, away from the direction of Mrs Mirabeau's office, and walked along the corridor toward the dining room. James tried a few door handles along the way, but each of the doors was locked.

"This hotel must have a basement, don't you think?" he said.

"Yes, I suppose it must have."

"I wonder where the staircase is. I was hoping one of the maids might show us."

"We could try the back stairs."

"How do we get to those?"

"We'd need to go back to the main foyer and turn left. There is a corridor there that leads to them."

"There's a risk that we might bump into Mrs Mirabeau."

"I don't understand, James. What are you planning to do down there?"

"I have a hunch that something has been hidden in the basement."

"Such as?"

"The lack of papers in Mr Gallo's office concerns me, Penny, and I think if we were to look inside his attic rooms we would find a similar story there."

"But Chief Inspector Fenton and his men may have taken them, as you suggested earlier."

"They may have, but I feel sure that Mrs Mirabeau is hiding something. I want to find out what it is before she realises I'm looking."

We reached the main foyer and I was pleased to see that there was no sign of her.

"This way," I whispered, scurrying along on my tiptoes to prevent my boots from echoing on the tiled floor. We reached the carpeted corridor and strode as quickly as possible toward the set of swing doors that led to the back staircase.

"I came this way the morning after the murder," I whispered. "I was hoping to take a look at the Venetian Suite."

"I'm pleased you know where you're going, Penny. It's terribly dingy, isn't it? I wonder whether there are any lights in the basement."

"I hope so, otherwise there will be little point in us going down there."

I pushed open the door to the back staircase, where the thin grey daylight filtered in through a window.

James paused to look at it. "The killer discarded his bloodstained overcoat through one of the windows on this staircase. We think he must have done so from the second storey, as that window appeared to have been recently opened." He leaned over the bannister and peered down. "It looks quite dark down there."

I felt a shiver down my spine. I had never felt at ease in this hotel, and the thought of climbing the stairs down to a dark basement was unappealing. I had no wish to accompany James there, but neither was I prepared to wait for him alone in the stairwell.

The gloom intensified around us as we walked down the stairs. There was no sound except for our footsteps.

"Hello!"

My heart leapt up into my throat as I suddenly beheld Mrs Mirabeau in front of me. Her face loomed pale in the dark, and she held a lantern in her hand. An odd smile played on her lips.

"We didn't realise you were down here!" I said with a gasp.

"Are you looking for something?" she asked.

"Er, yes, we tried to find you upstairs. I'd like to take a look at the basement," said James.

"Really? What an odd request."

"Have you just come from there?" asked James.

"Yes, there are a few items stored down there."

"May I ask what?"

Mrs Mirabeau gave another involuntary blink. "Just some personal belongings of mine. I felt they would be safer locked away in the basement than in the office."

"May we take a look?" James asked.

"If you must, but you'll need to take a lantern with you. Here, have mine. The candle has almost burnt down, but there is probably half an hour or so left in it."

"Thank you, Mrs Mirabeau," said James, "that is most kind of you. We'll return it to your office when we're finished."

"I'll unlock the basement door for you."

CHAPTER 36

The flickering lantern light shone against the brick walls and columns supporting the vast building above our heads. These supports divided the basement into small bays, each containing piles of old furniture and furnishings. I had to duck my head to avoid the thick, dusty cobwebs overhead. The cold from the stone floor seeped through the soles of my boots.

"I don't like it down here at all," I said, clasping James' arm.

He laughed. "Don't worry, Penny, I'll keep you safe from the ghosts."

"Don't say that!" I scolded. "I cannot abide jokes about ghosts when I'm stuck in a place like this!"

We walked over to where grey daylight filtered through an iron grid of thick, leaded glass in the ceiling.

"A pavement light from the street above," said James, looking up. "People are walking over our heads."

My foot slipped in a slimy puddle of water that had accumulated from the drips between the gaps in the pavement light. "Yuck!" I exclaimed.

We continued on our way.

"Must we remain down here much longer?" I asked, still clinging on to James' arm.

"We need to find out what Mrs Mirabeau has been doing down here."

"Storing items which she doesn't want to keep in her office. She told you that."

"Yes, but what items? Perhaps there's a safe down here."

"If there is, it will no doubt be locked," I said. "Then you can ask her to open it for you. Ugh! You can tell there are rats down here."

James shone the lantern on a chair with horsehair stuffing protruding from the jagged holes in its brocade covering.

I clasped his arm even tighter and jumped when I saw a sudden movement. "What's *that*?" My voice was higher-pitched than usual.

"Only our reflection," said James. "There is an old mirror over there."

The air smelled of damp soil and decay, similar to the way I imagined a tomb would smell. And there was another aroma too, like cold cinders in an unswept fireplace.

"Can you smell that burnt odour?" James asked.

"Yes. It must be left over from when the hotel caught fire."

"I consider it unlikely. The fire occurred years ago, did it not?"

"Yes, it was four years ago."

"Could the foundations really retain the charred smell?"

"The hotel collapsed in on itself, right down into the basement," I said. "Did you never walk past the ruins?"

"I suppose I must have done, but I don't recall it in great detail."

As we continued walking, the smell of burning grew stronger.

"Are we really likely to find anything down here?" I asked, keen to leave at the earliest opportunity.

"There has to be a safe."

"But we've searched most of the basement now and there has been no sign of one. Couldn't we ask Chief Inspector Fenton and his men to come and conduct a thorough search? They could bring plenty of lanterns with them and make short work of it. There can't be much light left in the candle, and I need to get back to the office soon to meet with Miss Davies."

James turned to face me. "All right, then. I think I can see a substantial wall up ahead which could mark the end of this section. Let's have a look over there and then we can leave."

"Must we?"

"Come on, it'll only take us a minute." James smiled before leaning in to kiss me. "I don't often find the opportunity to do that," he said. "There are benefits to being alone together in the dark."

I laughed. "Can we find a friendlier dark place next time?"

"I'm sure we can."

We continued on for a few more steps.

"What's that on the floor?" asked James. He raised his lantern and I saw a pool of something dark. For a brief, terrible moment I thought it might be blood, but then I saw that it was powdery in texture.

"Ashes," said James, stooping down with his lantern to take a closer look. "So this is where the burnt smell is coming from." He set the lantern on the ground, put his gloves on and ran his hands through the pile of embers. Dust rose up in the flickering light. "It's very fine," he said. "Paper, perhaps?"

"Do you think Mrs Mirabeau has been burning papers down here?"

"I would say so, wouldn't you? It certainly explains why there are so few papers left in the offices upstairs."

"We mustn't jump to assumptions, though. There may be another explanation for it."

"There may be." James stood upright again and picked up the lantern. "We need to ask her about it. Maybe we could make enquiries with the maids first, and hopefully one of them will let something slip. Either way, I think you're right about getting Fenton and his men down here. This basement needs to be properly searched. Mrs Mirabeau clearly has an unusual interest in the place, and we need to understand why."

"I'm surprised Chief Inspector Fenton's men didn't search here immediately after the murders."

"They may well have done, but once they found the murder weapon and the discarded overcoat and gloves, they had the most important evidence. Searching the basement probably wasn't much of a priority after that. The killer doesn't appear to have made it down here."

"Unless the killer is Mrs Mirabeau."

"Good point. Come on, let's go. I can't wait to find out whether Miss Davies will have something useful to tell you about Clara Hamilton."

We walked briskly back toward the door we had entered through.

"I'm looking forward to seeing daylight again," I said. "Even if it is grey and cloudy."

James laughed. "This is the right door, isn't it?" he said, holding his lantern up so we could see it more clearly.

"It's the only door, I think."

"I don't remember us closing it. Do you?"

"I thought we had left it open, but never mind. Perhaps it has swung shut by itself."

James stepped forward and turned the handle.

Nothing happened.

He tried again, turning the handle both ways. Then he

pulled at the handle before pushing against the door with his shoulder.

I felt a ball of panic grow in my chest.

"Is it not opening?" I said, my voice rising in pitch again.

"No, it's not," said James. "I think we have been locked in."

"Please don't say that." I tried to calm my rapid breathing.

"Mrs Mirabeau unlocked the door for us, didn't she?" said James. "And I'm sure we left it open when we stepped inside. I think she must have come back and locked it."

"But she can't have!" I cried. "Why would she do such a thing?"

"Hello?" shouted James, thumping on the door with his fist. "Can anyone hear us?"

"Hello?" I shouted, joining in with the thumping. "Hello! Is anyone there? Oh, James, it's hopeless! How will anyone ever hear us down here? Has she really locked the door on us? But why? Why would she do it?"

"Because we are close to finding her out," said James.

"So now what?" I cried. "How will we ever get out of here?"

CHAPTER 37

"I s there anything we can use to break the door down?" I pleaded.

"It would be difficult as the door opens inwardly."

"Could we smash the door frame with something?"

"It would have to be something heavy but portable."

"An axe!" I said. "Perhaps there's an axe down here."

"I can't recall seeing one."

We searched for an axe or anything else that could be used to damage the door frame, but nothing we found was of any use.

"There has to be another way out of here," I said, becoming increasingly flustered. "There must be. There can't only be the one door, can there?"

"I don't think there is any other," said James.

We walked the length and breadth of the basement, searching for another way out.

"What about the pavement lights?" I asked. "Surely we could smash one of those?"

"That leaded glass is a good few inches thick. It's designed to bear the weight of countless people walking over it."

"Surely we could smash one and shout for help!"

"We could try, Penny, but I don't even know what we would smash it with."

"I'm sure I can find something."

James gave me the lantern and I searched around the old pieces of furniture. The best option I could see was a bronze candlestick. I dragged a chair so that it sat beneath one of the pavement lights, then climbed onto it and began hitting the glass above my head. I only had to do it a few times to realise that any attempt to break the window would be futile. The candlestick simply bounced off the thick glass and began to bend. My arm soon ached.

"Would you like me to try?" offered James.

I could tell by the tone in his voice that he considered it a useless idea but was reluctant to tell me so.

He stood on the chair and struck the glass above us so hard with the candlestick that the noise was almost deafening within the echoing surrounds of the basement.

"I don't think it's doing any good," he said, examining the bent candlestick before clambering down from the chair.

"It was a foolish idea," I said, a heavy sensation settling in my stomach. "How long are we to be trapped in here, James? I'm supposed to be meeting Miss Davies. What time is it?"

James looked at his pocket watch. "Half-past three o'clock."

"She'll be at the office within half an hour!" I said. "I knew we shouldn't have come down here."

"I don't remember you saying so at the time."

"Perhaps not, but I thought it."

"You didn't have to come down here with me."

"I didn't want to stay upstairs on my own."

"As I see it, we both made the decision to come down here, and we couldn't possibly have predicted that we'd be locked in."

"We never should have trusted her."

"It didn't feel as though we were placing a great trust in her at the time; I just never foresaw this happening. She will be in a great deal of trouble when this comes to light."

"And when will that be? How will anyone find out that we're here?"

"They'll come looking for us before long."

"*Before long?* How long will that be? And even when they do come looking for us, when are they going to realise that we are down in the basement? Oh, this is awful, James." I began to pace the floor. "We could be here all night. And all day tomorrow! And another night! We're *prisoners*. Why has she done this to us?"

"To protect herself."

"Meanwhile, Miss Davies will think that I'm no longer interested in meeting with her. How long will she be prepared to wait for me, James?"

"Penny, you need to calm yourself. Fretting about the situation won't help us."

"What do you expect me to do?" I snapped. "Make myself comfortable on a chair with all the rats and patiently wait for someone to find us?"

"We may have no other choice. We could make as much noise as possible, but no one is likely to hear us. So we will either have to wait until someone notices that we are missing or until Mrs Mirabeau's conscience gets the better of her."

"I'm beginning to think that she doesn't have a conscience."

"We need a distraction. Let's sit down and take a look at the copy of the *Morning Express* you brought with you. There is very little life left in the candle now, but it might last long enough for us to find something useful."

"I'd like to sit up on the steps by the door," I said.

We walked over to the door and I tried the handle again, but it still wouldn't budge.

"Let's sit down and look at this newspaper," James said gently.

"I've already looked at it."

"And now we're going to look at it together. Come on."

James began leafing through the pages, and I sighed as I glanced at the familiar articles I had looked at countless times before.

"This edition was printed three days before Clara Hamilton stayed at the hotel," I said. "There was nothing particularly newsworthy that day."

"A report from the House of Commons..." said James, holding the lantern above the paper. I could see that there was barely any wax left in the candle. "The Congo Conference... Egypt... What news was there? A collision between two ships on the Thames, in which no one was hurt. Money markets... law intelligence... sporting intelligence... police intelligence... And then foreign news. Something here must have interested her, but there's no telling what, is there? We don't even know the lady. Unless..."

"What is it?"

"Unless there's another hidden message here. That must be it, Penny! Did you read through all the advertisements?"

"Yes I did, and there were hundreds of them."

"And the personal messages?"

"I read those, too."

"Are you sure?" James turned to the advertisements section and ran his finger down them until he reached the column of personal messages.

"Yes."

"Are you sure you hadn't dozed off by the time you reached this section?"

"I cannot recall falling asleep."

"I think you must have, because there does seem to be something significant here."

"Really?"

James held the lantern close to the paper and pointed to a single line of text, which was nothing more than a string of jumbled letters.

"That has to be why she kept an old copy of the newspaper," he said. "This message was for her."

"Of course!" I said. "It must be the Vigenère cypher again. If we assume the keyword is nemesis again, we can try to decypher it!" I opened my carpet bag and pulled out my pencil and notepad. "All we need to do is write down the grid of letters Mr Hobhouse showed us and then we can work it out! I'm so pleased you spotted it, James, and to think that I didn't notice it there!"

I wrote down the alphabet in a row, then began the second row with the letters shifted along by one.

"You'll have to do that twenty-six times," said James resignedly.

"I know."

It was then that the candle in the lantern spluttered out, rendering the task impossible.

CHAPTER 38

Voices woke me, and a flickering light threw disorientating shadows around. Startled, I began to sit up.

"What's happening?" I asked.

"We're being rescued," James said gently.

"Thank goodness!"

I had fallen asleep resting up against him. Once the candle had gone out, we had placed another chair beneath the pavement light and tried, but failed, to decypher the code in the fading daylight.

"Who is it?" I asked. I could see a dark figure holding a lantern over by the doorway.

"He told me he was Mrs Mirabeau's solicitor," replied James. "She's refusing to speak to the police now, or so he tells me. At least he has agreed to let us out. Come on! Do you have your bag with you?"

"Yes."

I picked up my carpet bag and we rose to our feet together.

"How long was I asleep for?" I asked.

"I don't know. An hour, perhaps."

The lantern moved away from us.

"This way," a man's voice said brusquely.

I held James' hand as we walked toward the door and climbed the dingy steps that led out of the basement. I felt a weight lifting from me as I did so. Ahead of me was the dark silhouette of the solicitor, and the windows on the staircase revealed a night sky.

"What time is it?" I asked James.

"Just after ten o'clock."

"Then we were trapped in there for approximately eight hours! It could have been worse, I suppose. At least it wasn't all night."

The solicitor led us along the corridor toward the grand foyer.

"You'll want to visit the washroom, no doubt," he said without turning to look at us.

As I splashed my face with water in the washroom, I wondered whether the hotel would ever host guests again. I felt a pang of sadness as I thought back to Mr Gallo's optimistic outlook that fateful night. He had held such high hopes for this place, yet his dreams had so quickly crumbled into nothing.

Mrs Mirabeau's solicitor was keen to swiftly escort us out of the hotel as soon as I returned to the foyer.

"Here's my card, Inspector," he said as we stood beside the entrance. He wore a top hat and his face was cloaked in shadow, but I could just about discern dark whiskers. "I have instructed my client to refer any further police enquiries to me."

"You do realise you would be committing an offence if you

deliberately impeded a police investigation, don't you?" said James.

"It is not my intention to impede, Inspector, but to protect my client from undue harassment."

"She detained us unlawfully!"

"That was not a course of action I would have advised her to take, but she carried it out under duress."

James gave a snort. "There was no duress! I merely asked her a few questions and then asked to take a look at the basement. She realised we would discover that she has been burning papers down there, and that's when she got you involved."

"She sought my help as a last resort, Inspector. For two weeks she has been assisting the police with their enquiries without complaint, and now she must be left alone. If there is evidence of her having committed any wrongdoing, do please bring it to my attention."

"There is the destruction of evidence and unlawfully detaining a police officer and a news reporter," retorted James. "Two very serious examples of wrongdoing so far, and I'm confident that we will discover more. I think you are likely to find yourself becoming quite busy, Mr..." James glanced down at his card for the name. "Tennant."

"Good night, Inspector," replied the solicitor, holding the door open for us.

"Shoeshine, sir?" asked a boy standing outside Temple train station.

"No, thank you," replied James. "Is this your regular pitch?"

"Yessir. Is you a copper, sir?"

"Yes, I am. For some reason, boys like you have a knack of spotting us even when we are wearing plain clothes."

"I've been 'ere fer over a year, sir, an' I ain't never done no 'arm to no one!"

"I'm sure you haven't. You're not in trouble, so please don't worry. What is your name?"

"Kit, sir."

James glanced back at the Hotel Tempesta, which sat directly opposite the station.

"There is a lady who works at that hotel, Kit."

"That's the place where that gen'leman got murdered, ain't it?"

"That's right."

"It won't never open again now. It's cursed!"

"So they say. There's a lady who is still living inside it; you may have seen her. She has auburn hair, wears rouge and smokes cigarettes."

"Yeah, I seen 'er sir."

"Good. I'd like you to watch out for her and keep an eye on anyone else who visits the hotel. Report back to me in a few days and let me know what you find out, will you?"

"Report back ter you where, sir?"

"At Scotland Yard. Do you know where that is?"

"Yeah, I knows it."

"You can get there quickly if you take the train from here to Charing Cross. It's the next station along."

"Yeah, I knows all the stations."

"Let me give you some money for your fare."

The boy's eyes widened as James handed him a few coins.

"And you'll want a half-crown for your trouble, no doubt."

The boy grinned. "Cor, yessir!"

"Now, there will be plenty more of that if you're willing to do a little work for me. I don't know how much you earn shining shoes, but as you're still out here late at night I'm guessing it's not much. Perhaps you'd like to do this work for me instead for the next few days? Follow the auburn-haired lady if you can, but don't let her see you."

"No, sir. I won't."

"And let me know where she goes."

"Oh, yessir. I will, sir!"

"Ask for me directly at Scotland Yard when you come. Look, I'll show you my warrant card. Inspector Blakely's my name."

"'Spector Blakely. Yessir!"

CHAPTER 39

My head felt heavy with tiredness the following morning as I walked past the grass oval of Finsbury Circus. The trees were bare of leaves, but the weak sunlight and soft birdsong cheered me a little. My destination was the nearby Broad Street station, from where I would board a train to Islington to meet James and Margaret Davies, whom I had missed meeting with the previous day.

During the train journey I leafed through the pages of *The Times*. A twelve-line paragraph on page three stated that Chief Inspector Fenton had arrested a man in connection with the murders, though the report declined to name him. I felt a snap of irritation as I read this. Mr Blackstone had clearly ingratiated himself enough with the chief inspector to get the exclusive news.

"Did you know that Chief Inspector Fenton has arrested a suspect?" I asked James when I met him outside Highbury and Islington train station.

"Yes, I heard it first thing this morning. He has taken Mr Goldman into custody, apparently."

"What possible motive could Mr Goldman have?"

"I don't know, but perhaps Fenton is on to something. I'll visit him later to find out. I suppose it isn't a big surprise, really. He was muttering on about Goldman yesterday, wasn't he?"

"I should like to know what evidence he has that Mr Goldman was responsible."

"Let's find out as much as we can about Clara Hamilton for the time being. How are you faring this morning, Penny?"

"I feel rather tired after our ordeal in the basement," I replied. "But I'm enjoying the sensation of sunlight on my face after all that darkness."

"What sunlight?"

"The gentle patches that appear from between the clouds now and again."

"I'm disappointed to hear that you consider our time in the basement an *ordeal*," said James. "I quite enjoyed having the opportunity to spend some time alone with you." He grinned.

"It's kind of you to say so, James, and I enjoyed your company." I smiled. "However, the circumstances could have been a little better."

"What's wrong with a damp, dark, rat-infested basement?"

"Nothing, I suppose, but let's take the key with us next time."

We both laughed.

"Which property does Miss Davies live in?" he asked.

I fished her letter out of my bag and looked at the address written on it.

"Swan Yard."

. . .

Miss Margaret Davies was a tall, slender lady with brown hair and looked to be about thirty years of age. She invited us to sit in a small parlour, which was simply furnished but clean and tidy. Several framed photographs hung above the fireplace.

"I must apologise for missing our appointment yesterday," I said once the introductions were completed. "I was detained... by, er, a case I'm reporting on, and I was unable to get a message to you to explain."

"Please don't worry, Miss Green. Your colleagues were very accommodating."

"Mr Fish and Mr Potter? I hope they weren't too irreverent."

"No indeed. They kept me entertained. I must say that I admire you for doing the work of a news reporter. You must be the only lady who works there."

"There is also Miss Welton, the editor's secretary."

"That must help, I suppose." Her hands fidgeted in her lap as she addressed James. "I hope you don't mind me asking, Inspector, but why you are here? Has something bad happened?"

James shifted uncomfortably in his seat. "Before we begin, we need to establish that we are talking about the same lady. You wrote to Miss Green to say that you had recognised the description of Miss Hamilton, I believe."

"Yes, it sounded just like my sister."

From the glance James gave me I could see that he was relieved to hear this, though the slight furrow in his brow suggested that he was concerned that we would now have to tell Miss Davies the unfortunate news.

"The purse with the initials A.D. convinced me," she continued. "Her name is Anna and her maiden name was Davies. What's happened to her?"

"I'm terribly sorry," I ventured. "I don't know how to say this, but—"

"You're going to tell me she's dead, aren't you?"

I gave a nod and felt my throat tighten as I did so.

Miss Davies shifted her gaze across the room as her eyes filled with tears. "I think I somehow knew that she was," she said quietly.

"I'm so terribly sorry," I replied.

There was a pause while Miss Davies dried her eyes with a handkerchief. "Let me make some tea. I could really do with a cup of tea," she said.

"Would you like me to make it?" I asked.

"No, I'd like to do it myself. I'll be fine, thank you," She stood to her feet. "After that you can tell me what happened to her."

Margaret Davies maintained her composure quite admirably as I explained to her the events of that tragic night at the Hotel Tempesta. I had no idea how much she knew about her sister's life, but I felt that it was only fair to explain everything rather than attempt to hide anything to spare her feelings.

"When did you last see your sister?" James asked.

"A long time ago. It must be about two years since the last time we met, and we haven't kept in touch. She was terribly affected by grief for her son. He died about four years ago, you see, and she never came to terms with it. Her husband had also died, and she felt so alone. She told us she wanted to do something different with her life, and after that she moved away. Everything changed, even her name."

"So her birth name was Anna Davies, which would explain the initials on her purse," said James. "What was her family name when she married?"

"O'Riley."

"And her husband died, you say?"

"Yes, shortly before the boy. He had rheumatic fever and the boy... well, sadly he was never well."

"What was his name?"

"Simon. They were both called Simon. I've had this strange feeling for a while that something wasn't quite right with Anna. I think about her every day, you know. I have a photograph of her."

She got up from her seat, then unhooked one of the framed photographs from above the fireplace and handed it to me.

Anna O'Riley had dark, intelligent eyes, a long face and wavy dark hair, which was pinned back behind her ears. Her brow and the corners of her mouth were lifted in a faint smile. She had a pleasant face and I felt an instant warmth toward her.

"That photograph was taken before she was married," said Miss Davies.

"What was she like?" I asked.

"She was three years younger than me, and very clever. Anna was always reading books. She had a restless mind and was never quite content with things to remain the way they were. Oh, and she used to frustrate Ma and Pa with all her questions! There were eight of us: three boys and five girls. Two of my siblings died young, and I'm the only girl who has never married. I'm also the only one still living in Islington. We grew up in a house on Compton Terrace, which is very close by. Anna spoke of marriage when we were young, but she also dreamed of becoming a doctor one day. She had read about the 'Septem contra Edinam', the 'Seven against Edinburgh', at the University of Edinburgh. Do you recall those seven female medical students who fought to qualify as doctors?"

"I certainly do," I replied.

"There was no chance Ma or Pa would ever have allowed her to study medicine, but it remained a dream of hers."

"And then she met her husband, did she?" James asked.

"Yes, Simon O'Riley. Before that she almost got engaged to someone else, but he fell onto a railway track one night and was hit by a train."

"Goodness! He lost his life?" I asked.

She nodded.

"How terribly tragic."

"Soon after that she met Simon O'Riley and married him very quickly. I wasn't convinced at the time that they were a good match, but she claimed to love him, and it wasn't long before little Simon was born. She seemed happy for a time."

"Less restless?"

"A little. Although she used to leave little Simon with Ma now and again, so she could go into town and do things. I couldn't tell you what those things were. She thought again about becoming a doctor and was interested in studying at the School of Medicine for Women, which had been founded by one of the Septem contra Edinam. Only she was married and had a son, and she fully expected to have many more children. She admitted to me that she was envious of men because they could have professions, and I told her that being a lady needn't stop her, though we both agreed that it was much more difficult for women. As I'm saying all this, I'm very aware that I'm speaking to a lady news reporter, Miss Green. I think she would have liked to meet you."

"And, likewise, I would have liked to meet her," I replied.

"It sounds as though she found herself a profession in the end," said James.

Miss Davies sighed. "It seems she did, though not a particularly admirable one."

"It's not what you might think," I said. "It's more complicated than that. We believe she was obtaining secret information for people."

"On whose behalf?"

"We're not sure yet, but we think she was some sort of spy."

"Really?" She gave a slight smile. "I can imagine she would have enjoyed being a spy. I expect she was quite convincing at it, too."

"She was! She pretended to be a..." I struggled to think of a word that wouldn't offend Miss Davies. "A courtesan. We think she was spying on Mr Gallo, and we feel sure that it had something to do with him buying forged paintings. We're still trying to find out more, but she was extremely secretive about the details of her private life."

"She would have needed to be. Was that why someone killed her? Because of her spying work?"

"We believe so," said James.

"She must have put herself at risk." Miss Davies shook her head sadly. "I suppose she only had herself to think about with her husband and son gone. Perhaps she wasn't so worried about the risks she was taking. I can imagine her being like that. She most likely put all her efforts into obtaining the information she needed. She would have been a good spy; I feel sure of that. Oh, I wish I had known all this while she was alive..." She paused to wipe her eyes. "I would have loved to have spoken to her about it all. She kept everything secret, you say?"

"She must have done, as it has proven difficult to find out anything about her," I said. "We're extremely grateful that you contacted us, otherwise we still wouldn't know her true identity."

"We have come across a message we believe your sister wrote," said James. "Can you tell me if you recognise this handwriting?" He opened his notebook, removed the folded scrap of paper with the coded message on it and passed it to Miss Davies. She stared at it with a puzzled glance.

"It looks like her handwriting," she said. "But it makes no sense!"

"It's written in code. Do you think Anna might have written this?"

"Was this part of her spying work?"

"We think so."

"I had no idea she was doing something like this. How did she learn to write in code?" She shook her head. "There was so much I didn't know about her."

"Is the handwriting familiar?" prompted James.

"Yes, I'm quite sure that Anna wrote this." She passed the message back to James. "I have a few letters she sent me some time ago. I can fetch them to compare the handwriting if you wish."

"That would be extremely useful, thank you. Do you happen to know where your sister was living before her death?"

"I've no idea, I'm afraid." She sighed. "I feel as though I don't really know the lady she became. And I suppose there are practicalities to take care of now: the funeral and such-like. It's fortunate that Ma and Pa are both dead, as I don't know how I ever could have explained this to them—"

Her words were cut off by a choke and she dabbed at her eyes once again.

CHAPTER 40

"Another one, young Blakely?" asked Mr Hobhouse. "What do we have here, then?" He held his magnifying glass over the message we had found in the *Morning Express.*

"Is it the Vigenère cypher again?" James asked.

"I can't tell from taking such a quick glance. It could be anything!"

"Miss Green and I tried to decypher it, but we were working with limited lighting. We were trapped in a dark basement, in fact."

"In a basement? With this sweet young lady?" Mr Hobhouse looked me up and down, then tutted. "You're as bad as your father! I don't know how you attempted to decypher this if you couldn't even be certain that it is Vigenère."

"The lady who was in possession of the previous message also had this edition of the newspaper with her," I said. "We believe the message you decyphered was likely to have been her response to this coded message recorded in the newspaper."

"Ah, I see. So there is some rationale to this, after all. But you don't know what the keyword is, do you?"

"We thought it might be nemesis again, but we haven't been able to solve it using that word," said James.

"Not as easy as it first seems, is it? I'll take a look at it for you, Blakely."

"Thank you, Mr Hobhouse."

* * *

"A lady came to visit you yesterday, Miss Green," said Edgar Fish, "but you didn't turn up!"

"Thank you, Edgar. Inspector Blakely and I have just visited her."

"So where were you?"

"Locked in the basement of the Hotel Tempesta."

"How unfortunate! How did that come about?"

"It was a malicious act carried out by someone who was trying to protect herself from falling under suspicion," said James.

Edgar laughed. "Locking an inspector of the Yard in the basement isn't going to help, is it? Have you arrested her?"

"We shall be addressing the matter in due course," replied James, "but for the time being we have something rather more pressing to work on, and I'm hoping Miss Welton will be able to help us."

"Miss Welton is always able to help," said Edgar. "I can't say that she does it with much of a smile on her face, but she helps all the same."

Miss Welton's dark dress was buttoned up to the neck and her grey hair was pinned neatly on top of her head. She peered at us over a pair of pince-nez.

"Good afternoon, Miss Welton. We're looking for the person who came in and placed this notice in the personal advertisements section," I said, showing her the coded message in our copy of the newspaper.

"Oh yes. One of those messages young lovers always seem to be placing."

"We don't believe it was a young lover on this occasion," said James.

"Do you know what the message means?" she asked.

"Not yet," replied James. "But we've already come across something similar."

"I suppose it could be one of those common declarations of love," I said. "We don't know for sure at the moment."

"No, but we need to find out," added James.

"All the young lovers are doing it these days," said Miss Welton, "and I've heard that some people are making a hobby out of deciphering them. I'd say that there is little point if one's efforts are only likely to yield a silly message about matters of the heart."

"You don't have much time for such messages, Miss Welton?" asked James.

"I suppose I must have once, back when I was young myself. But then I was just as silly as everyone else at that age."

"I don't believe it," said James with a smile.

"Are you sure you cannot recall the person who placed this notice?" I asked.

"I can't recall the individual, no, but I keep detailed records. Most of these notices are sent in the post these days; only a few people present them in person. I keep the original message and the record of payment for six months. What is the date of this edition? The eighth of November... Ah, you're in luck, then."

"Wonderful!" I said.

I grinned at James as Miss Welton got up from her chair and walked over to a cabinet of drawers. She opened one, took out an envelope and returned to her desk with it.

"Here are all the notices placed on the eighth of November," she announced, carefully emptying the notes out onto her desk. Each message had a slip of paper attached to it with a piece of thread.

"Do you record the name and address of each person who places a notice?" asked James.

"Yes, we do," said Miss Welton.

"Perfect!" I said, my heart skipping excitedly as she looked through the messages. "Who sent it?" I asked.

"Patience, Miss Green," she replied. "Ah yes, here we are."

She handed me a note, and I was delighted to see the handwritten cypher on it. My fingers fumbled with the attached slip of paper, desperate to see who had placed it.

"Cooke," I said. "Craig's Court."

"Cooke?" said James. He laughed.

"Have you heard of him?" I asked.

"Let me take a look at it," he said.

I handed him the note, along with the attached slip of paper.

"If this is the chap I think it is," said James, "he recently left Scotland Yard to set up what he calls a 'confidential inquiry office'. Do you know where Craig's Court is?"

"No," I replied.

"Directly behind Scotland Yard!"

I looked at the note in his hand, its letters jumbled just as they had been in the notice published in the newspaper.

"Does that mean that Anna O'Riley was working for him?" I asked.

"There's only one way to find out, and that's to ask him directly," said James. "However, I should like to wait until Mr Hobhouse has decyphered the code before we do so."

"Must we wait?"

"I know you're impatient to get to the bottom of this, Penny, but I would prefer to speak to this Cooke fellow once we have discovered what his message says. Cooke may have placed many other messages in your newspaper. Would you mind if I arranged for some officers to search through your records, Miss Welton?"

She sighed. "Of course I mind. They'll be a major disruption to my work. But I don't expect I'll have much say in the matter, will I? You'd better ask Mr Sherman."

CHAPTER 41

As I worked on the book about my father that evening, I decided to re-read the last letter he had written. The final paragraph described his imminent plans:

'Tomorrow I plan to ride twenty miles south-west of Bogota to the Falls of Tequendama. I have heard a great deal about the orchids and tropical birds there, and am looking forward to the spectacle of the River Funza plunging from a height of five hundred feet. It must be a tremendous sight to behold!'

It was incredible to think that Francis Edwards was now searching in the very same location. It was only three months since he had left for his adventure, but I felt sure that he must have stumbled upon some news about my father by this point. I desperately wished to hear more from Francis, but when I looked again at his latest letter I realised I had only received it ten days previously. I took a deep breath and reminded myself to be patient.

Tiger climbed onto my lap and I let her rest there, concluding that I was too tired to do any further work that evening.

Hurried footsteps on the staircase made me jump.

I moved Tiger onto my bed and reached the door just as three sharp raps were planted on it. My sister almost fell into the room the moment I opened it. Her eyes were red and she held a newspaper in her hand.

"Ellie!" I cried. "What has happened?"

"Have you seen this?" She waved it at me and tried to suppress a sob.

"No, what is it? Come and sit down!" I guided her over to the chair beside my writing desk. "Is that *The Holborn Gazette* you have there? What on earth are you reading that nonsense for?"

She fumbled through the paper before thrusting an open page at me.

"What am I supposed to be looking at?" I asked.

"There!"

Her finger jabbed at the comment section, and I began to read the relevant piece of text:

Readers may recall that just last week a news reporter for the Morning Express, *Miss Penelope Green, caused a breach of promise action to take place against an inspector of Scotland Yard, Inspector James Blakely.*

News this week has cemented the reputation of the Green sisters as saboteurs of matrimony. Miss Green's sister, Mrs. Eliza Billington-Grieg, has long been married to a lawyer in the City, Mr. George Billington-Grieg. The latter is no doubt ruing the day he allowed his wife to establish the West London Women's Society, *an association that champions causes such as women's suffrage, rational dress and the abolition of the opium trade.*

I felt my teeth clench in anger as I read on.

Mrs. Billington-Grieg's strong opinions have led to the decision to divorce her husband, an action she has almost certainly been encouraged to take by her sister, Miss Green. There is no doubt that the two daughters of esteemed plant-hunter Frederick Brinsley Green have done for matrimony what the steam train did for the stage coach.

Counsel for Mrs Billington-Grieg has cited her motivation for pursuing a divorce as 'unreasonable behaviour' on the part of Mr. Billington-Grieg. In our view, there is no behaviour that could be considered more unreasonable than the rational dress movement.

"Oh, ignore it!" I cried, scrunching up the newspaper and throwing it onto the floor. "It's Tom Clifford again, and he doesn't know you at all, so he cannot possibly comment. He has only done this because you're my sister, Ellie, and I'm truly sorry for it."

"Just think of all the people who must have read it!"

"Most of them will already have forgotten about it. It's not even news!"

"But what about the people who know me?"

"Do any of them read *The Holborn Gazette*?"

"I don't know."

"If they've read it they may mention it to you, and then you can tell them it's nothing more than a vindictive article aimed at your sister rather than at you. There was clearly a gap to fill in today's edition. You read what Clifford wrote about me last week. The unfortunate little man obviously has nothing else to think about."

"It's so unfair," said Eliza, drying her eyes with her handkerchief.

"You didn't deserve it, Ellie. Notice how he makes no mention of George's criminal activity; the very reason you cited unreasonable behaviour as your motivation for divorce. George's behaviour hasn't been called into question at all! This article has been written by a man who is evidently frightened of women who exercise a modicum of independence. With any luck his own wife will request a divorce from him in the near future!"

"And then you can write something awful about him!"

"I could, but why sink to such depths, Ellie? It's better to simply ignore it. If he knows we're upset by it he'll feel victorious, won't he?"

"Yes, he will. You're quite right, Penelope. We should pretend this silly article didn't bother us in the slightest."

"How did you even know he'd written it? You don't usually read *The Holborn Gazette,* do you?"

"Absolutely not! It was brought to my attention by my employer, Miss Barrington."

"Well, tell her not to read such a worthless newspaper in future!"

Eliza gave a laugh. "I shall do!"

"Now, let's burn it on the fire," I said, retrieving the screwed-up newspaper from the floor and throwing it into the little hearth. I watched with satisfaction as the flames leapt up and devoured Tom Clifford's words.

"Oh, what a silly mess," said my sister. "All I'm trying to do is begin a new chapter in my life. Why is it so difficult?"

"Because that's just how it is sometimes," I said. "But you have family and friends who love and support you. Please remember that."

"Thank you, Penelope. Sometimes you really sound quite wise."

"*Sometimes* is better than never, I suppose."

"I need some news that will cheer me up. Have you heard anything from Francis recently?"

"As it happens, I was just looking at his latest letter."

"When did we last hear from him?"

"About ten days ago."

"Oh, I thought it was much longer ago than that. I suppose we shouldn't expect anything more for a while yet."

"Do you remember him mentioning a telegraph office in western Colombia?" I said. "Hopefully he'll travel in that direction and send us something new from there. It would be quite exciting to receive an immediate message from him rather than having to wait for a whole month! I just hope he has something to tell us soon, but I suppose I'm being impatient as usual.

"I struggle terribly with my patience levels. I already cannot wait for tomorrow to arrive, as I'm hoping we'll find out more about a mysterious message James and I are trying to decypher."

"Which message?"

I gave Eliza an update on the case concerning Mr Gallo and Anna O'Riley, and explained how desperately I hoped to find out more about Mr Cooke and the message he had written.

"You were locked in a basement for eight hours?"

"Fortunately, James was with me."

"Without a chaperone?"

I felt a sudden warmth in my face. "If you must know, we passed the time trying to solve a coded message."

"While locked in a basement together?"

"James is a gentleman, so he did nothing to take advantage of the situation," I said. "And he was also extremely comforting. He helped calm me when I became fretful about being locked up in the dark."

"I would have completely lost my mind," said Eliza. "I think I would have screamed the place down!"

"So would I, had James not been there with me."

"When will he propose marriage, do you think?"

"Neither of us have even considered it, Ellie! The breach of promise case was only last week, and we have both been extremely busy working on this murder case."

Eliza laughed.

"What's so amusing?" I asked.

"If you did marry, I wonder what the conversation would be like beside the fireplace in the evenings. Neither of you would ever stop talking about your work!"

I smiled. "No, I don't suppose we would."

"Hopefully that means you are well suited and will be very happy together."

CHAPTER 42

"Good heavens! What's happened?" asked Edgar the following morning. "The *Morning Express* offices have been raided by the police! What have you been up to, Potter?"

Four police constables sat in the newsroom with us, looking through the many envelopes contained in the stack of drawers taken from Miss Welton's office.

"We're looking for coded messages," I explained. "We need to locate all of them."

"Would you like me to help?" asked Edgar.

"That's very thoughtful of you, Fish," said Mr Sherman, "but only when you've submitted your article on the rowdy behaviour at the recent Covent Garden Promenade Concert."

"I need Miss Welton to typewrite it for me, sir, but she's busy with the police."

"How about you have a go yourself?"

"I would sir, but I'd be unlikely to get it finished before Christmas. Perhaps Miss Green could—"

"I'm just about to leave," I said. "I need to speak with a private detective in Whitehall about the Gallo case."

"You've been spending rather too long on that case, Miss Green," said Mr Sherman. "I'm concerned that it's taking up the majority of your time."

"Not at all, sir. I've been meeting the deadlines on all my other work."

"I realise that, but you are employed as a news reporter, Miss Green, and I fear that you're doing more than straight-forward news reporting."

"What do you mean, sir?"

"I wonder whether you fancy yourself as a detective."

"I think I do a little," I said with a smile, "but reporting requires a certain degree of investigation."

"It does indeed. You need to be aware of where the roles of detective and reporter begin and end, however."

"I am aware, sir, but this case is extremely relevant to me, not only because I was at the hotel when the crime took place, but also because the private detective we're interested in chose to place his messages in our newspaper."

"Yes, yes, I know all that," said Mr Sherman. "But I don't want this taking up too much of your time, especially when your acquaintance with Inspector Blakely is clearly blossoming."

One of the constables glanced up with interest and I felt a flush of embarrassment.

"I can assure you, sir, that I both value and respect my profession, and will continue to apply myself as best I can to my work at the *Morning Express*."

"That is reassuring to hear, Miss Green," replied my editor with a nod. "But do have a think on what I've said, won't you?"

"Why didn't Mr Cooke use a false name and address when he

placed his notice in the newspaper?" I asked James as we met under dark grey skies outside Mr Hobhouse's office.

"Perhaps he thought his messages would go undetected. He must have assumed that nobody's attention would be drawn to a line or two of jumbled text in the notices column."

"It was certainly difficult to find. It will be interesting to discover whether Miss Hamilton placed any messages in the newspaper. I suppose the constables working in the office today will find out."

"Mrs O'Riley, you mean?"

"Oh yes, of course. It's difficult to accustom myself to calling her by that name."

"I was up working on it most of the night," said Mr Hobhouse, "but I think I've managed to solve it for you."

"Thank you!" said James. "What does it say?"

Mr Hobhouse handed us the piece of paper.

Nemesis: American received new delivery. Find out what he has. RDV Thursday Charing X, platform three, eleven am.

"Does it make any sense to you, young Blakely?"

"It makes a lot of sense. I cannot thank you enough, Mr Hobhouse. What was the keyword?"

"Hypnos. The Greek god of sleep. When you told me the message was likely to be linked with the previous one I made an assumption that the keyword could be a Greek god or goddess. Fortunately I was correct, which meant that I was able to solve it a little more quickly than on the previous occasion."

"This is perfect. Thank you again, Mr Hobhouse," said

James. "Now we can go and ask Mr Cooke what this is all about."

"Who might he be?"

"We believe him to be the sender of the message," I said.

"Is that so? Then why didn't you simply ask him what it said?"

"We wanted to be well informed beforehand."

"I see."

"We may have a few other messages that will need to be decyphered," said James. "I have some men looking for them as we speak."

Mr Hobhouse frowned. "I haven't a huge amount of time on my hands, and I'm not getting any younger, you know."

"I'm sure Scotland Yard will reimburse you—"

"I won't hear of it!" Mr Hobhouse held up a hand. "I refuse to accept any form of payment. I'm doing this because you're Roger's boy."

"Well, thank you, Mr Hobhouse. If the other messages have been written by Mr Cooke, he may have used the same keyword each time. That would make the work a little quicker, would it not?"

"Possibly. But you should never be too hopeful, Blakely. Just let me know what else you find."

"So Mrs O'Riley was known as Nemesis and Mr Cooke called himself Hypnos," I said as we walked up from Westminster toward Whitehall.

"It's possible, isn't it? I'm making the assumption that the message was an instruction from Cooke for her to investigate the paintings Mr Gallo had just bought. And then it requested a meeting with him at Charing Cross station on Thursday, which Miss Hamilton sadly never made."

"What does RDV mean?"

"Rendezvous, perhaps?"

"Oh yes, of course," I said. "Presumably Mr Cooke would have been waiting for her on platform three at eleven o'clock on the Thursday after she died. I don't suppose he realised what had happened to her, given that only Mr Gallo's death was reported in the newspapers."

"Let's go and discuss the matter with Mr Cooke, and hopefully we can get to the bottom of it. Is that snow?" James held out a gloved hand and a tiny snowflake landed on his palm.

I had walked past Craig's Court a number of times without realising it was there. The narrow alleyway led from the main thoroughfare of Whitehall and opened out into a dingy little courtyard. Mr Cooke's small yet immaculate office was on the third floor of a red-brick building.

"Inspector Blakely, isn't it? Yes I recall you joining Scotland Yard a few years ago."

Mr Cooke was a broad, square-faced man with narrow eyes, thick grey whiskers and a crooked nose, which looked as though it had been broken at some point in the past.

James introduced me. "And now you have a confidential inquiry office, Mr Cooke," he added. "Is business booming?"

"It is indeed." He gestured for us both to sit. "And I hope to keep a few people from having to bother the Yard."

"For a fee, of course."

"Yes, for a fee. I can't do it all out of charity, can I?" He rested his thick-fingered hands on his desk. "Why have you brought a news reporter with you?"

"Miss Green has worked with me on a number of cases. Don't worry, she can be trusted. She was staying at the Hotel Tempesta on the night of the recent murders. You've heard about the murder of Mr Gallo, I presume?"

"I have indeed. Has there been any progress in the case?"

"Some, though our work would be far easier to carry out if people came forward with any information at the first possible opportunity."

"Isn't that always the way?"

"You're familiar with the difficulty, I'm sure. Did you not feel prompted to contact the Yard yourself when you learned of Mr Gallo's death?"

"Why should I have?"

"Because you knew the identity of the lady who had been murdered alongside him."

"What are you talking about, Blakely?"

"I'm talking about Nemesis."

Mr Cooke gave a sniff and sat back in his chair. "What on earth do you mean?"

"You know full well what I mean. She was Nemesis and you are Hypnos, and if you deny it you will only be embarrassed by the further proof I have of your involvement."

Mr Cooke shook his head. "Inspector Blakely, I'd like to help if I could, but I am bound by client confidentiality."

"Even when failing to come forward delayed the identification of a lady whose body lay unclaimed in the mortuary for two weeks?"

Mr Cooke said nothing.

James sighed and pulled the message Mr Cooke had placed in the *Morning Express* out of his notebook. He laid it on the desk.

"We know what you've been doing, Mr Cooke. You employed a lady who called herself Miss Hamilton to find out about the forged paintings Mr Gallo bought. On the night of Tuesday the eleventh of November she managed to write down the names of those paintings. And she did so after you had placed this message, written in a cypher, in the *Morning Express*. You had asked her to meet you at Charing Cross station the following Thursday morning, but unfortunately she was unable to keep the appointment because she had been brutally murdered that night."

"I didn't know she was with Gallo that night."

"But you did know Miss Hamilton."

"She was a colleague."

"And you asked her to find out which paintings Gallo had bought. Your message states that '*The American received a new delivery*'."

"I will admit that much."

"Then you admit that you placed this message in the paper?"

"It has my name and address attached, so I can hardly deny it, can I? When I heard about his death I had no idea that she had died alongside him. It wasn't reported anywhere."

"That information was withheld to save the deceased man's reputation and protect his family. Presumably you grew increasingly concerned for Miss Hamilton's well-being when she failed to keep the appointment at Charing Cross station."

"I guessed that something had happened, but I couldn't have imagined what. I had no idea the woman was dead."

"What else do you know about her?"

"I know her name – Miss Clara Hamilton – and that is all."

"When did you first meet her?"

"I only met her once."

"Did you learn anything at all about her?"

"Only that she had been doing this sort of work for a year or two."

"What sort of work?"

"Investigative work."

"Was she a spy?"

"You could call her that, I suppose. She obtained information for people, and being a woman she was able to use her feminine charms to do so. That's an indispensable skill that a chap hasn't a chance in hell of acquiring."

"And how did you come to be introduced to her?"

"The introduction came from another member of my team."

"Who might that be?"

"I'm sorry, but it would be impossible for me to disclose that information."

"Even to a former colleague?"

"I cannot possibly identify the people who work for me. It would place them in great danger."

"You don't have to give me a name. You could simply arrange a meeting between me and this mysterious colleague."

"That would be quite impossible."

"It is *not* impossible!" James slammed his hand down on the desk. "We need to discover more about Miss Hamilton, as in doing so we will learn more about her killer. For a long time we believed we were searching for the killer of Mr Gallo, but I'm beginning to think that Miss Hamilton was the intended victim that night. Tell me who else was acquainted with her!"

Mr Cooke leaned forward and cracked his knuckles before resting his fists on his desk. "It's not that straightforward, Blakely. You're an intelligent man, and you must fully appreciate the sensitivities involved in my line of work. Let me speak to a few people. I want to help, really I do. And I am desperately saddened by the news of her death. I just need some time—"

"Whom are you working for?" James demanded. "And who wanted to know about the paintings Mr Gallo bought?"

"You know that I can't answer those questions."

"You do realise you can be subpoenaed if needs be? We shall obtain this information from you one way or another."

"I'm sure that it won't come to that." Cooke's manner appeared calm but there was an angry glint in his eyes. "Neither of us wishes to take this to court, do we, Blakely? Just give me a chance to speak to my connections. You have my word that I will help you in whatever way I can."

"How long will that take?"

"Give me two days."

CHAPTER 43

"Everything was going rather well until the pair of you turned up at the Hotel Tempesta and upset Mrs Mirabeau," said Chief Inspector Fenton. "Now she's refusing to speak to any of us, and we have to put up with that dreadful solicitor of hers, Mr Tennant."

"Arrest her, then," said James. "You do know she has been burning evidence in the basement, don't you?"

"How do you know that it's evidence she has been burning? It could have been anything."

"If it was nothing suspicious she would have thrown it straight into the fire in her office," said James, "but she evidently didn't want anyone to see what she was doing. And now we have no idea what has been lost."

"My men removed all the relevant papers from the hotel some time ago," said the chief inspector.

"How could they have decided so early on what was relevant and what wasn't?" retorted James. "All of it must be considered relevant until we have an idea of what has really happened!"

"Arguing about this won't get us anywhere, Blakely. The

fact of the matter remains that Mrs Mirabeau has become most uncooperative."

"She wasn't your main suspect in any case, was she?"

"No. We've had Mr Goldman in custody for a few days now."

"And what might his motive have been?"

"He has a keen interest in art. I believe he wanted to take possession of the paintings we discovered in Mr Gallo's room."

"Then why didn't he take them?"

"Because his plan went wrong. He hadn't expected Gallo to escape. By the time he had finally committed the dreadful deed he was terrified someone would discover Mr Gallo at the foot of the stairs, so he ran back to his room and hid for a while before disposing of the coat, gloves and knife."

"What is Goldman's history? Is there any evidence that he has stolen artworks before?"

"Not that we know of."

"Is there any connection between him and the master criminal Jack Shelby? Or Rigby Pleydell-Bouverie, as he calls himself?"

"None."

"Has he shown any previous propensity for violence?"

"We are still conducting our enquiries, Blakely. You're beginning to sound like the chap's defence counsel."

"And you do not think that Mrs Mirabeau's conduct is at all suspicious? Despite the fact that she has been burning evidence and has hired a solicitor?"

"I have been keeping a close eye on her, but thanks to you my work has become rather more difficult."

"I'm beginning to think that Miss Hamilton was the murderer's intended target," said James. "She was carrying out some investigative work for a private detective named Mr

Cooke. Do you recall Chief Inspector Cooke of Scotland Yard?"

"I do, as a matter of fact. He hired Miss Hamilton, did he?"

"Mrs O'Riley was her real name. She was a widow, and she decided to pursue this line of work following the death of her husband and son."

"So she was more than just a fallen woman?"

"Much more. She had several colleagues, who I'm hoping will be able to tell me more about her. I'm waiting on Cooke to arrange an introduction with them."

"So your theory, then, is that one of the guests murdered Miss Hamilton, or whatever her real name was, that night because she was a spy?"

"Yes."

"And Gallo?"

"He was a witness to the murder. Perhaps Mr Goldman wished to put a stop to Mrs O'Riley's work."

Inspector Fenton leaned back in his chair to consider this. "Well, it's possible I suppose, but we would need to understand why."

"Of course. I shall let you know of anything else we learn about her."

"I see you are still accompanied by the ink-slinger."

"I must ask you not to speak about Miss Green in derogatory terms," snapped James. "She has been closely involved in this case from the beginning, and continues to be of great assistance to me."

I tried to ignore Chief Inspector Fenton's sceptical expression.

"You seem to have a close acquaintance with Mr Blackstone of *The Times*," I ventured. "I cannot see how that is any different."

Chief Inspector Fenton gave a loud, unpleasant laugh.

"But it's completely different! And besides, I should be worried indeed if my acquaintance with Mr Blackstone bore any resemblance to the relationship between you and Blakely." He shook his head incredulously. "What a ridiculous thing to say."

"Perhaps the comparison between myself and Mr Blackstone wasn't so wise after all," I said quietly as we left Bow Street station.

"It was amusing to witness his reaction, though. He'll be out of sorts for some time now." James laughed. "The shoeshine boy, Kit, visited me first thing this morning. Apparently, Mrs Mirabeau has been coming and going from the hotel, often in the company of a man. I assume the man is her glum solicitor, Mr Tennant. Kit also followed her to Mayfair on Tuesday, but it seems she was undertaking little more than a shopping expedition on that occasion."

"It sounds like he has been doing good work."

"Yes, he has. He's a good lad. I've paid him a little more and asked him to keep at it. I was also told this morning that Inspector Raynes has an update for me. Shall we walk down to the Yard and find out what it is? Perhaps he has news on Shelby."

"I have good news and bad news," said Inspector Raynes in his familiar nasal tone. "We've arrested one of Jack Shelby's associates, and he seems willing to talk in exchange for leniency. He claims to have evidence that Shelby forged paintings in America, which means that Shelby can be arrested and extradited to his home country."

"That is good news indeed," said James. "And the bad news?"

"Shelby has escaped to Paris."

"Oh dear! So there is still no knowing whether he had anything to do with the forged paintings that were sold to Mr Gallo?"

"Not yet. The Pinkerton chap, Mr Russell, has followed him there."

"He may have an interesting tour of Europe on his hands!" said James. "Perhaps you can encourage this associate to tell you everything he knows of Shelby's dealings with Gallo. After all, Shelby was seen visiting the Hotel Tempesta."

"We'll keep working on it, and I shall let you know how we get on."

"Thank you, Raynes. It's interesting to hear that Shelby fled just after Fenton arrested Mr Goldman. Perhaps Shelby is concerned that Goldman will incriminate him."

"It certainly is a coincidence," I said. "Mr Russell seemed to think that Shelby would be staying in London for a while longer yet."

"There is also some other complicated news," said Inspector Raynes.

"What do you mean by that?" James asked.

"I visited the Hotel Tempesta to take possession of the forged paintings and they have mysteriously vanished."

"When was this?"

"Yesterday."

James muttered a curse under his breath. "Did no one think to recover the paintings from the hotel before then?"

"Apparently not."

"Well, I'll tell you where they are, Raynes. They're in a pile of ashes down in the basement."

"Ah."

"Yes, that must have been what Mrs Mirabeau was burning. Those paintings must incriminate someone, and she has removed the evidence. Oh, how I wish I had picked them up and taken them with me! You'll need to speak to Fenton down at Bow Street about this."

"I shall do so."

"Immediately!"

"Good idea."

James gave a sigh as Inspector Raynes left the room. "I cannot help but think that the guilty parties are a step ahead of us all the time. Do you have that same feeling?"

"It certainly feels as though there is a lot to keep up with," I replied.

"I have some good news, at least," he said. "I've been meaning to show you these." He scooped a large envelope up from his desk. "In here are the twenty-seven coded messages Mr Cooke has placed in your newspaper over the past six months. I shall take them down to Mr Hobhouse now."

"He won't thank you for bringing him twenty-seven messages!" I laughed.

"I'll buy him a bottle of whiskey on the way. How would you like to meet me at East India Dock tomorrow?"

"The dockyard? Why?"

"Mr Cooke sent a telegram to say that someone would meet us there."

❧

Tiger didn't seem her usual self when I returned to my room that evening. She was hiding under the bed; a move she usually reserved for times when someone she disliked had visited.

"What's the matter, puss?" I tried to coax her out, but she wouldn't come.

I hung my coat on the back of my door and looked around the room. It was only then that I noticed a few items were out of place. Francis' latest letter was on the floor next to my writing desk. I would have assumed that Tiger had knocked it off if several other things hadn't also been out of place. My father's diaries were not in the order in which I had left them, and a drawer in my writing desk had been left slightly open, as if someone had hurriedly looked inside it. Something didn't feel quite right.

"Mrs Garnett!" I called as I dashed down the stairs. "Mrs Garnett!"

"Oh my goodness, whatever has happened? Has there been another murder?" She scurried into the hallway, her dark eyes wide with concern.

"Have you been inside my room?" I asked breathlessly.

"No! I never go inside your room when you're not here. Well, only sometimes, to check that everything is in order. But rarely, and certainly not today. Are you talking about today?"

"Yes. Tiger is hiding under my bed and someone has looked through my writing desk. Perhaps other things have been moved as well, I don't know. I haven't checked everything thoroughly yet."

Her mouth hung open. "Has anything been taken?"

"Not that I've noticed. I don't really have anything worth taking."

"And you're sure that someone has been in there?"

"Yes!"

"But when?"

"Between the time when I left for work this morning and the time I returned here, which was about six o'clock. Have you been at home all day? Did you see anyone loitering about?"

"Let me think now." She stared at the hallway floor as she recalled her movements from earlier in the day. "I went out at ten o'clock to the market in Whitecross Street, and then I dropped in on Mrs Wilkinson. She's not been good recently with her cough."

"I'm sorry to hear it. What time did you return?"

"About a quarter after one o'clock. Do you think someone entered the house while I was out?" Her eyes widened further.

"We'll have to ask the other tenants," I said. "But are you quite sure that you didn't see or hear anyone who shouldn't have been here?"

"Quite sure! Do you think I would allow such a person to go wandering around unchallenged? And besides, no one could have come through the front door without a key!"

CHAPTER 44

"Someone broke into my room yesterday," I told James the following day. "They didn't take anything, but they had moved a few things around. Poor Tiger was terrified."

"How did they get in?"

"We don't know. My door was locked, and so was the front door. I'm wondering whether the intruder somehow clambered up onto the roof and got in through the window."

"Really?"

"It's quite easy to slide the window open from the outside."

"You should have a lock on it. You can't have people climbing into your room, Penny!"

"Mrs Garnett has asked a man to come and do just that. I cannot understand it, though. What do you think they were looking for?"

"I've no idea. Perhaps it was someone who wished to frighten you."

"Well, they've succeeded in doing that all right."

A cold wind blew across the West India Dock to where

James and I stood on a swing bridge over a lock. Small flakes of snow carried on the breeze, and gulls wheeled and cawed above the warehouses and cranes. Little rowboats paddled among sail ships and steam barges, and the quayside was busy with the transporting of sacks and crates. Beyond the warehouses we could hear the rumble and whistle of trains carrying goods to the depots in central London.

"You must be careful," said James, shaking his head. "I really don't like the thought of someone getting inside your room."

"Whom are we meeting?" I asked.

"I have no idea." He gripped his bowler hat to prevent it blowing off into the water.

Despite wearing a pair of warm winter gloves, the tips of my fingers already felt cold.

"So do we simply stand here and wait?" I probed.

"What else can we do?"

A group of dark-skinned sailors walked past us, conversing in a foreign language. I guessed they were on their way to a public house I had seen beside West India Dock train station.

"Do you think our meeting might be with a sailor?" I asked with a laugh.

"Anything's possible, isn't it? I can't help thinking that you should move to new lodgings, Penny. I don't like the idea of you being at risk."

"I couldn't possibly move! It's my home!"

"A home someone can get inside without detection. It is extremely worrying."

"I shall be fine once the window lock has been fitted."

"It may not be enough."

"What do you mean, not enough? You're frightening me, James."

"Inspector Blakely?" a female voice called out from behind us.

We spun around to see a lady of about fifty with sharp, lined features and grey eyes that had a diamond-like sparkle to them. She was dressed in a long, dark overcoat and wore a simple black felt hat.

"Let's keep moving," she said, walking past us and heading toward a bridge over another lock.

"Can I first establish that you are acquainted with Mr Cooke?" asked James, quickening his step to catch up with her.

I followed closely behind.

"I am."

"May I ask your name?"

"You can call me Mrs Adams for the purposes of this meeting."

James gave me a bemused glance as we strode between two tall warehouses.

"Did you know the deceased lady as Miss Hamilton or Mrs O'Riley?" I asked.

"You're a reporter, aren't you?" She stopped and gave me a direct stare.

I felt as though I were standing before a strict school teacher. "Yes. I work for the *Morning Express* newspaper."

She offered no reaction but continued to stride ahead. "I knew her by both names."

"When did you first meet her?" asked James.

"Early last year."

"Where?"

"At Le Croquembouche restaurant."

"We know it well," said James. "I believe Mr Gallo enjoyed dining there. Did she meet him there, too?"

"I believe so."

"She dined there a lot, did she?"

"No." Mrs Adams stopped and glared at James this time. "She *worked* there." And off she marched again.

We were walking briskly along the quayside, dodging the oncoming men, horses, carts and trolleys.

"She was popular with the clientele there," Mrs Adams continued, "including the politician Mr William Macmillan. He was someone we were interested in."

"Who might *we* be?" asked James.

"I'll keep my responses relevant, Inspector. There is no need for me to give away superfluous information."

"But it might be relevant."

"It won't be."

"So Mr Macmillan was of particular interest to you."

"Yes, he was, and when I saw how well he had taken to Mrs O'Riley she also became interesting to me. She was already calling herself Clara Hamilton by then. After engaging her in conversation I found her to be an erudite lady, capable of far more than basic waitressing work. I learned of her sad past and deduced that she was a lady of ambition. She told me she enjoyed conversing with the learned gentlemen at Le Croquembouche because they were interesting men of high standing. During another visit I asked Clara whether she thought she might be able to encourage someone to talk. Her rapport with Mr Macmillan presented the perfect opportunity."

"And she agreed?"

"Yes, she did. The prospect of doing this sort of work excited her immensely, and she excelled at it. We were able to obtain all the information we needed."

"Did you meet with her often?"

"As little as possible, for obvious reasons. I only met her on three occasions after she began working alongside me."

"What did you know about her?"

"She told me about her husband and son. She liked to keep herself busy in order to avoid dwelling on what she had lost. She liked to socialise and had an enquiring mind. She was perfect for the job."

"And when did you learn of her death?" James asked.

"Mr Cooke told me she hadn't arrived for their meeting. I had heard about Mr Gallo's death by that point, and I suspected then that something had happened to her. Mr Cooke confirmed it to me after you had spoken with him. It was devastating news."

"We assume the killer didn't want her telling anyone about the forged paintings Mr Gallo had bought."

"What have you learned about the people he bought them from?" she asked.

"There is a possibility that an American criminal by the name of Jack Shelby was involved."

"How interesting. We had hoped that Clara's relationship with Gallo would yield some useful evidence. We had known for some time that he was acquiring forged paintings but we couldn't discover where he was obtaining them from. Clara was perfect for the job, Gallo was extremely fond of her. We all were."

"Why do you think Mr Gallo bought paintings that he suspected were stolen?" I asked.

"Some people are so intent on collecting these paintings that they care very little about how they come by them. Mr Gallo was one such man, and I believe that he once bought a stolen painting for his hotel in New York. It was spotted hanging on a wall in one of the lounges. He claimed he hadn't realised it was stolen, but I strongly doubt that. The sale must have been discreet, and he must have purchased it at a low price; much lower than it would have fetched through a legitimate sale at an auction house. The forgeries he bought would have been spotted sooner or later, but I suppose he didn't give much thought to that. Mr Gallo was rather a spontaneous man. He often acted first and thought about the consequences later."

"Mr Cooke is a former colleague of mine," said James. "How did you come to meet him?"

"That's irrelevant to your investigation, Inspector, and it's time for me to go. Was there anything else?"

"Do you know where Mrs O'Riley lived? We have spoken to her sister, who has sadly had no contact with her for the past two years. If we can locate Mrs O'Riley's home, her sister will be able to deal with any personal effects."

Mrs Adams gave a solemn nod. "She rented rooms on Westmoreland Place. Number seven."

"Where is that?"

"In Pimlico."

I watched James as he took out his pencil and notebook to make a note of this.

"Thank you for your help, Mrs Adams. Would you mind...?" His voice trailed off as he looked up. "Where did she go?"

We both glanced up and down the busy quayside, but she was nowhere to be seen. Around us, the bustling work of the dockyard continued, and a man shouted at us to move out of the path of a crane, which was being shifted along a track.

"What was it you wanted to ask her?" I said.

"If she minded us contacting her again. I can only imagine that she did!"

CHAPTER 45

"Yes, this is her residence. And she owes me rent!" fumed the large, red-faced lady who had opened the door to me, James and Margaret Davies in Westmoreland Place.

"Miss Hamilton is sadly deceased, Mrs Reagen," I said. "We have already tried to explain that to you."

"Have yer? What's 'appened to 'er, then?"

"My sister was murdered," said Miss Davies. "But I'll make sure that you receive the full amount you were expecting in rent."

Mrs Reagen's face paled and she took a step back. "Oh no, I don't want ter trouble no one at a time like this. I didn't understand yer properly the first time. When I 'eard the word *police* it stopped me listenin' proper. You'd better come in."

"Are you all right, Mrs Reagen?" I asked as we moved into the hallway.

"I'll be a'right in a bit. I weren't expectin' it, yer see." She twisted her hands in her apron. "A sweet girl like that? I can't 'ardly believe it. I'll tell you the truth, I was angry to start with 'cos I thought she were tryin' to escape payin' 'er rent. I've 'ad no word from 'er or nothin' for over two weeks! I never would've thought summat like this would 'appen to 'er. I've never thought it at all. She kept 'erself to 'erself most times, and some evenin's she'd get dressed up, but no friends or gentlemen ever called round for 'er, and I wondered to meself what she did. I've 'ad a few guesses an' all, an' maybe I was right, but I never liked to ask too many questions. I only asked 'er if she were lookin' after 'erself and bein' careful, and the suchlike. It weren't no good 'er bein' out after dark on 'er own like that."

"Which room did she rent from you, Mrs Reagen?" asked James.

"Top floor." She nodded toward the staircase.

"Thank you. I've brought the key we found in a bag she had with her when her body was discovered." James pulled it out of his pocket and showed it to Mrs Reagen.

"Looks about right," she said, emitting a deep sob and pulling her apron up to wipe her face. "I'm so sorry for yer loss," she said to Miss Davies.

Mrs Reagen showed us to Anna's room on the top floor and James unlocked the door.

"Do you mind if I step inside first?" he asked Miss Davies. "I'd like to check that the room is in order if that's all right. Given the tragic nature of your sister's death I can only hope that there is nothing in the room that might be distressing."

"What do you mean?" asked Miss Davies.

I wondered whether James was worried that the room had been ransacked, or even worse, whether there might be another victim inside.

"Do let Inspector Blakely check the room, Miss Davies," I

said. "I'm sure everything is fine, but he just needs to be certain."

Miss Davies gave a nod and I held my breath as James pushed open the door and stepped inside. After a brief moment he called us in.

"Everything appears to be fine," he said.

I glanced around and saw a tidy bedroom with a bed, dressing table, washstand and wardrobe. A faint scent of perfume lingered in the air.

Miss Davies gave a little gasp and walked over to the dressing table, upon which a hairbrush and comb had been neatly placed. She picked up the hairbrush and I felt a lump in my throat as I saw the long, dark hairs caught in its bristles.

It was an ordinary room, which appeared to be just as Anna would have left it. I pictured her here, unwittingly readying herself for her final evening with Mr Gallo.

Miss Davies dabbed at her eyes with her handkerchief.

"We'll need to look through the drawers and cupboards, Miss Davies," said James. "We'll be as careful as we can with your sister's belongings, and when we've finished I'm sure most of her possessions can be handed over to you. We may need to borrow anything that might be useful for the investigation, but it will all be returned to you before long."

Miss Davies gave a faint nod, and there was a pause before anyone touched any of Anna's possessions. I felt as though we were intruders, and that we had no right to be looking through her personal belongings.

"I hope we are able to find something useful," I said in an attempt to justify why we needed to go looking through every drawer and cupboard.

"I'm particularly interested in finding any documents, notebooks, letters or diaries," said James. "Anything that might help to explain who attacked her."

"Given the nature of her work, she was probably careful not to leave too much evidence lying around," I said. "An accomplished spy would be unlikely to leave many clues."

"Unfortunately, you're right," replied James. "But I should like to have a look through the writing desk in any case."

"I'll sort through her clothes," said Miss Davies, "and then I'll start packing them away if that's all right with you, Inspector. Do you think you could fetch down that trunk from on top of the wardrobe? It would make sense to pack them straight into that."

James obligingly lifted down the trunk. When he opened it, we discovered several rolls of letters inside.

"Just what we were looking for!" said James. "If you don't mind, Miss Davies, I'd like to collect together all the personal documents we find here so I can take them away to read. I will, of course, return them to you as soon as I have finished. I can already see that I wouldn't have the time to read them all right now."

"That's quite all right," said Miss Davies.

"A diary would be particularly useful," said James as we looked through the drawers. "But so far there has been no sign of one."

Before long everything was packed away, and James and I had bundled up all the papers with some string we had obtained from the landlady. Miss Davies wiped her face with her handkerchief once again.

"Are you all right?" I asked.

She nodded in reply.

I imagined how I would feel if I were packing away Eliza's things, and a lump rose into my throat.

"Thank you for your help, Miss Davies," said James. "I cannot think how difficult all this has been for you."

She nodded sadly again.

"My colleague, Chief Inspector Fenton of Bow Street, has

arrested a suspect, but there is quite a bit of evidence to gather yet. If he decides to charge him with your sister's murder I will let you know as soon as possible."

"Thank you, Inspector."

⚜

James cleared some space on his desk at Scotland Yard and we began to lay out Anna O'Riley's papers.

"There are some receipts here that may prove useful," he said. "She had some boots re-heeled at a place in Panton Street... And she bought a hat from a milliner in Lexington Street."

"I have some more receipts here," I said. "She appears to have kept everything of a practical nature, but very little personal information."

"I'll keep looking through the receipts," said James. "Would you be able to look through the letters? From what I can see here, Anna O'Riley's main correspondent was a lady named Elizabeth Radnor."

I spent some time reading the letters from Elizabeth Radnor but found them to be fairly conversational and unremarkable.

"What have you found out?" asked James as I folded up the last one.

"Mrs Radnor lives in Wimbledon with her husband and five children. She seems to have been a neighbour of the Davies family at one time. She expresses surprise at Anna's decision to change her name."

"Do you think Anna explained why she did so?"

"I don't think she did. Mrs Radnor was aware that Anna was working as a waitress at Le Croquembouche and commented a few times on how she enjoyed hearing Anna's interesting news, as her own life in Surrey was rather dull in comparison."

"Perhaps Anna told her about the wealthy, powerful men she had befriended."

"Yes, I get the impression that she did."

"How far do the letters date back?"

"Two years. That seems to have been the time when Anna left Islington and became a waitress."

"And the mysterious Mrs Adams met her a few months later, at the beginning of 1883. Is there any suggestion that Anna and Elizabeth have met together in the last two years?"

"No. Letters appear to have been exchanged once every month or two, but there has been no mention of any meeting."

"Anna O'Riley kept her distance from most people, didn't she? Elizabeth must have been quite important to her if she kept up the correspondence. After all, it was more contact than she had with her own family."

"I think Anna may have confided in Elizabeth more than she confided in anyone else. Elizabeth's final letter was received last month, and in it she asks Anna to be careful and to look after herself."

"Which suggests that she was worried about her," said James. "Well, there's only one way to discover more, and that is to visit Elizabeth ourselves."

CHAPTER 46

"I received a telegram bearing good news this morning," said James the next day as we took the train from Waterloo to Wimbledon. "It came from Inspector Raynes and informed me that Jack Shelby has been arrested in Paris."

"That is excellent news!" I said. "So the Pinkertons finally got their man!"

"They did indeed. It will be interesting to see how willing he is to talk. I replied to Raynes, asking him to remind Mr Russell that we would like to know whether Shelby sold those forgeries to Gallo."

"That would be of great help to the investigation," I agreed.

"Last night I read through the rest of the papers we found in Anna O'Riley's room," he continued. "I brought a few with me that looked interesting."

"Most of these are receipts," I said once he had handed them to me.

"But they are interesting, nonetheless," said James, "as they allow us to identify her movements during the last few weeks of her life. I spent some time looking up the different shops on a map, and it seems that she spent a good deal of time around Mayfair and Covent Garden."

"What does that tell us?"

"Not a great deal at the moment, but it might tie in with something we discover later. There are also a few letters from a chap named Augie."

James handed them to me and I began to read.

5th September 1884

> *Dearest Clara,*
>
> *What a pleasure it was to make your acquaintance again after all these years! Must I really address you as Clara from now on? It feels rather peculiar when I have only ever known you as Anna. That said, perhaps it is no different from me using my pen name.*
>
> *I think it was fate that drew me to Le Croquembouche. Never could I have imagined that I would set eyes on you there! The timing couldn't have been better, as I have been feeling the recent loss of my dear mother quite keenly. We laid her to rest in the catacombs last week, and I will freely admit that I have since visited the place every day. There she lies in a casket, as if she were still here among us in the land of the living. It would be far easier had she chosen to be buried instead. If she were deep in the ground I feel sure that I would be more accustomed by now to the fact that she is gone forever.*
>
> *Do write and send me your sympathy. I shall remain at this address for a few days longer.*
>
> *Your affectionate friend,*
> *Augie*

"What a dreary letter," I commented.

"It's clear from the other letters that she did not respond," said James.

"I'm not surprised," I said. "She appears not to have encountered him for several years, and then he expects a sudden outpouring of sympathy from her. I feel sorry that his mother has died, but there was no need for him to be quite so self-pitying. It's interesting that he mentions a pen name, however. It suggests that he's a writer."

I quickly read the next letter Augie had sent.

21st September 1884

Dearest Clara,

I was disappointed not to receive a reply to my last letter. Perhaps you didn't receive it. I hope you gave me your correct address and not a false one! Such a deceit would be most harmful to a fellow in my current state of mind. But I shall give my Anna (I simply cannot get used to Clara!) the benefit of the doubt. Are you still employed at Le Croquembouche? I dined there yesterday evening in the hope of seeing you.

I had a dream last night that we were flying a kite together in Highbury Fields once again. Do you remember that afternoon? It always seemed to be summer in Highbury Fields. I yearn for those years when life was simple and each new day was filled with something new. Oh to be young again! Not that we're old, Anna, but I noticed there were more cares in your face when I saw you last. If anything is troubling you, you can tell an old friend. Please remember that. Perhaps you would consider taking a stroll with me one afternoon to the catacombs where Mother has been laid to rest. She was so fond of you.

Your affectionate friend,

Augie

I gave a shiver. "What an invitation! Imagine being asked to visit Augie's mother in her catacomb!"

James gave a laugh. "It's rather morbid, isn't it?"

"Who is this Augie, I wonder?"

"I'm hoping that Mrs Radnor might know something of him."

I looked at the address written on his second letter. "It's a different address from the last one. He appears to have been staying in boarding houses on both occasions."

"And both are in West Norwood," said James.

Elizabeth Radnor lived in a large, detached house on a hilly, tree-lined street in Wimbledon. A light dusting of snow had frozen overnight, making our way rather slippery.

"Oh dear, what has happened?" asked Mrs Radnor as the maid led us into the drawing room and announced who we were.

Mrs Radnor was a plump lady with fair hair. She wore a pale blue satin dress with lace at the throat. I could hear children playing somewhere in the house and a pleasant smell of baking wafted up from the kitchen.

James asked her to be seated before breaking the news that Anna O'Riley was deceased. She held her head in her hands for a while, and her shoulders shuddered. James rang the bell for the maid.

"What's 'appened, ma'am?" the maid asked, rushing to her mistress' side.

"I'm all right. Thank you, Katie."

"Would you like your salts, ma'am?"

"I shall be fine in a moment." Mrs Radnor sat upright and began to compose herself. "I have just received some sad news, but I shall be quite all right. Please will you fetch us all some tea? Make sure that the sugar bowl is nice and full."

"We have been reading your letters to Anna O'Riley," I

said once she was more composed. "That's how we found out about you. She led a secretive life, on the whole, but you appear to have been one of the few people she confided in."

Mrs Radnor gave a sad smile and clutched her handkerchief tightly in her hand. "I can't say that she completely confided in me, but she gave me some idea of what her life involved. I grew concerned when she told me she had changed her name to Miss Clara Hamilton. I realise it was because she didn't want people to know she had once been married, but it seemed most odd to me at the time.

"I'm lucky, I suppose, because I have my husband and my children, and Wimbledon is such a delightful place to live. I don't need anything else. She could have had all that, but then she lost her husband and her little boy too, and it was just all so awful. That's when she first wrote to me. I hadn't heard from her for a while, though we had been good friends when we both lived in Islington. We were neighbours in Compton Terrace."

"Was she on bad terms with her parents and siblings?"

"I wasn't aware of them falling out, and they seemed to get along. But she had enjoyed the closeness of her marriage, and the love she felt for her son was all-consuming." She paused to wipe her eyes. "It must have been devastating for her."

"What did she tell you about her life, Mrs Radnor?" asked James as the maid brought in a tea tray.

"She told me she made a good income, and that was important to her. After her husband died she had been worried about not having enough money. She had briefly lived with her aunt and uncle after she was widowed, but she had no wish to make it a permanent arrangement. Her parents had both died by then, which was a sad shame. Mr and Mrs Davies were lovely people.

"Anna found herself some work at a restaurant in Westminster, and she liked the people she met there. She told me she enjoyed their company. It was clear from her letters that she was impressed by some of the important men who dined at the place, and she was flattered whenever they showed her any attention."

"Do you still have the letters she sent you?" James asked.

"Yes, I kept them all." Mrs Radnor rang for the maid and instructed her to fetch the letters from the desk in the morning room.

"I looked forward to reading her letters, because one day can be very much like all the others when you're running a household," she continued. "Sometimes my life can feel rather dull. I wouldn't change it for the world, but I must say that I liked reading Anna's stories about the people she had met, the places she had dined and the hotels she had stayed at.

"I asked if I could visit her a few times, but she didn't agree to a meeting, and I surmised that she wished to keep her work a secret. She preferred to keep me at arm's length, I suppose. Some would say that it was perhaps inevitable that her profession would lead to immorality, but I was surprised by it, as she had never seemed to be that sort of woman. I couldn't help thinking that there was more to it than she had shared with me."

The maid returned with the letters.

"Thank you, Katie." Mrs Radnor began to leaf through them. "This is an interesting one... particularly this part here: 'I receive invitations to dine at exclusive restaurants, and I've been to parties in all manner of locations. I have seen the insides of many fascinating homes and palaces now, and have made a number of interesting acquaintances. I cannot call them friends, as this is not a way of life in which one makes close friends. But my assumed name allows me to inhabit a world that is so unlike the one I'm from. There is no need for my new acquaintances to know anything about me. All that matters is how I make them feel. I can assume a completely new identity; one that fits with the locations and the parties and the people I encounter. Few of them are interested in me, but they like talking to me because I listen. They enjoy my company, and it matters very little to me that they don't know who I really am.'"

Mrs Radnor paused as she folded the letter back up. "It's not a way of life I would choose myself, but it obviously interested her. It took a great deal to hold Anna's attention, as she grew bored rather easily. I only began to worry when she told me in later letters that she felt fearful."

"Could you find one of those letters for us?"

"I think so. Let me have a look."

We waited as Mrs Radnor leafed through the pile. "Here we are. This was the last letter I received from her, dated the thirteenth of October: 'I no longer work as a waitress, but I have continued my work as a paid companion. I am able to earn a decent wage doing this sort of work; however, if anyone asks me I still tell them I am a waitress. Thank you for reassuring me that you won't breathe a word of this to anyone else. I have always been able to rely on your confidence, and I am so happy that you continue to be a good friend to me.

"'Much of my life requires some sort of pretence. I must pretend to the outside world that I still work as a waitress, and I must pretend to my patrons that I find every ounce of their conversation fascinating. I'm happy to be able to send money to my aunt and uncle each month. They were so terribly saddened by Ma's death. I have made excuses not to see them because I know that they will ask me where the money comes from and what sort of job I have. Although I am quite good at pretending these days, I am hopeless when it comes to the people I care about the most.

"'There is another reason I pursue this sort of work, and perhaps I will explain it to you some day in the future. Although I am not breaking any laws that I know of, and am freely entering into it, I sometimes worry about the risks I have to take and the possible consequences.'" Mrs Radnor folded up the letter and placed it on the table. "I wish she had been able to explain that more."

"Anna was working as a spy," said James.

"Was she?" Mrs Radnor had a dubious expression on her face. "Are you quite sure about that?"

"We know it for certain, and have already spoken to some of her colleagues."

She gave a sigh. "Well, who would have thought it? I suppose it makes sense when you think about it. Perhaps I can understand now what she really wanted from these men. I think she would have enjoyed the challenge of obtaining important information from them. It was such a dangerous job, though, and I can only suppose that someone found her out. People don't take too kindly to being deceived, do they?"

"They certainly don't," said James.

"Do you have any idea who might have murdered her?" Mrs Radnor asked.

"There are several suspects," said James. "My colleagues at Bow Street station already have a chap under arrest."

"Oh, that is good news."

"But there is a lot of work to be done yet."

"Did Anna mention anyone she had met by name?" I asked Mrs Radnor.

"I don't recall many names being mentioned. I think she was keen to keep their identities a secret."

"Did she elaborate any more on the risks involved or the possible consequences?" I probed.

"No. That was the most she ever said on the subject."

"Are you aware of anyone in particular she felt threatened by or worried about?" asked James.

"No one I'm aware of. If there was, she didn't tell me about him."

"Do you recall Anna being acquainted with a man who called himself Augie?" I asked.

Mrs Radnor shook her head. "No, I'm not familiar with that name."

"What about Augustus?"

"Oh, of course. That's what it's short for! Yes, there was an Augustus. He and his family lived in the same street as us in Islington."

"Compton Terrace," confirmed James.

"Yes, that's the one."

"Can you recall his surname?"

Mrs Radnor thought for a while. "I really don't remember, and I wonder now whether I ever knew it. I don't believe I did, come to think of it. I only ever knew him as Augustus. He was a little older than Anna and me."

"What was he like?"

"Quite tall. And pleasant enough, although I think he was rather shy. He seemed to be very fond of Anna."

"Was the feeling reciprocated?"

"No, I don't think it was. She was polite to him and would converse with him when the necessity arose. We didn't like to upset him because he had a bad temper."

"Did you ever witness an angry outburst?"

"A few times, but it was only ever short-lived."

"We have already spoken with Anna's sister," said James.

"Which one?"

"Margaret. She still lives in Islington."

"Oh really? I must visit her. I haven't seen her for many years now. With this awful news in mind, I must go and pay my respects."

"I'm sure she would appreciate that," said James. "She told us Anna had once fallen in love with a man who lost his life on a railway track."

"Oh yes, that was absolutely dreadful!"

"When did that happen?"

"About a year before she married Mr O'Riley. It must have been about seven or eight years ago. His name was Walter Campbell."

"Was his death an accident?"

"Yes. He had been drinking at the Drayton Park Hotel in Highbury. On his way home he fell off the bridge that crosses the railway line where the track runs beneath Drayton Park."

"How did he manage to fall off the bridge?"

"People say that he was walking along the wall. It's the sort of foolish thing men do when they've had too much to drink, isn't it? Then he fell, and a train came and... Perhaps someone could have climbed down and saved him if a train hadn't got there first. Or perhaps he was already too injured by then. I don't know. Anna was distraught."

"Do you know who was with him that evening?"

"I couldn't tell you, Inspector."

"Was Augustus there?"

"I really wouldn't know."

"Is there a possibility that he might have been?"

"Yes, it's possible. I think a group of them had been out together that evening."

CHAPTER 47

"We need to find this Augustus fellow," said James as we travelled back to Waterloo by train. "I don't like the sound of him at all. And I intend to ask the Islington Coroner for details of the inquest into the death of Anna O'Riley's fiancé, Mr Campbell."

"Presumably his death was recorded as an accident."

"I'm sure it would have been. But don't you agree that there could have been something suspicious about it?"

This sounded like unnecessary work as far as I was concerned. "We're still trying to establish who murdered Mrs O'Riley and Mr Gallo," I said. "We mustn't get distracted by this other death." I noticed that the man sharing our train compartment was reading the *Morning Express*.

"But what if Augie, as he calls himself, is behind all three deaths? According to Mrs Radnor he was rather fond of Anna O'Riley."

"And it seems the affection wasn't reciprocated. Do you think that he had something to do with Mr Campbell's death, killing him out of spite?"

"Exactly. It must have upset him a little," continued

James. "His recent letters suggest he had maintained a rather twisted affection for Anna, even many years later. Doesn't that strike you as odd?"

"The man's general behaviour definitely strikes me as odd."

"If he was upset that she did not return his affection all those years ago, he must have been even more upset when he heard that she had fallen in love with Walter Campbell. I cannot imagine him liking the man, and Mrs Radnor didn't consider it inconceivable that Augie was present that evening. That's why I should like to hear further details from the incident. The coroner's records should be able to tell me what I need to know."

"But why would this Augustus chap murder Mrs O'Riley? And Mr Gallo, too? How did he even know she was with him that night? How did he get inside the hotel?"

"I cannot explain why he would wish to murder the pair of them. Not yet, anyway. But I dare say that he gained entry to the hotel because he was invited there. I'm fairly sure that we already know him."

"Mr Goldman?"

"It could be. Unfortunately, we're going to have to ask Fenton for his help in this area."

"Where does Mrs Mirabeau fit into all this? It seems incredibly suspicious that she has chosen to protect herself by hiring a lawyer."

"She has something to hide, there's no doubt about that. And we need to know who Anna O'Riley was working for. We know she worked alongside Mrs Adams, but someone requested that she find out more about Gallo's paintings, and that person must have instructed Mr Cooke to carry out that investigation. We need to go back to Cooke and make him speak up."

We glanced out of the window, watching another train

move alongside us as we travelled through busy Clapham Junction. Once it had passed by the rooftops came into view again, and the recent snow gave them the appearance of having been lightly dusted with flour.

"There is a good deal more snow on its way, apparently," said James. "They say that it's coming from the north."

"Doesn't it always come from the north?" I said with a smile.

I welcomed the opportunity to talk about something other than the Gallo case and relaxed back into my seat a little, allowing my shoulder to rest gently against James.

"All cold air comes from the north?" he said.

"Yes. Wet air comes from the west and warm air comes from the south."

"Is that a fact?"

"I don't know, to be completely honest. I think I heard it somewhere once."

"What about the east?"

"That's a good question. I'm not entirely sure."

"Has Mrs Garnett had a lock put on your window yet?"

"Yes, she had a man come and do it yesterday. I feel much safer now."

"That's good news. And your door is kept locked all the time?"

"Yes. Even when I'm in the room."

"And you still have no idea who broke in?"

"No. But if they were trying to frighten me it won't work."

"It frightens me a little," said James. "I want to be able to protect you."

"Thank you, James."

We exchanged a smile, and I suddenly wished that we had the train compartment to ourselves.

"I've been meaning to tell you that I asked for the charges against Mr Jenkins to be dropped."

"But he hit you!"

"And I deserved it."

"No you didn't. You'd already been ordered to pay him six hundred pounds. That was punishment enough!"

"If the case proceeded against him I would only have had to face him again in court. There was no need for it. Hopefully I shall never set eyes on the man or his daughter ever again."

"Let's hope not."

I rested my hand on his and glanced at the man reading the *Morning Express* once again. He was holding the newspaper up so that it shielded his face. I might have been mistaken, but it almost appeared as though he were listening in to our conversation. I gave James' hand a gentle squeeze and nodded in the man's direction. James surveyed him and seemed to share my suspicion.

"Excuse me, sir," said James. "My watch appears to have stopped. Do you have the time, please?"

"Half-past twelve," came the reply.

The newspaper hadn't moved an inch.

"Thank you. I must say that it's quite a feat to be able to check your pocket watch without moving your hands."

There was a pause before the gruff voice replied. "I looked at the clock when we passed through Clapham Junction station."

CHAPTER 48

As soon as I had read the telegram awaiting me at my lodgings that evening I travelled by cab to my sister's home in Bayswater.

"Look at this, Ellie!" I cried, brandishing the message in my hand. "Francis wrote it just yesterday!"

"*Yesterday?* From Colombia?"

"Yes! Isn't it astonishing? Look, it says the twenty-ninth of November right there."

"Goodness! His message has travelled all that distance in just one day. I cannot understand how telegrams work. I know they lay the wires down, but how are the messages sent along them?"

"Let's not worry about that now. Read what it says."

Report of European orchid grower living in Cali. Trying to arrange meeting. Letter on its way.
    F. E.

. . .

"He must know more than he has been able to say in this brief message, Penelope. Something about the reports he has heard concerning this European orchid grower must have suggested to Francis that it could be Father. Do you think it might really be him?"

"I don't want to have my hopes raised too much, Ellie, but it's a possibility, is it not?"

"I only wish he had been able to write more. Now we can only speculate until his letter arrives. It must have cost him a fortune to send a telegram all the way from Colombia!"

"This was sent from Buenaventura, which is on the east coast of Colombia," I said. "Look, here's one of the maps Francis drew." I opened it out and pointed at Buenaventura. "And I think Cali must be this place. He has written Santiago de Cali on the map, but I think it must be the same town. It is just west of Buenaventura, though I don't know how far. A hundred miles, perhaps."

"We'll have to wait at least a month until the letter materialises!" lamented Eliza. "It will practically be the end of the year! Oh dear, I cannot possibly wait that long. I'm beginning to wish that he hadn't sent the telegram at all."

"Why?"

"Because I cannot wait so very long for his letter! What if it is lost somewhere? Then we shall never find out who this man is!"

"We will, Ellie. We'll just have to be patient."

"Since when did you have more patience than me?"

"I don't, but I also know that there is nothing we can do other than wait."

"And what happens if this European orchid grower has no wish to meet with Francis? Imagine it is Father and he refuses to have anything to do with him."

"We discussed this before, Ellie. We've always known

there was a possibility that Father might not wish to be found."

"I cannot believe that it is him, Penelope."

"What makes you say that?"

"Look how far Cali is from the Tequendama Falls on the map."

"I'd say that it is between two hundred and fifty and three hundred miles."

"Which is a great distance when you consider how primitive the roads must be."

"But he's had nine years to travel it!"

"I suppose so."

"Anyway, I shall assume that it is not Father, but I feel pleased for Francis that he has identified someone who might be of interest. Now all we can do is wait."

CHAPTER 49

I told James excitedly about Francis' telegram the
following morning.

"That is excellent news!" he said. "Francis is doing
sterling work, by the sounds of things. Hopefully this orchid
grower will know something about your father's whereabouts.
Or it may even be him!"

"I realise there is a good possibility that it isn't, and am
trying my best not to become too hopeful. I was incredibly
impressed to have received a telegram all the way from
Colombia. Francis only wrote his message two days ago! Can
you believe it?"

"That's the wonder of telegrams."

"It was simply astonishing to be able to read his words so
soon after he had written them all that distance away!"

"I think South America has had telegraph cables for a
good few years now."

"But don't you think it incredible?"

"It is, Penny, and it has brought wonderful news indeed. I
hope Francis' forthcoming letter brings you the tidings you
wish to hear."

"You seem rather subdued, James."

"No, not at all. I'm very happy to hear that there may be news of your father."

"It's because it's from Francis, isn't it?"

"What do you mean?"

"You're envious of his ability to send telegrams from the other side of the world."

"I'm not envious, Penny. Why should I be envious? I'm standing here looking at you right at this moment, while he is far away from you in South America. I think my position is far preferable!"

"I sometimes feel that you become a little curt whenever Francis is discussed."

"That is simply not the case. Now, can we please go and speak to Mr Cooke? It's rather cold standing out here, and we need to get the people involved in this case talking."

❦

"Thank you for the introduction to the lady who calls herself Mrs Adams," James said to Mr Cooke. "Thanks to her we were able to visit Miss Hamilton's home and then find a long-lost friend of hers. We understand a great deal more about her now."

"Very good," replied the private detective. He sat with his hands resting on his desk, the thick fingers of one hand rubbing over the knuckles of the other.

"But we still don't know enough," continued James. "Why was Miss Hamilton – or Anna O'Riley as we have come to know her – with Mr Gallo that night?"

"To find out whom he had purchased the forged paintings from."

"And you asked her to do that work via the coded message in the *Morning Express* newspaper."

"That's right."

"But who hired you to commission the work?"

Mr Cooke sat back in his chair and gave a dry smile. "You know that I am bound by confidentiality, Inspector."

"I understand that, Mr Cooke, but two people have already lost their lives. We need to find out who's behind this."

"It wouldn't help even if I told you."

"How do you know that?"

"I just do."

"As a former police officer you have been in my position many times during your career. Surely that is enough for you to understand how important this piece of information is."

"I assure you that it will mean nothing to the investigation, Blakely."

"I must decide that!" snapped James.

"Don't you feel any sort of responsibility for Anna's death?" I asked.

"Anna?" he queried.

"Miss Hamilton, as you knew her. You sent her to that hotel to retrieve this information and she lost her life in the pursuit of it!"

"I couldn't possibly have known that I was sending her into any danger."

"Could you not?" demanded James. "Given that you clearly know more about the situation than you are letting on, perhaps you intentionally sent her to her death. Either that or you knew that she was at risk and simply turned a blind eye."

"How ridiculous!"

"But you cannot blame us for making that assumption, can you? By imparting so little to us you will appear to have been complicit in these murders before long."

Mr Cooke thumped his desk. "I am *not* complicit, Inspector! I conduct all my business with honour!"

"Then why maintain this silence?"

"Confidentiality, as I have already explained."

"It will remain confidential, even after you have divulged it to me," said James.

"And what about this news reporter?" he spat, giving me a sidelong glance.

"You may be assured of my discretion," I replied.

He gave a sceptical snort.

"So that is your reply, is it, Mr Cooke?" asked James. "What do you suppose I am likely to deduce from this?"

"That I am not caught up in this sorry business, Inspector."

"But you most certainly are. Anna O'Riley died while carrying out a job you had instructed her to do. You cannot wash your hands of this."

Mr Cooke rose to his feet. At full height he was substantially taller than James, who remained calmly seated.

"And who are you, eh, Blakely? Some young upstart who got promoted to inspector because of his father's rank rather than his own abilities. Are you really going to stand there and speak to me like that? A man with more than thirty years' experience in the Metropolitan Police Service?"

"I have tried appealing to your better nature, Mr Cooke."

"And I have told you why I must keep the information to myself!"

"You have, and I would say that it is a convenient excuse for a man who wishes to cover something up."

"I am not covering anything up!"

"But you are protecting someone: either yourself, your client or both. Why?"

"I am bound by the contract I have with him."

"Even when questioned by an officer of the law? Perhaps you are concerned that you will implicate yourself?"

"I am *not*! This conversation must come to an end, Blakely."

"That's a great shame, although perhaps I should be pleased that we have one more person of interest to us in this case."

"What do you mean by that?"

"A new line of investigation to pursue."

Mr Cooke snorted again.

"Thank you for your time, Mr Cooke." James stood to his feet. "We have found the twenty-seven coded messages you placed in the *Morning Express* newspaper, and I am delighted to tell you that a good friend of mine has managed to decypher them all."

Mr Cooke's left eye twitched.

"I noticed that not all of them were addressed to Anna O'Riley," continued James. "There were other recipients too, so we have a few more people to question."

"There is no need for you to investigate my business, Blakely! Everything is conducted just as it should be."

"It is up to you to convince me of that, Mr Cooke."

I rose up from my seat, and James opened the office door for me to step through. We had almost closed the door behind us when Mr Cooke finally spoke.

"I suppose there can be no great harm in telling you, seeing as he has already been arrested."

James pushed the door open again. "Telling me what, Mr Cooke?"

"Shelby. He was the one who asked me to carry out the surveillance on Mr Gallo."

"Jack Shelby?"

He nodded.

"But why?"

"Because he wanted to find out who was taking the business away from him. Shelby was supposed to be the master forger, but there was someone out there who was better than him."

"Who?"

Cooke shrugged. "I don't know. We were hoping that Mr Gallo could tell us."

CHAPTER 50

I worked in the reading room that afternoon, carrying out research for an article about the increasing wages of domestic servants. It was difficult to concentrate on such a dull topic when thoughts of Anna O'Riley whirled around in my head. I felt immensely saddened that she had lost her life while working for a known criminal such as Jack Shelby.

Why had Mr Cooke agreed to carry out the work for him? Why had he not collaborated with Inspector Raynes and Mr Russell to have Mr Shelby arrested? I reasoned that he had been paid a large a sum of money to remain loyal to the American criminal.

There was still a great deal about the case that I didn't understand, yet somehow I realised that I undoubtedly knew the murderer. It had to have been one of the people staying at the Hotel Tempesta that evening, but which one?

Francis' telegram was also occupying my mind. *Could my father really be alive and well, and living in Santiago de Cali?*

I put down my pen, rose from my seat and climbed the steps to the upper gallery, which encircled the reading room.

I knew the Colombia section well, as Francis had famil-
iarised me with the many books and maps stored there. I
found one of his favourites, a heavy tome titled *An Historical, Geographical and Topographical Description of the United
States of Colombia*, and sat down on the floor with it to look
up Cali.

The town was more than three thousand feet above sea
level, a fact I knew Francis would have looked up himself at
some point. It was situated on the River Cali, and I was
surprised to discover that it was quite an old settlement,
having been founded in 1536 by Spanish conquistador
Sebastián de Belalcázar. I wondered whether Cali was filled
with old, beautiful buildings. If my father happened to be
there I knew that he would appreciate them. It was home to
just over twenty thousand inhabitants, which gave me hope
that the European orchid grower Francis had heard about
would be reasonably well known.

"Madam!" exclaimed a sharp, whispered voice.

I looked up to see Mr Retchford, Francis' miserable
dough-faced replacement.

"What on earth are you doing sitting on the floor like a
slum-dweller?"

"I'm conducting some research on the Colombian town of
Santiago de Cali."

"May I ask that you conduct your research whilst seated
at a desk? It is entirely improper for our visitors to sit upon
the floor. I am quite astounded, in fact. I don't believe I have
ever seen such behaviour from any of our readers. What is
your name?"

"Miss Penelope Green of the *Morning Express* newspaper."

"You are learned enough to know better, in that case!"

I clambered to my feet and handed the book to Mr
Retchford for him to place back on the shelf. As I walked
along the gallery to the staircase I noticed a familiar figure in

a dark blue suit and bowler hat entering the reading room. I dashed down the steps to meet James.

"Come with me," he whispered. "Kit has some news for us!"

I quickly gathered up my belongings from my desk and looked up to see Mr Retchford still scowling at me from the gallery as I departed.

"What news might that be?" I asked once we had left the quiet of the reading room.

"He visited me with an update on Mrs Mirabeau's expeditions. She has repeatedly journeyed to Mayfair, and when I questioned him further he told me she has been frequenting an art gallery there."

"The Calthorpe Art Gallery?"

"The very same."

We made our way down the steps of the British Museum, which were lightly carpeted in fresh snow.

"Has she been speaking to Mr Court-Holmes?"

"Quite regularly, it seems. It's all so suspicious that Inspector Raynes has managed to obtain a search warrant for the gallery and is already on his way down there. I thought I'd come and find you first. Here's my cab. I asked him to wait for us."

We climbed inside.

"So what do you think Mrs Mirabeau has been discussing with Mr Court-Holmes?" I asked. "It must have something to do with paintings."

"I should think so. Stolen paintings, forged paintings, burnt paintings... And to think that Jack Shelby hired Cooke to investigate for him! I wish I knew what was going on, Penny. I feel as though we are running around in circles."

Kit was waiting outside the Calthorpe Art Gallery with a

bemused expression on his face. Inside, Inspector Raynes was speaking to Mr Court-Holmes while three or four police constables conducted a search. At the far end of the room I saw a lady in a dark dress seated on a chair and smoking a cigarette.

"You honestly think that I would steal my own painting?" Mr Court-Holmes asked scornfully, his chin jutting out at Inspector Raynes.

"In light of what we have discovered here, I believe that anything is possible, sir." He turned as we approached. "Oh, good afternoon, Inspector Blakely. Miss Green."

"What have you found?" asked James.

"The five forged paintings Mr Gallo bought," replied Raynes. "And two forgeries of the *Madame Belmonte*."

"What?!" James gave an incredulous laugh.

"And they weren't particularly well hidden, either," continued Inspector Raynes. "I don't suppose you imagined we would ever search your gallery, did you, Mr Court-Holmes?"

"I really don't know what you're talking about, Inspector. All I know is that the *Madame Belmonte* is still missing and is probably somewhere in Paris."

"There's no use in trying to blame Jack Shelby," replied Raynes. "I have a feeling that the real *Madame Belmonte* cannot be too far away."

"And Mrs Mirabeau?" asked James, nodding at the figure in the far corner.

"We are fairly confident that she removed the paintings from Gallo's attic room and brought them here. It seems Mr Court-Holmes was beginning to feel nervous about someone discovering their provenance while they remained at the hotel."

"So she didn't burn them after all," commented James.

"Although a few people are probably wishing now that she had!"

"Are you suggesting that Mr Court-Holmes not only sold the paintings to Mr Gallo but also forged them?" I asked.

"That's what we believe," said Inspector Raynes.

"But you have no proof!" snarled Mr Court-Holmes.

"We will have in due course, sir."

"And Mrs Mirabeau knew all about this scheme?" I asked.

"Yes, we think so," replied Inspector Raynes. "She's a good friend of yours, isn't she, Court-Holmes? In fact, I believe she was the one who introduced you to Mr Gallo."

"You must have been very pleased to be introduced to a new and wealthy customer," said James.

"I've heard enough self-satisfied comments from you gentlemen," retorted Mr Court-Holmes. "Please leave my gallery at once! You will be hearing from my lawyer in the morning."

"You forget that we have a warrant to search these premises," replied Inspector Raynes. "My men will remain here for as long as it takes."

I glanced over at Mrs Mirabeau again. She returned my look with a cold, unblinking stare.

"Thank you, Kit," said James, handing the shoeshine boy a few more coins. "That was exceptionally good work you did for us there."

"I ain't sure exac'ly what I done, sir. I jus' followed the lady like you said."

"Well, I couldn't have asked for anything more," replied James. "I may be calling on you for help again."

The boy grinned and walked off into the thick swirl of snowflakes descending from the dark clouds.

"Here's your snow," I said to James. "From the north."

"Always from the north," he replied with a smile.

"So it's a surprise to discover that Mrs Mirabeau was colluding with Mr Court-Holmes."

"It is rather, isn't it? We knew she was hiding something didn't we? And it turns out that she was assisting Mr Court-Holmes with his forgeries. It seems that he was the master forger who Anna O'Riley was trying to find."

"And lost her life in the process," I added.

"Sadly, yes."

"Jack Shelby employed Mr Cooke to find out who the forger was, then Cooke recruited Anna O'Riley. And Jack Shelby had nothing to do with the theft of *Madame Belmonte* after all?"

"No it seems that was Mr Court-Holmes all along."

"Fancy stealing his own painting!" I scoffed. "Mr Gallo could have chosen better friends than him and Mrs Mirabeau."

"They both deceived him for their own gain. And even though we've discovered this, I don't feel we are any closer to discovering who murdered Mrs O'Riley and Mr Gallo."

"Could Mr Court-Holmes have ordered their deaths?"

"He might have done, and perhaps he asked Mr Goldman to do it for him. If so, our case is solved, but I don't think it's as simple as that."

"There's still the Augie fellow to consider."

"Yes there is. And regarding him, I sent a man up to Islington to speak with the coroner there. Fortunately, he was happy to share the papers from Walter Campbell's inquest, which was held in the August of 1877. The verdict was accidental death, as Mrs Radnor told us."

"Were there any witnesses?"

"Yes, just one. A man named Augustus John Smith, who was a recent graduate from the University of Oxford. His address was listed as Compton Terrace in Islington."

"Where the Davies family lived. It has to be the same man!"

"Smith made a deposition at the inquest, describing how Mr Campbell had drunkenly clambered onto the wall of the bridge that ran above the railway line."

"Why didn't he try to stop him?"

"He did, apparently, but Campbell was determined to walk along the wall, and according to the report there was very little Smith could have done to prevent him."

"And presumably the jury believed his story."

"They had no reason to disbelieve it. Besides, we cannot know for sure that Mr Smith pushed him off that wall. It just seems rather coincidental, considering that he harboured such strong feelings for Anna O'Riley.

"There's something else that will interest you to hear. Our friend Augie Smith has a violent past. One of my men had a conversation with the chaps at N Division in Islington, and it turns out that a short while after Mr Campbell's death Mr Smith stood trial for a violent assault. He was cleared of any wrongdoing, but the jury may have been influenced by his impressive academic background."

"They didn't believe a graduate from the University of Oxford would do such a thing?"

"It seems not."

"Do you know any other details about the assault?"

"Nothing more than that at the moment."

"He may have been innocent, of course."

"Possibly. But if this is the same man who has murdered three other people in cold blood, I'd say that it is highly unlikely."

CHAPTER 51

I sat at my writing desk that evening and watched as the snow accumulated on the ledge of my window pane. Under normal circumstances I would have drawn the curtains to keep out the cold, but I was enjoying the spectacle, as was Tiger, who tapped her paw at the window when a particularly large snowflake became stuck to it.

"It's rather late," I heard Mrs Garnett say. "I'll need to accompany you."

There were footsteps on the stairs, and I reached my door just after the knock sounded.

"Penny!" James smiled and removed his hat, which glistened with flakes of snow.

"What brings you here at this hour?"

"Nothing serious, don't worry. I have something quite interesting to tell you, in fact."

Mrs Garnett stepped into the room behind him, her lips resolutely pursed as though to ensure nothing of an affectionate nature would pass between us.

"Mrs Reagen visited the Yard while we were out today. You remember Mrs Reagen, don't you?"

"Yes. Anna O'Riley's landlady."

"That's right. She found this torn-up letter in Mrs O'Riley's wastepaper basket."

Mrs Garnett peered over my shoulder as James showed me a piece of paper, onto which he had glued ripped fragments of a letter.

"She showed excellent presence of mind to spot the letter and bring it to me. I feel rather annoyed that we forgot to check inside the wastepaper basket!"

"The handwriting seems familiar somehow. Is it from Augustus?" I asked.

"It is indeed."

31st October 1884

Dearest Clara,

I am disappointed to hear that you have continued with your so-called profession, which is entirely unsuitable for a lady. What sort of gentlemen do you suppose them to be if they are happy to pay for your company? Your reputation is beginning to suffer, and it won't be long before you are deemed 'untouchable'. As I told you earlier today, I cannot bear the thought of that happening to you.

I apologise that my temper got the better of me when we spoke, but I must urge you once again to do the right thing. Perhaps it is difficult for you to fully comprehend the complexity of your situation, but I believe that you will thank me once you have taken heed of my warning.

It should be a comfort to you that there is a gentleman who wishes to marry you, and I would strongly advise you to take advantage of the opportunity while it is available to you. This may be the final chance you have to save yourself.

Your affectionate friend,

Augie

. . .

"Gentlemen were paying for her company?" exclaimed Mrs Garnett. "What a scandal!"

"The situation is not quite as it seems," I said.

"Well, it doesn't sound right to me. It's no wonder people get themselves murdered sometimes."

I bit my tongue, and James and I exchanged a bemused glance.

"This was sent just eleven days before Mrs O'Riley and Mr Gallo were murdered," I said.

"And the tone of this letter is more hostile than the earlier ones," said James. "It appears to have been written after a confrontation between the two of them. But whether he actually carried out the attack... who knows? It's imperative that we find him."

"The letter bears no address," I said. "Do you have his other letters with you?"

"I do."

"Maybe there is something in them that could give us a clue as to his whereabouts."

James reached beneath his overcoat and pulled the other letters out of his jacket pocket. "We have the addresses of the two boarding houses he stayed at so we could make enquiries with them."

"That sounds like a good idea." I re-read the two earlier letters. "He gives away very little about himself," I added. "Why was he staying in boarding houses, anyway?"

"Perhaps he usually lives outside London."

"The first letter was written shortly after his mother's funeral. Perhaps he was staying in London for the funeral."

"He might well have been. But he cannot live too far from London, as we know that he visited Le Croquembouche on several occasions."

"Perhaps he usually lives somewhere else in London and needed to be in... Where was it again?"

"West Norwood."

"Perhaps he only stayed in that locality for his mother's funeral."

"He was visiting her resting place every day, wasn't he?"

"So presumably he was staying close to the cemetery."

"Probably Norwood Cemetery," said Mrs Garnett. "That's the big cemetery down that way."

"Thank you, Mrs Garnett. Do you happen to know whether there are any catacombs there?"

"Isn't that where the bodies just lie in a crypt without being buried?" She gave a shiver.

"Yes."

"There's something very odd about that. People should be buried properly, I say."

"But do you know whether there are catacombs at Norwood Cemetery?" I probed.

"How would I know?"

"We'll need to find out," said James. "We're looking for a Mrs Smith who was laid to rest there at the end of August or the beginning of September. How about we go down there tomorrow, Penny?"

CHAPTER 52

"I t doesn't appear as though many people have ventured down to the cemetery this morning," said James, surveying the few tracks in the snow.

Thick snowflakes fell from the low, grey cloud as we stood beside the grand stone entrance of Norwood Cemetery. Several horses and carriages were labouring along the steep high street behind us.

A stone lodge lay just beyond the cemetery gates, and James made some initial enquiries with the cemetery warden there. The tall, sallow-cheeked man confirmed that there were catacombs beneath the chapel in the cemetery, and that the charge to visit would be sixpence.

The warden strode on ahead of us, wearing a wide-brimmed black hat. His long black coat billowed in the breeze as we made our way through the silent cemetery. Everything lay beneath a blanket of snow, and I could feel the damp seeping through my boots. I rubbed my hands together to warm my gloved fingers.

"I sent a telegram to P Division asking for their assistance," said James. "They have a station close by on Knight's Hill. Let's hope they can meet us down here. Once we've seen Mrs Smith's resting place, we can visit the boarding houses which Augustus stayed at."

The snowfall lent a serene beauty to the ornate tombs and headstones. A robin observed us from a nearby cross and made a tiny disturbance in the snow as it flew away. The warden turned right and led us uphill, the snow ahead of him lying smooth and untouched. We were the only people present, and there was so little movement around us that I jumped when a tiny avalanche fell from an overburdened branch.

"Will Mrs Mirabeau and Mr Court-Holmes appear in front of the magistrates today?" I asked James.

"They certainly will. I should have liked to be there myself."

"So should I! Perhaps there will be time once we've finished here. I would like to find out exactly what they got up to."

"I've heard word from Bow Street that Fenton has released Mr Goldman without charge."

"That's interesting," I replied. "Presumably for lack of evidence?"

"I should think so. And possibly lack of motive too. Hopefully our investigation into Augustus Smith this morning will yield something, I don't like the tone of his letters to Anna O'Riley."

"They're horrible," I agreed. "And although he needs to be apprehended, I can't say that I would like to meet him."

"I think it's likely that you already have."

I gave a shudder. "I think you're right."

. . .

The chapel finally came into view. Its arched windows stared darkly at us; its spire too steep for any snow to rest upon it.

The warden stopped at an iron gate and fumbled for the key that was stowed on his belt to open it. Then he lit his lantern and asked us to follow him down a stone staircase.

The staircase descended to the left and brought us to another locked gate, beyond which lay complete darkness. Once we had stepped through the gate, the warden raised his lantern so that the candlelight flickered against a long, stone corridor lined with arches.

I felt a prickle at the back of my neck as we followed in his footsteps. I could see that some of the arches led to further dark corridors, while others housed family vaults decorated with carved stonework and elaborate iron grilles. I hadn't minded walking through the cemetery, but the dead felt a little too close for comfort down in the catacombs.

"Remind me who it is yer lookin' for." The warden gave us a grimace rather than a smile.

"Mrs Smith," replied James. "She was laid to rest here at the end of August, or possibly the beginning of September."

"I remembers 'er," he replied, turning into a corridor to our right where the brick bays were lined with shelves. Rested upon each shelf was a neat row of coffins. Some were fronted with small headstones, while others were labelled with brass plates. Withered flowers lay in various stages of decay, and the air smelled of damp earth.

"Is it safe to be down here?" I ventured.

"What d'yer mean?"

"I mean the miasma from... Is there a risk of disease?"

"All the caskets is lead-lined, so nothin' can get out of 'em," replied the warden. "Yer quite safe."

I hoped we would find Mrs Smith's casket swiftly and be on our way without any delay. Being down in the catacombs gave me a tight sensation in my head and throat, and I was keen to be back in the land of the living as soon as possible.

"Are you acquainted with Mrs Smith's son?" James asked the warden.

"Yeah, I seen him."

"What's he like?"

"What's 'e like? I dunno what 'e's like. 'E pays me a sixpence like ev'ryone else does."

James and I exchanged a hopeful glance in the gloom.

"'Ere she is," said the warden, holding his lantern up beside a shiny new coffin, which lay at the height of our heads. Fresh flowers rested against a brass plate, which read:

Mrs Octavia Hannah Smith
    Died 25th August 1884

"Smith is quite a common name," James said to the warden. "Could there be another Mrs Smith who was laid to rest here at around the same time?"

"I don't remember no one else."

"Do you happen to know anything about Mrs Octavia Smith?"

The warden scratched his chin. "She were a widow. Lived local."

"Did you ever meet her?"

"Can't say as I did."

"Can you tell us anything about her family?"

"Only 'er son, like I told yer. Comes 'ere reg'lar, 'e does. Keeps 'imself to 'imself."

"What do you know of him?" James asked.

"That's all I knows. 'E ain't much of a talker. D'yer want ter look at anyone else while yer down 'ere?"

"No, that will be all. Thank you for your time."

"Now what?" I asked once we were out of the crypt and stood watching the dark, retreating form of the warden. I noticed the snow was falling more heavily. "Shall we visit the boarding houses? Or do you think this snow is going to impede our way?"

"It's possible isn't it?" said James, squinting up at the sky. "It's showing no sign of stopping. But we need to find Augustus Smith as soon as possible, when we pass the lodge on our way out I'll ask to see the burial record for his mother. It'll have her address on it, and maybe there will be some other documentation that displays the details of her son's lodgings. Perhaps I'm being too optimistic, but it has to be worth a try."

We began to follow the warden's fresh footprints.

As we walked, a tomb bearing the surname Green caught my eye.

"Look at that," I said, stopping suddenly. "Five family members with the surname Green. I wonder if they are distant relations of mine."

"It's possible, isn't it?" said James. "Look, I think those are the men from P Division." Three figures came into view ahead of us on the path. "I don't think many other people will be venturing out in this weather. I'll go and see."

I paused for a moment to finish reading the names on the tombstone, then began to follow James. I had only taken a couple of steps when my eye was drawn to another set of fresh footprints in the snow. They led up the path toward the chapel, but then diverted away from it and moved in-between the headstones.

I called out to James, but he was already speaking with the trio of men up ahead.

I examined the footprints again. They appeared to be the shape and size of a man's shoe, and had been made very recently; within the past twenty minutes, I conjectured. I glanced around but could see no one other than James and his colleagues. *Was it possible that the warden had walked this way?*

I took a tentative step off the path to peer around some of the taller headstones but saw no one wandering nearby. The footsteps followed an intriguing, winding path around the graves, and their owner appeared to have paused beside a tomb before continuing on his way.

I guessed that the footprints could only have belonged to someone who was searching for a particular grave. *But what was he doing here on such a snowy day? And where was he now?*

Feeling an uneasy shiver run down my spine, I quickly returned to the path and began to walk toward James. I had just regained sight of him through the thickly falling snow when a gloved hand was clamped over my mouth.

CHAPTER 53

"Not a sound," hissed a voice in my ear, "or I'll kill you!"

I froze, staring straight ahead at the distant figures.

"Step to your right."

My heart pounding, I did as I was told and stumbled over to a tomb on my right-hand side. My neck hurt as he continued to hold my head in a tight grip.

He pulled me down behind the tomb to shield us from the view of James and his fellow officers.

"Keep your eyes fixed straight ahead," he whispered. "Whatever you do, don't turn around."

I stared at the side of the tomb and the carved stone frieze that ran along the side of it. He slowly released his hand from my mouth and I took in a deep, shaking breath.

"Keep looking ahead!" he hissed.

"What do you intend to do to me?" I whispered.

"Quiet!"

My knees were cold and wet from the snow, and my entire body trembled.

"What do you...?"

"If you speak again I shall cut your throat. I didn't want to do this, but I had to stop you visiting my mother. What does any of this have to do with her?"

I heard the crunch of feet on snow nearby.

"Penny?" It was James' voice.

The gloved hand was clasped over my mouth again before I could reply.

So this was Augustus Smith. I tried to place his voice, knowing that I must have heard it before. *Who was he?*

"Penny?"

James' voice sounded further away this time.

"Penny? Where are you?"

Although I desperately wanted James to find me, I was terrified by Augustus' threat to cut my throat. *Would he harm me if James discovered us here? Did he really have a knife, or was he only bluffing?* I reasoned that he had not hesitated to kill Mrs O'Riley and Mr Gallo, and that I was of no importance to him at all. I concentrated on trying to breathe through my nose and tried not to consider how great a danger I was in.

I could hear distant voices and presumed that James had asked his colleagues to search for me. *Who was the man who held me here?* I thought about the guests at Mr Gallo's dinner. *Which one of them was he?* The hand was lowered from my mouth again, and I felt him shift his position. He was probably as cold and uncomfortable as I was. I knew that it would be completely impractical for us both to stay here much longer, and decided I could perhaps talk myself out of the situation.

"If you loved Anna," I ventured in a whisper, "why did you kill her?"

My question was met with silence.

"I saw the letters you wrote to her," I continued cautiously. "You cared about her very deeply, didn't you?"

There was still no reply.

"I should have liked to have met her. I learned about Anna from her sister Margaret and her friend Elizabeth. Do you remember Elizabeth? You both lived in Compton Terrace."

"Why have you been trying to find out about me? Why did you visit my mother?"

"Because you killed Anna. And Mr Gallo."

"I warned her it might happen. She didn't listen to me."

I felt a chill run through me as he made this confession. *Who was he?* Although I recognised his voice, I couldn't put my finger on who he was. *Perhaps Mr Goldman had found his way here? Or could it be Mr Bolton?*

"Here!" came a sudden voice, so loud that it startled my captor as much as me.

The hand was clamped over my mouth once again and my head pulled back. I tried to make a sound, but then I caught a glimpse of the shiny blade close to my throat. My stomach churned with dread.

"Fresh footprints!" came the voice again.

I squeezed my eyes shut, sure that Augustus would harm me if the police officer happened upon us.

My assailant suddenly rose to his feet, pulling me up with him. I felt a sharp pain in my neck, while my legs felt weak and cramped with cold.

"Stop!" he shouted, pulling me back onto the path in front of a young, shocked-looking police constable.

The constable stared at me in horror, his lips moving silently as he recovered his senses.

"Let her go!" he ordered.

"No!" came the response.

"Over here!" shouted the constable.

The hand covering my face tightened its grip and I battled to draw enough air in through my nose. The harder I tried the more difficult it seemed. I slowed my breath as much as I could and resisted the urge to struggle.

James and two other men came running into view. I held up a hand to stop them, not knowing what Augustus would do should they come too close.

"Good God!" exclaimed James, his face ashen. He swiftly unbuttoned his overcoat to reach beneath his jacket, where I knew his revolver sat inside its holster.

"Fetch your gun, Inspector, and I shall cut her throat," replied Augustus, resting the blade against my neck.

I fixed my eyes on James and silently urged him not to do anything rash. He raised his hands deferentially.

"I shan't touch my gun," he replied. "Just let Miss Green go and we can discuss this in a sensible fashion."

"If I let her go you'll shoot me."

"I won't shoot." James kept his hands raised. "You have my word."

Augustus' hand released its grip slightly but still covered my mouth.

"Why are you doing this?" James asked.

"Because you visited my mother."

James gave a hollow laugh. "Is that really the reason?"

"You must stay away from her!"

"Were you following us, Mr Smith?"

"I've been following you for days."

"*Days?*"

"I heard your plans. I heard you discussing this case. I shared a compartment on the train with you."

"So that was you," said James. "We knew there was something odd about the man behind the newspaper. I must ask that you remove your hand from Miss Green's mouth and allow her to breathe properly."

"I shan't let her go."

"Please release your grip just a little."

Mr Smith did as James had asked and held his arm across my shoulders instead. He made sure that the knife remained close to my throat.

I wished I could turn my head to look at the man who was holding me. *James and the constables knew what he looked like, but did James know which guest he had been at Gallo's dinner?* With the sharp blade still so close by, I didn't dare move my head to take a look at him.

"Tell us about Anna O'Riley," James said gently.

"Stop asking me about her!"

"Did you kill Mr Gallo because he was a witness?"

"He deserved it! You should have stayed away from here. Both of you!"

"And you should have stayed away from Anna."

"I needed her to listen to me. I warned her that something terrible would come of her foolish actions. She could have had a husband and a family; she didn't have to do what she was doing."

"Anna was not what you think she was. She was being paid to spy on Mr Gallo."

"She was no spy!"

"You're wrong, I'm afraid." James lowered his hands, and I silently prayed that he would be able to move his hand swiftly to his revolver at the right moment. "Anna was trying to find out who had sold Mr Gallo a number of forged paintings."

"She didn't mention that to me."

"She didn't mention it to anyone. She was very good at her job."

"Raise your hands, Inspector!"

Mr Smith had noticed, as I had, that James' hand was nearing his jacket.

James reluctantly did as he was told.

"You murdered Anna in a bout of bitterness and envy," I said. "She wasn't interested in you, and you wished to teach her a lesson. You also wished to punish Mr Gallo for seducing her."

"And what about Walter Campbell?" asked James. "Did you push him onto the railway track?"

"He was drunk."

"Did you push him?"

"He was the wrong man for her to marry. Anna was a lost soul; you didn't know her the way I did. I could have saved her."

"But instead you killed her!" James declared.

Augustus gripped me tighter in response to his words. "Stop saying that!"

I could tell that James was growing increasingly uneasy. Although he had successfully engaged Mr Smith in conversation, it seemed to be getting us nowhere. The constables appeared fidgety, presumably considering how to tackle the man who was holding me.

"You planned the attack very well," I said. "You knew that Anna visited Mr Gallo every Tuesday. I imagine you must have been following her to be party to that information. Perhaps you had regularly followed the poor lady since reacquainting yourself with her at Le Croquembouche. You came to the hotel that fateful night with an old overcoat and a pair of gloves to protect yourself and your clothing. You also brought a partially blacked-out lamp and the murder weapon.

"No doubt you panicked when Mr Gallo managed to flee from his room that night, but you were able to complete the dreadful deed regardless. And you conducted yourself with remarkable composure the following morning, having hidden the weapon in my bedchamber. How did you know that I had left the door unlocked? How did you find the time to hide the knife there?"

"My bedchamber was close to yours, Miss Green, I don't

think you realised that. Perhaps you'll lock your door next time?"

"I will, no doubt about that. You made the most of an opportunity. No one ever suspected that it was you who had committed the murders, you covered your tracks extremely well. Did you break into my home as well? I'm sure that it was you. Was the break-in supposed to have been some sort of warning or were you trying to find out what we knew?"

"I wanted to frighten you. I wanted you to stay away. But it seems you're not easily frightened, not unless I'm armed with a knife."

"If only I knew your pen name," I continued. "I know you by your pen name, don't I?"

"Most people do."

"Can we end this now?"

"And allow myself to be arrested? I'll let you go once the police officers have left." He raised his voice, directing his words at James. "I want you to leave, Inspector! Leave now and I promise not to harm her!"

"Will you let Miss Green go if we leave you alone?" asked James.

"Yes, but I refuse to be arrested! Get away from here and I shall release Miss Green unharmed. Do as I say! Now!"

James exchanged glances with the constables, and the four of them gradually began to retreat.

"Promise me you'll let her go, Mr Smith!" said James. He walked backwards, his eyes fixed on mine and his brow crumpled with concern.

"Don't even think about reaching for your gun, Inspector!" Augustus shouted out in reply.

James paused for a moment, clearly deliberating over whether to leave me alone with this man or not.

"Do as he says," I called over to him. "He'll let me go!"

"Penny, I can't..." James glanced at Augustus Smith and then back at me.

"Do as he says!" I ordered.

James took another step back.

"Please, James! He just wants to get away."

"That's right, Miss Green," added Augustus. His grip on me slackened as the men moved further back.

"If you harm even a hair on her head, I swear you shall hang for it!" shouted James. "As soon as we have gone, you will let her go so she can come and find us. You must let her go. Have I made myself clear?"

"As clear as day, Inspector."

As clear as day. I had heard the same phrase during that fateful evening at Hotel Tempesta, but who had said it?

James stepped back again, and it soon became difficult to distinguish his retreating form in the heavy snowfall.

CHAPTER 54

I suddenly became aware of the intense silence around us, though I felt sure that James would not have strayed far. *What was Augustus Smith's intent? He had threatened to kill me and now claimed he was going to let me go again. It didn't make sense. His actions suggested to me that he had a different plan altogether.*

I gently moved one hand to wipe my spectacles and adjust my hat.

"This way!" growled Mr Smith, pulling me back toward the tomb we had initially hidden behind.

His grip tightened again, and then he pushed me to the ground.

"I thought you were planning to let me go!" I cried.

"I lied," came the cold reply.

He pushed me back into the snow and held the knife blade to my neck once again.

It was then that I saw his face. He was clean-shaven, though I felt sure that I recalled him having whiskers. Black whiskers. His eyes were familiar.

It was John Blackstone, the reporter from *The Times*.

"Mr Blackstone?" I ventured. "Is it really you? But *why*?"

"Quiet!" he snarled.

I had no idea what he intended to do with me, but I was determined not to allow him to get away with anything further.

If I tried to fight back James would surely arrive quickly to help me... Wouldn't he?

"You don't need to hurt me," I pleaded. "Let me go now and I'll run away as fast as I can. You can get away too."

He shook his head. "If I let you go you'll never leave me alone. You and your friend Inspector Blakely will continue to pursue me. You'll come to this cemetery again and disturb my mother—"

"I promise we won't!"

"Quiet!"

He pushed the knife against my neck again. I felt sure that he was about to cut my throat, just as he had done with Anna.

Protruding from between the fingers of my right fist was the hatpin I had removed as I adjusted my hat a few moments before.

The time had come.

I gave a cry and launched my fist into his face as hard as I could. I screwed my eyes shut, not wishing to see the extent of the damage my hatpin had caused.

He recoiled with a blood-curdling scream, and I was up on my feet before I even had time to think about moving.

All I saw was white.

Slipping and sliding, I hurled myself forward into the snow, panting and crying and calling out for James.

Within a few seconds his arms had found me. "Penny!"

"Get him!" I shrieked. "Grab him before he gets away!"

CHAPTER 55

"So *The Times* has reported on the arrest of Mr Blackstone," said Edgar, as we sat in the newsroom, "but hasn't gone so far as to admit that he was one of its news reporters!"

"The editor is clearly too embarrassed by the whole affair," said Mr Sherman.

"I'm still struggling to believe that it was him," continued Edgar. "He always struck me as a dour, dull man. Rather quiet, too. I gather John Blackstone wasn't his real name."

"His name was Augustus John Smith," I said. "He chose to use a different name professionally after standing trial for a violent assault seven years ago."

"Quite sensible, I suppose," replied Edgar. "A news reporter should try to keep his reputation as untarnished as possible."

"I never considered that it could have been him," I said. "When he feigned drunkenness in the dining room he had us all fooled. Everyone assumed he was too inebriated to have carried out murder, so he was ruled out of the inquiries almost immediately."

"And by retiring early that night he gave himself plenty of time to prepare for the attack," added James.

Edgar shook his head. "I still cannot fully believe it. He always seemed so respectable."

"There are many seemingly *respectable* murderers," said James. "He was a clever man."

"A clever man and a lunatic," said Edgar. "Can lunatics truly be clever, though? I don't think they can, can they?"

"He wasn't a lunatic," said Frederick. "He was driven by love."

"He was driven by a conceited form of passion," I said. "And envy and revenge. It certainly wasn't real love."

"You thought it was all to do with stolen art, didn't you, Inspector?" asked Edgar.

"We felt that was a strong possibility," replied James. "That's why it took us some time to realise that Mrs O'Riley was the intended victim, not Mr Gallo. It was an error to assume that the attack had been directed at the hotelier."

"He was perceived to be the important person in this situation, while she was dismissed as little more than a loose woman," I said.

"I shan't be making that mistake again," said James.

"It wasn't only you," I said. "Chief Inspector Fenton and his men took the same approach."

"It was a natural mistake to make, Inspector," said Edgar.

"It is a stark reminder that all victims must be considered in a fair and equal manner," replied James.

"Has Blackstone confessed to the murders?" asked Mr Sherman.

"Yes he has," replied James. "With some rather twisted explanation that he was forced to do it. He seems to think that once the jury hear his explanation during his trial then they will spare him the gallows."

Mr Sherman gave a snort. "Quite unlikely."

"So what did he have to do with the stolen artworks?" asked Edgar.

"Nothing," I replied. "Anna O'Riley had been tasked by a private detective to find out who was supplying forged paintings to Mr Gallo. The private detective had been hired by the gentleman criminal Jack Shelby although there's no evidence that Anna knew this, she was just doing the job which she'd been asked to do. She had been visiting Gallo once a week and this caught the attention of Augustus Smith, or John Blackstone if you prefer. The obsessive affection he'd felt for her in their youth was re-kindled when he encountered her at Le Croquembouche restaurant a few months ago. When she refused him, he planned his revenge."

"And Mr Gallo got caught up in it," said Edgar.

"Unfortunately his fate was sealed once Mr Blackstone had persuaded Mrs Mirabeau to hold a dinner to promote the hotel's opening to news reporters," said James. "Although it was a clever ruse of Blackstone's, the man was ruthless and cruel. He subjected his innocent victims to a horrendous attack."

"And poor Miss Green was almost his next victim," added Mr Sherman.

"That was an extremely regrettable incident," said James, giving me an apologetic glance.

"No, it was quite necessary," I replied. "Neither of us could have known that he would follow us there, and the outcome was fortunate given that it resulted in his arrest."

"And the loss of his eye," said Edgar with a sharp wince. "Have you ever considered carrying hatpins around with you instead of a revolver, Inspector?"

Dirty snow had been shovelled into piles in Fleet Street, and the sun momentarily emerged from behind the clouds.

James checked his pocket watch. "The Holborn Restaurant is still serving its luncheon menu," he said. "Shall we... Oh, I don't suppose we can, can we? We'd need your sister here to chaperone us."

"She needn't find out," I replied with a warm smile.

"But it wouldn't be appropriate."

"It would be if we were discussing our work."

"Oh, I see. So we're working now, are we?"

"Yes. We're certainly not courting."

"We're just secretly courting, you mean."

"No, we're just working."

James' face fell. "Really?" He gave a sigh. "This all feels rather complicated at times."

"It does, but it doesn't have to remain complicated. There is a simpler way." I grinned.

"What do you mean by that?"

"Oh, James!" I laughed. "Under which other circumstances might a gentleman and lady enjoy each other's company without a chaperone? Let's see if you can work it out before we reach the restaurant."

I walked on ahead, stepping around a heap of grey snow.

"Are you suggesting what I think you're suggesting?" he called after me.

"I'm asking you to work it out," I replied over my shoulder. "And to tell me when you have an answer!"

THE END

HISTORICAL NOTE

A browse through newspapers from the late nineteenth century reveals that breach of promise cases were fairly common. Although usually brought about by aggrieved women, it wasn't unknown for them to be initiated by a man as was the case with fifty year old William Lister in 1867 who brought a case against the wealthy seventy year old, Patience Wray. One of the most famous breach of promise cases in the 1880s concerned the well-known actress Emily Mary Finney - stage name of May Fortescue - versus Lord Garmoyle or Arthur William Cairns, 2nd Earl Cairns. He appears to have cared a great deal for her but his aristocratic friends strongly disapproved of the union to a lowly actress and so he ended the engagement.

At the court hearing in 1884, Lord Garmoyle's counsel offered £10,000 (about $1.6m/£1.2m today) and the jury agreed to this amount. At the time it was the largest amount of damages ever recorded in a breach of promise case in the United Kingdom. May Fortescue used the payout to form her own theatre company and successfully toured Britain and America performing the plays of her friend, William S Gilbert - one half of the librettist duo Gilbert and Sullivan.

The character of Jack Shelby was inspired by the fascinating story of how Adam Worth was pursued by the Pinkertons and Scotland Yard. It's only briefly summarised here.

Pinkerton's detective agency was founded by a Scotsman, Allan Pinkerton, in 1850s Chicago. The agency expanded rapidly at a time when law enforcement and security in America was ad hoc and uncoordinated. From its inception the agency employed women detectives as well as men and involved itself in activities including the Civil War, chasing down outlaws and providing security for railroad companies and industrial disputes.

In 1873 William Pinkerton, son of Allan, worked with Inspector John Shore of Scotland Yard to convict an American gang who defrauded the Bank of England of around $13m/£10m in today's money. The two also worked together for decades on chasing down Adam Worth, the international 'Napoleon of Crime'.

Worth was a German-born American master criminal who stole around $100m/£77m (in today's money) in a thirty-five year career from banks and businesses across America and Europe 'without once resorting to bloodshed or physical violence' (*The Pinkertons* by James D Horan). Worth was clever, conniving and used a number of different aliases. He spent only six and a half years in jail and spent quite a lot of time in London. Worth had a lot of respect for his adversary William Pinkerton, but cared little for the Scotland Yard detective, Inspector Shore. One evening in 1876 the three of them met in London's Criterion Bar. Adam Worth later said of that evening:-

"I told Shore he didn't know anybody but a lot of three-card monte men and cheap pickpockets, and he could thank God Almighty the Pinkertons were his friends or he would never have gotten above the ordinary street pickpocket detective." (From *The Pinkertons* by James D Horan).

Twenty five years later, in 1901, Worth gave up his life of travel and crime and negotiated with William Pinkerton to return a famous painting, the *Duchess of Devonshire*, which he had stolen from a London gallery in 1876. He negotiated to sell it back to the gallery for $25,000 meaning that he did quite well out of his theft! During this time the detective and the criminal developed an unlikely friendship. Adam Worth died in London in 1903 and William Pinkerton looked out for his family - so much so that Worth's son, Henry, actually went on to become a Pinkerton detective.

Eliza's employer, Susan Barrington, is loosely based on the social reformer Octavia Hill. Her most well-known legacy in England is as a co-founder of the National Trust - an organisation which preserves historical buildings and sites. In the 1860s Octavia Hill was recruited by the social thinker and aesthete, John Ruskin, to manage housing in Marylebone for people on low incomes. Her work expanded and by the 1880s it was reported that she was managing homes in London for between three and four thousand low income tenants. Hill employed only women to collect the rent from these tenants and their role was to know the tenants personally and encourage their wellbeing by managing and promoting local associations, clubs and societies - many of them for children.

The 'Septem contra Edinam' or the Seven against Edinburgh University - admired by Anna O'Riley - were seven women who fought for the right to study medicine at Edinburgh University. They were: Sophia Jex-Blake, Isabel Thorne, Edith Pechey, Matilda Chaplin, Helen Evans, Mary Anderson

Marshall and Emily Bovell. In 1869 the women passed the matriculation exam and were admitted to the university's medical school, however hostility was rife with university staff refusing to teach them followed by the Surgeon's Hall Riot in 1870 when the women were pelted with rubbish by a mob of two hundred people as they tried to attend an anatomy exam.

The women were blocked from graduating and most continued their studies in mainland Europe while Jex-Blake helped found the London School of Medicine for Women. At the time of writing, it has just been announced that Edinburgh University intends to posthumously award the seven women with their undergraduate degrees in medicine at a ceremony in July 2019.

I use the spelling *cypher* in this book because it was more widely used in 1880s Britain than *cipher*. For now, though, I'll revert to the modern day spelling of cipher. The Vigenère cipher was invented by the Italian cryptographer Giovan Battista Bellaso in 1553. It was later misattributed to the French cryptographer Blaise de Vigenère who came up with a variation later in the sixteenth century. The code was considered unbreakable, earning it the name *le chiffre indéchiffrable* and was used by the Confederacy in the Civil War. The Union regularly deciphered the messages because the Confederates relied on just a few keywords.

A German army officer and cryptographer, Friedrich Kasiski, published a method for deciphering the Vigenère cipher in 1863 although it's thought that the British mathematician and engineer, Charles Babbage, found his own method of decoding it in the 1840s.

Francis Edwards was able to send a telegram to Penny thanks to the work of the Central & South American Telegraph

Company. The cable was laid in 1881 and 1882 from Mexico to Peru. With Mexico already connected to Texas by telegraph cable by this time, and the cables between America and Britain having been laid in the 1860s, swift communication between Buenaventura in Colombia and London was possible by 1884. Although it was probably quite expensive!

The Royal Aquarium was a Westminster entertainment venue built in 1876. The aquarium itself never took off - the water tanks ran into problems and it was a standing joke that the aquarium never contained any fish. In a bid to attract visitors the aquarium put on dangerous acts such as Zazel the human cannonball (a fourteen year old girl) and the tightrope walker, The Great Farini.

One of the stars of Beckwith's Great Swimming Entertainment was Agnes Beckwith - 'The Greatest Lady Swimmer in the World' - at the age of fourteen in 1875, she swam five miles in the Thames from London Bridge to Greenwich. Her swimming feats were numerous, including a twenty mile swim in the Thames when she was seventeen in 1878. Thanks to London's new sewerage system in the 1860s, the Thames was no longer an open sewer by Agnes' time, but it still can't have been very nice to swim in!

After a while the Royal Aquarium developed a seedy reputation and ladies of 'elastic virtue' were said to frequent the place. It closed in 1902, its theatre - managed by the actress Lillie Langtry - lasted until 1907. The buildings have since been demolished.

A magistrate's court was established on Bow Street, Covent Garden, in 1740 in what was then a crime-ridden area. It became home to London's first police force, the Bow Street Runners in 1749. In the 1830s the new Metropolitan Police Service built a station on the site and a new magistrate's court opened in 1881. Famous and varied defendants here included Oscar Wilde, the Kray Twins, Dr Crippen, Bertand Russell, General Pinochet and Emmeline and Christabel Pankhurst. The court closed in 2006 and the building still stands opposite Covent Garden's Royal Opera House. At the time of writing, the building is reportedly being redeveloped into a hotel and police museum by a Qatari investment firm.

West Norwood Cemetery in South London is one of London's 'Magnificent Seven' cemeteries which the Victorians built in the 1830s - 1840s when many of the church burial grounds were filled to capacity. There was a brief Victorian fashion for being laid to rest in catacombs: gothic, crypt-like structures where the coffins rest on shelves. The coffins had to be lead-lined to prevent any leaking of 'contaminants'. There are catacombs in a number of large Victorian cemeteries and many of them offer guided tours of their catacombs these days - including West Norwood.

The Twinings tea shop on The Strand has been in its current location for over three hundred years. Thomas Twining was a tea merchant who began serving tea in his coffee shop at the beginning of the 18th century. Twinings tea is a brand which is still going strong today and has held a Royal Warrant since the company began supplying Queen Victoria with tea in 1837 - it has supplied every monarch since. Jane Austen apparently wrote in her diary that her mother sent her to London to buy Twinings tea. Twinings is London's longest standing ratepayer with the company having occupied the same site on The Strand since 1706. The shop is worth a visit for tea tasting at the Loose Tea Bar and spending (too much) on tea gifts.

West India Docks is on the Isle of Dogs in London's former docklands. The dock is still there and is now a backdrop for the Canary Wharf business district. In the latter part of the twentieth century, much of London's docklands were redeveloped into offices and expensive apartments. Some older buildings and features of the area's past remain on the Isle of Dogs so it's an interesting place to visit and spot them.

If *An Unwelcome Guest* is the first Penny Green book you've read, then you may find the following historical background interesting. It's compiled from the historical notes published in the previous books in the series:

Women journalists in the nineteenth century were not as scarce as people may think. In fact they were numerous enough by 1898 for Arnold Bennett to write *Journalism for Women: A Practical Guide* in which he was keen to raise the standard of women's journalism:-

"The women-journalists as a body have faults... They seem to me to be traceable either to an imperfect development of the sense of order, or to a certain lack of self-control."

Eliza Linton became the first salaried female journalist in Britain when she began writing for *the Morning Chronicle* in 1851. She was a prolific writer and contributor to periodicals for many years including Charles Dickens' magazine *Household Words*. George Eliot – her real name was Mary Anne Evans - is most famous for novels such as *Middlemarch*, however she also became assistant editor of *The Westminster Review* in 1852.

In the United States Margaret Fuller became the *New York Tribune*'s first female editor in 1846. Intrepid journalist Nellie Bly worked in Mexico as a foreign correspondent for the *Pittsburgh Despatch* in the 1880s before writing for *New York World* and feigning insanity to go undercover and investigate reports of brutality at a New York asylum. Later, in 1889-90, she became a household name by setting a world record for travelling around the globe in seventy two days.

The iconic circular Reading Room at the British Museum was in use from 1857 until 1997. During that time it was also used as a filming location and has been referenced in many works of fiction. The Reading Room has been closed since 2014 but it's recently been announced that it will reopen and display some of the museum's permanent collections. It could be a while yet until we're able to step inside it but I'm looking forward to it!

The Museum Tavern, where Penny and James enjoy a drink, is a well-preserved Victorian pub opposite the British Museum. Although a pub was first built here in the eighteenth century much of the current pub (including its name) dates back to 1855. Celebrity drinkers here are said to have included Arthur Conan Doyle and Karl Marx.

Publishing began in Fleet Street in the 1500s and by the twentieth century the street was the hub of the British press. However newspapers began moving away in the 1980s to bigger premises. Nowadays just a few publishers remain in Fleet Street but the many pubs and bars once frequented by journalists – including the pub Ye Olde Cheshire Cheese - are still popular with city workers.

Penny Green lives in Milton Street in Cripplegate which was one of the areas worst hit by bombing during the Blitz in the Second World War and few original streets remain. Milton Street was known as Grub Street in the eighteenth century and was famous as a home to impoverished writers at the time. The street had a long association with writers and was home to Anthony Trollope among many others. A small stretch of Milton Street remains but the 1960s Barbican development has been built over the bombed remains.

Plant hunting became an increasingly commercial enterprise as the nineteenth century progressed. Victorians were fascinated by exotic plants and, if they were wealthy enough, they had their own glasshouses built to show them off. Plant hunters were employed by Kew Gardens, companies such as Veitch Nurseries or wealthy individuals to seek out exotic specimens in places such as South America and the Himalayas. These plant hunters took great personal risks to collect their plants and some perished on their travels. The *Travels and Adventures of an Orchid Hunter* by Albert Millican is worth a read. Written in 1891 it documents his journeys in Colombia and demonstrates how plant hunting became little short of pillaging. Some areas he travelled to had already lost their orchids to plant hunters and Millican himself spent several months felling 4,000 trees to collect 10,000 plants. Even after all this plundering many of the orchids didn't survive the trip across the Atlantic to Britain. Plant hunters were not always welcome: Millican had arrows fired at him as he navigated rivers, had his camp attacked one night and was eventually killed during a fight in a Colombian tavern.

My research for The Penny Green series has come from sources too numerous to list in detail, but the following books have been very useful: *A Brief History of Life in Victorian Britain* by Michael Patterson, *London in the Nineteenth Century* by Jerry White, *London in 1880* by Herbert Fry, *London a Travel Guide through Time* by Dr Matthew Green, *Women of the Press in Nineteenth-Century Britain* by Barbara Onslow, *A Very British Murder* by Lucy Worsley, *The Suspicions of Mr Whicher* by Kate Summerscale, *Journalism for Women: A Practical Guide* by

Arnold Bennett, *Seventy Years a Showman* by Lord George Sanger, *Dottings of a Dosser* by Howard Goldsmid, *Travels and Adventures of an Orchid Hunter* by Albert Millican, *The Bitter Cry of Outcast London* by Andrew Mearns, *The Complete History of Jack the Ripper* by Philip Sugden, *The Necropolis Railway* by Andrew Martin, *The Diaries of Hannah Cullwick, Victorian Maidservant* edited by Liz Stanley, *Mrs Woolf & the Servants* by Alison Light, *Revelations of a Lady Detective* by William Stephens Hayward, *A is for Arsenic* by Kathryn Harkup, *In an Opium Factory* by Rudyard Kipling, *Drugging a Nation: The Story of China and the Opium Curse* by Samuel Merwin, *Confessions of an Opium Eater* by Thomas de Quincy, *The Pinkertons: The Detective Dynasty That Made History* by James D Horan, *The Napoleon of Crime* by Ben Macintyre and *The Code Book: The Secret History of Codes and Code-breaking* by Simon Singh. The *British Newspaper Archive* is also an invaluable resource.

THANK YOU

Thank you for reading *An Unwelcome Guest*, I really hope you enjoyed it!

Would you like to know when I release new books? Here are some ways to stay updated:

- Join my mailing list and receive a free short mystery: *Westminster Bridge* emilyorgan.co.uk/short-mystery
- Like my Facebook page: facebook.com/emilyorganwriter
- View my other books here: emilyorgan.co.uk/books

And if you have a moment, I would be very grateful if you would leave a quick review of *An Unwelcome Guest* online. Honest reviews of my books help other readers discover them too!

GET A FREE SHORT MYSTERY

Want more of Penny Green? Get a copy of my free short mystery *Westminster Bridge* and sit down to enjoy a thirty minute read.

News reporter Penny Green is committed to her job. But should she impose on a grieving widow?

The brutal murder of a doctor has shocked 1880s London and Fleet Street is clamouring for news. Penny has orders from her editor to get the story all the papers want.

She must decide what comes first. Compassion or duty?

The murder case is not as simple as it seems. And whichever decision Penny makes, it's unlikely to be the right one.

Visit my website to claim your FREE copy:

emilyorgan.co.uk/short-mystery

THE RUNAWAY GIRL SERIES

❧

Also by Emily Organ. A series of three historical thrillers set in Medieval London.

Book 1: Runaway Girl

A missing girl. The treacherous streets of Medieval London. Only one woman is brave enough to try and bring her home.

Book 2: Forgotten Child

Her husband took a fatal secret to the grave. Two friends are murdered. She has only one chance to stop the killing.

Book 3: Sins of the Father

An enemy returns. And this time he has her fooled. If he gets his own way then a little girl will never be seen again.

Available as separate books or a three book box set. Find out more at emilyorgan.co.uk/books